DREADNOUGHT AND SHUTTLE

"If you love the kind of space story where ordinary people with flaws and fears are the heroes, and good people need to make choices in a messy and uncertain world, then DREADNOUGHT AND SHUTTLE is the kind of book you'll want to clear your evening for."

—Audrey Faye, author of The KarmaCorp Novels

"A fabulous and phenomenal tale! Cohen has delivered us an exhilarating one-two punch in this third book of her Halcyone Space series. Sci-fi lovers will geek out over all the techy-goodness. And for us adventure-seekers, there's a thrilling (and romantic) chase through space that will leave you happily satisfied!"

—Janet B Taylor, author of INTO THE DIM

"A fitting third installment to the Halcyone Space series, LJ Cohen's "Dreadnought and Shuttle" brings together again the team we learned to love in "Derelict" and "Ithaka Rising," for a rollicking adventure of rescue and justice."

—Lou J Berger, author of "Leaving Bordeaux" and other short fiction

ITHAKA RISING

"As the story unfolds and the pieces come together, the inexorable pressure of fine story telling, smooth characters, and compelling action rocket the reader into jump space where anything can—and probably will—happen."

—Nathan Lowell, Creator of the Golden Age of the Solar Clipper and the Tanyth Fairport Adventures.

DERELICT

"Cohen has real talent with character development and interaction, and prickly, defensive Ro is a sympathetic and interesting heroine."

—*Publishers Weekly*

"LJ Cohen deftly weaves together realistic teenage characters, futuristic technology, and big stakes for a real page turner."

—*Wen Spencer, Award winning SF&F novelist, author of the Ukiah Oregon and Elfhome series*

"Get on board Derelict, and you'll take an edgy, nonstop flight into an audacious SF future with unremitting danger as your pilot—and thrilling adventure your destination."

—*Lynn Viehl, NYT best selling author of the Stardoc and Darkyn series*

"A cracking yarn set in a lush future I'm hoping we'll hear more of."

—*Nathan Lowell, Creator of the Golden Age of the Solar Clipper and the Tanyth Fairport Adventures*

THE BETWEEN

" ... a moving tale of heroism and compassion. ... Lydia is a young woman utterly unprepared for the world she's about to enter—but she learns fast. She's a character you'll want to meet again, from a writer you'll want to read again. Take good note: LJ Cohen is a new voice to follow."

—*Jeffrey A. Carver, author of The Chaos Chronicles*

DREADNOUGHT AND SHUTTLE

Also by LJ Cohen

Halcyone Space
Derelict (book 1)
Ithaka Rising (book 2)

Changeling's Choice
The Between (book 1)
Time and Tithe (book 2)

Future Tense

Short Stories
Stranger Worlds than These

DREADNOUGHT AND SHUTTLE
Halcyone Space, book 3

LJ Cohen

Interrobang Books
Newton, MA

Published by Interrobang Books
Newton, MA

www.interrobangbooks.com

First print edition: June, 2016

ISBN-10: 1-942851-00-6
ISBN-13: 978-1-942851-00-4

Original cover art by Chris Howard, copyright 2016
www.saltwaterwitch.com

For Philip
for pushing me to go places I might not have gone

For Eric
who still has to write music the old-fashioned way

Chapter 1

THE LAST TIME Micah had been on Earth was for his father's corruption trial almost four years ago. While Senator Corwin Rotherwood's physical presence hadn't been strictly necessary, his father had been nothing if not fully invested in the theatrics. Certainly the grieving widower with his son made for wonderful vid coverage. Not that it changed the outcome or mitigated the man's humiliation, but Micah hadn't understood any of that at the time. Maybe that had been a gift.

New Chicago hadn't changed much, even if Micah had. He leaned his head against the shuttle's bulkhead and stared out the tiny viewport as they flew past the massive downtown region. Lake Michigan sparkled in the corner of his eye, the largest open space for hundreds of square kilometers. Then the shuttle made a wide, banking turn and glided south, leaving the rebuilt mega-city behind. It followed the maglev tracks past what had been the old border between Illinois, Indiana, and Michigan and toward the University—his new home for the next few years.

Micah was glad for the brusque professionalism of the shuttle crew. They hadn't recognized him, or at least they'd respected his privacy light. Either way, the journey had given him plenty of time to think, which was a mixed blessing.

The internal comms broke through the silence and the captain's voice announced the landing procedures. Micah blinked as the lights slowly brightened to match local time. By his reckoning, counting the debriefing and several days of depositions he'd given Commonwealth authorities at what was supposed to be a routine customs clearance, he'd been traveling for forty-seven subjective hours across more than a galactic week. The joy of wormhole travel.

As the shuttle eased lower, the University spread out below him in an organized grid of buildings broken up by sealed biospheres. The sun shimmered off the variable force fields that contained sample environments from multiple worlds. The sheer amount of diversity those habitats represented could keep any exo-botanist happy for a long time. But that wasn't why he'd come here.

Micah tapped the dark surface of his micro. While the data encrypted within it would be his true work, he couldn't deny that the University's collection was a treasure beyond price. In another life, it might also have been enough.

His ears popped as the shuttle landed. While he waited until the rest of the passengers exited his row, Micah tucked his micro into his jacket pocket before shuffling past the empty seats into the aisle. Pain lanced through his right foot. Swallowing a string of curses, he grabbed the seat back.

"Can I help you?" The steward reached over to steady him.

Micah shook his head and pulled away. Snarling at the man wouldn't make his damaged feet work any better. "Long trip."

"Starting at Uni?"

Micah nodded.

"Need ground transport, Mr. Chase?"

He started at the unfamiliar name he'd been traveling under. It had better become familiar and quickly. "No." Micah softened his voice and tried again. "No, thank you."

The steward smiled as he stepped aside.

The shuttleport was tucked in at the far end of the UCom–NorthWestern campus. A cluster of young students stood with their parents, talking and laughing in baggage claim. Micah hobbled past them, thinking of his mother. Nina Rotherwood had graduated from here with an advanced degree in neuroanatomy and then stayed to do research. Back then she'd been Nina Chase—Dr. Nina Chase. She'd met his father when he'd been placed as a legal aid attorney in the Uni-run clinic. Micah had a hard time imagining the senator being interested in helping anyone other than himself, but his mother used to tell stories of the brilliant young lawyer representing the indigent, who had charmed her into marrying him.

Micah had done everything his mother had asked of him and more. Now it was time to do what he had promised on her behalf after she'd died. But first he needed to get off his feet and hope his things had preceded him.

He waited outside the terminal for the monorail. It was a warm spring day and his nose was already clogged. His eyes watered and the pounding in his head nearly overwhelmed the ache in his feet. Some botanist he was. He squinted up at the sun. It would probably take a few weeks before he accommodated to unfiltered air and unmediated weather. He needed a shower, a change of clothes, and a place to lie down, and maybe not even in that order. If he was lucky, his bags would already have been delivered. If not, then all he had with him was his micro and what he was wearing.

On the ride over to campus, he powered up his micro and tapped his fingers across its edge as it registered itself on the campus network. Messages were waiting from his program administrator as well as housing and the registrar's office. Nothing from Jem, Barre, Nomi, or Ro. The disappointment was as unexpected as it was fierce. At least the Commonwealth had been good to its word. All the permissions were taken care of as well as his Uni ID: Micah Rotherwood didn't exist here. Michael Chase had taken his identity.

A map glowed across the screen with a blinking light for his quarters. Micah limped across campus ignoring the buzz of conversations around him. There would be plenty of time to meet his fellow students, but Micah didn't feel the need to be the senator's son anymore: the Rotherwood charm was something he was happy to jettison along with the Rotherwood name. Both had brought him misery.

They'd housed him in a small apartment that reminded him of his quarters on Daedalus. It had the same common space, the same kitchenette, and several doors branching off the main room that he'd explore later. Several pieces of luggage and sealed boxes sat in a neat pile next to one of them. Too bad they weren't his.

At least bureaucratic screw-ups were something he knew how to deal with. He collapsed on the generic sofa and removed his shoes and pressure-gradient socks. His feet throbbed with a strange mix of relief and pain. Closing his eyes, Micah propped up his legs, leaned his head back, and sighed. The issues with his bags would wait. So would a shower and a meal. For now, it was a gift just to be still.

"Didn't your mother teach you manners?"

Micah jerked upright, wincing as his unprotected feet thudded to the floor.

"I hope you aren't the kind of roommate who leaves his shit all over the place."

He blinked up at a tall, broad-shouldered girl standing in front of the window. *Roommate? What in the bloody cosmos?*

"What on earth did you do to your feet?"

Earth? Not hardly. Micah stared down at them as if they belonged to someone else. Dr. Durbin wouldn't be happy with the swelling that obliterated the contours of his ankles or the angry red mottling that reached to his toes. "Burns. Who the hell are you?"

She didn't seem to be deflected at all by his rudeness.

"Dev. Devorah Martingale Morningstar, actually. But it's a mouthful. A ridiculous name to give a kid, but there you have it." She stepped forward, eclipsing the sunlight pouring through the unshielded window and Micah blinked, trying to reconcile her bright, cheery voice with her strong frame. Short, spiky dark hair outlined a tanned face with high cheekbones. Dark eyes full of amusement studied him.

She stuck out a calloused hand. "Materials science, but I

dabble in urban archeology. You?"

"What?" He shook her hand on autopilot, feeling the solid strength to her.

"Do you have a name? Or at least a field of study?" She paused to cock her head and give him the once-over. "Definitely a spacer. And your hands are too smooth to be a field researcher's. Let me guess. Linguistics? No. Theoretical physics?"

He tried to shake the confusion out of his brain. "Micah ... Michael Chase. Exo-botany. And what are you doing in my quarters?"

"Well, Micah Michael Chase, exo-botanist, it's nice to meet you."

He tried to interrupt and correct the blunder he'd made of his name, but she just kept talking.

"Me? I like having a roommate. But not everyone can cope with sharing quarters. Consequence of the diaspora, actually. So much space. So few people. Most spacers opt out. Surprised you didn't."

"Opt out?" He felt as out of phase in this conversation as in a jump gone wrong.

"Ahh." Dev smiled. "Seems like someone didn't read his housing forms too carefully."

*

Moving slowly so she wouldn't wake Nomi, Ro slipped from the small bed and curled up on the sofa. The only light in Nomi's quarters came from the glow of Ro's micro. The cursor on the empty message blinked patiently. Every time she'd sat down to compose a message to Micah, Ro ended up deleting it, unsent. She knew she had to find a way to warn him about her father, but she didn't know where to begin. More than once, she'd started to ask Barre to do it for her. That would have been easier. And wrong.

For good or for ill, she was Halcyone's captain and it was her job to manage the crew. Even if Micah wasn't technically part of Halcyone's complement anymore, he was still involved in what was turning into some secret cabal. Their futures were linked by their fathers' failed smuggling operation, and while Senator Rotherwood had died in the aftermath, her father's reappearance posed a threat to them all. As much as Ro would have liked to keep Micah out of this, she knew that ship had jumped, in more ways than one.

Ro had read and reread the message from Dr. Ada May so many times, she'd memorized it: Her father's name. Nav coordinates. And a warning to be careful. As if she had never not been careful where her father was concerned. Unfortunately, the coordinates didn't translate to any known region of Commonwealth space. Which likely meant wherever they led to had been erased from official maps the same way Ithaka had been hidden.

May's intel was all the hard data Ro had on her father. She'd so far been unable to crack the security on the memory cube she'd lifted from his workshop before the Commonwealth had impounded all his possessions. And it wasn't for lack of trying.

They could run the coordinates through May's nav program. If her father was using the same trick to hide, it would probably be able to identify where he was holed up, but they couldn't risk it until they'd tested the hack Barre and Halcyone's AI had written. Otherwise, they'd broadcast a clear route directly to Ada May and Ithaka. And they couldn't test the hack while they were still tethered to Daedalus Station.

Her thoughts chased one another around her head like satellites and their primary. None of this was helping her figure out what to tell Micah.

"Hey. I thought I was supposed to be the nocturnal one."

Nomi stretched, arching her back in the bed, chin-length dark hair swinging away from her round face. An old quilt slid down her smooth shoulders. Bringing the worn blanket here had been one of the hardest things Ro had ever done. Nomi had simply smiled and spread it atop their shared bed without a word. Ro still didn't know what she'd done to deserve the woman's grace.

"I'm sorry. Couldn't sleep. If I'm bothering you, I can work back on Halcyone."

Nomi slipped out of bed and wrapped the quilt around her like one of her kimonos before padding over to where Ro sat on the sofa in the small common space. Nomi's quarters were barely big enough for one. There was no way this was going to work.

"If I didn't want to be bothered, I wouldn't have invited you in." Nomi's light brown eyes nearly closed when she smiled and tiny lines radiated outward from their corners like light from a star. She planted a quick kiss on the top of Ro's head and sat next to her, curling her feet beneath the quilt. "Can I help?"

Ro ran her fingers through the knots in her hair. "If I knew what kind of resources my father got his hands on, I'd have a better idea how much to tell Micah."

"He deserves to know everything," Nomi said, her gaze now serious and piercing. "Then he can decide what he needs to do."

"'Everything' includes a superhauler's worth of stuff. Look. He just started Uni. At least one of us has a chance to be free of this mess. Why shouldn't it be him?" Ro wasn't sure she even understood all the players or what the full stakes were. All she knew for certain was that it involved Ithaka—a planet that wasn't supposed to exist, her father, a black market not quite under the control of its founders, and Dr. Ada May, who was very much alive and well, despite Commonwealth history to the contrary.

"It's not your call, Ro."

She stiffened, shifted away from Nomi, and struggled to keep her breathing under control.

Nomi started to talk again, but Ro shook her head. The twin responses of fear and anger were nearly instinctual. But at least Ro was learning: it was her father's ghost still haunting her, and not anything to do with this woman by her side.

"No. It's okay," Ro said and leaned back against Nomi. "You're right. I'll tell him."

They sat in silence for several moments. Ro let her thoughts drift, knowing she couldn't hold onto this fragile peace. Problems she couldn't solve circled at the edge of her mind in unstable orbits. Figuring out what to do about Micah was the least of them.

Nomi exhaled softly before checking the time. "I'm on shift this morning. Will you be here when I get back?"

It was just a question. There was no judgment or criticism in it, yet Ro still felt her heart race in response. She made herself gently squeeze Nomi's hand. "Yes."

As Nomi got dressed for work, Ro sat in silence pondering the Micah issue. Well, it wasn't really him that was the problem as much as how she could safely communicate everything he needed to know without putting him at risk. Or at least more at risk.

And ultimately, if Ro was being honest with herself, it was really her own avoidance she wrestled with. Which wasn't fair to Micah. *Okay. Fine.* Ro looked up for Nomi. She deserved her "I told you so" moment. The small apartment was silent and empty. She smiled at the reprieve, turned to her micro, and composed the first of several messages to a certain Michael Chase, starting with an innocuous greeting that would run Ada May's secure messaging routine before decrypting Ro's mail.

He deserved to know everything. Fine. Everything it would be.

Chapter 2

BARRE FELT LIKE he'd been trapped in a strange kind of time loop. It had been less than a week since he'd had his head buried in this same console on Halcyone, splicing wires and tracing circuits. He didn't really mind. It was easier to tinker with the old ship than deal with a conspiracy forty years in the making.

After carefully backing out of the nav operator's station, he wiped his hands on the clean corner of a very grimy towel. Sweat beaded his forehead. He sent a quick musical query to the ship's AI. She knew exactly what he wanted.

Their direct communication had gotten much better, but Barre hadn't been able to link to his brother again through Halcyone for more than a brief brush of mind-to-mind. There would be time for exploring that path again, now that Jem was home and starting to integrate his neural implant.

In response to Barre's request, the air speed increased and the temperature dropped to something a little cooler than Ro seemed to like. Halcyone might be her ship, but she couldn't connect with the AI like he could. Smirking, he asked

Halcyone to lock the controls. Lucky for them, life support was one of the subsystems on the old freighter that worked reliably. Well, for the most part.

Having access to Micah's father's money made some things simpler and some things harder. The temptation to just purchase whatever Halcyone needed to do a complete refit was immense. But there was already enough scrutiny on their actions without having to explain where they had gotten the resources. In the brief time since they had found Jem on Ithaka and brought him home, the pressure on all of them seemed to intensify. Barre couldn't distinguish between his own necessary paranoia and an imagination on overdrive.

It remained abundantly clear that their parents didn't believe the cover story he and Jem had told them. There wasn't much they could do to Barre, but his little brother was still a minor and they were coming down pretty hard on him.

Barre whistled a second request to the AI, enjoying the resonance of the high-pitched sound in the bridge. An echo of what he thought of as Jem's theme played back to him. After a moment, Jem's voice crackled through the small space.

"What's going on, Barre?"

"Drone work. You busy?"

Jem paused before answering. "Sort of."

"Can it wait? I've got a job for small fingers."

"Fine. Might as well be useful somewhere."

As Jem dropped the connection, Barre sighed. He knew this wasn't the work his little brother wanted to be doing, but metaphorically beating his head against the metaphorical wall of his brain damage and still-healing neural implant wasn't going to help him.

He heard Jem's hesitant steps in Halcyone's corridor. "Bad brain day?" Barre asked as his brother slipped past the melted bridge doors. At some point they would have to replace them. Between the more recent blast burns and the forty-year-old damage to the bridge, Halcyone had definitely taken a beating.

"Not great. I don't want to talk about it."

Jem's eyes were downcast. He no longer had to contort his head and neck into a strange angle to keep the vertigo under control, which was a huge improvement. But he still struggled with balance and the tendency of his eyes to start their stuttering dance, especially when he was fatigued. Which seemed like all the time now.

Surely Jem knew he needed to rest his healing brain. But that didn't stop him from pushing himself and the limits of the neural implant during all of his waking hours. "You need to get more sleep, kiddo."

"Tell me something I don't know."

It was already an old argument. "Well, I'm sorry for giving you a task that's beneath you, but I don't have time to program a tech drone."

Jem lowered himself onto the floor of the bridge. "What do you need?"

"How are you at pairing with your micro?"

"It's tiring, but I can make the connection stabilize for a few minutes at a time."

"Good. There's a switch I can't reach without tearing the entire console apart." He waggled his big hands. Jem's hands were more delicate, like their mother's. Surgeon's hands. "If you can swap it out with a new one, it'll save me hours of work. I can ask Halcyone to push the schematic to your micro."

"Sure. Whatever. At least Mom backed down on the sedative ban."

That was a huge concession, given her reaction to Barre's bittergreen use. And probably too little, too late. Maybe if she hadn't freaked out over Jem using the neo-benzos to stabilize his nystagmus, he might not have been so desperate to get the neural. But that ship had jumped clear across the galaxy. His brother had a black market neural implant that so far hadn't been able to fully compensate for his brain damage and had left him with synesthesia bordering on sensory hallucinations.

Jem seemed to think it had been worth it.

"You know how to splice these in?"

Jem gave him a withering look and snatched the switch from his hand. "I didn't suddenly become inept."

"Touchy! Have you been hanging around Ro lately?"

"Ouch," Ro said.

Barre turned. She stood in the permanently open doorway.

Jem laughed. "Heya, Ro. Don't mind my brother. He's an idiot."

"I noticed. What's going on?" she asked.

"I'm outsourcing," Barre said, smiling. "How's Nomi?"

"Working."

Usually, mentioning Nomi would make Ro blush, but not this time. She brushed her hand over the melted doors and

14

stared past the darkened forward viewscreen.

"Everything okay?" Barre asked.

Her deep green eyes narrowed in thought. "I wrote Micah."

"Oh," Barre said.

Jem jumped up and then grabbed onto the navigation station's chair. Barre had to hold himself back from helping to steady his brother.

"What did he say? How is he? Has he started classes yet?"

Ro held up her hands. "Whoa, kiddo. I just sent it. It'll take a few hops to even get to him. And it's a lot to take in."

"Was that a good idea?" Barre asked.

"He needs to know."

"No. Not that. I'm just worried about our friends." Even aboard Halcyone, Barre was reluctant to name Ada May and the doctors and researchers they had met on Ithaka.

"She's not stupid. I bet she sent Micah Ada's encryption program first, right?"

Barre smiled. Jem still fairly worshiped Ro.

"What Jem said." Ro stepped into the bridge and over to Barre's little brother. "How are you doing?"

Jem shrugged. "It's slow. But I have a bigger window now before I hurl."

"Good," she said. "So you guys tracked down the nav station problem?"

"Burned-out relay. Jem's being my tech drone."

"Let me know when it's fixed." She turned to leave.

"Wait," Barre said. "So do we have a plan?"

"Keep fixing my ship."

"Sure. But then what?" Barre looked around the bridge.

15

Aside from the nav issue, much of what they needed at this point was purely cosmetic or a matter of upkeep and supplies. The old freighter was never going to win on speed or comfort, but she was space-worthy.

Her voice dropped to a whisper. "Run those coordinates? Find my father? I really don't know." She fiddled with her micro and glanced toward the corridor. "Can you finish here without me? Commander Mendez just shoved a bunch of priority work orders through."

Barre met Jem's gaze and raised an eyebrow. His brother nodded. "Yeah. We're good."

"Thanks. Meet you back here for dinner?"

"Are you buying?" Barre asked.

"Only the best for my crew," she called out from the corridor.

"Great," Barre muttered. "She's going to bring emergency rations again."

"Well, you could always have dinner with Mom and Dad."

"Shut up and get to work, drone."

Jem's lips twitched into the ghost of a smile. "Just a suggestion."

Barre triggered his connection with the AI and requested that she push the schematic over to Jem's micro. He could have sworn her musical reply had an amused overlay. How much did Halcyone really understand of the subtle interplay among her human crew? Even fully functioning AIs weren't all that skilled at the fine nuances of emotion. Sure, they had the benefit of huge processing speeds and the ability to replay and analyze interactions against a near-infinite database of norms, but there was still a cognitive schism between artificial and developmental intelligences. And Halcyone was first-gen. She had also been badly injured—first by the virus that had nearly destroyed her, and then by her original crew in an effort to stop her from crashing into the asteroid forty years ago.

Maybe Ada May would have some insight into the question. For now, he needed Jem to repair a switch. It was a simple problem that had a simple solution. There was something satisfying in that.

*

Nomi smiled and nodded at her station-mates as she made her way from the main commissary toward comms. A few weeks ago, all she had wanted was to truly become part of the staff. To make friends and feel connected. Now, she felt like a lone relay station; messages came and went, but she couldn't broadcast anything of her own. It gave her a strange sympathy for Micah.

In his old life, he'd had to spend too much of his time being the senator's son. She wondered how much of himself he could be in this new one. At least Ro was going to bring him on board with this whole Ithaka mess.

Her micro chirped its official station alert tone and Nomi stopped so quickly, one of the medics nearly ran her over. They both murmured apologies. As he rushed off, Nomi read the message.

/Report to command/

There was no evidence that linked her to The

Underworld, its black market, or Ithaka. Ro had taken care of that. Her micro had May's encryption program running and Nomi would sooner believe that gravity had reversed itself than Ada May's own program had been cracked.

Station personnel diverted around her on their way to their duties as she stood there staring at the display. If she was being reassigned, all of comms should have been notified and someone pulled in to cover. But if that's all it was, she would have simply been sent a link to the duty roster. It had to be something more. Her hands shaking, Nomi opened up a window to dash off a message to Ro.

After returning her micro to sleep mode, Nomi headed to the North Nexus. She'd been in meetings with Commander Mendez before. If they had any proof of anything, she'd have been escorted by armed security.

The station was kept at a constant twenty degrees, but it was as if Nomi had been standing on the sun side of the asteroid without an exposure suit. Her cheeks blazed and the back of her neck was damp beneath her hair.

Nomi walked into command. Her body chilled instantly as the lieutenant commander stood from her desk. She hadn't had any contact with Gutierrez since Ro and Barre had returned with Jem, and that was just fine with Nomi. The stern veteran unnerved her, and not because of the wicked-looking prosthetic arm she used with such precision. It was the woman's predatory gaze that seemed far more dangerous.

"The commander wanted to see me?" Nomi's voice remained steady. Maybe she was getting better at this compartmentalizing. It was confusing. Gutierrez should have been their ally. They all were connected to Ada May and all working to safeguard Ithaka, weren't they? So why did Nomi feel so off-balance in her presence?

"Follow me."

Nomi scowled up at the LC, hoping to get some kind of clue from her, but the woman's face was even more closed than Ro's. "Yes, sir." She trailed behind Gutierrez into Mendez's office. So this was official. Could it be a reprimand? But for what?

"Ensign Nakamura, please come in. Emma—please stay."

Gutierrez sent Nomi a sharp look. A warning? Was she worried, too?

"Yes, sir," the LC answered in her even voice.

There were two empty seats in front of Mendez's desk. They sat.

"I am concerned about security in comms," Commander Mendez said.

Nomi wiped her hands on her uniform top. "Sir?" There was no outward evidence either in her voice or her body of the sudden spasm of fear that surged through her. Ro would have been proud.

"It appears as if Lieutenant Lowell has taken an interest in you and your work."

Nomi's hands trembled. She pressed them against her legs. Had Lowell been reporting to the commander? Nomi had been sure he was simply looking out for his own interests, most especially the reward money for locating Ithaka. Even if he hadn't intimated a partnership with Ro's father, Nomi wouldn't have trusted him.

The LC must have shifted in her chair because Nomi

caught the glint of light off the woman's prosthesis.

"I think I've been assigned to his shift maybe two or three times since leaving nights. As far as I know, I performed my work to his satisfaction."

Mendez nodded, but her expression remained blank otherwise.

"Can you think of why he would have examined your employee file?"

She could think of several reasons, none of them benign. But then again, hadn't Nomi looked at Ro's father's? "They are a matter of public record. Perhaps he was curious about the newbie on his team."

"Fair enough, Ensign." Mendez drummed her fingers silently on the translucent surface of her desk. "But that doesn't explain him accessing our acting Chief Engineer's files as well."

Again, Nomi caught that flash of light from Gutierrez's arm. She wished she could make even momentary eye contact with the LC. Would the woman warn her if Nomi strayed into a mine field?

"Has Ms. Maldonado mentioned any concerns or connection to the comms supervisor?"

Heat rose to Nomi's cheeks again. Of course the commander knew about her relationship with Ro. There was nothing in the regs that prohibited it. They weren't at war, and the two of them worked in different areas. Besides, Ro didn't have an official Commonwealth commission. "No, sir."

The commander let the silence build in the office. What did she want? There had to be something Nomi could tell Mendez that would divert suspicion from Halcyone's crew.

Commander Mendez had to know about Lowell's search for Ithaka and Nomi had nothing to gain by pretending otherwise. Gutierrez was a silent shadow to Nomi's left. No help there. If the LC was using her Commonwealth position to protect Ithaka, she wouldn't risk her cover for Nomi.

"Lowell did mention another Maldonado, sir," Nomi said. The commander nodded for her to continue. Nomi hoped she was doing the right thing. "When Halcyone returned with Jem Durbin, Lieutenant Lowell pulled me aside and wanted me to remind Ro—Chief Engineer Maldonado—that he had worked with her father."

"And why would he say that?"

Nomi forced herself to look straight ahead and not glance at Gutierrez. The LC's words echoed in her mind: *because Ithaka doesn't exist and the Commonwealth isn't looking for it.* "He believed Ro had some new information on the location of the lost colony—Ithaka. He offered to split the prize money with her if she would help him."

"Why would he think so, Ensign?"

"I'm not sure, sir." It was the safest answer. And at least partially the truth. Nomi didn't know how Lowell had made the connection between Ro, the black market, and Ithaka. Unless it was something he'd picked up from Ro's father. At this point, Nomi wasn't sure who posed more of a threat to them: Mendez, Gutierrez, or Lowell.

"He has requested that you be permanently assigned to his shifts."

Lowell had had his "two crew"—Simon Marchand and Yizhi Chen—working the second shift for as long as Nomi had been on station. The only reason he would break up his team was to use her to try to get to Ro—and by extension, to Ithaka. Again, Mendez waited silently as Nomi struggled to organize her whirling thoughts. "Are you asking me to keep Lowell under surveillance?" Belatedly she added the "Sir." Gutierrez drew in a sharp breath.

Mendez gave no indication she heard Nomi's direct and less than appropriate question. "This will give you the opportunity to watch and learn from a seasoned officer, Ensign."

Nomi held her breath a moment while she parsed the meaning in what Mendez had and hadn't said. So her commander wasn't ordering her to spy on Lowell. But she figured Nomi would have good reason to be a careful observer. Did that mean she'd have to report to Mendez? No wonder Gutierrez seemed uneasy. One mistake and secrets would leak like atmosphere from a bad airlock seal.

"Emma, please reassign the ensign to Lieutenant Lowell's shifts."

Gutierrez made a notation on her micro. "Yes, sir."

Mendez held Nomi's gaze for a long moment. "Check the roster for your new schedule. Dismissed."

Nomi smoothed her uniform top and stood. Gutierrez also stood, nodded to the commander, and escorted Nomi out of the silent office.

At the anteroom's doorway, Gutierrez leaned close to Nomi. "That was risky, Ensign."

She didn't answer. The door hissed open and Nomi slipped into the corridor, her heart beating triple time.

22

Chapter 3

MICAH SPENT AN hour getting lost on his way to his adviser's office. By the time he arrived, a full thirty minutes late for his appointment, his feet ached, his head swam, and his eyes burned. All he wanted to do was sit with his legs elevated, but Dr. Parrish swept Micah out of the office with a curt "Walk with me."

Cursing beneath his breath, Micah struggled to keep up with the tall man's stride. Parrish didn't seem to notice and kept up a constant monologue during the forced march around the exo-botany administration building, past the endless greenhouses, and to the faculty club.

"I hope you're settling in," he said, peering at Micah over his anachronistic glasses. It appeared to be the style now on Earth, along with bow ties and faux-tweed jackets. But there was nothing retro about Parrish's research.

"I'm eager to set up my lab space," Micah answered. He wasn't sure how much Parrish had been briefed about him. Short of asking—which Micah was loath to do—he had to hope the Commonwealth had held to their part of the bargain. His new identity should stand up to most scrutiny. He just had to hope no one would be so interested in him they would go searching more deeply. And that included Parrish. "And get started on my studies. As you probably know, my schooling was delayed by my mother's death." Sticking to the truth was easier, but it still hurt to say it out loud, even after several years.

"Hmm. Yes. Shame about that. You have a bit of catching-up to do, I'm afraid." Parrish rummaged through his briefcase—another nod to the classical neo-academic style he had adopted—and pulled out his micro. Micah had half-expected a reproduction notepad instead. "I've had to rearrange your course load some."

Micah shifted his weight from right to left, hoping to ease the strain on his abused feet. Standing out in the bright sunlight wasn't helping. Sweat trickled down his neck. "Is there a problem with the schedule?" He had chosen those specific courses so he could most effectively hide his illegal experiments in plain sight.

"As impressive as your independent study has been, your core committee expressed some concerns."

"Sir?" Micah's voice rose and he forced himself to adopt his best impression of the senator beneath the scrutiny of his accusers. The irony was thicker than the pollution that swirled overhead and just as choking.

"They are recommending some remedial courses. To

ensure you get up to speed as quickly as possible."

Micah noticed the use of "they" and not "we." Parrish was distancing himself from the bad news the same way his father had always done. He wanted to permanently laser the pleasantly bland expression off the man's face.

"Here is your revised plan for the semester. Look it over. I'm available to hash out any scheduling snags, but I'm afraid the shift in your actual class assignments is non-negotiable."

Micah swallowed his fury as Parrish waved the file over. His micro beeped its passive acceptance.

"Can I offer you some lunch?" Parrish asked.

"No. I've already eaten." He hadn't, but the thought of sitting across from the professor and having to be polite and deferential after Parrish had just derailed his life for the next year was more than Micah could tolerate. Even after years of learning to swallow bad news and disappointment, he didn't trust his tenuous control. He added a belated "Thank you" because he knew it was expected.

Parrish nodded. "Well, good to have you here, Mr. Chase. I look forward to seeing where your scholarship takes you."

Micah nearly snarled at the man as he disappeared into the climate-controlled haven of the faculty club. His dorm was clear across campus. There was no way he'd make it without help. His feet throbbed in time with his heartbeat and he was hoping the slippery sensation he felt was sweat and not plasma seeping from the graft sites. Dr. Durbin would have his head if he'd opened up the wounds.

Admitting defeat, Micah reserved one of the little transpods available on campus. Not much bigger or much more comfortable than a trundle and about as slow, they were most often used to help haul equipment, though drunk students used them to get home from parties. Micah climbed in and turned the air controller to max cool. The soft hiss soothed him. His eye strain eased as the canopy closed.

He waved his micro over the control module. It read his dorm data and jerked its way to a speed barely above even his stumbling walk. But it was better than limping the whole way. The small bench seat forced him to hunch, his knees practically pressed into his chest. Outside its bubble top, Micah watched his fellow students meander their way from class to class, or gather in small groups in the abundant green spaces between buildings. He was glad for the tinted polymer that kept anyone from seeing in.

All the way back, Micah refused to look at Parrish's class reassignments. As if not seeing them would keep the reality of how he'd been screwed from taking effect. He needed those classes. No upper-level classes meant no designated lab space and no designated lab space meant, at best, his work on the bittergreen project would be delayed. Again.

Micah had had enough of waiting to last a lifetime. Waiting for his mother to die. Waiting for his father to self-destruct again and again. Waiting for his citizenship and his freedom. Well, he had that now, no thanks to his father.

The transpod stopped abruptly. The canopy slid open, letting in the oppressive heat and thick air. But at least it would only be a few steps into the building and up the maglift to his floor. Then he could rest his damaged feet and figure out something.

He wouldn't be Senator Corwin Rotherwood's son if he

couldn't come up with some way to get what he needed.

By the time he hobbled to his room, Micah's world had narrowed to the blood pulsing in his feet and a surging anger.

"Hey, Michael, how's things?"

Gritting his teeth, he nodded to Dev, not trusting his voice. It wasn't like she was noisy or deliberately disruptive, but she took up both physical and emotional space in the common area and other than the brief time he had to share his lab on Halcyone with Ro, Micah had never had to negotiate his living or working quarters before.

She was sitting with her long legs swinging over the side of an oversized chair, shifting her attention among three windows projected from her micro. Micah winced, not sure he could make it to his room at this point. He flopped onto the sofa and propped his abused feet on the coffee table. Getting out of his shoes and socks was a priority, but he was afraid he wouldn't be able to get up again without their support. And asking Dev for help was completely out of the question.

"Rough day?" she asked, looking over the top of her virtual display.

"Long day." He really didn't want to talk, but ignoring her was unforgivably rude, and it wouldn't fix what was wrong in his world. Hoping she would get the hint, he leaned his head back and closed his eyes.

"You'll get used to it."

Used to what? Getting screwed by his adviser? The unfiltered air? The crowds of people who all seemed to know one another?

"I have a cousin who was a spacer. It probably took him six, eight months to learn to be planetside again. He turned his quarters into a sensory-controlled space—auditory filtering, light modulation, the works. I can ask him the specs if you want."

"I'm fine." Micah's response was sharper than he'd intended. He shook his head and opened his eyes. "Just walked a little too far."

"You didn't say how your feet got burned." She tilted her head, waiting.

Micah stared past her, seeing Halcyone's storage bay filled with crates of illegal military-grade weapons under forged diplomatic seals. The memory of the shock-cuffs restraining his hands and feet was never very far away. His palms were slick with sweat. "You're right."

"Michael Chase, intergalactic man of mystery."

"What's that supposed to mean?" he snapped. Elevating his feet wasn't helping all that much. He was going to need to soak them. Maybe that doctor colleague of Durbin's could see him in the next few days. It wasn't like he'd be busy setting up his lab.

"Look around. What do you see?"

He really didn't want to play this game. He needed the throbbing in his feet to ease. He needed some privacy to review Parrish's changes. Then he needed to figure out an alternate plan for his research.

"Come on. It's not a trick question," she said.

It would be easier for Micah if Dev hadn't been so nice. In some ways, she reminded him of Nomi. Not in looks or even basic personality—Dev was brash in every way that Nomi was reserved—but there was something in the clarity and directness that the women shared. He could almost hear Nomi's voice in his mind: *you need to find friends. It'll be harder for you now with the things you'll be hiding.*

He let his shoulders settle. "Fine." He looked around the common space and at the door to his room. A stack of Dev's permapapers covered half the coffee table. Several holos of her family and of some of the old Earth cities where she'd been poking around between terms were arranged on the far wall on magnetic shelves. Her micro balanced on the arm of her chair. Other than that, the room was a standard-issue space. If it weren't for the window, he could have been back on Daedalus Station.

He listed off what he had inventoried. Dev nodded.

"What?" he snapped.

"You really don't see it?"

"Sorry, no."

"There's nothing of yours here. Well, except for you. No holos, no papers, no keepsakes. Not so much as a pair of shoes."

"Not true," he said, pointing at his heavy shoes.

She ignored him. "I've known spacers. Sure, payload is always an issue. But not even a single holo of home? There's a story in there somewhere, Chase."

Damn. He was going to have to manufacture some kind of past. He hadn't thought of that. Ro would have done it for him if he'd asked, but even if he had, she'd been so busy with Halcyone. "There was an incident. My stuff is gone. No mystery." He didn't want to meet Dev's gaze, but he could feel her staring at him. What he told her wasn't exactly a lie.

Alain Maldonado assaulting and imprisoning him certainly qualified as an "incident" and tossing the mementos of his old life in Daedalus's recycler meant it was gone.

"Hey, I'm sorry."

Now he felt like a jerk. But it was better this way. Sympathy, the habit of politeness, and good boundaries would keep her from poking more closely into his life. "It's okay. Really." He met her gaze. Her dark eyes were full of unwanted emotion. "I'm here. My feet are healing."

"Well, if there's anything I can do, just ask. This is my third term and I pretty much know where all the bodies are stowed."

"Bodies? I thought you were archeology, not anthropology." Micah pulled out the senator's full-on, vid-ready smile.

"That's just a minor. Materials Science, remember?"

Micah slipped his feet from the coffee table. As soon as they hit the ground, the pain surged. He gasped.

Dev sat up and leaned forward. "That doesn't look like such a good idea."

"Shit." He winced and levered his legs back up. A few days of walking on uneven ground had set him back weeks. Durbin had been right.

"Tell me what you need." Dev's voice cut through his self-pity like a laser scalpel.

"Fine. There's a basin and a bottle of tablets in the head. Fill the basin to the lower line with warm water and drop three of the tablets in." Micah pressed his lips together, leaned forward, and unzipped his shoes, dreading what he'd see once he peeled the socks off.

"Micah?"

"What now?" The pain was making him snippy.

"The door." Her voice stayed even and calm. It was more than he deserved.

"Sorry." Micah triggered the release from his micro. Well, if Dev had wanted to peer into his life, she wouldn't get anything more from his bedroom than from the common space. The only images he had of his mother were on his micro. Anything of the whole family or his father were long deleted.

By the time she returned with the filled basin, Micah had managed to remove the socks. His feet weren't the bloody mess he'd feared. They were red and swollen, but the dampness was sweat, not fluid from the graft sites. He'd take it and be grateful.

He slipped his feet into the warm, medicated water with a groan that embarrassed him. The mild anesthetic countered the pain from keeping them gravity-dependent for so long and the anti-inflammatory would work its magic. He should be able to walk a little within a half-hour.

"Better?"

"Yeah." Micah wriggled his toes in the slightly fizzy water. "Thank you."

She nodded. "What are friends for?"

Friends. Micah thought of the friends he'd left behind on Daedalus: Barre, Jem, Nomi, even Ro—they were more like family now. Maybe coming here so soon had been a mistake.

"I'm heading out for a bit. Can I bring you back anything?"

Micah stared out the window at the clear blue expanse of

sky. "You've done more than enough."

As she left, he realized just how harsh his reply had sounded. How much like Ro from when he'd first met her. Damn.

Chapter 4

ALL THROUGH THE first shift and well into second, Ro mulled over Nomi's terse message.

/Need to talk. Working 2nd shift. Will ping you when I can take dinner./

It was hard for Ro not to immediately hear her father's voice berating her for placing her trust in anyone. His lectures played on infinite loop in her head as she worked through the list of priority repairs for the day. Her logical brain knew she was overreacting, but that didn't help her concentration. Bitter experience translated Nomi needing to talk to Ro screwing up somehow. But what had she done?

Three times she lost track of the tiny drone she'd programmed to trace conduit deep inside of Daedalus's control levels. She had to focus. Besides, even if she'd wanted to, Ro couldn't reach out to Nomi now in the middle of her comms shift.

Ro crept through the access corridors far beneath the station, using her micro to guide the drone and draw a schematic of the current state of the power plant. It was uncomfortably quiet here, with only the harsh echo of her breathing and the occasional hollow thumps to keep her company as she banged into metallic surfaces. Several meters above her, station personnel moved through Daedalus, completely unaware of the network of narrow tunnels that had been carved out of the asteroid's rocky innards. And these were only the passages big enough for a person to access.

Her drone was the size of an Earth insect and was busy threading itself in and among the kilometers of conduit, looking for a specific broken coupling. At least once she'd mapped everything as it currently functioned, it would be simpler to do ongoing maintenance.

Her micro beeped. Ro jerked her head and slammed it against the low ceiling. "Shit!"

"Ro?"

It was Barre.

"What?" she snapped, rubbing at the top of her head.

"You sound like you're at the bottom of a mine shaft."

"What. Do. You. Want." She forced herself to talk slowly and calmly, when all she wanted to do was to swear at him for the interruption, unreasonably angry at him that it hadn't been Nomi calling.

"You're off the hook for dinner. Jem got it. Is Nomi coming? There's enough for her."

Ro closed her eyes. "How should I know?"

Barre fell silent, but she knew the channel was still open.

"Should we wait for you?" Barre asked after a moment.

"Whatever. I'll be there when I'm done. Ro out." She set

her micro to "unavailable, emergencies only" and continued down the corridor, filling the silence with a string of profanity that did nothing to make her mood improve.

Her knee scraped over a sharp seam in the corridor, ripping through her jumpsuit and to the skin beneath. A thin line of red marked the cut. She swore and rummaged through her multiple pockets, but couldn't find the antibiotic glue. "Great. Just great." She checked her progress on her micro. The drone had barely traced fifteen percent of the warren of conduit and hadn't found the break yet. Her stomach rumbled. She looked down at the offending floor.

The seam she had gotten snagged on was one of the many exit hatches that lined the access corridors, both top and bottom. Standard issue—they could be used on planet-based or space-based installations. This hatch led to nowhere, but the one above her head would take her back to the habitable areas of the station. And Barre, Jem, and Nomi.

According to the time on her micro, she'd been working steadily for ten hours without a break. Ro shook her head. She needed to eat. And clean off the cut. Nomi hadn't left a message for her yet. And if Ro were being honest with herself, that was the reason she'd kept at it for so long down here. Even with an entire team of engineers, this wasn't something that could be finished in a day. Surely Mendez didn't expect that.

Ro pinged Barre. "Did we ever lay in our own med supplies?"

"So nice to be needed."

She bit back the snippy response. "Still some food left?"

"Yeah. We decided to wait for you."

"Thanks."

Barre laughed, a deep rumble that filled the corridor. "Don't be too grateful. It's just a step above rations."

"Be there in five. Ro out." It took her more like fifteen to recall the drone, climb out of the maintenance levels and into the station proper, and make it back to Halcyone. As she stood by the ship's airlock, her micro buzzed.

Nomi's avatar on the screen set Ro's heart pounding.

/Meet you on Halcyone?/

/I'm here. Barre and Jem, too./

/Good./

The pressure in her chest eased a fraction. But if it wasn't about their fragile relationship, whatever had Nomi so concerned had to be about Ithaka. Shit. She signaled for access.

Halcyone welcomed her as the door opened. Ro limped to engineering, which had become their de facto meeting place and mess hall. Jem and Barre were sitting on the high stools that lined one side of the main engineering console, dark now since the ship was docked. Four stay-hot plates filled the display surface.

"Hey," she said.

The brothers turned toward her. Despite their difference in size and age, there was no denying their genetic bond.

"Nomi's on her way. Can you patch me up before we eat?" She pointed at her leg. There was no use getting them worried about whatever Nomi had to tell them. It wasn't like Ro knew anything anyway.

Barre stood and waved her to his stool. Ro rolled up her pant leg.

"That all you got?" Barre asked. "Hardly seems worth the fuss."

"I don't think anyone's been in some of those subfloors since the station was built. Who knows what's growing down there." She held out her hand. "If it's beneath you, I'll take care of it myself."

"Keep your p-suit on. I got this." Barre wiped his hands with aseptic gel before settling down on the floor in front of her. "It may sting." Ro held her breath as he patted the length of the cut with a sterile pre-treated gauze. The pain was manageable. The cloth's white surface turned red as it moistened and absorbed the dried blood.

Fresh blood outlined the slice in her knee. Ro looked away.

"It's deep, but I don't think it's an infection risk, since it's bleeding nicely."

"Nicely?" Ro's voice squeaked a little.

"Not afraid of a little blood, are you?" Jem said, his eyes sparkling.

She closed her eyes. "Well, I wasn't raised in a medical bay like some others I could name. Just seal the damned thing, okay?"

"Wow. She is human."

Ro smiled and opened her eyes. "Hey." Nomi stood just inside the doorway to engineering, her answering smile not quite masking the worry in her expression.

"Sit tight. We're not done here, yet," Barre said, as Ro leaned forward, ready to get up. She waited as Barre slathered on the antibiotic glue and sealed the cut. It burned a little, but it wasn't anything she couldn't deal with.

"Good?" she asked.

"Good," Barre replied.

Ro unrolled her pant leg, frowning at the grime embedded in the knees. At least Barre's treatment would keep the wound clean. "Thanks."

"No problem." He craned his neck, looking toward Nomi. "How's things?"

Ro gave him a hand up.

"Confusing," Nomi said. "I'm glad you're all here."

Jem snagged one of the plates and waved Nomi over. "If you have bad news, then can we at least eat while we talk?"

It was good to see him hungry. The dizziness from his head injury must be getting better. Ro hadn't eaten all day, but the smell of the food made her queasy. Barre was right—it was one step better than the meal ration bars, but only just. These were to-go meals, a basic mix of protein, fat, and carbohydrates, pre-replicated and stored in the commissary for active-duty crew to pick up during busy shifts.

Pausing, with his mouth half-full, Jem winked at her. "Courtesy of the Doctors Durbin. They asked me to pick up the meals for the infirmary staff. So I nabbed a few extra." He slid one toward Nomi.

She came over to the nav station—now table—and waved away the offered plate. "I don't know if it's bad news, exactly."

"We're as secure here as we can be." Ro had added a sweeper subroutine to Halcyone's autonomic functions, so unless Daedalus Station boasted a programmer-slash-hacker at least as skilled as her father, whatever they said on board the ship would be private.

Nomi gave her a quick hug and the tightness in Ro's throat eased. "I have to get back to comms soon."

"Wait." Barre paused, a fork midway between the plate and his mouth. "I thought you were on mornings."

"Until today. It's part of what I need to talk about."

Ro pushed her plate away.

"Mendez has set me up as Lowell's watchdog."

Ro's stomach lurched as Nomi told them about her meeting with Mendez and Gutierrez. "So she knows we're"—Ro paused to glance at Nomi's worried eyes—"together. And she suspects I know more about Ithaka than I'm saying. I don't understand. What does she hope to gain from putting you in the middle like this?"

"Well, Mendez knows she won't get anything from you, Ro. Sorry, but there are some ways you're like your father." Barre shrugged.

Ro returned the gesture. He wasn't wrong.

"And Lowell can't be trusted," he said.

"So, what's that supposed to mean?" Nomi asked, glancing between the two of them. "I'm the weak link? Thanks."

Ro squeezed her hand. "Not that. But you're the one she has leverage on. Lowell could walk away with his full retirement at any time. I'm not officially staff. You? The Commonwealth still owns you."

"This is going to get a lot more complicated, isn't it?" Nomi asked.

"Yeah. I think it already is." Ro turned to Barre. "You wanted to know what we were going to do next? Well, I think we need to figure that out."

"Does everything finally work on this boat?" Nomi asked.

"Mostly," Ro answered.

"Pretty much," Barre said, almost simultaneously.

"The equipment May gave us really helped. Jumps will be a lot more comfortable. And Barre has the Commonwealth security beacon isolated from Halcyone's main systems so they shouldn't be able to track us. We need to test it first, but if we have to get back to Ithaka, we probably can." Ro just wasn't sure that would be a good idea. And what she really wanted was to track down her father.

"We're down to busy work at this point," Barre said, frowning. "She's not a cruiser and she can't hold her own in a fight, but refitting her for either of those things would bring the Commonwealth down on us hard and fast."

"We don't need that kind of attention," Ro said. And neither did Ithaka.

Nomi exhaled heavily. "It's not like we can just pretend nothing's changed."

No. Everything had changed, but there was nothing they could do about it. Except watch and wait. Track those coordinates back to her father, or at least to where he had been. May had given them a start. There was strange comfort knowing for certain that her father was alive. It gave her a focus for her worry. Watch and wait. Ro pursed her lips. That's what Gutierrez had been doing for a lot longer than they had. Almost forty years longer, if her guess was right. "Nomi? Do you think Gutierrez knew what the commander was up to?"

"No. I mean, the LC doesn't give much away, but she seemed unsettled. And surprised."

"I don't know about the rest of you," Barre said, "but I think Lowell's just a wormhole to null space. Gutierrez is the one we need to figure out. What's her connection to Ithaka and Ada May? Can we trust her?"

"Can we risk not trusting her?" Ro asked. "Wow, I can't believe I just said that."

"So what do we do?" Nomi asked. "I've been reassigned to Lowell's shifts. He's my supervisor. How am I supposed to spy on him?"

Ro placed a hand on her arm. "You're not. Just keep your ears open. He already thinks you're an ally. Don't disabuse him. Just listen. You're a good listener."

Nomi sighed. "I can do that."

"What can I do?" Jem asked.

"Keep healing," Barre said.

"If you're feeling up to it, I could use some help." Ro watched Jem's eyes brighten. "I'm going to poke into Gutierrez's background." If she was on their side, the LC could help Ro use station resources to track her father. "Any objections?"

Barre opened his mouth to speak, looked at his little brother, and shook his head.

"Be careful, Ro," Nomi said.

"Am I ever not?"

Ro's face heated up as all three of them laughed.

*

Micah refused to give in this time and walked across

campus to his first class. The early morning sun seared his sensitive eyes. He sneezed several times in quick succession. The last time he'd lived planetside was when he was five or six. His parents had taken him on trips all through the Hub and beyond, but their home base had been a sleek cruiser for most of his younger life, interspersed with embassy accommodations before finally ending up on Daedalus Station.

He should be grateful for his place here, but all Micah wanted was sunglasses and a personal air filtration device.

This morning, Micah used his micro to find the shortest path to the academic quad, but he was still short of breath and his feet ached by the time he got to the classroom. He slipped inside the small amphitheater and found a seat in an empty row by the back. The buzz of conversations rose around him. Micah closed his eyes. This was going to be a lot harder than he'd thought.

The whole "gather in one room to learn" thing seemed quaint and more than inefficient. But here he was, in the place his mother had always wanted him to be, doing what she had dreamed. He thought about his encrypted lab notes. Well, she probably hadn't anticipated that part. Through his closed lids, Micah felt the lights brighten in the lecture hall. The voices around him fell silent. He opened his eyes and sat up.

"Welcome." Dr. Parrish's voice filled the whole auditorium. He triggered the display and the entire wall behind him now showed the logo of the Ucom–NW Exobotany program: a stylized biodome and the school's seal. "For some of you, this may be your first experience learning in real time and in a physical cohort. For others, being here is a continuation of your prior schooling. I trust that all of you will learn something from one another."

Micah triggered the note-capture mode on his micro. At least he would look the part, though intro to exo-botany was something he had the skills to teach at this point. His choice of specimen might be unorthodox, but his methods were state of the art. Except there was no way he had to prove it that wouldn't get him arrested. Or worse.

He stretched out his legs into the aisle, wishing he could prop them up on something. The throbbing in his feet made focusing on Parrish's lecture difficult.

"... different this term. A bit more project-based and interactive than in past years. And to keep you lot interested, I'll be offering a points bonus to the student who finds the most reproducible bugs in the program."

A buzz of excitement filled the room. Even Micah sat up.

"If you log in to your class server, you'll find your access credentials and an overview of the software. You will all be my alpha testers."

The rest of the class laughed.

"If you do your job well, I will, of course, reap all the rewards."

Another round of laughter. Micah wasn't amused. Ro would loathe this man and his insincere joviality. Parrish reminded him of his father; Micah knew how to deal with that. He logged in to the server and started poking around, keeping only a small portion of his attention on the professor. Anything important would be in the syllabus. Parrish just liked to hear himself speak.

What a waste of time. But he was a big name in the field. Maybe one of the biggest. His connections brought huge money to the University. What Micah couldn't understand was why he would be teaching this basic class.

Well, what mattered now was burning through the remedial work as quickly as Micah could in order to secure his own private lab space. If playing with Parrish's little toy was the way to do that, so be it.

From what Micah could tell through accessing the program on his micro's small screen, it was a plant modeling and growth simulator. His estimation of Parrish rose a few points.

"... allow us to compress several seasons' worth of growth into a matter of processor cycles. Certainly it should revolutionize the work of terraforming. And earn me the Nobel Prize in the process." Parrish laughed and the class laughed with him. Micah smirked. The man had an ego even larger than his father's.

Fine. So Parrish had issued him a challenge. After class, Micah waited until the amphitheater emptied before heading to the library. The sooner he tested this program to destruction, the sooner he'd get to the work that mattered.

He secured a private workstation, triggered the carrel's glass to opaque, and got to work. He wasn't as good as Ro with the heads-up displays, but he could manage. From where he sat, with his legs propped up on the desk, he read through Parrish's introduction while glancing frequently at the program's primitive user interface. While the rest of the class would have to start from nothing—either use dummy data and hope they would unearth something useful, or compare the program's output with some crop's real-time growth—Micah had years of data he could run and analyze.

After pairing his micro with the library's workstation, he opened the file with one of his earliest experiments. Of course it wouldn't be so simple as just pulling the data over. Parrish's program was primitive. Micah was going to have to reformat everything to make it work. Too bad Ro wasn't here.

But maybe she could help.

Micah opened his mail program and checked for new messages. There were several confirmations from the University and a bunch of junk mail and solicitations. "Wow, that didn't take long," he said, wiping them from the device. As he scrolled to the bottom of the inbox, he noticed Ro's message. He smiled.

Before he could read it, the screen on his micro blanked out, taking several virtual windows with it, including the screen with his bittergreen data. "Piece of shit device," he muttered, before hitting the reset. "Let's try that again."

Warmth pulsed through his chest as he opened Ro's message.

It faded as he read the opening lines.

If you're seeing this, then the encryption program is running. If you're not in a private space, shut down your micro. Now.

Sweat beaded across his forehead. Encryption program? That was pure Maldonado paranoia. The opaque carrel windows would keep anyone from seeing inside. When he got to the part about Ada May and Ithaka, he started to shake. Would the security program be enough?

This was bigger than his father. Bigger than his plans to take down the drug cartels with his bittergreen project. Bigger than the weapons they'd discovered on Halcyone. If the Commonwealth found Dr. May and discovered the path to Ithaka, there would be open war again.

War. All Micah could see was the stash of weapons his father and Alain Maldonado had been smuggling. Who had forged the diplomatic seals? Where had those weapons been bound?

Ignoring the pain in his feet, Micah stood and paced the small carrel, stopping to stare back at Ro's message every time he walked past the desk. He kept looking at the door, but he couldn't see out. At least no one could see in, either. He focused on getting his breathing under control. Ada May. Shit. Ada Fucking May. The co-inventor of the AI source code. The mother of wormhole travel. Even after reading through Ro's message a half-dozen times, he still didn't believe it.

And Alain Maldonado was alive. Yeah. That he could definitely believe. The man was far too vindictive to die so easily. But even if he was looking for Micah, that identity had disappeared on Daedalus Station. It was Ro who was in the most danger. If the Commonwealth did their job even half-decently, there should be no way Maldonado could connect Micah Rotherwood with Michael Chase.

The Commonwealth. The same Commonwealth that had suddenly become Ro's enemy. And by definition, Micah's. He dropped his head into his hands.

Well, now they all had more to worry about than Micah's database organization.

Giving Ro's message a final glance, he wiped it from his server. Even with Dr. May's security program, he didn't want to take any chances. Then he opened a new window to reply to his friends. What was he going to tell them? His frustration with Parrish and the program seemed pretty null compared with Ithaka. And Ada May.

Chapter 5

JEM WOKE, STARING at the ceiling in his room for a few moments before attempting to get up. "Daedalus, what's local time?"

"Zero six hundred hours and five minutes."

His parents would already be awake and having breakfast. As much as he'd rather avoid them, he needed to check in with his mother to get his meds. It was frustrating to have to be so dependent on her, but at least she was allowing him access. He yawned and considered sleeping for another quarter hour, but then he'd have to find his mother in medical.

He cautiously rolled over, kicked his legs off the bed, and levered himself to sitting. So far, so good. Maybe this would be a good brain day. "Daedalus, lights up twelve percent, please."

The room brightened slowly. The soft glow was accompanied with a gentle lavender-shaded hum that Jem knew existed only in his skewed sensory perceptions. Maybe later he could ask Barre what note it was.

Even getting dressed didn't trigger any vertigo. That was definitely a good sign. He tucked his micro in a pocket and opened the door. His parents had been talking quietly over coffee, but fell silent as Jem entered the common area. Which meant they were probably talking about him.

"How are you feeling this morning?" his father asked. His voice was too big for the room and filled with overly bright primary colors.

"Still tired." Ever since the neural procedure, he seemed to need a lot more sleep than he used to.

His mother gave him a lecture about brain plasticity and infant development that blurred past him in a hazy gray before she carefully doled out an exact dose of the neo-benzos. They helped with the dizziness, but made Jem a little sleepy, too. He figured it was worth it.

"Will you be home for dinner?" his mother asked. Jem could feel the pressure of all the questions she left unvoiced.

"I'll ping you when I know. I might eat with Barre. If that's okay." He'd have to stop into medical to get another dose in the afternoon. Maybe one of the techs could give it to him. Maybe he could convince someone to just let him manage the prescription on his own.

"Remember, you have another set of scans scheduled."

It was part of what he'd agreed to in return for being released from medical. Scans every three days for the next several weeks, or until his parents were satisfied his brain wasn't going to supernova. "Fine. I'll be by around shift change." That would give him plenty of time to work with Ro. If there was still work for him to do.

His mother nodded and Jem headed back to Halcyone.

There was more than a good chance that Ro had stayed up late into the quiet hours of third shift digging into Gutierrez's records. Or maybe not, if Nomi had anything to say about it. Jem smiled. Nomi was good for Ro. She smoothed out the engineer's ragged edges. At least a little bit.

On his way to Halcyone, Jem ducked into the commissary and grabbed a roll and a thermos of hot water. Coffee, the meds, and the vertigo didn't seem to all get along. He missed the caffeine, especially now that he was battling fatigue, but there wasn't anything he could do about that. Getting the neural had been his choice. And things were better. He just wished they would get better faster.

The ship's airlock opened for him before he had the chance to signal the door.

"Good morning, Jeremy."

The AI's vocabulary and response algorithms were getting more and more sophisticated by the day, but her voice still lacked the pitch and intonations of human speech. Barre must be working with her conversation skills. Not bad for a musician. "Heya, Halcyone. Is Ro onboard?"

"Captain Maldonado is in Ensign Nakamura's quarters."

Jem smirked. He'd called that one.

"Messaging her now."

"No! I mean it's fine. Can you just leave a note on her micro to meet me here when she's ready?"

"Affirmative."

Maybe he could take some time and see about integrating his neural with Halcyone again, now that he was feeling a little better. "Is Barre awake?"

"Affirmative. Officer Durbin is in engineering."

Officer. That was new. Jem trailed his hand along the burnished metal walls of the ship's corridor, wishing he were old enough to join his brother and Ro as permanent crew. But even if he were a full citizen, his parents would balk at his leaving their supervision now. Another reason that he needed to get the neural and his brain up to full strength.

Barre was standing with his back to the door in engineering. He didn't even turn when Jem entered. "Hey!" His brother still didn't notice.

Jem tapped Barre's shoulder and smiled as he whirled around, startled.

"Well, good morning, 'Officer' Durbin."

"Shut up, Jem."

Barre wasn't really grumpy; Jem could see it in the colors of his voice. "Halcyone give you a promotion?"

"She's definitely getting more talkative. Not my doing. At least not directly."

It was probably a combination of the SIREN code and Barre's neural link with the AI. Dauber and May had created their program to be self-learning, after all. "Should we be concerned that she's using your thoughts as source material?"

Barre snorted. "Waiting for Ro?"

"Yeah. Figured I'd get the most out of the meds Mom lets me take."

"I know Ro was here last night. Nomi showed up after her shift to drag her away."

"Well, if you're done talking about me, how about we get to work?" Ro stood just inside the doorway. The earthy scent of coffee wafted from her thermal mug.

Barre gathered up his micro and his empty plate. "I thought I'd do some work with Halcyone's musical triggers. I want to play with the nav defaults so we could run the Ithaka program if we needed to, but keep it hidden from curious eyes, otherwise. Especially handy if we have any guests on board."

Ro's eyes brightened. "I like. Let me know if you need any help."

"Nah. I got this. You and the wonder-boy have enough of a challenge here."

Jem wasn't sure if it was getting away from their parents, or what had happened on Ithaka, but Barre had a steadiness about him and a relaxed confidence now. He smiled up at his brother. "Catch you later?"

"You bet," Barre said as he headed out of engineering.

"You up to some screen gazing?" Ro asked.

Jem nodded. "I'll let you know when I need a break." He took small sips from his water before pulling out his micro. "Tell me what you need."

Ro sprawled out in one of the crew chairs, propping her feet on the console, her micro in her lap. "I did a little recon last night and found a few interesting things." She called up several virtual windows.

They buzzed in an irritating, intermittent pattern that threatened his equilibrium. "Can you dial down the contrast and brightness?" Jem sat beside her. It wasn't something he would have been comfortable requesting before, but she wanted his help.

"Yeah. Sure."

The displays softened. The vibration faded and Jem's eyes relaxed.

"So, I started with the publicly available stuff." Ro wiggled her fingers and two of the three windows dimmed. "Don't worry, I hid my query from the system."

Like that was ever in doubt. Jem squinted up at the one live display. There was a lot of text. "So give me the 'I'm out of air' summary."

"Emmaline Gutierrez. Age fifty-nine Earth solar years. Born in a shanty town around Old El Paso, Texas. Father unknown. Mother deceased. Enlisted in the Commonwealth Space Force when she turned seventeen and was granted full citizenship. Did her basic training in Fort Bliss. Was attached to the Twenty-Fourth Space Infantry and sent in as part of a peacekeeping force to the New Louisiana Colony. Then her record just fast-forwards to her post-war service. They node-hopped her all over the place, mainly as military liaison for multiple out-postings before she got assigned here with Mendez."

"How did she lose her arm?"

"No idea. Not in the records."

Jem studied the display as if he'd find the missing information there. "That's interesting."

"You know what else is interesting?"

"I have no idea, but you're going to show me, right?"

"Smart boy." Ro changed the active window to the middle display. "There's actually no record that I could find of Gutierrez's activities during the war."

"That doesn't make any sense."

Ro frowned at the display. "No, it doesn't."

"Do you think Ada vanished it?"

"Why? Even if she wanted to mask Gutierrez's record for some reason, she would have created a dummy history. In case someone got curious."

"Someone like you?"

"Exactly." She paused, lifted her arms as if she was going to manipulate the display again, then dropped them at her sides. "If May didn't make Gutierrez disappear, then it had to be the Commonwealth."

"Wait. I thought the LC was on our side," Jem said.

"Define 'our,'" Ro said.

"Well. Us, Ada May, and Ithaka, right?"

"And where does the black market fit in with all of that?"

Jem scratched his head, feeling the thickness of his surgical scars beneath the hair. Ada might have been gruff and cold initially, but Jem thought she was their ally. Their friend. Of course Ro was going to be suspicious, no matter how much Ada had given them. Ro's father was part of the black market. How far in, no one knew. But that meant he had ties to Ithaka, even if they were distant, tenuous ones. And even though Gutierrez seemed to be protecting Ithaka, she still took orders from the Commonwealth. Even without the brain injury, this was enough to give him a headache.

"It doesn't matter, kiddo. And it's not your problem to figure out." Ro rubbed the tight, springy coils of his short hair. He swatted her hand away. "We still need to keep digging. You up to it?"

He blinked a few times to clear his vision. "Yeah. So what's in window number three?"

Ro shifted focus again. "A closer look at Gutierrez's recent placements. I've gone back a decade and mapped out where she's been. That's as far as I got last night." She quickly called up a fourth window with a star map and circled several wormholes. "You're good at patterns. Anything scream out to you?"

It was an apt way to put it. Ever since he woke up from the neural implantation procedure, light did seem to have a sound. Jem stood and walked closer to her display until the stars became blobs of indistinct brightness. Then he stepped back, waiting for them to come into focus again. He raised his hands and paused. "May I?"

"Sure." Ro fiddled with her micro. "All yours."

Jem tagged Daedalus Station in yellow. Then he zoomed out so far the yellow circle became a tiny golden dot in an enormous galaxy of constellations. He circled Earth's solar system in green and mapped a path from the Hub through all of Gutierrez's postings in chronological order, ending at Daedalus. It was a drunkard's walk through the cosmos. Jem erased it and started again, this time just looking at her prior assignments in relation to one another. But there seemed to be no obvious pattern, no matter how he manipulated the map.

"There are a lot of Commonwealth bases managing a lot of wormholes, Jem."

"I know." He sighed, about to erase his highlights and paused, with his finger covering the indicator for Daedalus Station. "But if Gutierrez is connected with Ithaka, there has to be a reason she came here. I mean, with her seniority, she could probably have been stationed anywhere. Even back on Earth."

Ro stood next to him. It always surprised Jem to realize she wasn't all that much taller than he was.

"Let me check something." With a few deft gestures, Ro called up a fifth window. Text scrolled by so fast, Jem didn't even bother to try to keep up with it. "Well, there's nothing in her official service record to show she was demoted or reprimanded, so let's posit she requested to be stationed on Daedalus. What's so special about it?"

"It's where Senator Rotherwood ended up?" Jem suggested. Maybe she had wanted to keep an eye on him. Maybe she'd known about the smuggling ring.

"I don't think so. She got here long before Micah and his dad."

So that wasn't it. Maybe it was proximity. "Can you mark Ithaka's location on this map?"

"Not without setting up an actual jump and running the Ithaka program. Which I don't want to do even in a sandbox, not while we're attached to the station." Ro paused, pursed her lips, and studied the display. "But it's not more than a handful of jumps from here. Could Gutierrez be one of the fail-safes May told us about?"

"She does have access to travel logs and flight plans in and out of the region." That gave her the authority to reroute ships based on conditions in interstitial and jump space. No pilot would question a Commonwealth order regarding navigation.

"True, but wouldn't those orders be a matter of record?"

Ro chewed her lower lip for a moment before turning back to her micro. Again, her hands moved so fast, Jem couldn't track them. "No pattern of advisories that I can find."

"So, if it's not proximity to Ithaka and she's not monitoring jump traffic, why in the cosmos is she here?" The station really had only two functions: guarding the wormhole and acting as a relay for ansible traffic. "Ro? What about the ansible network. Is she tracking comms?"

"Here? Why? There's so little traffic that Nomi figures Lowell and the station AI could probably handle it on their own."

They slowly turned to one another.

"Lowell," Jem whispered, thinking about what Nomi had told them at dinner the night before. He focused on the star map and grabbed the edge of the console as a wave of vertigo made the stars seem to streak across the display. He closed his eyes, hoping it would pass quickly. If it didn't, he'd be of no use to Ro or anybody.

He groaned.

"Hey, you okay?"

"Yeah. I think I just timed out, is all." Jem focused on the cool blue of his breath, working to visualize the nanoemitters bridging the damaged sections of his brain. He'd been reading about positive and negative feedback loops; if he could just trigger something to tone down the reactivity of his visual cortex, he'd be able to quell the vertigo. It could work. Theoretically. It should work. The emitters focused his brain's own electrical output to the tiny transmitter just behind his right ear. That boosted the signal to any connected device. But what if he turned the signal back to the emitter array? Get it right, and it would set up the loop.

Get it wrong, and he'd probably end up on the floor.

Which wouldn't be the first time.

"Can I help?"

"Doubt it."

"What about your brother?"

His eyes snapped open. "Don't. Okay? I'm working on it." He would have liked to lie down on the floor before trying this, but Ro was already concerned enough. "Just give me a nano."

"Yeah. Sure." The orange of worry streaked through her voice.

Jem was so tired of people fretting over him. But that wasn't going to end until he fully integrated his damaged brain with the neural. Well, no time like the now.

Jem kept his eyes open and unblinking. The light seared his vision. It didn't take long before the nystagmus started.

Instead of closing his eyes and looking away, Jem let the pressure build and focused on imagining the waves of excitation and inhibition rippling across his visual cortex. He dropped into the relaxed-ready-for-input state that Dr. Land's aftercare exercises had taught him. They created the best conditions for the nanoemitters to transmit, but rather than trying to link with his micro, Jem focused on the chaotic signal his brain was producing and fed it back to its source.

His heartbeat deepened. Time expanded. He knew his eyes were still open, but the colors and lines of the display had vanished until all he saw was a pulsing blur. At first, there was no structure or pattern to it, reflecting his panicked response to the terrible vertigo that had ruled his life for far too long.

Dr. Land had been honest with him. There was a good chance Jem's mind would never fully integrate the emitters and the receiver into a functioning neural. Pushing the fear aside, Jem focused on his breath and the mental exercises.

A distant part of him was aware of Ro standing beside him. Her worry was a palpable thing, but it didn't belong to him. Jem's whole world shrank to the motion and intensity of the light. Slowly, a perfect circle softened in front of him. It was like watching an eclipse expand across his visual field, but instead of swallowing everything in its penumbra, it left the light behind, only taking all the harshness with it. His eyes relaxed. The rhythm of his near constant headache stuttered and stopped.

"Jem?"

"Yeah," he replied, still in the half-dream state. "I'm good." He took a deep breath and focused back on the external world. Ro was leaning over him, gently cupping his shoulders.

"Your eyes," she said. "They're not doing their stutter."

"Yeah." He blinked and looked away from her concerned gaze. "Wow. It worked." At least for now. Jem had no idea how long his little trick would buy him, but if he could silence the vertigo, he wouldn't need the meds anymore. "Wait till I tell Land." He turned back to Ro. "Okay. So where was Lowell posted before Daedalus?"

"Let's see."

It was hard to be patient and give up control to Ro, but even with the feedback trick, Jem wasn't sure how long his focus would last.

"Huh," Ro said, softly.

"What?"

"Hang on. I need to go back further." She paused again and Jem could imagine her flicking through data. "Okay. Check out this timeline!" Ro's voice climbed in pitch and was shot through with dark blue. "It's not an exact match. But then again, it couldn't be. He'd be suspicious."

"Of what?"

"Of Gutierrez. Over the past half-dozen years, all of the LC's postings have been in the same sector as his. The same ansible quadrant. Culminating in her placement here, on Daedalus, just weeks after he got transferred."

"There are a lot of people in the Commonwealth, Ro." Jem slumped back into his chair and leaned his head back. "What are the chances it's coincidence?"

"Look, I've mapped it out."

He forced himself to stare at the display Ro had created with both Gutierrez's and Lowell's assignments, hers mapped in red, his in green. Just as they had guessed, the two lines braided together in their journey through Commonwealth-controlled space.

Jem wasn't sure what he was more excited about—that they had found a connection between Lowell and Gutierrez, or that he could look at the data without wanting to hurl. "Okay, what's next?"

Chapter 6

AFTER STRUGGLING TO put his thoughts in order and reply to Ro, Micah had finally realized there was little he could do from here to help her. Neither the reality of Ithaka nor the threat posed by Alain Maldonado changed what he'd come here to do.

Besides, hurting the cartels would probably hurt Maldonado, too. It would be Micah's contribution to Ro's new crusade. He returned his focus to Parrish's program. It had been painstaking work, but he figured out how to create an input mask and a normalization routine so he could filter his old data and feed it into Parrish's program. He had run the first season's worth of growth through the simulator and even though he knew the outcome—those variants hadn't set viable seeds—it was still disappointing reliving his initial failure.

It was a good start and he needed to elevate his feet for a while before his next class. Dr. Durbin had been right, damn it. Micah really wasn't ready for this kind of demand on his healing burns. But that ship had jumped and he needed to make the best of it.

Still, Micah took the slightly longer path back to his dorm, the one that wound through meticulously maintained formal gardens instead of the one that directly crossed the quad. It wasn't so much that he was avoiding his fellow students—although he was—but being exposed under an open sky and in all that empty green made Micah's throat constrict and his heart race. It wasn't agoraphobia. It couldn't be. Micah could gaze out at the enormity of space from the bridge of a flitter without blinking. Like everyone who lived aboard ship or on a station, he had logged a minimum of EVA time in emergency drills. But this? This was unnerving.

At least he didn't run into any other students and the gardens were lovely. They reminded him of the hydroponics spaces at the heart of the two interlocking rings that made up Daedalus Station. Nomi would have enjoyed them.

His easier mood evaporated when he opened the door to his quarters. Dorm. Apartment. Whatever. Dev was sitting on the sofa, with her back toward him, swearing at what looked like a shiny metal cube resting on the surface of the coffee table.

He froze and glanced rapidly between the closing door and the door to his room, but there was no way of escaping in either direction without Dev seeing him. "Having a tough day?"

She whirled around, knocking the cube from the table. "Damn it, Michael. Don't do that!"

It was still strange hearing her call him that. "Do what?" Micah wondered if it was safe to come in and sit down.

"Startle me. My brothers used to compete for which of

62

them could make me jump higher." Dev frowned and retrieved the little box. "Never mind."

"Wow," Micah said. He stepped his careful way over to the living area and sat in the reading chair. "I didn't think it was possible."

"What?" she snapped, staring at the cube and turning it end over end on the table.

"You're grumpy. That's my job."

Dev smiled. "Here. Catch." She lobbed the small box toward him. "What do you make of it?"

It was cool in his palm. Micah took a closer look at it, surprised to find there were no seams or tool marks. "What is it?"

"Well, that's the problem. I have no idea. And I need to have something for class in two hours."

"This is your homework?"

"It is if you are unlucky enough to be in Sadistic Sellen's lab. Every class, she hands out a mystery material. If you can figure it out, you get a harder one next time."

Some prize. "What happens if you can't?"

"You fail."

"Ouch." Micah ran his thumbnail over all six sides, but there was no catch or trigger. So it wasn't a box—at least not something that opened. "Hacksaw?"

"It's generally frowned on to use destructive tests. But for this one, I might make an exception."

Micah propped his legs up on the table and tossed the box back and forth between his hands. "It's pretty light. Can't be solid."

Dev scooted over to the edge of the couch, leaned toward

Micah, and snatched the cube from him, mid-flight. "Plenty of metals this light. But I don't think it's the box I need to worry about."

"Then what?" Micah loosened his shoes, sighing with relief.

"It's the coating. I'm sure of it. Something about the coating."

"How long have you been working on it?"

She ran her fingers through her short black hair, making it stand on end. "You're right. Too long. Time for a break." Smiling, she knocked his feet off the table. "Come on."

"What are you doing?"

"Taking your advice."

Micah replayed their rapid-fire conversation over in his head. He hadn't given her any advice.

"Besides, there's something I want to show you."

"I have a class in another hour." He was planning on staying right here, in air- and light-controlled comfort, until he had to go. And it would give him time to check to see if Ro had replied to his message.

"Poor spacer. This'll be just what the doctor ordered. Promise." Dev stood, grabbed his hand, and tugged.

"I'm fine," he said, snatching his hand away. It had been a mistake being sociable with her. She had as much respect for containment as a nuclear meltdown.

She looked him up and down, her eyes narrowing when she got to his loosened shoes. "It's just a short walk and it'll be worth it. You're a plant guy, right?"

Micah couldn't help smiling. Plant Boy. It's what Ro liked to call him. He leaned over to tighten his shoes. "Fine." It was pretty clear Dev wasn't going to leave him alone until he acquiesced. "You have thirty minutes."

The smile that lit her face combined triumph and pleasure. She was the opposite of Ro. Everything showed on the surface. The two of them would probably loathe one another.

Dev rummaged around in the small galley. "It's an abandoned biodome. I think whoever was running it must have graduated or dropped out and it kind of got forgotten. It's a good place to study. And besides, I have lunch for both of us."

"Biodome?" He was up and across the room so fast, he didn't have time to register the ache in his tired feet.

"Oh, so you really are a botanist," Dev said, laughing. "I was beginning to think it was some kind of cover story."

His breath hitched in his chest. There was no way she could know. No way anyone could know. He leaned against the galley counter and closed his eyes.

"You okay?"

"Fine." He relaxed his shoulders. "Just got up too fast."

"We could take a transpod. At least partway."

Micah pushed away from the counter. "I'm good. Let's go." If he walked slowly, it should be okay. It was only pain and he was good at managing that. Hadn't Maldonado's stunt with the electrified cuffs proven it?

Dev pursed her lips for a moment. "It's not that far."

"I'm fine," Micah said, a little too loudly and definitely too firmly.

Dev's ruddy face flushed an even deeper red before she turned away. She grabbed the mystery cube and dropped it in her bag along with their lunches. Micah followed her silently from their rooms. They walked along the main pathway that led to the academic buildings, but before they reached the campus proper, Dev turned left, angling toward the biodomes. From the air, this part of the University had looked like a game board with domes strategically placed. On foot, it was more of a tangle of paths threaded through the narrow corridors between the individual habitats.

Some shone with reflected sunlight. Others were dark, coated with shielding. Micah presumed it was to modulate how much and what spectra of radiation would reach the plants inside. He paused to look at one of the clear domes. "Full airlocks? How much control over each habitat do you have?"

Dev squinted through the transparent windows. "No idea. But I'd love to get a look at some of those coatings." She tapped him on the shoulder and pointed past him. "See that overgrown hedge?"

He nodded.

"There's a dome in there."

Maybe Micah wouldn't have to wait to jump through Parrish's hoops after all. "Well, what are we waiting for?"

This time when Dev reached for his hand, he let her. They pushed through the greenery, taking care not to let the thin tops of the branches whip back at their faces. A few feet off the path, and everything fell silent. It was as if they'd stepped onto a different planet. Trees had grown up to partially shade the abandoned dome, but enough of the surface was still bathed in sunlight to allow a bittergreen crop to grow. Water and power would be the biggest problems.

"How long has it been like this?" Micah peered inside. The riot of green matched the thicket outside. A third problem: it would take him weeks to clean out the volunteers. Or remnants of someone's long-abandoned experiment.

"No idea. My brother Giles told me about it. Kind of a family secret. Here. Come on." She towed him over to the airlock and punched in a code.

"Old school," he said.

"Yeah. The rest of them have ident plates."

The door opened with a hiss. That meant power and atmosphere worked. They stepped inside the airlock and as the outer door sealed, Micah had a moment of nostalgia for Halcyone. He laughed and Dev shot him a questioning look. Nostalgia. For a broken-down ship that was, at least indirectly, responsible for his burns and his father's death.

Dev triggered the inner door and stepped through. "What do you think?"

Micah joined her in the biodome proper. The afternoon sunlight streamed through the southwest quadrant and shone down on a tangle of weeds and wildflowers interspersed with the evidence of a checkerboard of overgrown raised beds. Water was spraying in rhythmic spurts from what had been carefully planned irrigation line, now hopelessly torn. Of course there had to be water, or all the plant life in here would have died by now.

"So?"

"Yeah." It would do. It would definitely do. He could replicate the setup he had on Halcyone. All the basics were already here. He limped over to where the control module was bolted onto the inner wall next to the airlock trigger. There should be settings for atmosphere, humidity, light levels, temperature, and watering schedule.

"Cool, right?"

He turned around to face Dev. And his shoulders slumped. This was her place. She controlled the access. He couldn't grow bittergreen here without her consent. And it wasn't like he could hide what he'd be growing. "Yeah." Micah stared past her, letting his focus drift to the hedges outside the translucent dome. "I need to get back."

He took a step toward the airlock and tripped over a half-buried root. Cursing, Micah crumpled to the ground, the abused nerves of his right foot on fire. Over and over, he slammed his hand against the hard packed earth, welcoming the painful distraction. He shouldn't have come. Not with Dev. Not to the Hub. Not to Uni.

Dev crouched beside him and placed her hand on his shoulder. "Let me take a look."

Micah shivered at her touch. "It's only pain," he whispered, as much to himself as to her.

"Come on. There's a place to sit just over there. You can prop your legs up on one of the raised beds."

There was no way he could make it back either to their quarters or to the academic quad right now and lying in a crumpled heap was uncomfortable and undignified. He sat carefully, moving his right leg as gently as he could.

"Here. Lean on me."

He let her haul him to his feet and sling her arm around his back. Standing this close, Micah realized she was at least as tall as he was. And maybe even a little taller. She guided him over to a bench. By the time he sat, he was sweaty and a little lightheaded.

"You look like crap."

"Vaso vagal reaction." He leaned forward, rested his arms on his thighs, and let his head hang. "From the pain." He needed to elevate his feet, but he needed not to pass out more.

"So you're a doctor and a plant guy?"

"Not hardly." As the room settled and his pulse slowed, he thought of Barre, tending to their injuries after Halcyone's initial panicked flight. And later, to Micah's burns. He missed him. He missed all of them. He had spent a lifetime on his own. This, though, was the first time Micah was truly lonely.

"Here. You need some water. It's cold." Dev pressed a bottle against the back of his neck.

Micah sat up and carefully propped his legs on the edge of the raised bed before reaching for the drink. "Thanks."

"You going to be okay?" Dev asked.

"Can't see as I have too many other choices." He would figure it out. One way or another. His micro buzzed to remind him of his afternoon class. He looked up as he heard Dev sigh. She had taken the cube out of her bag and set it on the edge of the overgrown bed.

"You should eat something." She reached in her bag and passed him a sandwich before sighing again.

They sat in silence and ate as the sun slipped in and out of clouds, casting intermittent shadows inside the dome.

"I should get going," she said, brushing crumbs off her lap.

"Wait." Micah gestured at the cube. "What about your class?"

"I've analyzed that stupid thing every way I could, short of smashing it."

"But you said you'd fail ..."

"Unless it's one of Sellen's pranks."

"Seriously?"

"She's been known to give out inert objects just to drive her students to drink."

Something in Dev's voice made Micah think she doubted that. There was real worry there. "Can I take another look? We may have gotten off on the wrong foot." Micah looked over at his feet. "Pun intended. I'm sorry. Look. I'm a good listener. Tell me what you've already tried and maybe something new will shake out."

"Sure. Go for it," Dev said and reached for the small box. "Here. Catch." She threw it in an easy underhand lob that gave Micah time to watch it spin in the bright sunlight. It dropped right into his cupped hands.

Something had changed. The coating that had been dull and oily-looking in their quarters now reflected the sun's brightness and created dazzling afterimages everywhere he looked. Dev was talking, but all Micah's attention was on the box. Either his hands were warming the sample, or the material was heating up in the sun. "Dev?"

She looked up, her head canted to one side.

"I think ..." Micah scowled at the box. A slight whine came from inside it and the surface shimmered.

He picked it up with his right hand and lifted it closer to his eyes. The coating was definitely changing. "Did you see that?"

Dev scrambled over to him. "Ha! It's photosensitive! Sneaky Sellen. The light levels in the dorm wouldn't have enough UV energy to trigger it. Here. Let me ..."

The sound the box made climbed in pitch and cut off so abruptly, Micah's ears rang. His hand tightened reflexively around it. As he made full contact, a jolt of electricity zapped him. His arm spasmed and the box flew past Dev's shoulder. He dove to the floor, cradling his arm, his body coated with sweat again. For a long moment, he was no longer in an overgrown biodome with Dev, but back on Halcyone, enduring the brutal punishment of the security cuffs Maldonado had imprisoned him in.

He couldn't breathe. He couldn't move. Tears leaked from the corners of his closed eyes. A high-pitched whine pierced the room's silence.

"Michael? Michael? What's wrong?"

A hand gripped his shoulder and he swung wildly at it. Something grabbed both his wrists in an iron grip.

"Michael!" Dev's panicked voice cut through the vivid memory. He inhaled sharply. The sound cut out. It had been his own screaming.

"Fuck." He pulled out of Dev's hold and covered his face with his hands.

"You're shaking. What the hell did that thing do to you? If this was Sellen's idea of a joke, I'll have her brought up on charges."

Micah took huge gulps of air, and it still didn't feel like he could breathe. He wiped his face clear and scooted back until he could lean against the bench. It took three tries before he could speak. "It's not ... She didn't ... It wasn't the box."

"Talk to me. Do you need me to call campus security? Take you to the infirmary?"

"No. It's ..." He looked up. Her brown eyes were wide, the pupils dilated as if she, too, were in shock. Micah stared at the tangle of greenery all around them. He couldn't help feeling this was a huge mistake, but he owed her some kind of explanation. "You asked me how I got burned. Did you really want to know?"

Dev nodded slowly.

There was the short version and the long version. "It's complicated. And there are parts I can't tell you. Can't tell anyone." He wanted to tell her everything. Which felt like a crazy, reckless move. He was so tired of holding on to it all on his own, but some of his story intersected with Ro's and with the additional secrets of Ithaka. Ithaka and Ada May. Those weren't his to share, no matter how much he trusted Dev.

He trusted her. It was something he had never expected to find here.

"I was sort of a stowaway on a small freighter that was being used to smuggle weapons and other contraband. One of the smugglers took me captive."

He paused to meet Dev's eyes. Would she think he was spinning an old spacer's tale? She kept her gaze level and unblinking.

"He shackled me in military-grade wrist and leg cuffs. That shocked me whenever I moved."

Dev reached out to him. "It's okay. You don't have to tell me any more."

Micah's hands shook. He didn't want to relive it. Not here. Not now. Not ever. But he couldn't stop. He owed her this much, at least. "That's why I freaked out about the box. It zapped me."

"Oh. I'm so sorry."

"I wasn't alone on the ship. Besides the smuggler, I mean. My friends ..." There were still too many nights when he woke sweating and shuddering from the remembered pain. The electrical shocks were bad, but what followed was even worse. "I knew they were in danger. Did I tell you the ship's hold was full of weapons?"

Dev nodded, her eyes bright and opened very wide.

"I used a plasma rifle to cut the cuffs from my feet." Micah fell silent, gripped by the memory of that moment: his hands slick on the smooth surface of the weapon. The barrage of punishment from the cuffs. The whine of the rifle powering up. The stench of burning polymers and flesh.

"Oh," Dev repeated softly. She took his hand in hers and sat in silence.

The sun shifted slowly across the dome. Micah didn't know what he had expected from her, but it wasn't this patient waiting. Her presence and the quiet of the greenery soothed him. Sitting here with Dev, it was hard to believe in the horror of those moments.

"Thank you," he said. His voice was hoarse and his throat was dry, but the tightness in his chest he'd been carrying since that day had eased.

"Your friends. Are they okay?"

"Yeah." They were, for now. Even if Alain Maldonado was out there somewhere, Ro had Halcyone and her father was a wanted man in the Commonwealth. It would be okay. The pain, the damage, the rehab—it had all been worth it in the end. Barre and Ro saved him and he saved them. Together they found their way back to Daedalus. Now he was here and even if everything else was venting atmosphere, at least he'd found a friend. He squeezed Dev's hand. "Don't you have a class to get to?"

Chapter 7

OUT OF THE corner of her eye, Ro caught Jem shaking his head and frowning. "Well, this still doesn't get us any closer to the LC's past. We have a whole load of vacuum here," she said, as she collapsed all of the overlapping displays with a sweep of her hand. "May as well take a breather."

"Well, not exactly vacuum. But yeah, the air around Gutierrez is pretty thin." Jem rubbed his eyes before turning away.

Ro stomped on the urge to ask him if he was all right. Sometimes the compassionate response was the wrong one. She wondered what Nomi would say to that. "I'm going to grab some lunch before I start tracking down Lowell's history." Given that he wasn't career military, that should be pretty routine. "Want to join me?"

"I wish. I have an appointment in medical. Probably easier to do that on an empty stomach."

They headed out of engineering in silence. There was nothing Ro could say that would ease the tensions between Jem and his parents. *Look on the bright side, at least your father didn't try to kill you.* Yeah. Neither relevant nor helpful. "Hey, thanks. We make a good team."

He paused at the airlock and gave her a huge smile. The kind she remembered from his impossible exuberance. From before Halcyone's wild burn slammed his head into the ship's corridor. He used to drive Ro mad with his endless barrage of questions and ideas. Ro smiled back. It was good to see that Jem again.

After he headed off to medical, Ro meandered through Daedalus Station toward the commissary. Her micro buzzed. Mendez had pushed through another set of work orders. If Ro could prioritize them, she could balance what needed to be done for Daedalus with her own work. It wasn't going to be easy.

"Maldonado."

Ro jerked her head up and stopped short, nearly walking into Gutierrez. Her micro slipped from her hands and tumbled to the floor. Cursing, Ro crouched to pick it up. The LC knelt down beside her and placed her prosthetic claw on top of Ro's hand. The cold metal pressed down, pinning Ro in place.

"Let go." Ro had seen Gutierrez handle delicate instruments, exerting only the exact degree of force needed to keep them stable. That arm could also crush the bones in Ro's hand without much effort. Members of the crew passed them by without a glance, but the longer the two of them remained there, the more notice they would attract.

The LC shifted her artificial grip to Ro's wrist and pried her hand aside with deceptive ease. Gutierrez's intact hand palmed the micro. It seemed like minutes, but it was only a few seconds before she released Ro and stood, holding the small device just out of reach. "I believe you dropped something."

"I believe you're threatening me." Though even if she could prove it, reporting the LC would only increase Commonwealth scrutiny on all of them. Surely, Gutierrez didn't want that.

"Have you had lunch yet?" Gutierrez asked, slipping Ro's micro into her pocket.

"What?" Ro rubbed her wrist. The prosthetic hadn't even left a mark.

The LC nodded as if Ro had agreed to her invitation and strode down the corridor toward the officers' quarters. Ro couldn't risk an open confrontation here. Besides, Gutierrez had her micro. "Fine," Ro muttered. "Be glad to." She lengthened her stride to catch up.

Gutierrez nodded to staff members as they passed but didn't say anything. As they walked side by side in silence, Ro reviewed her recent searches. She'd employed all the safeguards she could. There was no way Gutierrez could have known Ro had been poking into her records unless May had given the LC the tools to protect herself from any virtual incursion.

Would May do that? There was no doubt the brilliant co-inventor of the SIREN code could create hacks Ro could only dream of. She thought she'd been careful, but careful hadn't been enough. What was the real connection between May and Gutierrez? How did the LC lose her arm? That was at the heart of the lost service record. It had to be.

Gutierrez paused at the door to her quarters and waved

Ro inside. Her prosthesis gleamed in the overhead light. Ro hesitated on the threshold before meeting the woman's steady gaze with her own. The time for being subtle was long gone. "How did it happen?"

"Curious about my missing records?"

Ro stepped inside. "You could say that." She stopped short. Instead of the utilitarian decor Ro expected, Gutierrez's quarters were filled with brightly colored wall hangings and art. Two tall stools sat at the counter by the kitchen area. The LC steered her past them toward several soft chairs facing a low table that appeared to be carved from real wood.

The cost of the furniture was one thing. The cost of transport had to have been astronomical. Astronomical. Ro snorted to herself. "Nice cubicle."

"It serves."

"And you?"

Gutierrez raised an eyebrow. "I have served longer than you've been alive." She sat in one of the chairs and rested her manufactured arm along the red upholstery.

"That may be true, but it's irrelevant," Ro said, sinking into the other seat. "What do you want from me?"

"I want you to stop poking at things you don't understand."

So Gutierrez had discovered her incursion. It meant May was definitely protecting her. And it meant Ro had to be a lot subtler in the future.

"I understand more than you realize. I understand that you're part of Ithaka, somehow. And if that's true, we should be allies."

The claw at the end of the LC's arm snapped shut. "You have no idea what you're doing, Maldonado. Just go back to playing with your ship and find your way off of Daedalus. It'll be better that way. Trust me."

"Seriously?" Ro shifted forward on the overly soft chair, pressing her shoes into the floor. "After finding Dr.—"

"Don't." Gutierrez cut her off. "Just don't. Even I don't trust my own security that much."

They had been talking freely on Halcyone. Too freely? Had they betrayed May already? "How can I walk away now?" Ro asked, softly. What she knew—what they all knew—put her friends at risk. It put Ithaka and May at risk, too. Yet May had let them go, even though they knew the secret of Ithaka and The Underworld.

"It's easy. You have a ship. You have skills. You can go anywhere."

"I have responsibilities here." Barre wasn't going to want to leave Jem, at least not until he was fully healed. Besides Ro wasn't going anywhere without Nomi. "And my father is still out there." Ro didn't care if Gutierrez believed she was afraid of him. Now that she had a lead, she wasn't going to lose it.

"You've blundered into something far bigger than your issues with your father."

If Gutierrez was trying to make Ro angry, it wasn't going to work. Ada May and the silent struggle between Ithaka and the Commonwealth were far more important than any one of them. Her father posed a clear and present threat, not only to Ro and her friends, but to everything May was working for. Gutierrez had to understand that. "We're on the same side."

"Are we?" Gutierrez leaned forward. Her intense gaze had the energy of a plasma arc. "Do you even know what the sides are?"

Of course she did. There was Ithaka and the Commonwealth. Gutierrez folded her arms and kept silent as Ro frowned, thinking. So where did Mendez fit in? The commander either knew or at least suspected Ro had connections to Ithaka, but officially, the rogue planet didn't exist. So what was Mendez doing? And then there was Targill, captain of the Hephaestus, the ship that had come looking for Halcyone at Mendez's request. Targill and Mendez were both Commonwealth, but Ro got the sense Mendez didn't trust him. Which brought her mind jumping back to Daedalus and Nomi's comms supervisor, Lieutenant Lowell.

"Lowell is a Commonwealth officer, but the commander assigned Nomi to spy on him. Why?"

Gutierrez nodded. "A minor question, given everything else, but at least you're asking them."

"Okay, fine. Then what's Mendez's connection to Ithaka?"

"There isn't one. But she's ambitious and wants to escape this rock. That makes her a threat, not an ally."

So that was Gutierrez's world. Threats and allies. "And what about me?" Ro asked.

"You? I have been told you are an ally."

It was a careful answer.

"But I have been burned by allies before." Light glinted off Gutierrez's prosthesis.

"Does our mutual friend know how you were wounded?"

"She knows." Gutierrez paused, stared past Ro, her eyes distant. "She was there." Before Ro could say another word, Gutierrez pulled out the micro she'd taken and offered it back, using her intact hand. "But she is far too trusting for her own good. And she doesn't always understand the calculus of war. I do. I will keep her safe."

Ro nodded. At least she knew where Gutierrez stood.

*

Dev tossed the bag holding the little photoactive cube in one hand, waiting for her coffee to cool enough to drink. Professor Sellen had chosen another student to publicly humiliate in their materials lab yesterday and she had done such a thorough job of it, class had ended before Sellen had gotten to Dev.

The cube was silent now, covered and insulated. Without something or someone to complete the circuit it was inert. As Michael had figured out yesterday. His door was shut. Either he had gotten up far earlier than she had and was already gone, or he was still asleep.

She wasn't sure what to think of the story he'd told her in the dome, but she did know she believed him. His panicked reaction was too primal to be anything but a traumatic memory. Damn. It wasn't the full story, and there was still too much he kept hidden, but Dev was patient. She would unearth the truth the way she pieced together remnants of old, abandoned cities.

The door buzzed and Dev jumped. The cube tumbled

from her hand. She scooped it up and tucked it into her pocket before querying her micro. An image of a tall man displayed across the screen. No one Dev recognized. "Can I help you?"

The man stepped back and checked his micro, frowning. "I was told Michael Chase lived here."

"And you are?"

"A family friend."

Well, that would be one way to gather some intel. She smiled and triggered the door release. "It's open."

She held out her hand as he stepped inside. The man was even taller than his image suggested—easily fifteen centimeters taller than Dev. And she was definitely not petite. The next thing she noticed was his eyes. In the overhead light, they shone a deep green. His intense gaze locked on her. Just as Dev was beginning to feel awkward, he finally took her hand and shook it. His palm was calloused. His grip had the raw strength that reminded her of her brothers and the way they always tried to overpower her.

It didn't work then and it wouldn't work now. Dev held her smile and matched his grip. "I'm Dev. Devorah Martingale Morningstar."

He didn't react to her ridiculous name, but he released her hand abruptly. "You live with Michael?"

Long-time spacers were often rude by Hub standards. And there was no doubt this man was a spacer. It was evident in the way he kept his legs a little farther apart than normal, his pale complexion, and his nearly shaved head. "Roommate. And you are?"

The man studied the common room, but there was still

no evidence that Michael lived here. Dev would have to push him to change that. It wasn't good to always feel temporary.

"Maldonado. Alain Maldonado."

"Nice to meet you Mr. Maldonado. Come on in. Sit down. Let me see if Michael's actually here."

"I take it he hasn't mentioned me." The man's gaze didn't leave Dev as he moved over to the sitting area. Instead of taking a seat on the sofa, he pulled one of the galley area stools over.

"He's a quiet one." Dev shifted away from Maldonado. It wasn't anything he said, but she had a feeling that Michael might not be happy to see him. She knocked on his door. "How did you say you were connected to his family?"

"I worked with his father. Shame about the man. How's Michael holding up?"

That was more than she learned from her roommate in days. "He seems to be doing okay. His feet are still a problem." She knocked again. Still no answer. "Sorry, he must've had an early class, Mr. Maldonado. Do you want to wait, or should I text him that you're here?" Dev reached into her pocket for her micro.

The man's hand clamped around her wrist. Her micro tumbled to the floor. Before Dev could react, something pricked the side of her neck and burned its way inside. She had time for one sharp indrawn breath before her legs went out from under her. *What the hell?* She reached her hands out to stop her fall, but they didn't respond. Maldonado kept her from slamming into the ground.

She tried to shout, but nothing happened. Maldonado hooked his arms under hers and grunted with the effort of dragging her across the room. Her feet bumped along the floor. Her head lolled to one side. All she could see was the small section of flooring directly beneath her. Dev could blink and breathe, but that was all.

Holy shit. He paralyzed me. He paralyzed me!

As if he had heard her panicked thoughts, Maldonado spoke. "The effect is reversible. It's a neuromuscular inhibitor that targets only the voluntary muscles. Much more effective than the cuffs."

Dev's heart seemed to slam against her chest. *The cuffs. Michael's feet.* This was the smuggler he'd told her about. *Shit. Shit. Shit.*

Maldonado dropped her to the floor. Her head bounced off the faux-wood surface with a thud that blurred her vision for a moment. The dull pressure of a headache bloomed behind her eyes. She couldn't activate a muscle, but she could feel pain. That seemed absurdly unfair. The need to move, to do something flooded her with adrenaline. Waves of heat and cold washed through her, but her body was a distant, heavy shell. What did he want with her?

The door opened, but Dev couldn't turn her head to see what was happening. She struggled to cry out, to make any kind of noise. If it was Michael, then there would soon be two bodies on the floor. A low hum came from the hallway. Her skin broke out in gooseflesh.

A large trundle moved into her limited line of sight. Its top flipped open with a bang. Her apartment door swung closed. No Michael. Dev didn't know whether to be relieved or terrified. Maldonado's rough hands rolled her over onto her back. She couldn't close her eyes, even if she wanted to.

The ceiling swung into view. Dust motes swirled inside the light panels. She should have someone clean that. The pressure to laugh built up deep inside her chest, but nothing emerged from her throat. Tears blurred her sight and burned her eyes.

As if from a distance, Dev felt her body being lifted from the floor. Her head flopped backward. Maldonado's sour breath triggered dry heaves. If she threw up now, she would choke. She was going to die and no one would ever find her. Her lungs continued their relentless tide without her control. Her eyes blinked automatically, but not enough to clear the tears.

"You were a surprise," Maldonado said. "But I think it's actually better this way."

Her stomach fluttered as he dropped her. It seemed to take forever to hit the bottom of the trundle. The impact forced the breath out of her and pain bloomed in a dozen spots along the back of her body. If he wanted her dead, he could have killed her already. Dev could think of several ways and her mind pictured them in horrific detail: one of his large hands over her nose and mouth and she would suffocate. A simple twist to her neck would do it, too. As would pushing her from a height.

And in each scenario, Dev would be helpless to fight back, helpless to do anything but count the seconds until her consciousness dimmed for good. Inside her mind, she screamed—an impotent mix of fear and rage. Then the cover swung shut, leaving her in utter darkness.

Chapter 8

NOMI WOKE TO the flowery scent of jasmine tea. She rolled out of bed, grabbed a clean uniform, and padded across the small living area to the head. Ro sat perched on a stool sipping tea from one of Grandmother Nakamura's cups.

"Good morning, starshine!" Nomi sang out. It was closer to afternoon, by station reckoning. Nomi had adjusted to second shift far more easily than she had to the third. And it had been lovely and peaceful to walk the gardens beneath a manufactured night sky. She had even gotten Ro to come with her yesterday evening after work.

Ro tried for a scowl, but failed, laughing instead.

So it was true: You *could* retrofit an old shuttle. Nomi smiled as she brushed past Ro, and left a kiss on the top of her head. Ro was still sitting, staring into the bottom of the squared-off cup when Nomi finished dressing. "What time did you get to bed?"

"I didn't."

Nomi sighed. Ro had planned to reorient herself to match Nomi's schedule, not eliminate sleep.

"Be careful. Lowell can't be the harmless crank he looks like. Not if Mendez is having you spy on him." Ro set her cup down, picked up its mate, and poured Nomi some tea. "Especially since Gutierrez has been following him across the cosmos."

"It doesn't make sense." Nomi inhaled the fragrant steam before taking a sip. If she closed her eyes, she could see her grandparents' house and the small garden of miniature trees her grandfather had tended. Things had been so much simpler then, when her main worry was figuring out which of the tiny branches to prune and avoiding Daisuke's elaborate pranks.

Now everything was layers of secrets and lies.

"I'm sorry," Ro said.

"Everything that malfunctions in the cosmos isn't your fault."

Now it was Ro's turn to sigh. "No, but you being in the middle of this mess is."

It was a familiar and uncomfortable conversation that Nomi had hoped Ro had moved beyond. "Fine. You're a terrible person and I should never have thrown my lot in with you. Better?" Nomi tried to keep her tone light and teasing, but some of her annoyance must have crept in.

Ro tightened her hands around the empty cup.

Nomi gently pried the cup from her and refilled Ro's tea. "I'll meet you back on Halcyone for dinner, okay?"

"Okay."

"Try to get some rest. The conspiracies will wait for you. I promise."

She had time to grab some breakfast before second shift

started. Maybe Lowell would be in the commissary. Nomi figured she had a better chance overhearing something of interest there than in the midst of a comms shift.

The commissary was a lot busier now than it had been when Nomi had grabbed her meals in the past. Another change from the graveyard shift. One she wasn't completely sure she wanted anymore. Most of the tables were filled, both with staff taking their lunch breaks and with others just waking up for their days. Nomi grabbed a tray and moved through the line.

She jerked her head up from contemplating Ro's warning and the pureed soup of the day selection at the sound of someone calling her name. Simon Marchand was standing beside her, grinning.

"Wow. You were at least three jumps from here."

"Make any gumbo lately?" she asked.

"Would I be here if I had?"

"Guess not."

They both grabbed a bowl. Marchand took a few of the flatbreads. Nomi chose a plate of fresh greens, thankful for hydroponics.

"Want to sit with us?"

Lowell was holding court in the back corner table, sipping coffee. The crowd of mostly comms people standing around him parted to let her and Marchand sit. For whatever else Lowell's faults were, he could tell a good story. And he'd been around the cosmos on enough postings, he had a lot of stories to tell. It suited Nomi to listen.

Her grandfather had taught her that and it tended to get people to talk to her.

As Nomi ate, Lowell was telling what had to be an old spacer's tale about some ghost ship and his role on its salvage mission. Whenever he would ping the wreck, trying to establish a link with its AI, the ship would jump, causing the salvors to have to track it through half a dozen sectors. It reminded her a little of what happened to Ro and her friends on Halcyone.

Lowell was describing some clever maneuver he had done, when Nomi noticed Marchand's frown. He was watching Lowell, his lips twisted into a look of distaste. She didn't think it was the soup. As soon as he noticed her gaze, Marchand forced a smile. It wasn't exactly her "mission," but anything related to Lowell could potentially be important. She'd have to talk to Ro about it later. And maybe find an excuse to meet with her fellow "two crew."

"Are you ready for another thrilling shift moving messages from nowhere to nowhere?" Lowell asked. His tone stayed as light as it had for his earlier story, but Nomi could sense his real frustration beneath. The comms officer had never made a secret about his boredom here on Daedalus. Which only confirmed that he was here for a particular purpose—and it wasn't running comms.

Mendez wanted information. Nomi needed information, but she suspected that being under Lowell's direct supervision wasn't the way to extract it. The most useful data she got from him was when they were off shift and away from overhearing ears. It's how Nomi knew there was a link between Cam Lowell and Alain Maldonado.

"Each shift done is one shift closer to real gumbo," Marchand said.

"The Commonwealth, in its infinite wisdom and vast cosmic power, has deemed me crucial to the shifting of those very critical messages." Nomi lifted her hands. "Either that, or someone made a serious mistake in my deployment papers and when I find out who it was ..."

"You'll be in the Hub, enjoying nonreplicated food and not giving a thought to the peons you left behind." Lowell slapped her on the back. Nomi stiffened and then forced herself to relax.

As she reached for her tray, Marchand stopped her with a light touch. He looked like he was about to tell her something when Lowell turned back.

"Come on. Time to relieve the slackers on first."

A look of frustration crossed Marchand's face. He reached for Nomi's tray along with his own. "I got this."

"Thanks." Nomi pursed her lips. Now she had two mysteries to solve.

*

Dev's head throbbed. There was a strange metallic taste in her mouth and when she swallowed, her throat burned. The last time she'd felt this bad she'd been fourteen and she and her brother Giles had snuck out to a party with a bottle of their oldest brother's vodka and some fruit punch. If he had ever found out, he never let on. Dev and Giles had been sick for two days, both of them claiming the flu. She had rarely drunk since. She didn't remember drinking last night.

"Michael?" she called out. Her voice echoed strangely.

She opened her eyes to a dimly lit space. It wasn't their apartment. It was hard to concentrate, but she pushed through the pain and the strange lethargy that made her body feel so thick and heavy. *Where am I?*

"Hello? Michael? Anybody?"

Dev was lying on a cold, hard surface, looking up at a slightly curved metallic ceiling. She had no idea how she'd gotten here. Or where "here" was. Moving carefully, Dev rolled onto her side and pushed up to sitting. Everything ached. She reached into her pocket for her micro, but it wasn't there. Instead, she felt the outline of the small cube Sellen had assigned to her, snug in the bag she'd sealed it in.

Frowning, she looked around her for the micro. No joy.

Her body was one big bruise. "Okay, Dev. Triage time." She patted down her arms, legs, and torso. Nothing bleeding. Nothing broken. A head wound might account for her confusion. She palpated her head, wincing at several sensitive spots, but found nothing major. Her neck felt stiff and she tried to ease the tight muscles, yelping as she touched a sore spot. The skin was raw in a patch about three centimeters in diameter.

As she probed the outlines of it, she remembered.

Son of a bitch. Maldonado.

Ignoring the pain, Dev surged to her feet. A wave of dizziness nearly dropped her back to the floor. She blinked as the room spun. She lurched over to the wall. It was the only thing she could lean on. The room was bare except for what looked like a pile of blankets in the corner. A round doorway, more like an airlock, took up much of the far wall. Near where Dev leaned were the remnants of what looked like a small galley behind a half wall. There was a deep double sink and a cooktop with four induction coils. All the wiring had been exposed.

There were metal plates bolted to the floor where tables and chairs had once been secured.

A ship? She was on a freaking ship?

A speaker crackled to life. Dev nearly wet herself.

"There's a snug on the floor. I suggest you use it. We jump in under two minutes."

The speaker cut out, leaving her in silence again. How the hell did he get her on a spaceship? She strode to the door and hit the release trigger. Nothing happened. She slammed her hand against it again.

"Ninety seconds to jump."

Fuck. He wouldn't dare jump without her being secured. Dev pressed the heels of her hands against her eyes. Seconds fled past. He wouldn't dare. Would he?

"Sixty seconds. I suggest you don't delay."

Damn it. Dev unrolled what she'd assumed were blankets, but was an old jump snug. She'd done emergency drills with one on the single commercial flight she'd taken, but she'd never had to use one. They were supposedly idiot-proof. And a lot less comfortable than a jump berth. She jammed herself into the shapeless bag. How much time did she have left before Maldonado folded them inside a wormhole? A bolt in the floor pressed into her right shoulder blade. She wriggled away from it, but only succeeded in moving toward another one.

The snug felt loose around her. What if it malfunctioned? An alarm blared through the room. They were going to jump!

Shit. Dev struggled to remember what they had told her in the drill. Wait. It had to be triggered. Her hand shook as she groped around the opening for the pull-cord. She quickly tugged it before tucking her arm back inside. The nanofiber-laced fabric tightened with even pressure all over her body.

A vibration hummed through the ship. Dev closed her eyes and then snapped them open again, her heart racing. Jumpers were supposed to stare at something. There was no vid screen here, just the ceiling, made up of titanium and steel plate, embossed with a diamond-shaped repeating design that seemed to ripple as she watched.

The ship shuddered beneath her. Dev's mouth dried. Then she was falling. Her spine pressed into the floor. Through the thin fabric of the snug, the remnants of the table latches were imprinting themselves on her, but her senses told her she was falling down an endless well. Her stomach fluttered and her ears popped. If the snug hadn't been so tight, Dev would have yanked her arms from it to brace herself.

Even with her eyes fixed on the ceiling, she couldn't fight the certainty that she was spinning as she fell. The rest of her brain simply refused to believe the signals from her visual cortex. Closing her eyes would only make it worse, would only add nausea to the mix.

During one of her summer digs during high school, Dev hadn't been paying attention to where she stepped, and she fell through a weak spot in the floor down a full story in an abandoned house. She could smell the sour tang of mold spores and rotted wood.

Dev kept falling and kept jerking her body in a futile

attempt to right herself. That summer, she had hit the ground hard, her arm pinned beneath her, broken in two places. The ghost of that pain returned now.

The jump stretched out and her body fell more slowly and more quickly at the same time. The ceiling receded to a distant twinkle. Then reality slammed into her with the force of the floor on that long-ago dig. It shattered her concentration. She couldn't breathe. She couldn't move. The vertigo stopped, but she was flattened by a heavy weight.

They were accelerating.

The snug offered very little protection from the extra gravity. The floor offered none.

Dev fought to take in air, anger overriding her fear. The day of that accident, she had torn up her over shirt to splint her broken arm and walked out of that building under her own power, enduring the bumpy ride on her small transpod all the way back to base camp. Maldonado was the rotten floor. He had surprised her, but she was going to get out of here, too.

Chapter 9

FOR THE FIRST time since he landed back on Earth, Micah actually enjoyed the bright sunshine. Even the unfiltered, unprocessed air didn't bother him today. As he walked through the main academic quad, he nodded to his fellow students. Their smiles seemed authentic and he smiled back, more than a little surprised by his own good mood.

Telling some of his story to Dev had eased the terrible pressure in his chest. There were still secrets he needed to keep—both for his safety and hers—but as much as Micah hated to admit it, Dr. Durbin had been right. Talking to someone was helpful.

Classes were just as frustrating as they had been yesterday, but even that was more manageable. Micah would just keep running his archived data against Parrish's program and plan for next term, when he could start the work he knew would help him make his breakthrough. That was also something he couldn't share with Dev.

By the time he got back to their quarters, he was tired. Getting reacquainted with being planetside took more work than he had anticipated. Maybe he should take Dev up on her offer to contact her cousin the spacer.

"Dev?"

No answer. Maybe she was ensconced in her room. Micah knocked. "Hey, Dev, you here?" She was probably in class. Maybe when she got back, he'd ask her to post her schedule. It would be nice to plan communal meals, at least.

He headed to the sitting area, hoping to divest his shoes and prop his feet up for a while. One of their kitchen stools had been dragged over to the sitting area. Micah put it back. Dev had left a nearly full cup of coffee on the counter. She must have been running late to class. He set it down in the small sink before collapsing on the sofa.

Micah had to admit that having a roommate wasn't such a bad thing.

He could imagine Ro mocking him. Well, he probably deserved it. Smiling, he checked for any new messages from Daedalus. Jem had been on his mind and he hoped the kid was doing better. His micro buzzed for an incoming video. Talk about good timing! While Micah would love to do a live feed with Ro and the rest, he wasn't sure how good her security was. Encrypted plain text was safer, if a lot less satisfying. The video message would probably be something generic and mundane, but that was okay.

"Well, let's see how life on Daedalus is spinning along."

He propped his feet up, rested the micro on his lap, and triggered the playback.

"Hello, Micah."

Shit. He jerked upright. His legs slid off the table and his micro tumbled to the floor, pausing in mid-play. Alain

Maldonado stared up at him from the screen, his lips frozen in a self-satisfied smile. The urge to run flooded Micah's body with adrenaline and made his feet throb in time with his racing heart. How in the cosmos had the man found him? His identity should have been tighter than the vacuum seal on an airlock.

Micah reached for the micro with trembling fingers. He could leave. He could contact Ro and plan a rendezvous with Halcyone somewhere. It would only take minutes to pack anything that had any value to him. It would mean leaving Dev, just when he was getting used to the idea of having a confidante and friend in his life again, but the stark reality of Maldonado changed everything.

He triggered the playback.

"Or should I say Michael? You're probably wondering how I tracked you down. It wasn't that hard. Remember, I knew your father. He was usually such a careful drunk, but sometimes the self-pity would get the best of him and he'd talk about the lovely Nina Chase and their charming courtship at Uni. So I didn't even need to break the Commonwealth lock on your records."

His dad had screwed him again. Micah dropped his head in his hands. Great. Just great.

"I'll make this short. I don't care about you and your botany experiments. You think you can stick it to the cartels when so many others have failed? Go for it. I think you're chasing comet dust, but everyone needs a hobby."

Damn it. Was there anything Maldonado didn't know? Ro was right to be wary of him. They would all have been better off if he'd died after escaping Halcyone.

"I'm not even interested in revenge."

Micah looked up. What in the void did he want, then? Maldonado leaned back and the video tracked him, capturing what looked like a captain's chair on a small ship's bridge. Micah rubbed his temples. For all he knew, Maldonado could be orbiting Earth.

"This is a simple business transaction. My employers were not exactly pleased to discover that I couldn't deliver their shipment, and was unable to repay them their advance." He narrowed his eyes and sat forward again until his face filled Micah's screen. *"The Commonwealth froze my assets, but I happen to know for a fact that your recently departed father had some extremely clever ways of hiding his money, courtesy of his many interesting connections. Reimburse me for my inconvenience and you can go on with your new life."*

It had been blood money. Micah was glad he was rid of it. "Talk to your daughter. See if you can convince her to give it to you," he said to the screen and the empty room. "Good luck with that."

"Encoded in this message are the ansible coordinates for a dead drop." He paused. *"I assume you know what that is, given your father's history."*

Another dig. Micah paused the playback before the urge to throw the micro across the room for the satisfaction of seeing Maldonado's face shatter overwhelmed him. Micah's father had been an informant both for the Commonwealth and the cartels. Until everything had gone slipstream, thanks to Halcyone. Micah supposed his father wouldn't have committed suicide-by-soldier if he, Ro, Barre, and Jem hadn't discovered the weapons and the senator's part in the smuggling operation. So, yeah, Micah had some role in the man's death. But not the responsibility for it. Nor for Maldonado's present troubles.

He wished he could tell Ro's father to fuck off in real time, but he'd have to get the satisfaction in a message. Preferably one from somewhere off-planet, where Maldonado couldn't track him. Where Micah went after that was another problem. One he'd have to tackle after he'd talked to Ro.

"All right, finish your evil overlord monologue and be done with it." Micah triggered the playback again.

Maldonado moved off-screen for a moment, but his voice was still clear in the recording. *"If you are anything like your father—and I suspect you are—you're going to need a little incentive to cooperate."*

What did that mean? Was the man going to blackmail him? After saying he didn't care about the bittergreen?

"It's not the best quality, but I was rushed."

The image lurched and for a moment, the video showed a stainless steel floor.

"It's a recording of video I took with her micro. Make sure you look at the time stamp."

Micah jumped up, clutching his micro and staring into the still-empty screen. Her? He swallowed hard. Did he have Ro? The video focused on a second micro and zoomed in on the dark display. Maldonado triggered it. The light flare made Micah blink until the levels stabilized. He stared, unable to process what he was seeing. A woman lay unmoving on the floor of an empty room. Her arms were carefully folded across her abdomen, which rose and fell slowly. A shock of short, dark hair spiked out in all directions.

Micah sucked in a sharp breath.

The walls of his quarters pressed in on him.

His lungs burned as if the room had been scoured clean of air.

Not Ro.

Dev.

He had Dev.

"I look forward to hearing from you, Micah."

He was so unbearably polite. As if this was simply a business transaction. The recording ended and this time Micah did throw his micro across the room. The sturdy little device bounced and landed screen-side up, frozen on the image of his unconscious friend.

*

Ro slashed at the virtual windows around her. One by one, they winked out, leaving her in the silence and dim lighting of the bridge. Ever since her uncomfortable meeting with Gutierrez, she'd been digging into Lowell's background. The LC hadn't exactly dismissed him as a threat—only dismissed the importance of the commander setting Nomi to watch him. It was a subtle distinction, but Gutierrez had been following the man for years, so there had to be some connection.

It wasn't hard to trace his work history. What was

frustrating and just about impossible for Ro to believe was how little else she could find. Either Lowell had the most boring life in the cosmos, or someone had gone to great lengths to make it seem so.

"You busy?" Barre stood at the remnants of the blasted bridge door. They were going to have to deal with that at some point.

"Halcyone, ambient light up to fifty percent." She waved Barre in as the bridge brightened, illuminating the forty-year-old scars of weapons fire. "No. I could use the distraction. What's up?"

"Halcyone and I have been working on nav triggers."

Ro raised an eyebrow. It was still hard to accept Barre and the AI writing code together. "You're going to put me out of a job." She was only half-kidding. "Here's a sandbox. Show me what you got."

Barre pulled up a virtual window of his own to display next to the one she'd just created. "We've made a sort of dual boot routine. But it always defaults to the standard Commonwealth maps and includes a specific function call to the beacon."

"I still don't like it. Anything that activates the damned thing places us at risk." If Ro had her preference, she'd melt it into slag. Having it fully isolated from all of Halcyone's systems was barely an acceptable alternative.

"Do you think I'm happy about it? Think, Ro," Barre said. "Mendez knows it's installed. What do you think will happen if she pings the ship and it doesn't respond? She's already suspicious. Do you really want to be the target for every ship in the Commonwealth?"

"We're not that important."

Barre stepped through the displays, distorting them into a ripple of color with his body. "Yes, we are. And they're going to be watching us. The only reason Halcyone wasn't impounded and we're still free is they think we're stupid enough or naive enough to lead them right back to Ithaka."

"We're not ... I'm not ..." Anger heated her face. Halcyone was hers by right. She had earned this ship.

"We need to keep them believing we're harmless. Idealistic. They need to believe they can track us and control us. Otherwise, we're spaced without air."

Ro stared up at Barre's grim face. Her shoulders dropped. "Maybe even literally."

He nodded. "It could come to that."

"Out of the wormhole and into the supernova."

"Didn't see this coming when you started screwing around with the AI, did you?"

Ro cringed inwardly at the rebuke, but then saw his lips quirk into a smile. "All right, music-man, go ahead and run your hack in the sandbox."

His arms raised to shoulder height, Barre looked like a conductor about to lead an orchestra into musical battle. Where Ro used subtle gestures, Barre swung his hands around with furious precision. Once he superimposed his display on hers, he triggered the simulation and a virtual Halcyone prepared for launch. Ro watched the code view, looking for any anomaly when the program forced a response from the beacon. Whatever Barre and Halcyone had cooked up, it was seamless. She couldn't see where or how the program jumped into the routine they had created to isolate the Commonwealth hardware, but nav responded without a hitch.

"Now watch," Barre said. He whistled a series of notes that seemed to climb up and down the scale aimlessly. The display blanked out for an instant before rebooting the entire nav subsystem. Barre pointed to a corner of the running program.

"See? That's the beacon. It still thinks it's active. But it's happily playing in its own virtual reality. Sending and receiving data. The wrong data, but who's counting." Barre spread his arms out wide. "Ta da!"

"And the Ithaka program?" She didn't want to risk running it, even in a secure sandbox.

"Primed to go at any time. That's what the musical trigger allows."

"Huh."

"That's all? Huh? What about 'Barre, you're amazing. How ever did I program without you?'"

Ro smiled up at him. "You are something. I'm just not sure what." He was amazing and not for the first time, she was ashamed at her initial assessment of him, back before Halcyone was Halcyone.

"We're going to have to test it for real," he warned.

"I know. If you're right about how they see us, then anything we do is going to be under scrutiny. It's not going to be easy to get off Daedalus without triggering curiosity."

"You'll figure something out." Barre uncoupled his micro from hers and slipped it back into a pocket. "Are we doing dinner in engineering tonight?"

Before she could answer, her micro pinged. It was an

incoming message from Micah. "Hey, you might want to stay for this. Something from our favorite botanist."

Barre laughed. "Think he's obliterated the cartels yet?"

"Knowing Micah? Probably." Ro smiled and waited as May's encryption program rendered the message in plain text. Her hands trembled as she started to read it. "Shit." She reached for the support of a nearby console.

"What's wrong? Is Micah okay?"

"Read it. Just read it." Ro knew her father was out there, knew she and all her friends were at risk because of him. But she never imagined he would threaten a bystander to target one of them.

"Ro, we have to go after him."

She looked up, unblinking, hardly seeing Barre in front of her. "My father or Micah?"

"Both. We meet up with Micah and find your father."

"And where do you suppose we look for him?" Ro wanted to break something, but everything in the bridge was either already broken or bolted down.

Barre placed his hands on her shoulders. Ro struggled not to flinch. "We start with May's coordinates. If he was there, maybe he'll go back. Maybe there'll be some clue. It's the only solid lead we have."

"I can't let him hurt anyone else." She twisted away from Barre and rubbed at her upper arms. The bruises her father had left had long healed, but she could still feel them in her memory. "What should I tell Micah?"

Barre was humming something at Halcyone. A star map rendered itself on the cracked viewscreen. "Halcyone, display the fastest route between Daedalus Station and Earth."

The AI drew a bright yellow line across one corner of the display.

"Center on the target and redraw."

Ro had a moment of vertigo as Halcyone shifted the star map.

"Indicate the closest stable wormhole to any point on that path that is also a major transport hub."

Barre's deep voice calmed the panic that had overtaken Ro and caused her thoughts to scatter like light through a prism.

Halcyone circled a point in space.

"Magnify and identify."

The screen jumped again. Ro was getting used to compensating for the jagged crack.

"Wormhole designation: Epsilon seven seven three slash six two. Station designation: Eurydice."

"Tell Micah to book passage to Eurydice. We'll meet him there. It's big enough and there's enough traffic that we could get there and leave without being noticed."

Ro shook her head, but the dizziness she felt was internal. "How. How are we going to get off Daedalus without attracting a whole lot of attention we can't afford to attract?"

"I don't know, but we're going to need to figure out something."

"Okay. Send word to Jem and Nomi. We need all hands on deck for dinner tonight. I'll send Micah a reply." Ro grabbed her micro and headed to the melted and twisted remnants of the bridge door.

"Wait. Where are you going?"

"To talk to Gutierrez."

Chapter 10

WITHOUT ANY EXTERNAL cues, the burn seemed to go on for hours. The pain in Dev's shoulder blade and spine had passed through annoying throb, to numb, to a fierce burning. She fully expected to have the outline of the broken clamps permanently pressed as bruises onto her skin. But the pain wasn't the worst of it.

Her pulse seemed to speed up and slow down randomly, as if her body's local time kept changing, even though the jump was over. The air felt dense, her lungs stiff. Every breath was a battle. She counted each inhale and exhale, afraid if she didn't actively keep track, she would stop breathing. It was far too easy to imagine her heart giving one last surging beat before giving up, her blood stagnant, her body cooling. The snug would make a convenient shroud.

She struggled to force the vivid image from her mind of Maldonado tossing her body out an airlock. Given that he had warned her about the jump beforehand, it was clear he didn't want her injured permanently or dead. He wasn't going to run at this pace forever. He couldn't. She grabbed onto that thought like a belay line.

It took Dev several breaths to realize the weight had finally lifted from her chest. She choked back a sob of relief before rolling away from the shapes on the floor that had tormented her. Earth-normal gravity never felt as sweet or as light. She loosened the snug and wriggled out of it. The fact that she never got airsick was a definite blessing, but she still dreaded ever getting back in the now sweat-drenched fabric.

It was pretty obvious that Maldonado could watch her if he chose, so he had to know she was awake. She walked the perimeter of the room, pacing the confines of the former galley. It was too small to be a commissary, and she didn't think they called them "kitchens" on space ships.

The ocular was about two-thirds up the far wall. Decent enough for basic wide coverage, but it sacrificed pinpoint focus for the gestalt view. Which meant there would be blind spots in the room. She just needed to take advantage of those blind spots in her exploring.

From the time she'd turned fourteen and beat out her brother Giles for a spot on a dig site during a summer program, Dev had been comfortable working alone in abandoned places. Even he had finally admitted she was better at it than he was. This wasn't much different—an unknown space with potential resources and dangers. But here, her life might depend on what she found and how she used it.

She was used to looking for hiding places, thanks to being the youngest of four in her family. Giles was only two years older than Dev, but their two other brothers were nearly a decade older. The three Morningstar boys spent most of Dev's childhood in a futile attempt to keep her from following them from the settlement into the abandoned town nearby that became their playground.

Dev had quickly become more interested in the broken fragments of the past she uncovered there than in her brothers' endless games of extreme hide and seek. But that didn't mean she couldn't play that game here, now.

There was no food in the galley. Which wasn't a problem yet, but would be if Maldonado kept her here much longer. She rubbed at the sore spot in her neck where he had drugged her. Heat rose up through her chest. Her breath came in ragged gasps. Dev tightened her hands into fists and pounded them against the hard surface of the counter. The fresh pain focused her thoughts away from her captor and back to her examination of the ruined space. She had to stay in control. If she gave in to panic, he would win. And that wasn't going to happen.

The ship's air scrubbers had done a good job keeping the dust eliminated, but the rusted and sagging wire shelving meant the ship had been like this for some time. Even if there had been food here, Dev wouldn't have trusted it.

The door on the refrigeration unit had been twisted off its hinges. The place where the oven had been was a large hole in the thick wall. She leaned over and peered inside the dark space, groaning as her back complained. A wasted effort. Without a light, she couldn't see past the first few centimeters.

Neither an escape route nor an effective hiding place.

Dev cursed the lack of her micro. The light was the least of it. She was no hacker, but there were an array of programs and testing routines that would have been useful. All she had was the little photosensitive cube that Michael had helped her figure out.

She walked back into the seating area. Did he know she was gone? What would he do? They barely knew one another, but surely, he'd say something. Dev wasn't even certain how long she'd been missing. She risked glancing at the ship's ocular, but if Maldonado was watching her, he didn't reveal his presence. It was hard not to curse the man. Swallowing her anger, she turned away, not wanting to give him the satisfaction and forced her thoughts back to her roommate.

If she hadn't seen the burns on Michael's feet, she might have dismissed his story. And then there was the haunted look in his eyes as he had told her. Even in the warmth of the biosphere's sunshine, he had shivered, his face pale, his skin clammy. He had been hurt and hurt badly. By Maldonado.

Dev shuddered, part in sympathy, part in fear. When Maldonado warned her about the jump, she'd convinced herself that he wasn't going to harm her. But this wasn't one of her brothers' games. And at any time, she could become expendable.

She had to get out of this room. Then secure a hiding place. There had to be resources on board even a stripped-down ship. The silence pressed down on her and she paced the galley again. Was there anything she could use here? Waves of panic fractured Dev's focus over and over. Each time one hit, she would lean on the remnants of the counter and hang her head until the lightheadedness faded and her heartbeat slowed to something resembling normal. *Think,*

Dev. Think.

What would she do if this were one of Professor Sellen's tests? She blinked. Well, why not? What was a ship but a container full of materials? *Okay, then.* She looked at the kitchen area again, this time with an eye toward salvage. The heating elements were fractured, but some of the wiring that once had connected them to their power source remained. Wire was always useful.

Positioning herself with her back to the room's ocular, Dev wrapped a few loops of the exposed wire around her hand and yanked as hard as she could. A decent section of it came free from where it vanished behind the former cook top. Dev measured it against her body and coiled the meter and a half or so of length around her waist.

She had nothing to strip them with, except her teeth. That would have to do unless she could find something sharp. Which would be a good idea, no matter what. It would be far too convenient for some long-ago cook or salvor to have left a knife. She knew that, but searched anyway.

It gave her something to do and something else to think about other than what the hell Maldonado was doing.

It wasn't easy to be methodical and hide what she was doing from him. She had to assume he was watching, or recording security vid. But in the end, it didn't matter. He had to know that she would search her makeshift jail cell. Anyone would in her situation. Dev's thin hope was that he didn't know much about her. He had seemed surprised to find her in what he must have assumed was Michael's apartment. So he couldn't know about her background. And what Maldonado didn't know was most definitely going to hurt him.

Sharp. Something sharp.

No knives. No blades of any kind remained in the former kitchen. There wasn't so much as a spoon. The rusty bucket she found in an otherwise empty closet wasn't of much use. Dev examined the partially dismantled refrigerator. Part of the door still remained, hanging off half-torn hinges. A single hinge plate caught her eye. It was flat and thin enough that a corner of it might be able to be sharpened. If she could find something to grind it against. If she could find something to remove it with.

Okay. She prioritized. Get it off the fridge first. Then worry about turning it into a blade. As she renewed her search, now with a specific purpose and focus, Dev's hands steadied and her thoughts cleared.

She took a deep breath. Nothing had changed. But everything had changed.

*

Finding and booking a shuttle to Eurydice Station had been easy. The booking software accepted Micah's new credentials without a hitch, and even lacking access to his father's assets he had enough credit. He'd have to leave for the New Chicago spaceport in a few hours; that was the problem. His quarters felt like a prison, but there was no way he could cope with attending his afternoon study group.

Pacing the small common area had made his feet swell and throb, even in the custom shoes, but he had too much anxious energy to sit. Every minute he was trapped here waiting was a minute more that Dev was in danger.

They should have flooded Maldonado and the engineering compartment with radiation for real when they'd had the chance back on Halcyone.

Micah had picked up his micro nearly a dozen times in the past half-hour intending to report Dev's abduction. But to whom? His academic adviser? Dr. Parrish knew him as some first-year student, here for remedial work. Micah could figure out who Dev's adviser was, but what would he tell them? The only proof he had was Maldonado's recording; sharing it, along with the questions it would certainly raise, would only put more people at risk.

He lurched over to where Dev had placed a row of holos along the wall by her bedroom. He took one down. Dev squinted, smiling from the center of a group of three men, all of whom shared her height and her dark, sleek hair and dark eyes. They were clearly family and Micah wondered what it would have been like growing up with siblings. Dev talked a lot about her brothers, but he didn't recall their names or have any idea where he could find them.

Micah looked at the other holos. There were no images of parents. As open and as gregarious as Dev was, she had never mentioned them.

"Okay, then," he said to the holo. "I guess we both have parent issues. I'll tell you mine if you tell me yours." His hands gripped the edges of the holo tightly. *Damn Maldonado. Damn him.* Micah resumed his pacing.

He could ping his Commonwealth contacts. Maldonado was a wanted fugitive. They would have to follow up on it. He halted, mid-stride, and stared up at the blank wall. But he couldn't risk them connecting Ro with her father and, through her, finding Ithaka. There was too much Micah didn't know, but it was clear that the only thing preventing outright resumption of hostilities between the Commonwealth and the rebels they sought was Ada May's protection and whatever tenuous control she had over The Underworld.

Micah was reeling, a satellite wobbling in an unstable orbit. The wrong shift in any direction and he would either spiral into deep space or crash into a planet.

His father must have felt like this, tenuously balanced between the cartels and the Commonwealth. He shook his head. The last thing he needed was some complicated sympathy for the senator. He forced his thoughts back to Dev. They had to find her. Moved by an impulse he didn't really understand, Micah cloned the holo to his micro and set the image of his smiling roommate and her brothers as his backdrop before carefully placing it back on the shelf with the others.

He limped back to the sofa and tapped his finger on one of her brother's faces. Martingale Morningstar. A fairly unusual name. How hard would it be to find them? At least it would burn up the time he had before his flight. Settling the micro on his lap, Micah pulled up a window and a private search page. The cosmos was big, but he had some clues. They were Earthers. Raised in the Americas. And Dev was active in the urban archeology movement. That narrowed things down considerably. All of that, and her name.

There had to be a near-infinite number of Michael Chases

in the universe. Finding him in that amount of noise should have been like listening for one ping in a universe of ansibles. Except that Maldonado had known his father and his father had been an idiot. Heat rose up through his chest again and he forced himself to take slow, deep breaths to bring the anger under control. That wasn't going to help Dev.

Maybe this would.

He created a search string for her full name. The first bunch of results were academic papers where she was listed as co-author. All of them were from archeology journals. Not too shabby for a second-year Uni student—and not even in her main area of study. He grouped and set them aside before rerunning the search. Now the top result was a news story. A holo of a younger Dev stared out at him, smiling broadly. "Daughter of the Midlant Settlement earns full ride."

Huh. She hadn't mentioned that. The settlements were quasi-permanent refugee cities that grew in the years after so many of the old coastal cities were finally abandoned. The Midlant Settlement sprawled out in a series of shanty towns along the new coastline from what used to be Philadelphia all the way to Virginia. It was pretty much a miracle Dev got anywhere near Uni.

Micah did some quick calculations. Her grandparents were probably part of the initial diaspora, when the newly-organized Commonwealth Guard along with a mashup of relief agencies had set up a series of temporary shelters, each with tents for twenty thousand refugees. It had been utter chaos after the levees and dikes had finally failed and the cities drowned. The government of North America established martial law, essentially forcing the exhausted and newly homeless into manufactured groups at gunpoint, splitting communities and families randomly into hundreds of identical tent cities.

The food and water riots had caused nearly as many deaths and as much destruction as the flooding had.

After a while, when it became clear that the temporary arrangements were the new normal, some of the areas merged; others incorporated into small cities. They formed quasi-representative governments to negotiate for supplies and resources. The Midlant Settlement was the oldest and most well-established of them all, but that wasn't saying much. Even now, generations after the coastal flooding that had triggered the mass migration, the settlements were rough places to live. Micah wished that made him feel better about Dev's chances with Maldonado.

So many of the original refugees had volunteered to go off-world, figuring the mining colonies had to be better than the settlements. Given the benefit of hindsight, Micah didn't think that had panned out, but desperate people made difficult choices. He wondered why her family had stayed.

Refining the parameters, this time Micah searched for any mention of the family in the Midlant Settlement. If there was one thing the Commonwealth did well, it was record keeping. Even in the settlements. It only took a few moments to find her brothers and match names with the faces from Dev's holo. Giles was the brother closest to her age. Tanner was the next oldest, and the elder brother was Vic. Micah squinted at the display. Still no hint of their parents.

Now that he had her siblings' full names, he could, in

theory, find them. Then what? There wasn't much he could reveal without betraying too many confidences. But he couldn't stay silent. He was the only one who knew about Dev. If anything happened to him before he could find her— and Micah was under no illusions that Maldonado wouldn't kill him—that information would vanish.

He wasn't as good at creating hacks as Ro was, but the one he needed was pretty simple. A message triggered by an event was as basic as you could get. Far more difficult was composing the message his micro would send after he'd been out of contact for twenty-four hours. After appending Maldonado's vid to it, Micah returned to his search page and found contact information for all three brothers.

His little program would send the same message to all three. He hoped he would never need to have it trigger.

Chapter 11

RO PAUSED AT Halcyone's airlock. There wasn't a space on Daedalus she felt safe having the conversation she needed to have with Gutierrez. It was pretty clear from their last meeting that aside from her usual hostility and suspicion, the LC had similar reservations.

"Halcyone, open a live link to Durbin, Barre."

"Link active, Captain."

Looked like Barre had been tinkering with the AI's speech algorithms again. "You still on the bridge?"

"It's a lot easier to stretch out my legs here than in my quarters. Word from Micah?"

"No. It's Gutierrez. I think it's time she has a tour of the ship. Fewer eyes and ears on us that way."

"Do you want me to make myself scarce?"

"Actually, no." Gutierrez kept bumping Ro from her comfortable orbit. It was time for a little boost. "I could use your perspective."

"Aye, aye, Captain."

"Knock it off."

She expected Barre to laugh, but he fell silent for a long moment.

"I think she needs to see us as equals, Ro. And you are Halcyone's captain. Gutierrez may need to be reminded of that."

"So what then? You're my XO?"

"Well, if we are going by Commonwealth ranks, yeah, but maybe we don't need to be quite that formal yet. I don't think she'll want to be outranked by both of us. But every ship has a captain, even the dinkiest flitter. And that's you. So get used to it. "

"Yes, sir," she answered. "If the LC accepts my invitation, I'll meet you on the bridge."

"Barre, out."

Halcyone played a quick fanfare and dumped the link. Ro smiled briefly before turning her thoughts back to Gutierrez. And if she declined? That would make things even more complicated than they already were. Reluctant to connect to the station from within Halcyone, Ro squared her shoulders and ducked just outside the airlock.

"Daedalus, locate Lieutenant Commander Gutierrez."

"Off duty. Main commissary."

Good. Though Ro was certain the woman was never truly off duty. She woke her micro. Any message she sent this way would have to be generic and utterly innocuous. It was frustrating. Ro was certain Gutierrez would have an encrypted means of messaging, courtesy of Ada May, but without real trust between them, Ro was stuck using a route she was certain would be monitored.

Fine. At least this would be sure to get Gutierrez curious.

Ro tapped out her invitation. It would be hard for Gutierrez to pass up an opportunity to get aboard Halcyone. Barre was right. Ro was captain of this ship, and even docked, Halcyone was by Commonwealth law a sovereign space. Unless there was a declaration of hostilities, or she was served a warrant, the ship couldn't be boarded without a crew member's permission.

Well, this was Ro's official permission.

And after their earlier conversation, Gutierrez would have to be intensely curious about Ro's motive and timing. Good. She tapped SEND and returned to her ship. Her ship.

Her micro pinged for an incoming message. She smiled. That was fast.

Ro had the airlock open when Gutierrez arrived. "Welcome aboard Halcyone," she said.

The LC strode through, ducking her head slightly to avoid hitting the top of the opening. She waited, frowning, until Ro cycled the lock closed. "I hope you know what you're doing, Maldonado."

There was a time Ro would have flinched at the sound of her father's name. She simply smiled and corrected Gutierrez. "Captain. Captain Maldonado."

The LC raised a single eyebrow before nodding. "Captain."

"Follow me," Ro said. She turned and strode down the narrow corridor to the bridge, not bothering to look back at her guest. It was petty of her, but she hoped it would reinforce just who was in control here. Both for her and for Gutierrez. Ro paused at the melted mess of the bridge door, thinking of Micah. That's why they were all here. That's what

Ro had to focus on. Micah, his friend Dev, and her father—who was a threat to them all.

Barre was waiting just inside and nodded as Ro entered. Gutierrez paused at the threshold. For an instant, Ro saw the bridge through the LC's eyes. She had been part of the fighting during the war on the Commonwealth side, at least initially. Ro still had no idea what had turned Gutierrez into a double agent. Had she known this ship's former crew? Halcyone had been a rebel ship, destroyed by the AI virus Dauber and May had been manipulated into creating. The doomed crew's final panicked transmissions played in Ro's head.

"... *not responding! Interstitial engines off ... collision course. ... day, mayday, mayday, this is transport vessel ... Jesus, Merryweather is down. Halcyone's gone crazy.*"

She could almost hear the terrible buzz of energy weapons turned on their own equipment in a desperate effort to regain control from the damaged AI. Suddenly the war felt very present and very real.

"What do you need from me, Captain?" Gutierrez emphasized that last word.

Ro pulled herself away from the ship's past. "You wanted us to leave Daedalus. Well, something's come up and we need flight clearance. And it would be best if you helped us."

Barre sat in the navigator's chair and spun to face Gutierrez. "Please."

"Mr. Durbin," Gutierrez said, as she stepped farther into the bridge. "Or do you have a rank I'm unaware of?"

"Barre will do, Lieutenant Commander." He waved her to the chair next to him.

Gutierrez seemed to visibly soften. Barre was pretty good at this political stuff, for a musician.

The LC nodded her thanks and sat before returning her gaze to Ro. "So, Captain, what could possibly have changed so radically in a few hours?"

Ro met Barre's eyes. He nodded. She didn't trust Gutierrez. She didn't have to; she trusted Barre. There was a time that wouldn't have been enough, but too much was at stake to let fear hold her back. "My father is officially back from the land of the presumed dead."

"That's unfortunate, but not quite unexpected," Gutierrez answered. "I take it you wish to find him? You'd be better off letting Commonwealth enforcers bring him in."

"It's not that simple," Ro said.

Gutierrez leaned forward and canted her head.

Ro settled her hunched shoulders. "It's Micah. My father is threatening Micah."

"How much does your friend know?"

"Everything."

"That's unfortunate," Gutierrez repeated. "Let the authorities deal with it. The best possible outcome is for them to apprehend your father and he dies resisting capture." She leaned forward and pressed her hands on the chair arms. "I am sorry about Micah. The senator was an idiot, but that wasn't his son's fault."

"And that's it? You're done?" Ro stood in front of the still-seated LC, her hands on her hips. They both knew she wasn't much of an impediment to the tall soldier if she chose to leave. "I don't know what happened to you during the war, and honestly I'm not sure it matters. If you think I'm going to abandon Micah to my father again, you're crazy."

The LC's prosthetic hand tightened and the armrest creaked.

Barre came to stand beside Ro. "And this time, there's another life at stake. He has a hostage for Micah's cooperation. His roommate at Uni. She doesn't deserve this. She isn't any part of it."

Gutierrez looked up at them and for just a moment, Ro saw a flash of pain and of pity in her eyes. "I'm sorry. She is now and it doesn't change anything. A single life against the chaos of war?" Her expression hardened again. "You have no idea what that looks like. How can you?"

"We're not at war," Barre said softly.

Gutierrez drew breath to speak, but Ro cut her off. Heat rose from her chest up to her face. "And we're not going to walk away. Help us or don't, but don't you dare tell us to abandon Micah."

"Or Dev," Barre said.

Gutierrez stared at the dark viewscreen. "She was wrong to trust you."

"We have done nothing to betray that trust," Ro said. "And we will continue to do everything we can to safeguard both her and Ithaka. But we won't let my father win. He's the real risk here. And not just to us. Don't you see that?"

Gutierrez winced. "You think you understand the meaning of sacrifice." Pushing the two of them aside, she stood. Ro shrank away from the touch of the LC's prosthesis. "Do what you must. I won't interfere. If only because I'm wary of bringing any more attention your way. For *her* sake."

Her. Ada May. Even here, where Gutierrez had to know

Ro had employed every security measure in the cosmos, she was still hesitant to say the scientist's name.

"You're wrong about us," Barre said.

Gutierrez stopped and faced him.

"We understand sacrifice. And loss. We just refuse to concede defeat without even trying."

"Is that what you think?" Gutierrez's lips curled into a sad smile. "It's the calculus of war. By calling your friend here 'captain,' you agree to place your life in her hands. Can you be absolutely sure she will make the necessary choices when the time comes?" She turned to Ro. "Because that's what it takes to be in command. And to be commanded."

"We are not at war," Barre repeated. "And I trust Ro with my life."

Gutierrez lifted her chin. "Then I sincerely hope you will never have that trust tested." She took one last look around the bridge before striding out of the ship.

Ro and Barre stood in silence as the echo of her footfalls faded.

*

After breaking several fingernails, Dev resorted to exposing one corner of her little cube from its bag and using the edge to loosen the screws on the door hinge. Either its stored charge was dissipated, or the corners weren't poles. She had to hand it to Sellen. Whatever the photoactive material was that coated the metal, it was incredibly resistant to damage. Probably self-healing. It seemed almost barbaric to be using it this way.

Finally, the fragment of hinge was free. Dev pocketed the screws before examining the rectangular piece of flat metal. Now to sharpen it. Her grandmother used to tell her stories of the early days in the settlement, after the Commonwealth guards had left. After all, their mission had been to set up the shelters and move on. The grateful residents were supposed to wait patiently in their tents for the water to recede and for their homes to be rebuilt. Except it hadn't worked that way and by the time the government had admitted defeat and conceded the coastal cities to the sea, the shelters had become shanty towns. And whatever thin veneer of civilization the inhabitants once had, or tried to cling to, got worn away by months and years of empty promises, more extreme weather, and lack of resources.

Her grandmother's stories had been full of daring, sacrifice, and repurposing. The brutal times were softened by time and distance, but Dev knew the years between the mandatory evacuations and the formation of the official Midlant Settlement had been hell. Back in her dorm room, she still had an old wooden box filled with the blades her grandmother had made from the remnants of the large metal cans the occasional food rations arrived in. She could have used that box now.

What Dev had instead was the wreckage of a former galley—and motivation.

She examined the counter. A lot of the surface had been peeled away, presumably sold for scrap, but there was a small section next to the sink that was still mostly intact. She ran her hand over it. At the edge, a roughened strip caught her fingertip. She looked closer, wet her finger, and rubbed off a layer of grime to uncover the remnants of a ceramic sharpening steel. Well, that was better than a leaky rowboat without oars. She smiled at her grandmother's old expression and got to work.

Her back was to the ocular, but if the audio was working, there was a good chance Maldonado would figure out what Dev was doing. There was no help for that. She got into a rhythm, swiping the side of the hinge at a twenty-degree angle against the edge of the counter. The sound the metal made on the ceramic surface was a high-pitched rasp, almost like a bird call. After every ten passes, Dev would pause, wipe the emerging blade and the sharpening material with the hem of her shirt, shake out her hands, turn the hinge over, and keep going.

She counted to ten again and again, until time had little meaning. Her breath quickened and sweat dripped down her forehead to sting her eyes. Pressure in her bladder brought her back to her body. How long had she been here? How long was Maldonado going to keep her here? Now that she had stopped the mind-numbing routine of sharpening, Dev's hands cramped. The hinge was barely sharp enough to press a line against her thumb. She slipped it into her pocket and shook out her arms. This was going to take a lot longer than she thought.

If Maldonado thought shutting her up in here without even basic sanitary facilities was going to somehow break her spirit, then he definitely didn't know any Morningstars. She grabbed the bucket and set up the far corner of the galley behind the half wall as her latrine. If she was here for any length of time, it would get unpleasant, but Dev could handle unpleasant. She had grown up in Midlant.

After a short rest, Dev returned to her work. The muscles of her neck and shoulders ached and her fingers stiffened so badly she kept dropping the hinge. But still, she kept going. Ten swipes on one side of the hinge, ten swipes on the other. Her stomach rumbled, but Dev could deal with the hunger. It was thirst that could kill.

The sound of the galley door opening seemed as loud as the ship's engine. Dev's heart raced as she slipped the not-quite-blade into her pocket. Brushing off the metal dust from her clothing, she stepped toward the door. Damned if she was going to cower in front of him.

He stood just inside the galley. In one hand he held a small energy weapon. Its stubby shape belied its sleek efficiency. A bag hung from his other hand.

"Please stay where you are. I'd hate to have to shoot you."

His voice was pleasant, conversational, and Dev shivered, remembering how efficiently he'd paralyzed her and loaded her into his waiting trundle. Keeping the weapon trained on her, he dropped the bag to the floor.

"Water and emergency rations. I see you already set up sanitary facilities. We're going to be here for a few days, so make yourself comfortable."

Dev slid her hand into her pocket and ran her finger across the edge she'd been working at. It was barely sharp enough to cut anything, but there were plenty of places she could jab a body with it hard enough to hurt. Maybe even seriously. The question was, could she do it?

If Maldonado tried to drug her again, she would resist.

But if she rushed him now, she'd be hit before she could take more than a step or two. If he hadn't been armed? Dev could wrestle any of her brothers to a draw, but Maldonado's weapon changed the rules. This wasn't a game and she wasn't going to be able to tap out. If she went for him, it would have to be to disable or to kill.

Her heart raced and her mouth dried. She was no soldier. She'd gutted a snake on a dig site, but even that was self-defense. To stab a living, breathing person was a different matter. The threat Maldonado posed was less immediate than the snake's had been. She didn't believe he would shoot her now. Why would he? Maldonado controlled all the jump parameters here: it was his ship, he knew where in the universe they were, and he had access to life support, food, and water.

If he'd wanted her dead, he'd already had plenty of opportunities. At least for the short term, he needed her alive, unharmed.

Dev pulled her hand from the pocket, leaving the hinge behind. "I don't suppose you have my micro," she said.

"It's in a safe place."

It was too much to hope that he'd give it back to her. But then again, she hadn't had one for most of her growing-up years and managed just fine. Uni had softened her. This was a place for Midlant survival skills.

"No other questions? You are an interesting one. No wonder Micah ... Michael likes you."

She remembered when her roommate had first introduced himself. *Micah ... Michael Chase.* That same pause. So he'd changed his name. Huh.

Did Maldonado assume they were a couple? She wasn't sure if that would work in her favor, or against her, especially if Maldonado was counting on Michael's ... no, Micah's supposed emotional connection to her as leverage.

Her captor slid the supplies bag toward her before backing out the galley door. Before Dev could move a step forward, the door sealed again. The urge to test the lock mechanism was almost irresistible, but the need to eat and drink was even stronger.

He'd provided her with a carton of water bulbs and a flat of basic ration bars. Right about now, they looked like a feast. She tore into the water first and drank a full bulb without stopping. The water sloshed uncomfortably in her stomach. Dev cradled the empty container in her hand. Made from a modified polymer, it was light enough that it didn't add much weight to the water itself, and acted as an efficient insulator to keep the water liquid, even when exposed to extreme temperatures. It was a marvel of materials science—flexible and sturdy. Maldonado probably had no idea what he had just given her.

She pulled out her failed blade. More like an awkward screwdriver. Well, it hadn't been a total waste, but now that she had better source material, possibilities expanded in her mind. Food, water, tools, and time. She had what she needed.

Chapter 12

THE WORK IN comms was little more than a distraction. Nomi monitored incomings while Simon Marchand had the outgoings. Lowell never seemed to do much of anything. Mendez hadn't set up any sort of regular reporting mechanism, so Nomi had to figure out what could possibly be relevant and pass the information along. So far, there was nothing except for Simon's clear dislike of their supervisor. Which didn't prove treason. She needed more data.

She and Simon couldn't take breaks together— not while on the same shift—so that left off-duty time. Maybe she could do turnabout with some of the pickles her grandfather used to make. The hydroponics staff had been experimenting with some miniature vegetables. She'd gotten to be friendly with the lead tech. All Nomi would need was a large container and saltwater. Maybe some herbs, if any were ready to harvest. If nothing else, it would be a reminder of home. And a reason to talk with Simon "off the clock."

Nomi's micro pinged for her dinner break. She transferred her console to Lowell's before pushing back in her chair and stretching. Maybe Ro would have some other ideas for what to do about him.

"Nakamura, Konomi signing out, eighteen hundred hours thirty. Check and confirm." It seemed silly to go through the formal process when there were only three of them on duty. This wasn't something she'd ever had to do on nights. The station's AI would make a log entry anyway. It just seemed like make-work.

There was no response. Nomi swiveled her chair around and repeated the sign-out. Lowell shook himself away from whatever had engrossed him on his screen before releasing her from the shift. She and Simon shared a puzzled look. What could he have possibly been doing to distract him to that extent? It wasn't as if they were moving a lot of comms traffic. If Ro had been sitting in her chair, Nomi was sure she would have been able to hack into Lowell's workstation to find out. But all Nomi had were suspicions—hers, Simon's, and Commander Mendez's.

"Back in forty," she called over her shoulder.

"Say hi to Captain Maldonado for me," Simon answered.

Lowell jerked upright in his chair and shifted his gaze to Nomi briefly before relaxing and returning to his display. That was curious. All the way to Halcyone, Nomi puzzled over Lowell's behavior, but without anything more specific, she couldn't be sure she wasn't imagining conspiracies where none existed.

The ship's AI greeted her, the artificial voice seeming warm and pleasant. "Nice to see you, too, Halcyone," she answered. In engineering, Barre and Jem were sitting at adjacent consoles, their chairs turned to face each other, identical glum looks on their faces. Ro was pacing the center of the room.

"What happened?"

"Micah's in trouble," Jem said.

"My father." Ro nearly spit the words out.

Nomi stood in front of Ro and blocked the tight line she'd been tracing up and down the narrow aisle. "What about your father? What kind of trouble?"

Ro's cheeks were flushed. "Gutierrez can jump in the wrong end of a wormhole. I'm going to find him and when I'm done, he won't be able to hurt anyone or anything."

How was Gutierrez involved? "Barre? What's going on?"

He passed Nomi his micro and her breath hitched as she read the message chain with Micah. "So, what's the plan?"

Ro stopped short. She clenched her fists. "We get off Daedalus. We meet with Micah. We find the bastard."

"Good plan. It just could use some specifics," Nomi said, trying to ease the tension.

"We need a plausible reason to get off Daedalus. One that won't trigger suspicions," Barre said. "The last thing we need is to be followed because someone thinks we'll lead them to Ithaka."

"I'm telling you, we should contact Ada. She'll help us," Jem said. It was clear from his frustration and Barre's sigh that they'd already been through that argument.

"I'm sure she would, Jem," Nomi said. "But anything that involves Ithaka is a risk we can't afford to take."

"We have to help Micah!" Jem jumped up and took a step toward Ro.

"You think I'm not trying?" Ro shouted back. "If we're not

careful, we could make things worse than they already are. For Micah, for his friend, and for Dr. May."

"Wait. Just wait a minute." Nomi moved between the two of them, thinking furiously. "Eurydice Station is hardly a hotbed of black market action. Do you really think Mendez will call in the cavalry to tail you there?"

"I don't know. Maybe? Probably?" Ro threw up her hands. "But from there, we're going to make for the coordinates May sent us and we can't risk being followed. If my father is there, and he thinks we've set the Commonwealth on him, the girl he abducted will be a liability he can't afford."

"Dev," Barre said. "Her name is Dev."

"Besides, we have to get to Eurydice first."

"It's a major spaceport," Nomi said. "They do all the refits for the entire sector."

"So what?" Ro snapped.

Nomi caught Ro's hands and held them gently. "So, Mendez doesn't know how much you've been able to do on Halcyone. As far as she's concerned, you've been busy doing work for Daedalus. Eurydice has everything from the big parts suppliers to bays you can rent for do-it-yourself fixes. And you have a spaceship in need of repair."

"Oh." Ro blinked. "But will she let us leave?"

"Me? Probably not. I don't have several consecutive days off for another week or so. I'd have to check my schedule. But you? You're not really beholden to the station proper, right? Besides, you're a ship's captain. There are certain privileges that come with the title. Maybe you should try them out."

"Oh," Ro repeated. The red in her cheeks faded. She squeezed Nomi's hands before bringing them up to her lips. "I'm an idiot."

"What can I do?" Jem asked. "He's my friend, too."

"Mom and Dad aren't going to let you off station. You know that."

Jem sat down again, his shoulders slumping.

"But you can be our eyes and ears here in a way even Nomi can't. She's official. You always seem to be able to slip under the sensors. Mom and Dad are part of the senior staff. If something explodes here, you'll be the first to know."

He nodded, his gaze downcast.

"He's right," Nomi said. "I'm already maxed out trying to keep tabs on Lowell. I could use your help."

"Fine."

"All right, then," Barre said. "Do we have Micah's ETA?"

Ro checked her micro. "If he's not delayed, his shuttle gets to Eurydice at zero six hundred local time. Assuming we get flight clearance tonight, we can meet him there right around the same time."

Nomi had to bite her lip to keep from asking Ro when she'd last slept. "Log your request. Get out of here. We'll be waiting for you."

"I'll walk you back, Jem," Barre said. He met Nomi's gaze and nodded.

She was grateful for the few minutes she'd have alone with Ro. When the brothers left, she slipped into Ro's arms. "Be careful," she whispered.

Ro rested her head in the hollow of Nomi's shoulder.

Nomi kissed the soft silk of Ro's hair and breathed in her

scent. "Please."

*

Micah had booked the first shuttle from the Chicago Spaceport to Eurydice Station without even looking at what he would be flying. It didn't matter. Speed was far more important than comfort. He slid into his row past the other three passengers, barely paying attention to the pre-flight orientation instructions. He'd heard them so often, he could have given them himself by now.

The woman sitting next to him fumbled with her straps. Micah sighed, loosened his harness and leaned over to help her.

"Thank you."

Micah turned away and secured himself again. He turned to the window and stared at the tarmac far below.

"It's my first jump-flight."

She was a woman in her forties or fifties. First flight? Even for an Earther, that was rare.

"I guess I'm a little scared."

Micah really didn't want to talk to anyone, but he realized he was committed now. What was the old superstition about being responsible for someone whose life you'd saved? There had to be some corollary for helping with shuttle seat harnesses.

"Take a space-sickness tablet. Trust me, it'll make things better." Both for her and for all of them in her row.

"What if something goes wrong?" Her hands gripped the

arm rests so hard her knuckles were blanched.

Micah's first response—it doesn't matter, we'll be dead—wouldn't have been at all helpful. "These commercial shuttles have redundancies for redundancies. They can pretty much fly themselves. And worst case scenario, all Commonwealth ports have jump-sickness treatment facilities. Just keep your gaze on the display. You'll be fine."

She patted his hand. "Sounds like you've done this a few times."

"You could say that." Micah rolled his eyes. "Look, I don't mean to be rude, but I've got some things to figure out."

"Oh, I'm sorry." Her hand receded.

"Hey, it's okay." She looked nothing like his mother and his mother was never anxious about anything, not even her own death, but something about this woman reminded him of her. He turned back. "Really."

With part of his mind, Micah listened for the pilot's announcements. She was calling for the flight attendants to confirm passenger loading and to secure themselves. The engines whined as they spun up. His seat neighbor drew her breath in sharply.

"We're going to take the space elevator up in a few minutes. There'll be a lot of vibration. Then everything will go silent after we break orbit until the first burn." The next commercial flight he took, he was definitely going to make sure he got a private cabin.

"And the jump? They'll give us plenty of warning?"

"Yes."

She fell silent for some time. The windows darkened as the ship broke through the cloud cover and the sun hit the photosensitive coating. It reminded him of Dev. He clenched his teeth and willed the shuttle to go faster.

"It's my daughter."

"What?"

"She's due to deliver any day now. Her husband is meeting me on Eurydice. I'm kind of nervous."

"Really?" Micah said, smiling, "I'd never have noticed."

She laughed, a high, shaky sound. "It's more than the trip and being a grandmother for the first time. It's just that I've never met him. I want to make a good first impression."

Micah wondered if Dev had ever been off-world before. If not, she must be terrified. Waking up to being Maldonado's prisoner was terrifying enough. He should know. Bastard was due for a lot of payback. Micah curled his hands around the molded plastic armrests hard enough for them to creak in protest.

"Hey," the woman said. "You're supposed to be the seasoned traveler. Is everything okay?"

Micah released the tension in his shoulders and hands. "I have a friend. She's in trouble." He turned his face away from her and stared out the window. The play of light and shadow reminded him of the biosphere and the afternoon he'd spent talking with Dev.

The woman slipped her hand beneath his and held it in silence until the first burn warning sounded. Soon after, they jumped. One long, stable wormhole took the shuttle from Earth's solar system on its twisting way bypassing interstitial space and folding time. Ro could probably explain it better, but all that mattered was that Halcyone would be meeting him and they could go after Maldonado.

By the time they docked at Eurydice Station, the cabin smelled faintly of stale vomit, despite the air-handling system. His nervous neighbor thanked him over and over again. Micah waited until the row emptied and he let her disembark ahead of him. She paused at the airlock to wave and wish him good luck.

It wasn't luck he needed.

He didn't have any checked baggage. All he had taken with him was a change of clothes, a cleansing kit, and his micro. After the bulk of the passengers had left the ship, Micah cleared customs easily. His Commonwealth-issued ID didn't raise any suspicions. He hated leaving a trail to follow, but at least this one would end here.

As soon as he pinged the station, his micro updated to local time and swamped his display with local news and ads. He swiped them away, impatient for word from Ro. When he used to travel with his father on diplomatic credentials, they were whisked from a private docking cradle to a reserved lounge area. It was strange being nostalgic for something he'd despised, but negotiating the crowded arrivals area made him jumpy. There were too many people here. All the shops that lined the travel corridor from the gates to baggage claim tried to claim his micro's attention with personalized sound and images. There had to be a way to block all of it without turning off the device completely, but that was Ro's department. And until he heard from Halcyone, Micah was prisoner of the cacophony.

His body clock was completely off. Subjective travel time through jump space never synced up with galactic time. And the longer the jump, the worse the discrepancy. They had left

Earth orbit in the early evening. His body was convinced it should still be in bed, but according to the clock, it was morning.

It could have been worse. Jump space compressed years of travel into hours. Which worked in Maldonado's favor as well: he could have taken Dev anywhere.

The terminal was so noisy, he almost missed Halcyone's message when it pinged him. Micah stopped suddenly, his heart racing, and several irritated travelers plowed into him. He waved them past, stepped into the entrance of an access corridor between several stores, and opened the text message.

/Here. Docking bay Epsilon 704/

/On my way/ He opened up a station map. It was hard not to run and push through the milling crowds, but Micah was wary of calling attention to himself. He walked briskly, but carefully down the arrivals corridor and into the station proper. The noise and congestion dropped significantly. Micah took the most direct line to the public docking bays, ignoring the itch between his shoulder blades, certain it was only his own paranoia making him feel as if he were being surveilled.

The Commonwealth authorities could certainly have followed him here, but for what reason? They had to be confident that they could find him at any time. There was no evidence that tied him to Maldonado. As far as they knew, Maldonado had vanished and was presumed dead. His communications with Ro were secure and even if anyone suspected anything, once Halcyone left Eurydice, he and the ship would effectively vanish. At least that was the plan.

By the time Micah got to the Epsilon level, he was alone. He turned down the access corridor for bay 704 and broke into a run. Through the airlock, he saw the battered freighter. The tension in his shoulders and his chest eased. Halcyone's hull was dented and scraped, her shape an ungainly blot against the backdrop of space behind her, but Micah had never seen anything so beautiful.

He triggered the door release. "Ahoy, Halcyone, permission to board?"

The Eurydice side of the lock opened. He stepped inside.

"Permission granted, Micah Rotherwood. Welcome back."

He smiled. Halcyone's voice had smoothed considerably since the last time he'd heard her. The inner door swung open and he entered, remembering the first time he'd been aboard. She hadn't had a name, then. She was simply an old wreck he had repurposed for his makeshift botany lab.

"Good to be back, Halcyone. Where is Ro?"

"Captain Maldonado is on the bridge."

Micah smirked. Captain. Huh.

"Barre Durbin is also on the bridge."

His friends had come. It was going to be all right. He ran up the corridor to the bridge and stopped short at the remains of the blasted door. The smell of charred flesh and melted polymers overwhelmed him. It didn't matter that it was only in his mind. He stumbled and nearly fell through the open doorway, his feet throbbing. The memories of that day were never far from his conscious mind. Anything could trigger them: the scent of cooking meat, the metallic flash of a blaster, even the whine of a power tool could bring him back to this place, on that day.

It followed him through dreams, where his feet bubbled away as he stood firing at the door. Only then, the door kept regenerating, sealing his friends inside, permanently, while somewhere behind him, Maldonado's laughter came closer and closer.

He shivered even as sweat beaded across his forehead.

Micah shook his head to clear away the images that mixed memory with nightmare. He looked up to see Barre's concerned face in front of him. His large hands dropped onto Micah's shoulders with welcome warmth. "Hey, man, it's good to see you."

Micah returned Barre's smile. Ro walked up to him and took his hands.

"I love what you've done with the place," he said.

*

"You look like crap," Barre said. Dark circles lined Micah's eyes and his shoulders drooped with fatigue. Barre didn't like the way he limped as he entered the bridge.

"Well, it's great to see you, too," Micah answered.

"Sit. I want to take a look at your feet."

"We don't have time for that."

"Don't be an idiot," Ro said. "Listen to Barre. Besides, we have another fifteen minutes before we're cleared for pre-flight."

Micah jerked his hands from Ro's. "You filed a damned flight plan? What in the bloody cosmos were you thinking?"

"Easy there, space ranger." Barre placed a hand on Micah's chest. "How do you think you leave a major port like Eurydice without permission? We'll take a jump and then recalibrate to follow May's coordinates. We have it covered."

"And what if he's not there?"

"We'll find him. I know my father. He'll have pissed someone off enough that they'll remember him. It's what he does best."

Barre pointed to a seat. "Sit. Shoes off."

"Man, you really do take after your mother."

There had been a time when hearing that would have really bothered him, but there were circumstances where her brutal efficiency and ability to push emotions away came in handy. "This is what you can do to help your friend. So quit whining."

"Fine." Micah yanked at the shoe closures, removed the shoes, and tugged his socks off.

Barre sat on the floor and examined his feet, looking for pressure points and tracing the graft scars. His parents had done a good job with the repair. Micah might have problems with swelling for the rest of his life, but at least he'd have working feet. There were red marks where a sock bunch had dug into his left instep.

"I'm going to attribute the extra swelling to sitting in a jump-seat and the acceleration burns, but you need to check your socks before you put on the shoes. Every time."

"It's my fault. If anything happens to her, I swear, I'll kill him."

"It's not. It won't. And get in line." Barre handed Micah his pressure-gradient socks. "You're lucky you didn't break the skin. Not feeling pain isn't the same thing as healing. Don't be an idiot."

Micah looked away, his face flushed.

"We'll find her. You know Ro won't stop until we do." Barre watched her move around the bridge, a model of efficiency wrapped tightly in barely controlled rage.

"Station control just gave us our three-minute warning," she said.

Micah put on the socks, smoothing them carefully before slipping his shoes back on. "There. Satisfied?"

Barre nodded.

"We have to be somewhere where I can send him a message in less than three hours," Micah said. "I have no idea what in the cosmos I'm going to say to him."

"We need to buy time. Demand proof that Dev's unharmed."

Barre winced, noticing the slight hesitation in Ro's voice before that final word. They had to act on the assumption Maldonado would keep Dev alive until he got what he wanted. Otherwise Micah would go completely nuclear.

"And who thinks that he'll release her after he gets what he wants? You? You?" Micah gazed at each of them in turn. "No? Me neither. And just how long can we string him along?"

"Long enough," Barre said.

"Do you really believe that?"

Barre was saved from answering by an alarm blaring through the bridge.

"Okay, crew, strap in. We've got a short trip through interstitial before we reach the jump point."

Micah and Barre followed Ro's lead and snugged their harnesses. Newer ships had temporal-damping mesh built into the command chairs, but they hadn't had the chance to retrofit Halcyone with them yet. If they had been putting her in the repair dock for real, they could have. When it was time to jump, they'd have to use the berth cushioning May had given them. It left the bridge empty during their wormhole transit, but it was a huge step up from the snugs.

"Eurydice Station, this is the Commonwealth freighter, Halcyone. We are secure. Release docking clamps."

"Halcyone, this is Eurydice Station. Acknowledged. Docking clamps releasing. Safe travels."

A series of hollow clangs echoed through the ship.

"Micah?" Barre said, softly.

He stared straight ahead at Halcyone's cracked viewscreen. A muscle in his jaw twitched.

"We'll find her," Barre said, again. His voice was swallowed up by the growl of Halcyone's interstitial engines.

Chapter 13

DEV WOKE, HER body stiff and cold. Without her micro or any external cues, she had no idea how long she'd slept. Before exhaustion had taken control, she'd organized her inventory: her cube, the mostly useless hinge, wire, three empty water bulbs, and a rations wrapper.

They were all tucked around her and the nest she'd made of the jump snug.

She swore as she stretched. The bruises from being trapped on the chair clamps during the jump were even more painful this— she would call it—morning. Her hair was a matted mess that she ignored. A cleansing kit would have been nice, but she didn't think Maldonado was in the business of being nice. At least she had food and water.

Okay, Dev, wash, eat, drink, plan.

There was enough water to spare some for washing. Anything that made her feel more like herself was a win and whatever Maldonado's game was, Dev needed to be at her sharpest to play it. She considered using her shirt for sacrificial towel material, but she was barely warm enough as it was. The outer layer of the jump snug would work just as well and didn't interfere with the functional inner weave. It might also be useful for wrapping tool handles.

Hacking at the fabric with the sharpest bit of her hinge, Dev got it to start to split. After that, it tore easily into strips. At least now when she used her makeshift head, she could clean herself up. She emptied her waste bucket in the galley's sink. There was a good chance that since the water wasn't flowing, the reclamation circuits weren't working either, but that would be Maldonado's problem, not hers.

Breakfast time. Dev chewed and swallowed a meal bar, washing it down with plenty of water. The bars had the requisite amount of nutrients and calories to keep a body functioning, but also the texture and likely the taste of pressed insulation foam. Unpleasant, but working hungry was never a good idea.

She gathered up her materials. If she'd had access to a heat source and a makeshift forge, she might have been able to make the hinge into a proper blade, but still, the hours she'd spent yesterday weren't all wasted. Between the metal edge and the counter material, Dev had what she needed to shape the polymer water bulbs into things she could use.

The only way she had to mark time, besides the fatigue in her body, was taking note of hunger and thirst. After what was probably three or four hours of work, Dev had transformed the polymer bulbs into several decent screwdrivers, a blade, and an awl. She shook out her hands, frowning at the incipient blisters. It had been a long time since she'd been in the field. Not that this was anything like any of her dig sites.

Dev arched her back. It felt as if her spine were one big solid block of ache. She crouched to give her leg muscles a rest, then sat for a while, rolling her new tools around in her palm. *Now what?*

There was no way to know when Maldonado would check on her again. He'd given her what looked like more than a week's worth of supplies. Maybe they were going to be here for a while. She rested her head on her knees. How many classes had she missed? Would they think she'd dropped out like her brother? Just another settlement rat washing out of every opportunity handed to her. Shit. Had Micah even reported her missing? His story and Maldonado's actions made her think it was unlikely. He seemed to have as much mistrust of the Commonwealth as most of the settlement folks.

If he had said something, then maybe her scholarship would still be there. Which also meant the school would have notified her brothers and they would be frantic. If her grandmother had still been alive, Dev wouldn't have liked Maldonado's chances to get out of this unscathed, but it was just the four of them left. Their parents had split for the colonies not long after Dev was born, when it was clear they couldn't support the family on the jobs available for them on Earth. Her grandparents had raised them, but both of them had died when Dev was young. Her brothers were her entire family, now.

It was a good thing Maldonado didn't expect any of them to ransom her back. Of the four of them, Dev and Giles were the only ones to make it to Uni. Giles had managed to blow his own scholarship after less than two years. Her brothers were scattered around different areas of the Midlant Settlement, scraping together enough credits to live, but not doing much better than that.

Dev was supposed to have been the one to change everything.

She slammed her fist into the floor beside her. A hollow clang reverberated through the galley. Dev drew her breath in sharply and ignored the throbbing in her hand. Snatching up one of her newly made crude tools, she tapped it against the flooring, listening intently. The sound was different for about a third of a square meter around her.

An access hatch. Of course. There had to be service tunnels for water and power and repair access all through the ship. Now all she had to do was get it open. Ignoring the grime on the floor, Dev crawled around examining the metallic tiles. They looked solid, each piece abutting the next with the thinnest of seams. The metal was treated with the same almost holographic patterning as the ceiling, giving it a three-dimensional effect and making it hard to study closely. She closed her eyes and ran her hands over it instead. What her eyes had missed, her fingers found: small plugs set into the corners of the tile. When she looked at them, she couldn't see them at all.

Letting her hands be her guide, she slipped the tip of her thinnest screwdriver along the edge of the seam and slowly pushed on its makeshift material-wrapped handle. The polymer tool bent in a shallow arc as she pressed down. "Don't break, please don't break," she whispered. The bulb's material was strong and resilient by design, but if the plug covers were sealed in place, the polymer wasn't going to stand up to whatever alloy they'd made the floor out of.

She released the pressure on the tool and pulled it free. Her forehead beaded sweat. Her hands were trembling. Moving quietly, she repositioned to the opposite corner and tried again. Again, the screwdriver started to warp before there was any sense of movement from the plug. With deliberate care, Dev set it down and wiped her hands on the bottom of her shirt. Then she picked up the tool and went to the third corner.

In her mind, she was uncovering a precious relic, and this was a dig site, not a prison. Slowly, carefully, she could loosen the plugs. She had to.

It was just going to take time. Dev had plenty of that.

She lost track of how long she circled the small area of floor, applying minute amounts of pressure to each of the four plugs in turn, before one shifted. At first Dev thought she'd cracked the screwdriver, but when she looked down, the pattern of the flooring had been disrupted and the tiny disk was now ever so slightly raised up above the level of the tile.

"Fuck, yeah," she whispered, before attacking the remaining three with a new energy.

*

As soon as the burn ended and Halcyone had reached her cruising velocity, Micah flung off the restraints and paced the narrow confines of the bridge. Ro and Barre both remained seated, watching him try to wear a path in the decking plates. "Where in the universe are we going, anyway?"

Ro shrugged. "It's hard to tell. Wherever May's coordinates lead, they're not on the Commonwealth charts. I'm assuming it's hidden the way Ithaka is."

"And you trust her?"

She and Barre shared a look Micah couldn't interpret. "She helped Jem. And she let us go," Barre said.

"She's Ada May." Ro spread her arms wide. "What choice do we have?"

It was dangerous to have heroes and trust was too easily broken. Micah paused to glance at his micro for probably the hundredth time. Still more than two hours before Maldonado expected his message and he was no closer to figuring out what to say. "If it's not on the map, how do you know we're not going to jump into oblivion?"

The two of them glanced at one another again before Ro nodded to Barre.

"Ro instructed Halcyone to let us know when we were clear of the main shipping routes and far enough from any major wormholes that we wouldn't show up on any routine scans. Then we can run the Ithaka program and reboot nav. We'll have a better idea then."

"Look at you, talking all engineer-speak. When did that happen?"

"When you helped my brother run away to The Underworld and we had to rescue him."

Micah clenched his jaw to keep silent. It didn't help that Barre was right, but it had turned out okay for Jem in the end, hadn't it?

"Hey, guys, friends here, right?"

And having Ro be the mediator was new, too. Nomi must be a good influence. "Where are we now?"

Barre whistled a few notes to get Halcyone's attention. Micah didn't see Ro make any gestures, but the map on the forward display centered on a dot in space surrounded by a lot of emptiness.

"Here," Ro said. This time she did gesture and circle another spot on the top left-hand corner of the display. "And heading there. That's when we'll reboot nav and take a blind jump."

Blind jumps. That's what they had all been, once upon a time. Before Dauber and May had created the self-aware computers that were powerful enough to run the quantum calculations. If May had given them the coordinates, Halcyone shouldn't end up a micron thin and smeared along the interior of a wormhole, and neither should they.

Was he doing the right thing? Maybe he should have just turned this over to the Commonwealth. They were gambling with Dev's life. He stopped and slammed his fist against the nearest console.

Ro propelled herself out of her chair and stood in front of him. "Hey." She grabbed his hands. "Hey. Look at me."

Micah looked up. Her eyes were open wide and very, very green.

"It's going to be all right. We'll find her."

"They could be anywhere." Micah pulled his hands from hers and turned away. "She could be dead."

"Stop it! You think you're the only one with a monopoly

on guilt?" Ro shifted so she was directly in front of him again. "And no one knows my father as well as I do. He may be vicious and ruthless, but he's not a casual murderer. Alain Maldonado is far too concerned with manipulating people. It's hostages he wants. I should know. After all, look how long I was one."

All Micah could do was stand there and shake his head.

"Remember, he could have killed any of us when he was on Halcyone," Barre said.

Micah made a rude gesture and pointed to his feet. "And see where that got me?"

"Maldonado was just keeping you in storage. The aftermath was your brilliant idea."

Micah strode to where Barre was lounging, his feet up on the console and curled his hands into fists. Heat pulsed through his face.

"If it would make you feel better, go ahead." Barre opened his arms.

"Fuck." Micah loosened his fists and tugged his shaking fingers through his hair. "How much longer until we're out of Eurydice's ansible range?"

Ro checked her micro. "We should be close to handover any minute."

"Fine. As soon as we're picked up by one of the outer satellites, I'll send Maldonado his damned message. The quicker we make the jump, the better. Assuming there's something useful on the other side of those coordinates."

"Handover in three, two, one. We are out of Eurydice's coverage."

There were more basic repeaters out here, this far from

anywhere useful. If anyone was tracking his messages, they'd only get the remote beacon's address, but would have no idea where Halcyone was pinging it from. Running his reply through the encryption program would help. And Micah had to believe that Maldonado would have safeguards on his end as well.

He slumped in the nearest chair and leaned over his micro, his hands hesitating on the text input. There were so many things he wanted to say to Dev, but this wasn't for her and Maldonado would never pass along Micah's regret and apology. Fine. He wasn't going to send a video. The fewer clues the man had to Micah's location, the better.

I can get access to my father's accounts, but he hid them beneath layers of security. It will take some time to drill through and establish control. That wasn't true, but Maldonado couldn't know that. And he would believe his father had been just that suspicious. *I need to talk to Dev. In real time. I won't release the money without proof that she's unharmed.*

Ro craned her neck to read over Micah's shoulder. "Soften that last bit."

Micah wanted to scream and rage at Maldonado, the way he had never had the chance to do after the cuffs started torturing him. "Fine." He deleted the sentence and started again. *Show me proof that she's unharmed and I'll release the money.*

"Better. Let him believe you're cooperating. That you're under control."

"I'm not." Micah nearly snarled in her face.

Ro placed a hand on his shoulder. "Just as long as he

believes it."

"Can you get Halcyone to send this?" Micah pasted the dead-drop headers to the message.

"You should still be paired with the ship. Just ask her," Barre said.

"Okay." He took one final look at the message, but there was nothing else that needed to be said. So much was in Maldonado's hands. Micah didn't even have any way of checking if and when it would be received. "Halcyone?"

A bright musical tone filled the bridge.

"Send outgoing message. Set up comms to check for reply every sixty seconds. Notify on new mail."

The tones sounded again. "Message sent. Checking remote mailbox."

Halcyone's pause could have been measured in scant seconds, but the time seemed to stretch in uncomfortable silence.

"Remote mailbox empty."

"Thank you."

"You are welcome, Micah Rotherwood."

"Wow, you've really done a job on that computer," Micah said. Not that he was surprised. He'd seen Ro pretty much perform magic with just a micro and her waving hands.

She nodded to Barre. "Not me. Him."

"Barre?"

"Not you, too," Barre said.

"No offense, man, but you're the musician. I just thought ..."

"It's all good. Halcyone and I—we have an

understanding."

Micah's mouth fell open as Barre told him about contacting Jem neural-to-neural through Halcyone when they were "guests" on Ithaka. "Wow. That's quantum. Do you have any idea what this means?" It was the holy grail of the singularity, the direct fusion of an AI with a human mind.

"It seems to work better when Jem's not conscious. At least that's when he's been able to link back with me. We haven't had much time to figure it out."

"But you can hook directly into the AI. That could be worth a small fortune to the right people."

"And how do we figure out who the right people are?" Barre asked quietly.

The black market would kill for that kind of information. And if it meant that someone like Maldonado would benefit? Micah fell silent.

"Besides, I'm not even sure how I did it. It started with the music. Maybe it's something related to that and Halcyone's specific damage. At least it means I can help Ro with her."

"Speaking of which," Ro said. "Are we ready to reboot?"

"Are you sure this is the best way to help Dev?" Micah asked.

Ro squeezed his hands. "I think it may be the only way."

Micah nodded. "Then let's do this."

"Barre?"

He whistled a series of repeating notes. Halcyone used the synthesized tones to play it back. Then the viewscreen went blank. The crack that zigzagged across it stood out starkly. The lights on the bridge flickered. Micah started, but neither Ro nor Barre seemed alarmed.

"Ithaka routine initiated. Stand by for nav control."

Brightness flooded the bridge as the screen blazed a harsh white. Micah blinked away afterimages, like impossible dark stars against a dazzling sky. When he was able to focus again, there was a different map on the display.

"Nav control enabled."

"Good girl," Barre said softly.

Ro pulled up a window showing a long string of coordinates. "Halcyone, plot a course, minimize interstitial transit. Display."

The map wavered for a moment. Their current position showed up as a small ship icon. A series of dotted lines stretched from the ship to a circled wormhole.

"Expand trip parameters."

Text scrolled next to the map. Micah had no idea what the nav shorthand meant. "A little help here?"

"Halcyone calculated a brief burn at three g's. Everyone okay with that?"

Micah and Barre nodded. A little discomfort was more than a fair tradeoff against the clock and Dev's safety.

"Then a single long jump. Barre—we'll need a trigger with a short buffer. Micah, there's an extra berth in Barre's room that has adequate cushioning."

"Ro, we have no idea what we're jumping into," Barre said.

She held Micah's gaze for a long moment before answering. "I know, but we don't really have much of a choice. And really, do we ever?"

*

As Ro settled into the jump foam, she reviewed the parameters. It was easier to focus on the details of the trip than on what they would do once they arrived. There was no information on the maps—only a numerical designation and the schematic of a small star system with several planets and their satellites. Surely May would have warned them if they were jumping into an armed resistance stronghold or an active smuggling operation.

If May even knew.

Ithaka was one tangled mess, a tensegrity web where pulling on any of the nodes—the Commonwealth, Ada May's quiet insurgency, the black market, the cartels, and the smugglers—tugged on each of the others. She understood why Gutierrez was so reluctant to either get involved or have Ro disturb such a tenuous balance.

But that didn't mean Ro agreed with the embittered old soldier.

"Alert. Burn commencing in thirty seconds."

Leave it to Barre to have included a countdown. She closed her eyes, grateful for his friendship and his skill. Nomi would be pleased. Ro snapped her eyes open. Nomi. She hadn't checked in with her. And now it was too late to manually compose a message.

"Alert. Burn commencing in twenty seconds."

"Halcyone. Send message to Nakamura, Konomi, text

only, encryption on."

"Affirmative. State message."

"Send detailed navigation parameters. Include the following ..."

"Alert. Burn commencing in ten seconds."

What could she say in ten seconds? "Include the following text: Talk soon. Be careful. Message ends."

As Halcyone counted to zero, Ro thought of all the things she'd left unsaid, hoping Nomi would hear them. Then the ship's interstitial engines powered up and all she could focus on was the mechanics of breathing.

Either the burn wasn't as bad as she'd feared, or Ro was getting used to travel on Halcyone. The jump wasn't even all that torturous. Certainly May's donated cushioning helped. As soon as the AI gave the all-clear, Ro scrambled back to the bridge. Micah and Barre had beaten her there.

Halcyone had changed the screen to show local space. In the distance, clouds obscured the daytime side of a planet. There was no evidence of orbiting ships or artificial satellites.

"Where are we?" Micah asked, frowning at the display.

"Cosmos knows," she said. If this was anything like Ithaka, someone would have been alerted to their arrival. She couldn't imagine an unattended wormhole. "Nowhere the Commonwealth can find us, I suspect."

"Is that a good thing?" Barre asked.

"Honestly? I don't know." She shared his concern. They were flying blind in more ways than one.

"You'd think May would have given us more than a location," Barre said.

"Unless that's all she had." May's lack of intel was a

bigger problem than Barre seemed to realize. It meant the woman had even less control of the various forces in this confused constellation than she'd led them to believe. "Well, there has to be something here."

"We have to keep moving. If our elapsed subjective time is right, your father's deadline has come and gone, which means he's gotten my reply. You know better than any of us. He's not a patient man."

There was a countdown running and Dev's safety hung in the balance. The problem was, Ro had no idea how long they had before the zero mark.

"If the wormhole is abandoned, then this is a dead end," Barre said.

"I won't accept that!" Micah shouted.

"Hang on." Barre lifted his hands and gestured at Micah to relax. "If. And I don't believe that. Ada May isn't some all-seeing eye, but she isn't without her resources, either. If she says Maldonado was here, I believe it. And I think it has to be more than just a random bolt-hole. So let's take a closer look."

Micah wanted to argue, but Ro knew that was more about his frustration than any issue with Barre's logic. They had one and only one lead: this one. If it didn't pan out? Despite her reassurances to Micah, she had little hope that her father would honor any agreements he had made, even if he did get what he wanted.

"Okay," Ro said. "Halcyone, bring us around to orbit the nearest planet." The ship's sensors were primitive, but if there was a city or a settlement here, they should be able to detect it.

The planet grew in size and in detail as they got closer, and it was pretty clear that if there were people down there, they were pretty effectively hidden. Or gluttons for punishment. The planet was one big storm system and active volcanoes glowed anywhere the fierce winds dissolved the cloud cover. It looked like a map dotted with red pins.

"Well, that's unpleasant," Barre said.

"How much do you trust the good Dr. May? Could she be working with your father?" Micah asked.

"Not a chance." Ro may not have understood all of what May was after, but there had been no mistaking her moral outrage when she'd found out what Ro's father had done.

"Well, what do we do—"

Halcyone interrupted Micah with its implacable voice. "Incoming hail."

"On speakers," Ro snapped.

"... state your business. Unidentified vessel, you are trespassing on private space. Identify yourself and state your business. Unidentified vessel—"

"Halcyone, end playback," Ro said. "Looks like we tripped some kind of beacon. How do you want to answer?" Her inclination was to lie, but if this was more than an automated repeater, they—whoever they were—might be able to decrypt Halcyone's comms headers. The question was, could they risk using the Maldonado name? It could give them access. It could also get them killed.

"We don't have time to be subtle," Micah said.

"We also have no way to protect ourselves if they decide to blow us out of the sky." Ro picked at the ragged edge of one of her cuticles. "Barre?"

"Someone knows we're here, even if they don't know who we are." He shrugged. "And Micah's right. Time is critical. I say we throw the biggest rock we have and watch the ripples."

She didn't need to outline the risk. "Halcyone, open a channel and keep it monitored."

"Channel open."

"This is Captain Maldonado of the freighter Halcyone." Ro squared her shoulders, hoping this wouldn't be a disaster. "Commonwealth registry Epsilon Delta niner seven niner requesting permission to dock."

Invoking her father's name and identifying as a Commonwealth ship were equally risky propositions. Maybe between the two of them, someone behind the beacon would be more curious than threatened.

Moments passed. Halcyone orbited the volcanic planet, each revolution creating a metronomic beat as they waited.

"Halcyone, break orbit and change course to three eight two, mark seven. Ground control will direct you to an open berth. Welcome back, Captain Maldonado."

"Halcyone, close channel." Ro pressed her hands against the nav console to steady them. "Shit. Now what?"

Chapter 14

THE WORDS OF Ro's terse message echoed in Nomi's mind all shift. *Talk soon. Be careful.* Nomi wasn't the one who needed to be careful.

"Up late last night, Nakamura?"

Nomi jerked upright in the comms chair as Lowell's voice reverberated both in her headset and through the room.

"You have incomings to log."

She shifted her attention to the ansible display where several message alerts were blinking. Most were the green of routine traffic, but there were a few amber lights, too.

"Got it, sir," she said. It was more traffic than they usually received in a single shift. She frowned and caught Simon's gaze.

"Need help?"

"Nah. I'm good."

The routine of work crowded out her worry over Ro until she logged the headers of several more amber-level messages. They were all from Commander Targill of the

Commonwealth ship Hephaestus, all for Commander Mendez, and all encrypted.

Nomi had been temporarily assigned to the Hephaestus during the search for Ro after an out-of-control Halcyone had blasted free of Daedalus. This flurry of comms traffic wouldn't have set off any alarms for her, except for the fact Alain Maldonado had also been aboard Hephaestus and had used his position there to get on Halcyone to threaten Ro, Barre, and Micah.

Targill seemed to have more than a passing interest in Ro and Halcyone, and through them, Ithaka. Nomi was grateful for the commander's actions in locating the damaged freighter and in helping get Jem home after his head injury, but anything and anyone connected to Alain Maldonado was suspect.

She hesitated for barely an instant before her hands resumed the work she'd been trained to do, automatically, smoothly, as if this were an emergency situation. But her mind raced.

"Something wrong?" Lowell was staring at her.

"No, sir."

Was Targill working with Maldonado? Even if he was only what he appeared to be—a high-ranking Commonwealth officer and a war hero—she was wary. Now that she knew the truth, how could Nomi continue to blindly trust a Commonwealth that had manipulated the war on every level and continued to extend its control over an entire galaxy?

There was a break in the messages and Nomi squinted up at the representation of the ansible network that looked so much like a vast starscape. Ro was out there, somewhere. And Hephaestus was sending urgent messages to Commander Mendez. Nomi wasn't naive enough to believe that was total coincidence.

"Ready for your break, Nakamura?"

Again, Lowell's deep voice startled her. She nodded, signed out her station to him, and walked out of comms without any destination in mind. What was Hephaestus doing out there? And where was Ro? It had been hours since Nomi had read her all-too-brief message. She looked up to find her wandering had taken her to the sealed airlock at the edge of the station. There was a vast space where Halcyone should have been. She traced the large window with the tip of her finger before turning back to the main corridors of Daedalus.

Nomi passed by the commissary and headed toward her quarters, not wanting to be surrounded by station chatter. There was enough food in the small galley to put together a small plate. Not that she was very hungry. When she got to her door, she kept walking. She didn't want to be there, either.

Her micro beeped and Nomi grabbed it, but it was just a station announcement. A quick glance at the time showed her she'd wasted half her break in aimless wandering. Ro hadn't sent another message and Nomi was no closer to puzzling out what Hephaestus was up to. She had a brief fantasy of hacking the messages or simply asking Mendez, neither of which was anything near a viable option. But maybe there was someone she could ask.

"Daedalus, locate Lieutenant Commander Gutierrez."

A recording of the LC's clipped voice replied. "Off duty. In quarters."

Looking up, Nomi realized she was already near the command nexus, where the upper echelons of the station staff had their quarters. Would Gutierrez be curious enough to see her? Nomi straightened her uniform top and strode through the corridor. She hesitated at the LC's door before announcing herself. The door slid open and Gutierrez stood just inside. The woman stared at Nomi, her thoughts hidden behind the highly practiced neutral mask that was her typical expression.

Hidden, Nomi thought. *She's learned to stay hidden in plain sight.*

"How can I help you, Ensign Nakamura?"

"I'm on break." Nomi realized how stupid and irrelevant that must have sounded, but the longer Gutierrez stood in the doorway, staring, the more uncomfortable Nomi became. "There's something I need to ask. Can I come in?"

The LC nodded and stepped back. Nomi wiped her hands across her shirt.

As the door sealed, Gutierrez cautioned her. "While what is said in this room is in all likelihood private, your visit will have been logged. I hope you know what you're doing."

Did she? Nomi studied Gutierrez's quarters, trying to gather her thoughts. Warm artificial daylight flooded the walls, illuminating colorful paintings and wall hangings, rather than the more typical holos or programmable displays. The furniture was equally classic—a rich red sofa and chairs around a highly polished wooden table that looked like it had been created from an old tree burl. The table alone had to be worth more than a year's salary. The LC's salary, not Nomi's.

She studied Gutierrez's prosthesis, seeing it in perspective with the woman's quarters. Simplicity. Function. Craftsmanship. Permanence. The artificial arm was anything but primitive; it worked and it suited her. Like everything else she'd surrounded herself with.

It may have been a different aesthetic, but it reminded Nomi of her grandparents' home.

Nomi stood at attention under the LC's steady gaze. "She's gone after her father."

"And?"

"To coordinates somewhere in the vast diaspora of The Underworld. I just logged more than a dozen priority messages from Hephaestus to the Commander. Tell me I'm wrong for seeing the connection."

Gutierrez didn't move. Neither did Nomi.

"Why did you come here?"

A memory from another meeting with Gutierrez flashed through her mind. Ro had gone after Jem and had found Ada May and the conspiracy they were now all drawn into. The LC's words hung over the room like a ghost. *"... if they unmask Ithaka, the war that follows will make the one I lost my arm and my innocence to seem like a skirmish."* A cold sweat broke out on Nomi's forehead. "I thought ..." She took a deep breath and started over. "You said you'd do anything you could to prevent another war. Well, here's your chance."

Gutierrez nodded. Her dark eyes seemed to burn into

Nomi's. "Anything. Including sacrificing your friends."

Heat rose to her face. "And how, exactly, will that prevent a war?" Nomi took a step forward. "Ro is protecting Ithaka! Do you think Doctor—"

"Don't." Gutierrez's voice was a warning shot.

Nomi took another step closer, backing Gutierrez into the living space. "If Ro could find her, others will, too. Right now, Ro's in the best position to keep her safe."

A darkness shaded the woman's eyes. "Others have found her. I protect her. That's my job."

"Your job." Nomi echoed Gutierrez's words in a hoarse whisper. "Your job. You're not going to help us, are you?" She didn't wait for a response. "You're just going to stand by and let Ro get killed. And for what? So someone like Alain Maldonado can run weapons? So more innocent lives get tangled up in the process? I haven't met your doctor, but I don't think that's what she created Ithaka for, do you?"

"You have no idea what's at stake."

"Yes, I do."

"Your friend was doomed the moment she woke that ship. It would have been better for all concerned had she failed."

"But she didn't."

"And we all have to deal with the consequences." Gutierrez turned aside.

Nomi hesitated, holding back her response. The LC stared across the room; she wasn't focused on the colorful artwork, but gazed past the enclosed space. Her discomfort made Nomi break out in gooseflesh. Another memory surfaced: *"I owe a debt. I mean to pay that debt even if it costs the lives of your friends."*

"Your debt. It's to *her*, isn't it?"

Gutierrez froze.

"You said there were others." Nomi's voice cracked. "You've killed to protect her."

Still the LC kept silent.

The equivalent of a star map assembled itself in Nomi's head, disparate coordinates suddenly forming one coherent image. It was almost too big to hold on to. "Ro. You would have killed her, but May told you not to."

As Gutierrez whirled to face her, Nomi realized she'd said the doctor's name aloud. It didn't matter. If these rooms were under surveillance, they had already said enough to incriminate themselves several times over. And the chances were the Commonwealth knew Ada May was alive. Or suspected it. The LC strode over to Nomi and stood centimeters from her. The prosthesis glittered in the too-bright light.

"Leave."

Nomi opened her mouth to reply.

Gutierrez's claw hand opened and closed once. "Now."

Nomi fled.

*

Micah stared, unblinking as one of the planet's moons loomed larger and larger on Halcyone's broken viewscreen. According to galactic time, they were nearly an hour past when Maldonado had gotten his reply. Had they pushed back too hard? There might have been a dozen reasons he hadn't answered, but Micah kept imagining only one: that Dev was already dead and this was all for nothing.

As Barre and Ro maneuvered the ship—Ro with quiet and economical commands, Barre with strange not-quite-melodies—Micah struggled with memories of the last time he'd been here. It was nearly impossible not to relive the desperation and the terror of his escape from Maldonado. He had thought he was getting over it until his most recent flashback in the abandoned dome, triggered by Dev's little box. He slammed a fist against the top of the nearest console.

"You might want to sit down." Ro was buckling her chair harness. "We're on a glide path down to the surface. It should be a smooth landing, but you never know."

Nothing seemed smooth anymore. But nothing had been since his mother got sick all those years before. He nodded and took a seat.

Between the two of them, Ro and Barre had figured out how to make Halcyone dance. Their landing was as professional as any experienced pilot's. There was a series of clangs as the landing and stabilization clamps engaged. Then everything fell silent.

They looked at the sensor data. It was about the size of a mining outpost, but there were a lot more docking bays than Micah expected. The moon had breathable atmosphere and nearly the same gravity as Earth, so either it had been a lucky find or it was terraformed. Micah was betting on terraformed, courtesy of deep pockets.

Barre frowned at Ro. "Now what?"

She picked at a ragged cuticle. "Thought there would be a welcoming committee when we got here."

"Welcome back. They said welcome back. So the son of a bitch was here." Micah flung off the restraints and paced, halting at the partially melted door.

"Wait," Ro said.

Micah stopped, halfway into the corridor.

"We need a plan."

"Shouldn't you have thought of that before we got here?"

Her voice, when it answered, came from behind him. "It won't help her if we get ourselves arrested."

"Or worse," Barre said.

"Fine." Micah still didn't turn around. He didn't think he could face his friends without breaking down. "So what do we do?"

"I don't think you're going to like it."

"I already don't like it."

"We trade on our fathers' names. You're the senator's legal heir and you have control of his money."

Micah gripped the edge of the door frame, feeling the twisted polymer dig into his palm. "I don't want his fucking money!"

"Hey. We know that." Barre had come to stand near Ro. "But whoever's out there? They don't. And the only way we're going to get answers is to bluff our way into them. We know Maldonado's being hounded by his former business associates."

"And that helps us, how?"

Ro rested her hand on his shoulder. Micah forced

himself not to shake her off.

"Think, Micah. This could take one of two jump paths. Either this is my father's hidey-hole, or it's where he ran from to escape his creditors. If it's the first, then we play his agents. If it's the second, we get to sell him out."

"Okay. Okay. I can do that." He tapped his micro. "For what it's worth, I still have the private little last will and blah blah blah he left for me."

"I'll stay here and keep Halcyone ready to fly. I want both of you to keep a live link open. If things start to go critical, get back to the ship as fast as you can."

"What are you going to do, sing at them?" It was more than likely that the denizens of this moon would all be armed. Suspicious. He had his father's money and charm on their side. Ro had her father's name and her hacking skills. All of which were dubious gifts.

"You'd be surprised," Barre said.

"Fine. What are we waiting for?"

"Are you sure you're ready?"

Micah looked back into Ro's worried gaze. "Are you?"

She nodded and swept past him into the corridor.

They paused at the airlock. "Comms check. Barre? How do we sound."

"Five by five."

She stared through the porthole, frowning.

"What's wrong?"

"No guards."

"And that's a bad thing?"

"It's puzzling. And I don't like things that don't make sense."

Understanding people was a soft science. One he'd learned alongside his father's unintended lessons of charisma and manipulation. It wasn't anything like Ro's logical programs. No wonder she was uneasy. "It just means they don't consider us a threat. Come on."

She cycled the lock and they stepped out into the docking bay. Instead of the large open space he'd expected, they were in a small anteroom with a touch screen on the far door. As they approached, it triggered an auditory message.

"Welcome, Captain. Please select required services and length of stay."

"Seriously?"

"It makes sense, Ro. The place is anonymous, doesn't take a lot of personnel to run, and if you can't pay, you can't play."

"How do we know how much it is?"

"We don't." If this was truly a black market outpost, anyone who asked that question didn't belong. "I got this." Micah paused and smiled grimly. "Or my father does." He made sure all the auxiliary services were unchecked. All they needed were the docking clamps. Halcyone was self-sufficient otherwise. At least for the short amount of time they'd be here, if all went well.

"Select three days," Ro said.

"Three?" If they didn't get what they needed within the hour, staying here longer wasn't going to help them. In fact, even an hour might be too long.

"We don't want them to think we're nervous."

Maybe Ro understood people better than Micah

thought. "Okay." He entered in the information. The screen blanked and was replaced by a single input box. He keyed in his father's information. The long series of alphanumeric characters specified a particular account in a particular institution. Once he entered in the passcode, whatever this place charged for a ship's docking would be automatically transferred.

He hesitated before the final digit. "No refunds."

"Funny."

The computer's voice read out a confirmation. "Do you accept, Captain?"

"I accept."

"Select number of idents."

Micah chose two. He and Ro each pressed a hand to the screen.

"Biometrics confirmed. You are cleared for unlimited access to and from docking bay three two Alpha. Your credentials will expire in seventy-two galactic standard hours and fines will accrue."

The door to the anteroom slid open. They stepped out into a wide corridor lined along one side with numbered entrances, presumably to other docking bays.

Micah scanned up and down the empty hallway. "Barre? How's our signal?"

"Five by five," he repeated.

"You ready to show them the old Rotherwood charm?" Ro asked.

In the end, it hadn't been enough to protect his father. He only hoped it would get them the information they needed and off this moon in time. Both for their sakes and for Dev's. Micah checked his micro again, but there was still no word back from Maldonado. "Let's go."

*

Jem tossed his micro aside and collapsed across his bed, trembling with exhaustion as if he'd just spent an hour sweating in an EVA suit. The only person he could ask about the neural integration process was Barre. And even if his brother were here, Barre's experience would be relevant only to a point. No one—not even Doc Land—knew for sure how well the implant would work in his damaged brain.

So Jem kept at it, a little at a time, and there were glimmers of hope. He could pretty routinely link with his micro and do simple tasks, like play back a vid, or check his mail. It's just that it took about ten times the mental energy it would have taken to do it manually.

His micro vibrated against the headboard. Instead of grabbing it, he concentrated, pretended his thoughts were a tractor beam that he threw at the small device. A neutral voice echoed in his mind.

"Incoming voice call."

It wasn't exactly his own voice, but it wasn't the artificial voice of Daedalus Station either. Jem subvocalized a single word, "Answer," knowing he should be able to control the micro more easily and with less of a conscious effort than that. At least it seemed that way for Barre.

There was a pause and then Nomi's voice poured through his mind. That was cool. It was close to what it felt like when

Barre had spoken directly with him on Ithaka. Jem tried to answer her without speaking, but all it accomplished was trigger a slight headache.

"Jem? Jem, are you there?" Her voice was rushed, breathless.

"I'm here. Are you okay?"

A long pause. "No. Can we talk? Face to face?"

Cold washed through him. "Is it Halcyone? What happened?" He sat up quickly and had to put his head between his knees as the room spun.

"No. It's not that. But I need ... I need to talk to you. I ... It's complicated."

She sounded scared. Nomi was never scared. If it wasn't Halcyone, then what was it? "Come by my quarters. My folks are both at work."

"On my way." The relief was evident in her voice.

Jem rubbed a cool cloth across his head and face. Even that amount of mind-work was wearing. If this was as good as it got, would he be satisfied? He studied his face in the small mirror hanging above the sink. At least his eyes weren't moving. That was a good sign. It was weird not being able to feel what was going on in his brain even as the nanoemitters were busy working to bridge the damage in there. He wished he could talk with Dr. Land.

The door chime interrupted his brooding. He triggered the release to let Nomi in and stopped short, just inside the living room as she stepped inside. His micro was still in his pocket. He hadn't told Daedalus to open the door. That was him, using his neural. Seismic!

The moment he met Nomi's gaze, his excitement faded.

Her face was flushed and she was breathing hard as if she'd run all the way here.

"What's wrong? Aren't you supposed to be in comms?"

She pushed her hair from her eyes before shaking her head. "I told them I was ill."

"You look like crap. Do you want me to take you to medical?"

She shook her head.

Jem took her hand and tugged her over to the sofa. Her hands were void-cold. She sat staring straight ahead, her lips pressed together, trembling, but he couldn't tell if it was from anger or fear.

"I think they're in danger."

Cold settled in the pit of his stomach. It was far worse than the persistent symptoms of his head injury. "Wait." Not trusting his nascent skills with the neural, he manually shuffled through the programs he had access to on his micro until he found a kind of white-noise hack. It wouldn't completely mask their conversation, but it would blur it, in case anyone was combing Daedalus's passive logs for keywords.

"But you said it wasn't Halcyone."

"It's not. It's Gutierrez."

"Wait. The LC? You're not making any sense."

"I know. I'm sorry." Nomi curled her long legs beneath her on the sofa. Hugging her arms across her chest, she told him about the messages from Hephaestus and her meeting with Gutierrez.

"It could be coincidence. It's a big universe."

"This is Ro we're talking about."

"Fine. You're probably right. So where does that leave them?" And what could they do about it? They had a set of coordinates, but without a ship and the Ithaka protocol, they wouldn't be able to find where they led.

"I don't know. But I'm sure Gutierrez knows more than she's saying. As far as she's concerned, if Ro gets herself killed, it's one less threat to our mutual friend."

They should be on the same side. Ada trusted them. She trusted him. The old scientist might be a little suspicious and jaded, but she had let them leave. Had helped Jem get his neural.

Nomi rocked back and forth. "I don't know what to do. There isn't even any specific warning I could pass along to Ro. But she's somewhere out there, asking questions about her father in a place where those questions could very easily get her killed. And she doesn't have any backup."

"She has Barre and Micah."

She answered him very softly. "I'm sorry, Jem, but that's not backup. If anything, they're just collateral damage."

Jem winced, but he knew she was right. They'd been stupidly lucky up until now, but not every wormhole opened into clear space. "It doesn't make sense. The doc wouldn't have given Ro those coordinates just to send her into a trap."

"But you said it yourself. She's not truly in charge. Not if someone like Maldonado can use the black market for his personal gain."

It wasn't Ada's fault. Programs were neutral constructions. It's how they were deployed that was the problem. If anything, she had been dangerously naive when she enabled the code that hid Ithaka and allowed The

Underworld to function. Or maybe just desperate. Either way, she'd saved a lot of lives.

Jem stared at Nomi, going back over what she'd said about Gutierrez and what he knew about Ithaka and its structure. Ada May was Ithaka's nominal head. She'd created an incubation hub that funneled tech through the black market into the Commonwealth, and money back to the colonies that still opposed it. They had no real weapons other than stealth, so it was not so much war as a constant eroding of Commonwealth control.

The doc had people loyal to her. People like Charon who risked moving in and out of Commonwealth space. It was Charon who'd escorted Jem to Ithaka. He'd looked up the mythology when he got back to Daedalus Station. According to some ancient beliefs, Charon was the Ferryman who guided the souls of the dead across the river Lethe—which was the name Ada May had given her AI. It was all connected. If Charon was Ada's Ferryman, that made Gutierrez Cerberus, the three-headed dog and guardian of The Underworld.

"She called her off."

"What?"

"The doc. You said it yourself. She told Gutierrez that Ro wasn't a threat. That she had safe passage."

Nomi stood and paced the tight living area. "So what? Gutierrez may not directly harm Ro, but she isn't planning on helping her, either."

"What if she's ordered to?" It would have been simpler to have his micro accept voice commands, but he didn't trust his sound-masking hack for this and he didn't yet have the stamina to only use his neural. His eyes burned from the effort of focusing. It was better than the double vision and the nausea, but he didn't want to push his luck. He configured the secure message program and handed the small device to Nomi. "Tell her. Tell her what's going on."

Her eyes widened when she read the message headers. Jem knew exactly when she got to the subject line because she gave him a strange, confused look.

"Curb your dog?"

"Don't worry. The doc will understand."

Chapter 15

DEV STARED DOWN at the open access hatch and the square of darkness that fell away from her. It wouldn't be pleasant skulking around in the dark through the service corridors of an unfamiliar ship, but it was better than staying trapped in Maldonado's cage. She glanced up at the ocular, then back toward the hatch. There was no way of knowing how closely he was watching her. This was only going to work if he was effectively blind.

How to shut it down?

Returning to the dining area, she lifted the edge of the snug and looked over her pitiful collection of tools and supplies. Well, not quite pitiful, but certainly primitive. She nibbled at the edge of a food bar. It would make a decent cement in a pinch. Certainly coating the ocular with it would block Maldonado's view, but it was less than elegant and more obvious than she wanted.

She picked up Sellen's cube by two of its corners. How much of a charge did it still have after Micah triggered it? The thing had been sitting under the ambient room light for hours, but Dev had no idea how efficient the photosensitive coating was. It hadn't picked up enough charge when she'd had it in their apartment. The only way she could check would probably use up whatever juice the thing had stored.

Six sides. Which ones were the poles? When Micah had caught it, he'd tightened his whole hand around it and it had zapped him. Could Dev use the test device to create a small EMP? That should fry the ocular. If. If there was enough stored charge in the cube. If she could discharge it all in one go without using her body to close the circuit. If she could get close enough to the ocular.

That was a lot of ifs.

Everything was one big variable. And one more crucial one: how long would it take before Maldonado checked back on her? She set the cube back down on the ground and walked back into the galley section. Gently, she put the tile back in its place and pressed the plugs into the corners.

Time to get to work.

Sitting against the wall just beneath the ocular, she hoped she'd done a good enough job at figuring out its blind spot. In the end, she didn't have much choice but to try to disable it. Dev cut off a length of the salvaged wire and stripped the insulation off its ends with her polymer knife. It was such a familiar ritual. She could almost imagine she was back home, scavenging tools and supplies from abandoned homesteads to build surprises for her brothers. Her hand tightened around the thin handle. This was no game and she needed to stay focused if she wanted to see them again.

She set down the blade and prepared wire. Her neck ached, cracking as she stretched it. Grabbing a length of spare cloth, she sheathed her hand in a makeshift mitten. It was thin enough that she should still be able to feel the wire, but would provide enough insulation that when she held the cube, her fingers wouldn't complete the circuit. Dev needed to get close enough to the ocular so the resulting pulse would kill it. And she had to do it so Maldonado didn't suspect anything. Which meant keeping her back to the ocular's ever-present eye.

The cube sat in her shielded hand, a small, seemingly innocuous silver shape. With any luck, not so innocuous. She grabbed her prepared wire and, with her thumb, carefully held one exposed end to the side she mentally labeled as "top," letting the other end drape over her hand. Then she stood and paced the room, getting closer and closer to the far wall on every pass.

Aware that she might be putting on a show for nothing and no one, she sighed dramatically and slid down the wall to the floor, looking the picture of the dejected prisoner.

The ocular was about two meters directly above her.

Would she be close enough, if the cube even discharged?

Only one way to find out.

Dev carefully pinched the insulated section of the wire's free portion and, holding her breath, touched its exposed end to the side facing her. Nothing. She exhaled. One down, four to go. Then she would repeat the whole series testing one of the other faces. There was a finite number of combinations and at least one would complete the circuit.

With steady hands, she ran through each combination with the stable end of the wire at the top position. Still nothing. She wriggled her thumb before pressing the wire to the side facing her and running through the options again, in clockwise order. Either these combinations were inert, the wire was broken inside the insulation somewhere, or she had miscalculated and the box hadn't had enough time or light to store sufficient charge.

She held her breath and moved the stationary wire to the third side. Skipping the first two combinations, Dev pressed the wire to the fourth side. A low hum rose from the cube as heat sank through the cloth covering her hand. She would never badmouth Dr. Sellen again.

The hum rose in pitch until Dev was sure Maldonado would hear it and then the box emitted a bright flash as if it had been struck by the full glare of the sun. She winced, nearly dropping the cube. Her arms and the back of her neck tingled as the box created a local static charge. Would it be enough? She kept her hands curled around the box until the sensations faded and the sound died away.

The cube's coating seemed dulled now, a pewter gray rather than the almost liquid silver of mercury.

If it had done its job, Maldonado would have to physically check on her. Again, she went over the "ifs" in her head. They were all the certainty she had.

Dev covered the box and slipped it back in her pocket. Then she unwrapped her hand before sweeping the rest of her supplies under the jump snug. The next move was

Maldonado's.

She didn't have to wait long. He strode into the room, grabbed her arm, and dragged her to her feet. Dev stiffened and pulled against him. His gaze burned into hers. Had he seen her? She thought she'd been so careful, working where the ocular couldn't monitor closely.

He shoved her against the wall and paced to the far side of the room.

She stumbled and fell in a heap next to the jump snug. Dev rubbed her arm. Heat spread out from where his fingers had pressed. Without taking her eyes off of him, she felt beneath the snug and palmed the small blade.

Maldonado reached into a pocket. Dev held her breath, tightening her hand around the polymer tool, for whatever good it would do against a real weapon.

"Talk."

"What?"

"Talk." Maldonado's voice was a low growl. "Talk to your friend. Tell him ... Actually I don't care what the fuck you tell him." Her micro was dwarfed in his calloused hand and he pointed it at himself. "Hello, Micah. The timestamp is accurate. I'm certain Ro will corroborate that. Here's your proof." He turned the device toward her. "Your turn."

Proof. Proof that she was still alive. For some reason, that chilled her more than being Maldonado's prisoner did. Dev's breath hitched in her chest. It was hard not to glance up at the ocular, but the last thing she wanted to do was give him a reason to think she'd taken it out. Keeping her hands in her pockets, she fingered the slim blade and stared directly into the micro, imagining her roommate listening at the other end of an ansible transmission. If Maldonado was transmitting live, there was a chance Micah could trace the message at least to a sector. Her shoulders slumped. And do what? Besides, Maldonado said something about a timestamp. It had to be a vid, then.

"I'm okay." She had this overwhelming impulse to reassure him. "Really. He hasn't hurt me." Not beyond the drugging and his rough handling. That would be too much and the wrong kind of information right now. She glared at her captor. What did he want? There was too much Dev didn't know, but it had to be related to their history. The weapons. Micah's burns.

"It's not your fault."

She desperately wanted to send him some kind of message, but didn't know him well enough to know what to say. The pocketed cube pressed into her leg as she shifted on the snug. She tapped it with her free hand and flashed a quick smile.

"Whatever you think, there's no static between us, right?" She took a breath and sneaked a glance at Maldonado. He was still filming. "Tell Sellen I'm okay."

Dev wasn't sure if Micah would even have the slightest clue what she was talking about, but she wanted him to know she wasn't helpless. That she had tools. That she would fight back with them.

Another variable she had no control over.

Maldonado grunted something and shoved her micro back in one of his coverall's pockets. He spun on his heel and strode out of the room without another word.

Dev took her hand out of her pocket, opened it, and let

the slim blade tumble to the floor.

*

This part of the station—or whatever it was—seemed to be made up of endless identical branching corridors that went on as far as Ro could see. She paused at the end of the one that led back to the docking bay. "No convenient 'you are here' signs."

"Almost as if they want us to be confused," Micah said.

"Yeah. Well it'll be a problem if we need to get out of here fast." Ro paged through the hacks on her micro, but none of the mapping services would work without a handshake with the local AI. "They didn't even offer us a map."

"What a shocker. Definitely not getting a five-rocket rating."

"Barre? You listening?"

"Not much else to do. What do you need?"

"Have Halcyone make an approximate map from the location data on our micros. It won't have local features, but it will at least give us a trail to follow back to the ship. In case."

"Good idea, Cap. On it."

"Make sure the ship follows each of us."

"I don't think it's a good idea for you to split up."

"Trust me. Not planning on it." It was odd that they hadn't met another person yet. It suggested possibilities that Ro didn't want to dwell on.

"Right or left?" Micah asked.

Barre had already pushed a quick and dirty map to her micro. It didn't show any details of the station or settlement, but it did leave a ghostly trail in the hazy nothingness Halcyone used to visually represent missing data.

"Not sure it matters."

"Then right." Micah strode down the corridor as fast as his damaged feet in their clunky shoes could manage.

Ro followed, profoundly uneasy with the empty silence. Surely, they were being watched. But by whom? It was hard to play a game when you didn't know the players or what side they were on. At the end of the short corridor, they reached a small nexus. If this place followed any of the conventions of typical Commonwealth installations, there should be branching choices off the nexus. One of them had to lead to something inhabited here. And the someones who were behind it. "Ready for this?" she asked.

Micah squared his shoulders and nodded. The way he stood, the set of his mouth and the glint in his eyes suddenly resurrected his father. "I hope you know what you're doing, Ro."

She didn't answer. They both knew what the stakes were.

They entered the nexus. It was empty. Three airlocked exits led out from the roughly circular structure. Ro slapped her hand on the rightmost ident plate.

"Access denied."

She and Micah shared a look.

She tried the middle exit.

"Access denied."

The artificial voice faded, leaving her and Micah in unnerving silence in the harsh, bright space. "Third time's

the charm," Ro said, as she touched the final plate, half-
expecting to hear the local AI repeat the same message. This
time, the door seal slid open.

A short corridor ended at a major junction ahead. Ro
exhaled. She'd begun to think the place was deserted.

"Feels like they wanted to quarantine us or something,"
Micah said.

Ro looked behind her to the nexus door and then down to
her micro. It would be a long retreat back to Halcyone if
something went wrong. Which was probably the point.

Before entering the inhabited part of the station, Ro
paused. It looked like any one of thousands of anonymous
transit points in the cosmos. Shopfronts and kiosks lined the
main corridor. The lights were set to emulate dusk. There
were more than a handful of fellow travelers, but far less
than she had expected. None paused to glance at them. If
this were just some out-of-the-way hole her father had
stumbled onto, then the chances of any useful intel on him
were going to be slim.

For Micah's sake, she hoped she was wrong.

"Hungry?" Micah asked.

"Seriously?"

"My father was a huge proponent of bar diplomacy."

She waved him in front of her. This wasn't the ship and
her skills weren't the important ones here.

Micah raised an eyebrow, but kept silent as he led her
toward a dimly lit storefront, its holographic display set to
some historical facsimile of a pre-diaspora pub.

"Quaint," she said as they walked in. The low buzz of
conversation stilled. Ro blinked furiously to accommodate to

the darkness of the entryway. It gave whoever was already there the distinct advantage. Well, they'd wanted to be seen. "What next?"

"Grab a table. I'll get us something to eat and drink. I suspect once I wave around the senator's money, we won't have long to wait."

If Ro had any sense at all, she'd call him back. This was a terrible idea. But, it was the best one they had. As her eyes adjusted, she studied the room. A narrow rectangular space, it had the one public exit. At the far end, a door labeled "staff" probably led to the galley or storage. The bar area took up most of the space at the front of the pub, leaving an even narrower passage back to the handful of tables and shadowed booths. A tactical disaster.

As she stood there, laughter and chatter resumed. Fortunately, the place wasn't packed so Ro chose the table closest to the exit and against the wall. She still didn't like the escape route. While she waited for Micah, she studied the handful of people sitting in the room. It could have been any spaceport, except for the weapons. Commonwealth ports were interdiction zones unless you were in uniform. No uniforms around here. Just plenty of well-worn sidearms.

The people seemed just as well-worn. A few groups of space-pale men and women sat drinking in the back booths. Most of the other tables had one or two occupants who watched the room with studied disinterest. Nearly everyone had already assessed her and Micah before returning to their own glasses and micros.

Micah sauntered over to their table, his body a study in casual confidence. Only Ro knew the price he paid to walk that smoothly. He set down a platter of something that looked fried and slid a drink in front of each of them. "Synth-cider. Enough alcohol to kill whatever local germs might be lurking, but not so much we'll lose our edge."

She downed a sip. Sharp but smooth. Not bad. Better than the potato-like lumps congealing on the plate. "How long do you think until someone notices us?"

Micah emptied his glass. "Oh, they noticed us. As soon as we walked in. When I used my father's account to pay our bill, that sealed the deal."

Nothing had changed in the room's dynamics that she could see. "So why are we still sitting here talking to ourselves?"

He stared across to the bar. "Not for long."

The bartender walked toward their table with three full glasses on his tray.

Ro raised an eyebrow. "We didn't order this."

The tall, lean man nodded to Micah and sat down. "Don't worry, I put it on his tab." No one in the rest of the bar looked in their direction.

She swapped out the slightly warm dregs for the new glass.

"You work for Maldonado?"

Ro managed to bring the glass to her mouth and take a sip without spilling any or choking on it. "Not exactly. But he and I do have unfinished business."

The bartender nodded. "Fair enough." He turned to Micah. "Pretty bold flashing the Rotherwood name and coin around. Last I heard there was a bit of that unfinished business between the senator and Maldonado. You involved in their mess?"

"You could say that," Micah said.

The three fell silent. Ro studied the water ring her glass had left on the table.

"Then I'll give you the same advice I gave him."

Ro stiffened.

"Debts in this part of space have a way of getting personal. And trying to jump ahead of them usually turns messy."

"Are you threatening us, Mister ...?" Micah asked.

"Larson. And that depends. Will the warning suffice?"

Micah smiled. "That depends."

He canted his head. "On?"

"On what kind of relationship you had ..." Ro trailed off and took a steadying breath. No reverse in a wormhole. "With my father."

"Ahhh," Larson said, before leaning back in the chair and contemplating his now empty glass. Its facets threw sparkles in the dim light.

She didn't want to risk taking her gaze off the bartender. If that's what he truly was. Certainly not all of what he was. He didn't wear a holster and had no obvious weapon, but that didn't mean he wasn't protected. Her left hand curled around her micro. At least Barre was listening. As much good as he would do if things here got complicated. But, he was listening and somehow that made Ro feel safer.

"Now, that's interesting." Larson turned from contemplating Ro to look at Micah. "And now I see the resemblances. I won't ask how you found this place. Clearly, you're both as resourceful as your fathers."

Ro snorted. She still couldn't figure out what side Larson was playing for.

"I don't have the patience for the late senator's games." Micah slammed his glass down and leaned forward on the table. "We have funds and need information. Let's trade."

Larson smiled. "Direct. Refreshing. I like it."

Now that Micah had committed them, it was time to jump.

"I need to find my father," Ro said quietly.

"How lovely to see filial devotion." Larson made a show of wiping his hands on the towel he had tucked into his waistband. "And if he doesn't want to be found?"

"What he wants is irrelevant," Ro said. "His former business associates are looking for him, too. It would be better for all concerned if we found him first."

Larson fell silent again, studying her and Micah. His bland expression gave nothing away. He could have been considering his inventory for all she knew. Or figuring out any number of ways to get them killed.

"I'm a broker. There's little that moves in and out of this rock without me knowing about it and facilitating it."

"And taking a cut."

He nodded. "Transaction fees. I also hold funds in escrow for more complex exchanges. There are considerable costs associated with keeping this facility neutral territory."

Ro snorted. "I'll bet."

"I don't discriminate amongst buyers and sellers. My reputation depends on that neutrality and honesty."

"Meaning you cheat all comers equally."

"Exactly."

She was surprised at his lack of reaction to her taunt.

"I will tell you this much on the house. Your father approached me to make a deal on his behalf. I intervened with his business associates—"

"Weapons buyers." Ro and Micah said it simultaneously.

"Semantics." Larson smiled before continuing. "As part of my usual job, I make certain assurances."

"For a fee."

"Of course. These arrangements tend to be mutually beneficial. This one would have been no different."

"Would have been?" Ro asked.

Larson tented his fingers in front of him. "I have a problem that I think you may just be the solution to."

"What do you want from us?" Micah asked.

"Understand, my work is a delicate balancing act. Buyers look to cheat sellers. Sellers search for any advantage over buyers. Typically, the demands of the marketplace work it all out. Homeostasis. But, not in the elder Maldonado's case. He placed a ship in escrow, against his promised payment. A few days ago, he stole that ship out of my personal impound and left here precipitously. Which irritated his business associates and left me without any financial leverage."

"So?" Ro prompted.

"It has a tracking device on it."

Her heart raced. Halcyone could find him. And Dev. "And you're telling us this because?" Ro asked, keeping her voice low and calm.

He folded his arms across his chest and smiled.

Micah hadn't taken his gaze off the bartender. "Because he wants us to pay off your father's obligation."

"Why? He could just give the frequency to the buyers and let them exact their revenge." If it weren't for Dev, she would be more than okay with that. Let her father face the disastrous consequences of his own dealings and then he'd be out of her life for good.

Larson canted his head toward Micah. "Well?"

Micah ticked off the reasons on his fingers. "One. He knows I have the credit to pay off the debt and that we're not in a great position to bargain. That saves Larson's reputation. Two. Say the buyers go after your father. If they don't destroy the ship in the process, they'll take it as part of the debt, but that won't be enough for them. Our bartender here is still liable for the remainder. Three. In that case, he ends up looking incompetent to any potential customers." He turned to Larson. "How did I do?"

"You missed the part about me losing my commission. From both parties. Otherwise, spot on."

"How do we know you won't sell the frequencies to the buyers as soon as we leave?" Ro asked.

Larson placed his hands over his heart. "You wound me."

"He has no reason to," Micah said. "Once I transfer over the funds, Larson can pay the buyers on your father's behalf. Except it'll be on ours. But they don't need to know that. And for them, it's just a business transaction. They don't care where the money comes from."

"Well done. Well done, indeed," Larson said. "So, shall we conduct business?"

"Micah?"

He slid out his micro, his smile nearly a grimace. "Yeah. I'm ready to own your father."

The bartender paired his micro with Micah's. "A pleasure," he said. "I've taken the liberty of passing along the tracking frequency."

"That's it?" she asked. "My father's debt belongs to me?" Now it was time to make him pay.

"You've discharged his obligation." Larson studied the two of them for a long moment. "I think you'd best be shoving off now."

Another warning? Ro started to reply, but he cut her off.

"Using the Rotherwood name got you noticed. And not only by me."

Micah stood, shoving his chair back from the table so hard it nearly toppled over. The rest of the room fell silent as vacuum.

The bartender smiled sadly. "I'm not the one who used those credentials so openly. I've already received several inquiries."

"Which you will have no problem selling to the highest bidder." Ro's hands twitched, but her weapons were computer routines and they weren't going to be effective here.

"What can I say? I'm a businessman." He tucked his micro back in the large pocket of his apron. "But, I am also quite busy at the moment. I'm not sure I'll get to my messages right away."

So, a brief reprieve. But for how long? They raced through the silent warrens of gleaming corridors, tracing the path back to Halcyone.

"Barre? Get the ship ready for takeoff."

"That was fast. Get what we needed?"

"Yeah."

"How quickly can you configure a tracer?" Micah asked.

"I'll do it when we're underway." She squeezed his shoulder. "We'll get Dev. I promise."

"It's more than that." Micah shuffled down the corridor faster. "We need to get to your father before Larson sells him out."

The bartender couldn't be trusted to do anything but cater to his own self-interest. For the moment, his self-interest included keeping his reputation intact. "No. He can't risk going back on his word. My father is ours now. For good or for ill."

He turned back toward her without slowing down. "It's not the buyers I'm worried about. Larson never said anything about not contacting the Commonwealth. Remember, there's still a price on your father's head."

Chapter 16

JEM DIDN'T KNOW what Ada's response would be, but he was sure there would be one. Throughout the last of the afternoon shift and well into the evening, he kept waiting for some kind of message from Ithaka, but nothing came.

She had to help. She just had to.

He had dodged his parents at dinner again, pretending to be asleep. When they returned, they kept their voices low and retreated into their bedroom. There was still no word from Nomi or any contact from Ithaka.

Unaccustomed hunger drove Jem to the commissary, but even if anyone noticed him there, station staff had gotten used to his odd hours and frequent bouts of insomnia. He slipped inside the dimly lit common room and grabbed one of the redi-meals they kept available for quick reheat. For a change, the smell didn't turn his stomach. Maybe the feedback-loop trick he'd been practicing was helping.

A few lone staff sat scattered at empty tables, their faces lit by the glow from their micros. No one spoke as he found a seat in the back corner. Jem shoveled the generic meal into his mouth and realized it was about the best thing he had tasted in months. Go, nanites.

The whoosh of the commissary door and the angry click of boot heels startled him. A glint of light on metal captured his gaze. Gutierrez. She grabbed a coffee and strode to the back of the room, sitting, as usual, with her back to the far wall. He didn't think she'd seen him, but it was hard to tell with Gutierrez.

His belly comfortably full, Jem stifled a yawn. But, he didn't want to return to his quarters. Not until he heard from Ada. And since Gutierrez might just be their conduit to her, he could keep an eye on the LC, too.

He checked his micro, but there was no word from Ro, either. Jem could have used some caffeine, but he didn't want to risk attracting notice by getting up. He leaned back in the hard chair and watched Gutierrez from the shadows.

Her keen gaze swept the room, not settling on anyone or anything. Jem looked at her prosthesis, wondering if she had a neural, too. He thought of the briefing Land had given him before his procedure and realized she had to have one. She'd lost her arm in the war and that's when they started to implant the first-gen neurals. So they had something in common. They were both damaged. Both patched together. He wondered if she'd had any of the problems he did.

If she were anyone else, he could ask her.

A loud bang startled him. Gutierrez had stood abruptly and her chair had slammed into the wall behind her. Without a word to the other staff members who stared her way, the LC strode from the commissary. Anything she reacted that strongly to had to be important.

Jem slipped from the room and followed her, careful to keep one turn away in the corridor. It wasn't hard to track her. The sound of her sharp footfalls echoed in the silent station. And her path was all too familiar. She was headed to where Halcyone lived when she was docked here.

Ro couldn't be back already, could she?

Raised voices stopped him at a junction. Voices. Plural. The only place a second person could have come from was a ship. If it wasn't Ro and Halcyone, who was it? Commercial and military ships docked on the other side of the station.

He couldn't get close enough to see who Gutierrez was talking to without being seen. And there was no place to hide. He couldn't get close enough, but a drone could. Jem smiled. He had done this before. The two drones Ro had him modify were still tooling around the station. That would definitely do.

Jem closed his eyes and linked with his micro. Instead of pretending that he was activating the kinesthetic commands, or even tapping his way through menus, he just thought about what he needed. An image of the drone flitted through his mind.

The micro beeped and Jem froze until he realized he hadn't heard it with his ears. He relaxed his shoulders. Confirmation. Cool.

A small drone rolled to a stop at his feet as the voices at the airlock rose and fell. Jem didn't want to push his luck with the neural. He manually paired the drone with his micro, sent it toward Gutierrez and her companion, and retreated several turns in the station's corridors.

Now all he needed to do was wait.

Raised voices crackled through the small speaker.

"... think she's doing?" Gutierrez demanded. "This violates every protocol I can think of and probably some I don't even know about."

"Keep your engines cool." It was a man's voice, a familiar one. But, the tinny reproduction of the micro made it impossible for Jem to pinpoint it.

"How dare you." Gutierrez's voice was as cold as metal in space. "I warned you the next time I saw you, I would kill you myself."

Jem jerked his head up, as if he could see through the bulkheads and into the airlock area. And then he realized he could. A few quick commands and the primitive ocular built into the drone streamed to his micro. The footage was small and grainy. Gutierrez seemed impossibly tall, the perspective of the drone distorting her prosthesis into an enormous claw. The man next to her was equally pulled out of perspective but Jem would recognize his scars anywhere. It was Ada May's enigmatic courier, the Ferryman.

"That was a long time ago. I've done my penance and she's forgiven me," Charon said.

Gutierrez drew her sidearm with her intact right hand and pinned Charon against the bulkhead with her prosthesis.

Charon smiled. "Really, Em?"

Her face darkened. Jem gasped.

"And in front of an audience? How unlike you." Charon gazed down, his twisted smile filling the small camera eye.

Jem swore.

Gutierrez released Charon's neck, clacking her claw hand open and shut several times as he rubbed this throat. Then she turned her weapon on the drone and fried it. Jem's micro's screen flared before turning dark. He froze against the wall, but there was nowhere to really hide. If he retraced his way back to the nexus, they would trap him there. If he stayed here, Gutierrez would find him.

Shit. He should have ghosted. Jem scrambled to get Ro's little hack running.

Footsteps reverberated down the corridor. Jem gathered himself to flee. But to where? His heart pounded and his breath hitched. A dark shadow stood in the intersection.

"Hello, Jeremy," Charon said.

Jem shrank back against the wall.

Gutierrez turned the corner, still holding her weapon. He couldn't keep his eyes off it. The gun matched the dangerous silver of her prosthesis.

"Were you always a righty?" Jem asked. He shivered. It was as if his fear was utterly disconnected from his thinking and while part of him had already mobilized to flee, there was part that really wanted to know the answer.

Charon laughed. Gutierrez glared at the Ferryman before glancing back at Jem and holstering the gun.

"You're as bad as Maldonado," she said

Jem drew his breath in sharply before he realized she meant Ro. He smiled. "Yeah. And you're just as confusing and unhelpful."

"For your sake, I hope that was a simple feed hijack and not recorded."

Gutierrez didn't need to touch the gun to deliver the threat.

"Just a hijack. Unfortunately," he said. He hadn't had

enough time or focus to do anything more elaborate. He shifted his attention back and forth between them. Gutierrez stared straight ahead as if Charon wasn't there. "So, I was right. You do have history."

"You could say that," Charon said.

Gutierrez narrowed her eyes.

The tension in the corridor was ratcheting up, but Jem realized it had little to do with him. Well, maybe some. He was the one who contacted Ada May. This had been her answer.

"Do you have any idea what you've triggered?" Gutierrez asked, her voice a low growl.

Jem stared at her. It didn't matter. Not if his brother was in danger. He turned to Charon. "Take me with you. To their rendezvous point. Or whatever. Wherever those coordinates map to. I can help." He paused. Did Charon know about the link he and Barre had started to share? Could Jem even get it to work? Another bunch of things that didn't matter.

"You're staying put. I need someone in a whole different weight class." Charon nodded to Gutierrez.

"You've got to be fucking kidding me," she said.

It sounded like Gutierrez had swallowed glass and every word hurt.

"And you."

She turned on Jem. He tried to step back, but he was already pressed up against the wall.

"It would be best for all concerned if you spent some time in sick bay." She pulled out her gun again.

Jem's body shook. Sliding to the floor, he braced for the impact. He was unable to look away from the gun barrel. It was a tiny black hole in the harsh glare of the corridor.

"Em, is that really necessary?" Charon stepped closer to her and placed a hand on her shoulder.

Her face stiffened into a mask of rage. Her gun hand swept up in a controlled arc that struck Charon's cheek at the top of its swing. He crumpled to the ground beside Jem. Gutierrez swore and barreled down the corridor back to the station.

Charon pressed his hand against the deep cut dripping blood onto his coverall. "I guess it was," he said and laughed until he couldn't breathe.

*

Barre paced the bridge until Halcyone announced that Ro and Micah were back on board. He didn't hesitate to start the ship's takeoff procedures. There was an economy to his communication with her now. A few musical phrases, and the AI read his intentions easily. As the interstitial engines warmed up beneath his feet, they played a thrumming counterpart to the notes in his mind.

"Good," Ro said as she burst through the door. Micah limped in behind her. Both their faces were flushed. "Definitely past time to go."

"The bridge is yours, Cap." He didn't even mean it ironically.

She took her place behind the captain's chair and gripped the high seat back. "Halcyone, open a channel to the port facilities."

"Channel open."

"This is Captain Maldonado of the freighter Halcyone. Requesting permission to leave. Release docking clamps."

Her voice was steady and strong, but two bright patches blazed on her cheeks and her knuckles were white. Barre held his breath as the silence went on longer and longer.

Micah looked around the bridge, wide-eyed.

"This is Captain Maldonado. Of the freighter Halcyone. Release the docking clamps on bay three two Alpha."

They waited again, staring at one another.

"Request denied. Please power down your ship."

"What the fuck?" Micah looked as if he was ready to break something.

"Halcyone, close channel," Ro snapped.

"Channel closed."

"Fucking bartender sold us out." Ro stared up at Micah.

"It doesn't make sense," he said.

Barre had heard the entire conversation with Larson. Micah was right. It didn't make sense. He survived and thrived on his reputation. Selling out customers wouldn't help him.

"Ro's father wasn't the only one with enemies," Barre said softly.

"What choice did I have?" Micah's voice exploded through the bridge.

"None," Ro said. "But I think we've just traded a supernova for a black hole."

Halcyone's alert tone sounded in Barre's mind. "Incoming message."

"Open comms."

"Commonwealth freighter Halcyone, shut down your engines. You have three minutes to comply."

Ro slashed her hand across her throat. Barre closed comms again.

"Real threat or bluster?" she asked.

"Real," Micah said. "Look where they quarantined us."

"Can you hack your way in and disable the clamps?" Barre asked.

"Not in three minutes."

"But you think you could?"

"I don't know, Barre. Probably." Ro tugged her hands through her hair. "Maybe. If I don't trigger some fail-safe and blow us all up in the process."

"I doubt it would come to that," Micah said. "The ship is worth more intact. And so are we."

The three of them looked at each other. There was no blame. They had all known the stakes of the bet and the dangers of following this particular ion trail.

"Shut down the engines," Ro ordered.

"Aye, aye." Barre sent Halcyone a quick command. The slight vibration at his feet quieted. "How much time do you think we have?"

"Until what?" Ro asked.

"Until whoever wants me gets here," Micah said.

"I have no idea," she said. "But I don't think it'll be long."

"Then you'd better get to work," Barre said. "How can I help?"

Ro set her micro down on the main command console and pulled up several virtual windows. Smears of color trailed from her hands. "Monitor the station's comms.

Things may get messy."

"Messier than they already are?"

"There's nothing I can do here. I'm going to try to reach the son of a bitch," Micah said.

Barre nodded. At least it would keep Micah busy and out of Ro's way. Barre double-checked Micah's permissions. "You're all set. Just use your micro's interface."

"If you need me, I'll be in engineering."

Ro barely grunted, already engrossed in planning her hack.

"Keep us posted."

Micah nodded. "Same."

"I think you'll know if something goes wrong."

"Then it's just business as usual, right?"

Micah smiled and it was the senator's smile. Self-deprecating and smug at the same time. It was only there for an instant, but seeing his friend disappear like that sent a chill down Barre's spine.

"It's going to be okay," Barre said, but Micah had already left the bridge and Ro didn't hear him. He shivered again. It had to be okay.

*

Micah triggered his micro in the corridor on his way to engineering. "Halcyone, check remote mailbox."

"Message waiting."

He closed his eyes briefly. The soft whoosh of the door opening startled him. "Playback," he ordered as he stumbled inside and fell into the nearest chair, propping his aching feet on the console.

Maldonado's voice filled the small space. Micah gripped the edges of his micro until his hands cramped.

"She's alive and unharmed. Contact me when you're ready to transfer the money."

Then there was a brief pause when the playback hitched. Then it resumed, this time with a video feed. Maldonado's thin face filled the small screen.

"Hello, Micah. The timestamp is accurate. I'm certain Ro will corroborate that. Here's your proof."

The video lurched and Dev looked up at him. Her dark eyes were shadows. Her spiky hair stood up in all directions. There was a smudge on her cheek that Micah hoped was only dirt. She kept her hands out of view, tucked in her pockets. Micah curled his into fists.

"... I'm okay, really."

He blinked. Her voice was strong and sure. Her stare, defiant. He was suddenly sure he didn't want to see her angry.

"... hasn't hurt me." Her gaze flicked away from the camera and back again. There was a brief flare of fury in her eyes, before they softened. *"It's not your fault."*

Micah slid his feet to the floor and jumped out of his chair. But it was his fault. If he hadn't tried to run from his past, she wouldn't have gotten tangled up in it. It was all he could do not to smash his micro against the console. But she was talking again.

"... there's no static between us, right?"

She didn't have to blame him. He had enough guilt for

both of them and then some. Micah focused on the video.

"Tell Sellen I'm okay."

Sellen. Why did she mention Sellen?

"Halcyone, pause playback. Repeat."

The screen blanked and Maldonado's face appeared again. This time, he focused only on Dev. What was she trying to tell him? They had only known one another for a matter of days, but he already knew she was resourceful. Strong. Fierce. He smiled. He almost felt sorry for Maldonado.

Okay. Her hands were in her pockets. It wasn't a posture of fear. Her shoulders were set and her chin upraised. No. That was defiance. So she had something in her hands that she didn't want Maldonado to see.

Static. The static charge that had nearly turned Micah catatonic in the biodome. Static. Sellen. Static. It was a message. Micah smiled. It had to be. He stopped the replay and zoomed in on her lap. The quality of the vid wasn't good enough to focus in that far, but he was sure she had the cube. And, had a plan to use it somehow.

"Be careful, Dev," he whispered, as if she could somehow hear him. Maldonado wasn't stupid. He wouldn't hesitate to hurt her if it served his purpose. As long as he thought his payday was dependent on her, she was safe. As safe as she could be. He just had to delay him long enough so they could get off this moon and track his ship. Then payday would turn into payback.

If Ro could get them free.

Micah swallowed the lump in his throat. The longer they were stuck here, the more danger Dev was in.

He ran through the entire brief vid one more time, frame by frame, making sure he hadn't missed anything, but there was nothing else he could find. Dev had told him what she could. It would have to be enough. Now it was time to vent plasma and surrender. Delay until they could get out of here and locate Maldonado's ship. And, Micah had better make it good. As good as his father had been, Micah knew he could be better. He had no choice. Dev's life depended on it.

Stick to the truth as much as possible. They were in a kind of impound. And they would need to shake any pursuers before it was safe to initiate a handover. Micah just had to spin enough of it for Maldonado to buy without giving away their position.

Micah looked around engineering. It was all quiet. Too quiet. But that was probably a good thing. They were still here. Still alive. He didn't bother to check in with Barre and Ro. They had their jobs. He had his.

Composing himself, Micah triggered his micro to record. Dragged his hands through his hair. He didn't have to fake the fatigue that pressed on him as heavy as a five g burn. It was as if he'd been preparing for a performance like this his entire life. His father's placating voice was a whisper in the back of his head. Showtime.

Chapter 17

D EV SAT AGAINST the wall turning the knife over and over in her hand. There was no way of knowing if and when Micah would get her message. And even if he did, what would he do in response? Ultimately, Dev was on her own. But she had understood that from the very start of this particular adventure. Really, it wasn't much different than life in Midlant.

The ship was just another unexplored city. And it was time to map it out.

Maldonado was the biggest variable. Without a ready way to watch her, would he do physical checks? And if so, how often? But she knew the risks of sitting here. They were unacceptable.

She gathered her tools, wound the remaining wire around her waist, and opened the hatch in the galley again. The light only pierced a meter or so before the corridor angled away into darkness. With a last glance at her prison, she squeezed her legs through the opening and let them dangle, supporting her body weight on her arms. She scraped her toes back and forth against the wall searching for footholds that had to be there. Otherwise, she'd never get back into the room.

Her shoulders burned. She was out of shape for this. Grunting, she rotated a quarter turn and tried again. Sweat beaded on her forehead. Her arms trembled. The flexible toes of her shoes slipped into a narrow niche. She jammed her other foot below the first, exhaling heavily as the weight eased from her upper body.

Dev pulled her arms inside the access corridor and hooked them into the built-in ladder. When she reached the bottom rung, an extension slid down to the floor below. The only light was the square of brightness that leaked from the open tile an arm's length above her. It illuminated enough of the corridor to show her she wouldn't have to crouch. That was a gift. A headlamp would have been nice, but so would not being trapped on this ship. She had learned a long time ago not to wish for things she couldn't have.

Her eyes slowly adapted to the dark. There was a subtle glow up ahead. Behind her, the corridor ended in shadow. She headed forward, stretching her arms out to the sides and trailing her hands along both walls. Her right hand hit empty air and she stopped. A branching corridor disappeared into darkness. A step farther and her left hand registered another turn. A soft glow emanated from the ceiling. So another corridor to the port side. Time to count. *One right. Two left.* She kept walking. A blast of air hit her cheek just as her left hand hit emptiness. *One right. Two left. Three left.* Another glow strengthened ahead. And there was another corridor on the left. *One right. Two left. Three left. Four left.* A map sketched itself out in her head.

The brightness was coming from another grate set in the ceiling. A shadow occulted the light. The rumble of a deep voice echoed from directly above her. Dev froze, her heart racing. Maldonado. His footsteps rang over her head. Could he hear her? She struggled to soften her breath and listen.

He was swearing. Was there someone else on the ship? Shit. That would make things more difficult. Dev closed her eyes and concentrated, barely daring to breathe. One voice only. Maldonado's. Furious. Anything that snarled him up had to be good for her. The pressure in her chest eased. She crept closer to the grate, but she still couldn't make out what he was saying.

But at least she knew where he was. And judging by her internal map, this seemed to be a small ship. She tentatively labeled the room above her the bridge. What else could she find? Leaving Maldonado behind, she headed forward. The access corridor dead-ended a few meters ahead. She backtracked to the first turn past the bridge. In this direction, right. Reaching into her pocket, she fingered the handful of screws she'd liberated from the hinge. She placed one on the floor up against the wall, the tip pointing toward her starting point. A mental map was good. A map plus guideposts was better.

Another grate up ahead leaked light in striped bands across the floor. Standing below it, Dev listened intently. At least there weren't likely to be the kind of surprises she found in the desolate cities and towns she explored. No feral strays on a spaceship. No feral survivors either. She ran her fingers over the old scar on her left wrist, courtesy of a dog she'd surprised on a site the year she'd turned twelve. The rangy thing was as desperate and as much of a survivor as any Midlanter. Dev didn't blame the bitch for clamping down on her arm. You did what you could to protect your own. For the rest of that summer, even though the dog never let herself be seen again, Dev had shared her scant rations.

Her brothers were always hassling her for taking in strays.

Was that what Micah was? If so, maybe this was what she got for her pains.

She reached up to release the ladder and climbed up to the grate. Peering through the narrow slats, she saw the undersides of several consoles and a toppled-over chair. Navigation? Communications? Whatever it was, it probably was worth exploring.

Wedging herself against the narrow confines of the access tube, she ran her right hand along the edge of the grate, searching for the release that had to be there. Something sharp bit into her finger and she yelped, then bit her lip as the sound reverberated around her. Good thing her immune system was solid and she'd had all her shots. Moving more lightly, she found the trigger. The grate swung up. She shot her hand through the opening and grabbed it before it clanged back onto the metal floor. First, find the ocular.

It was set in roughly the same place, up on the far wall, as in the galley. She wriggled into the room and rolled behind the console, breathing heavily. Smeared blood stained her index finger.

Did Maldonado believe that Dev was trapped and helpless? Good. She would use that to her advantage.

Keeping her head low, she pulled out Sellen's cube. How

quickly would it recharge in this light? She squinted up at the ceiling. Unless Maldonado had cheapened out, standard ship's lighting was high-intensity full-spectrum UV. Otherwise, spacers went a little loopy, though typically the schedule was set to mimic a normal diurnal rhythm. Having the constant brightness was useful to charge the cube, but not great for long-term stability of people.

Dev unwrapped the cube and set it atop the console. She might not know its charge cycle, but at least she could assess its level of juice by the color of the coating. By the time she was done, she'd have a complete report for Sellen. Maybe that would redeem her from failing the semester.

If she got out of this ship alive.

She rubbed her wrist again. This time Dev was the cornered dog. Maldonado would feel her teeth soon enough.

*

Ro turned to her virtual windows. With enough time, she should be able to find a way in. She'd hacked freaking Ada May, hadn't she? It was all about finding the right leverage. Sifting through her toolbox, Ro considered several sniffer routines and set one running.

"Ro?" Barre's hand gripped her shoulder. "Ro!"

"What?" She turned her head to glare up at him, before the look on his face made her gasp. Ro quickly assessed her windows, but she hadn't triggered any alert as far as she could tell. "What's wrong?"

"News from Daedalus. You'd better read the whole thing."

She reached for his micro and scanned the words scrolling across its display. "What in the endless cosmic void does she think she's doing?"

"Which 'she'? Nomi, May, or Gutierrez?" Barre asked.

"All of the above." Ro reread Nomi's message. "This is complicated enough. May should know better than to add an unstable isotope to a chain reaction."

"That depends on where we are when the boom happens," he said. "Any progress?"

Her windows were quietly active, still running their little programs. "I should have a basic schematic in a few minutes." Unless their system was a lot more guarded than Ada May's. Which was hard to believe.

"Whatever you're going to try, sooner is better than later." Micah spoke softly from the doorway. "Your father is starting to get impatient for his money."

And they would need to locate his ship before that transaction was completed. As soon as her father had what he wanted, Dev was no longer a bargaining chip. He never kept things that didn't have value.

"We need to call off Gutierrez," Ro said, willing her program to run faster.

"Wait. What?" Micah asked.

"I don't have time for this. Barre? Bring him up to cruising velocity." She turned back to her displays as Barre showed Micah the news from Daedalus.

"We are so spaced," he said softly.

They had to get free. Once Halcyone was out of here and broke orbit, they could run the Ithaka program and even if Charon could track them, the cartels or the weapons buyers or even the Commonwealth—though Ro suspected there was a great deal of overlap—wouldn't be able to. That would simplify matters. At least she was pretty sure May didn't want them dead.

Her mapping program ended with a soft whine. That window flashed a sickly yellow. Ro swore and read the error message three times before she could make sense of it. "Son of a bitch. It's an isolated system."

Micah and Barre turned to her, identical blank looks on their faces. Ro wanted to scream.

"Isolated. An isolated system. The fucking docking clamps."

"You can fix it, right?" Micah asked.

"They have it rigged for manual release only."

"Then we release them. By hand. Barre and I can ..."

"No. You don't understand." Cold coiled in her belly. "Whoever releases the clamps is on the wrong side of the docking bay doors when they open. Once we're free, we catapult out of here. Who wants to be left behind?"

Shocked silence followed.

"Yeah, that's what I thought."

"We can't just wait here," Barre said.

She spun on her heel to face him. "Did I say we were going to wait? Did I fucking say that?" Fury rose through her chest and heated her face. Her body vibrated with the need for movement. "I need to talk to Gutierrez. Can you do that?"

"I can't promise you won't be overheard."

"Oh, they're going to hear me all right. Clear to the entire Hub and beyond." Ro's thoughts burned meteor paths across her brain. She was past the point of caring about secrecy and security. Gutierrez thought she was a rogue planet? The LC had no idea. "Just do it," she said.

"There's going to be latency," Barre warned. "Even with Ada's enhancements."

"Fine."

"For Dev's sake, I hope you know what you're doing," Micah said.

Ro swallowed her unease. It wasn't Dev she was worried about just now. "Barre? I need that channel." They had to get to Gutierrez before she left Daedalus. If it wasn't already too late.

The yellow warning continued to pulse in the live window at Ro's eye line. She crumpled it up and tossed the virtual trash at her micro. Then she picked up the little machine. Gutierrez first. Docking issue after. If there was an after.

Static crackled through the bridge. "... any idea ... risk you're taking?" Gutierrez's voice was still cold and sharp despite the poor quality of the connection.

"I know exactly what I'm doing. And it doesn't involve you. Or your chain of command." That was sufficiently generic. Ro wasn't going to needlessly involve Ada May if she could help it.

"I follow my orders." Gutierrez's snappy response was almost immediate. No garbling there. That message was loud and clear on all levels.

"Then stand down. This is a private matter. A family matter."

/not anymore/

Gutierrez had switched to the tunneled text that Ro had figured out and May had encrypted. Ro cocked her head.

Which meant Gutierrez had her hidden node address. How long has she had that? Could the LC hack into Ro's messages? Certainly not without leaving any traces behind. Unless it was something May had developed. But this was not the time.

Ro joined the text session. /do you have any idea what a mess you're going to make?/

/me? you're the one who triggered the unstable wormhole. i'm supposed to clean up after you. she wants you alive. she doesn't see how much of a liability you are./

Gutierrez's implication couldn't have been any clearer if she'd responded out loud.

/back off. there are lives at stake./

/at least we agree on something./

/i don't need your help./

/what you think is irrelevant. if you'd learned to follow orders, you wouldn't be here./

Ro thought of the LC's deadly prosthesis. /and how'd that work out for you?/

Their words slowly scrolled off the screen and vanished. There was no response for a long moment and Ro didn't know if that was because the LC was done talking or a random cosmic ray downed a message packet.

Ro typed again. /back the hell off/

/too late/

/what does that mean?/

/i follow my orders. Gutierrez out./

"Fuck."

"What?" Barre and Micah were staring at her, with identical wide eyes.

"Complications. They're coming."

"And we need to go," Micah said.

"I know. I know." Ro paced the bridge. "Get me the damned bartender."

"Channel open," Barre said.

Ro squared her shoulders. This should be interesting. "Larson. We had a deal."

"Sorry, Captain, but things escalated above my pay grade."

"So much for honor among thieves."

"Blame your friend. The Rotherwood name garners as much interest in some circles as the Maldonado one." Larson paused. "Maybe more."

Micah's face paled.

"We need those docking clamps released."

"Not possible, Captain."

"We can provide a significant incentive." Ro raised an eyebrow at Micah. He nodded. That would take a few zeros off his father's account.

"How about you join me for a drink. I'm sure things will be cleared up soon."

Ro signaled for Barre to cut the channel. "Does that sound like our bartender friend is bribe-able?"

"No," Micah answered, through clenched teeth. "If leaving me here gets the two of you on your way to Dev—"

"No," Barre said.

"No fucking way," Ro added. "My crew is not a point of negotiation."

"We have no choice!" Micah's shout filled the bridge.

"Oh, yes we do," Ro said. "Watch me. Barre?"

He opened the channel once more.

"Larson, it's nothing personal, but if you don't release those clamps right now, I'm going to fire up Halcyone's engines and melt this docking bay."

"I don't think so," the bartender said. "Your AI won't let you."

"Did you know my father restored the mechanics of this ship?"

"What does that have to do with anything?"

"He left the AI for me. I brought Halcyone back. Not him. Me. It was pretty well damaged but I reprogrammed it. This ship is, shall we say, pretty uninhibited. Forty years ago, it crashed itself on an asteroid and took the crew down with it. I don't think there's much this ship wouldn't do. Especially with my modifications and encouragement."

There was silence from Larson's end.

"But if you don't believe me, that's fine."

Barre stared at her, wide and wild eyes. "What are you doing?" he mouthed.

"Power up the interstitial engines. Ten percent only."

He held her gaze for another few seconds before something he did sent a vibration quivering through the floor of the ship. "Engines at ten percent."

"Captain, you're playing a dangerous game with an unknown opponent. Turn the engines off and let's talk."

"You have no idea, Larson. Barre? Engines up to twenty percent."

"Aye, aye, Captain. Twenty percent." The growling underfoot strengthened.

"Thirty percent."

"Thirty percent," came the confirmation.

Halcyone shuddered against the pull of the docking clamps. If Larson didn't blink, either Halcyone would break free dragging a significant chunk of the moon base with her, or the ship would be radioactive melted slag against the bay door. Either way didn't bode well for the bartender and his facility.

"Captain, you need to stop." Was she imagining it, or did Larson sound worried?

"Forty percent power, please, Barre."

"Interstitial drive at forty percent."

The heat from the engine outflow would really start to be a problem above half power. There was a good chance Halcyone would refuse to push past a certain threshold. AIs were programmed to be self-protective, but this one had already nearly killed itself. Clearly that programming wasn't working too well.

"Bring engines to fifty percent power."

"Fifty and holding."

"You're as crazy as your father," Larson said.

"Crazier, actually." Ro paused. "We have places to be, Larson. And you're about to get house guests you don't really want. Let us go. Let them all follow us off your little worldlet here. Trust me. You don't want to be in the middle of this trouble. Really."

She signaled Barre to hold.

Halcyone's engine whine rose to a higher pitch. Holding her micro with one hand, Ro gripped the back of the command chair with the other. If Halcyone broke free now, nothing was going to prevent them from being flung across the bridge. Micah and Barre wedged themselves against the nav console, each of them meeting her gaze. There was no doubt in their eyes. That degree of trust nearly broke her resolve.

She checked and the comms channel was still open. "Barre, increase interstitial power to sixty percent."

"Aye, aye, Captain."

"Wait!" Larson's voice crackled through the bridge speakers. "Check your sensors. Pod doors are opening."

Ro's entire body trembled in counterpoint to the ship. "Cut engines on my mark," she whispered to Barre.

A fine sheen of sweat glistened across his face. He nodded. A flicker pulled her attention to the forward display. Barre had configured it to show the bay. Larson was true to his word. The doors had opened.

"Captain?"

Ro smiled. He did sound worried. She let him wait a moment longer.

"After we throttle down, you have three seconds to get those clamps free before I fire the engines to max." She signaled to Barre. He cut the engines and the comms at the same time.

The sudden silence rang in her ears like a persistent alarm.

A clang reverberated through the ship.

"We're free!" Barre shouted.

"Engines up. Go, go, go!"

Halcyone leapt from the docking bay, growling like some caged animal. Ro knew exactly how the ship felt. They bolted away from the base. Ro held her breath, counting the seconds. How long before they were out of weapons range? Did they even have weapons?

It felt like an eternity—like the subjective twisting of time through a wormhole—until she heard Barre calling her name over and over again.

The viewscreen was full of stars. The planetary system May's coordinates had taken them to was receding in the distance.

She exhaled heavily. "Shit. Let's not do that again."

Chapter 18

IT FELT LIKE Nomi had just fallen asleep when her door chime rang. "What?" she called out, struggling to disentangle herself from the blankets. The chime sounded again.

More awake now, Nomi blinked and focused on the door. "Daedalus. Identify."

"Durban, Jeremy and unidentified guest."

She wrapped a kimono around her sleep clothes and triggered the door release. Jem stepped inside, leading a slight, narrow-faced man whose right cheekbone was weeping blood.

"Jem? What's going on?"

"Sorry. Medical wasn't an option. Or my quarters either."

Nomi grabbed a towel from the galley. "Don't bleed on the furniture. I'll get the first-aid kit."

Jem settled the man on her sofa while she rummaged in the tiny compartment above the sink. She tossed the standard-issue kit toward Jem. "Here."

He caught it, his eyes widening in surprise. "Hey, not bad."

"Oh, shit, sorry!"

"No. Really. I think the neural's helping." He bounced the kit in his hand. "A few weeks ago, it would probably have hit me in the face."

"Who's your friend?"

The man sat quietly studying her. If Nomi had been bleeding in some stranger's room, she would have been a whole lot less relaxed.

Jem turned to him. "This is Konomi Nakamura."

He bowed from his seat. "Charon. At your service."

Nomi drew in a breath. May's Ferryman. So this was Ithaka's answer. "What happened?"

Charon smiled and his expression transformed from somber to something just on the edge of uncomfortable. Old scars twisted his lips into a strained grimace. His eyes sparkled with hidden amusement that didn't match the stiff mask of his face. "Gutierrez. Emma Gutierrez happened."

"Jem?"

"It's complicated?"

Nomi stifled a yawn and turned to the galley and the waiting teapot. When was it not? "I'll make us some tea while you clean up your friend, here." She pulled out a strong black blend. If her sleep pattern was doomed to utter disruption, she might as well go with it.

Charon sat expressionless while Jem disinfected his hands before cleaning and examining the wound.

"It's not going to scar, is it, doc?" Charon's lips twitched into another twisted smile.

Jem ignored him and smeared a dollop of antibiotic glue across the wide cut.

The teapot beeped. Nomi offered a cup to each of them. Charon shook his head and stood. "Well, Jem, I guess it was a good thing I didn't dump you out of my ship's airlock."

"Probably."

"Yeah. Doc would have been moody."

"You're going to help our friends?" Nomi asked.

"I do what the doc tells me," Charon said, shrugging. "Even if it kills me." His casual, amused voice didn't match the intensity in his gaze or in his words. "And Emma just might." He laughed and bowed again, this time fully, a formal bow that reminded her of her grandfather.

Nomi studied Charon again, but there was no obvious stamp of Japan that showed through his DNA. She bowed back. When she stood up, the door to her compartment was sliding closed and he was gone.

"Do you trust him?" she asked.

"Not really. But Ada does."

"What's his history with Gutierrez?"

"I have no idea."

Nomi offered Jem tea. His hands wrapped around the mug and his long fingers overlapped. He had surgeon's hands. Like his parents. "Now what?"

He blew across the surface of the tea. Steam billowed toward her. He yawned.

They should have both been asleep. Nomi couldn't remember the last time she had a full shift's worth of rest and the circles beneath Jem's eyes still had a dark and bruised look.

Jem pulled out his micro. "I think we have work to do."

Nomi sighed. She could sleep later. "Okay. What's the

plan?"

"There are too many circuits we can't close. Ro and I tried to track down Gutierrez's past and got nowhere. At least until her path started converging with Lowell's."

"So we go after him." It's what Mendez wanted. Nomi was practically given access. "How's your brain, kiddo?"

"I can get the job done." There was a cold determination in his eyes.

She sat down next to him, moving the towel Charon had tossed aside. "I don't have your skills. Or Ro's. But I'm not totally useless. How can I help?"

Jem curled his body up against the corner of the sofa. "Help me figure out where to start. We can access his public records. I might even be able to hack into his private ones, but if I just start poking around randomly, it could get messy."

So many of her conversations with Lowell came around somehow to Maldonado. They were associates. At least distant ones. But maybe that was a way in. "We drop the Gutierrez angle for now. Can we correlate Lowell's postings and history with Alain Maldonado's?"

"Yeah. I think so."

Jem flicked his fingers in a way that reminded Nomi of Ro. Two virtual windows blinked into existence at their eye level. She didn't notice him running any query or typing in parameters, but data started marching across the windows.

"Maldonado's on this side. Lowell on the other. I'll run a convergence routine and have the program create a separate output."

He blinked up at her. "And would you mind turning the

lights down? They kind of sing, and the glare is still hard for me."

"Of course, kiddo." She dimmed the ambient lighting to dusk.

"Better."

Text scrolled across the screens in a blur. Nomi didn't bother to track it and neither did Jem. The raw data wasn't what counted. It was how the two men's lives intersected that mattered. Lowell had at least a decade on Maldonado, so they couldn't have had a school history together. What was the connection?

And if they found it, would it even help?

Nomi grabbed Ro's folded quilt from the back of the sofa and draped it over her lap. Maybe the search was a long shot, but it was the only thing they could do from their end right now. At least they had gotten through to May. Help was heading toward Halcyone. Nomi leaned over and squeezed Jem's shoulder. "It's going to be okay."

Jem yawned again. "Sorry."

The program was still sifting through data from all the various publicly available sources on all Commonwealth servers.

"This looks like it's going to take longer than I thought."

She tossed him a pillow. "Well, we should probably rest now while we have the chance."

"I'll set the routine to ping us when all the data is analyzed." Jem paused before shoving the pillow behind his neck. "Thank you." He leaned against the sofa back and was asleep.

If only it were that easy for Nomi. Worry about Ro kept

sleep a distant thing. The flickering windows cast an uneven light on Jem's face. Without the intensity of his roving, alert gaze, he looked far younger and more fragile than his twelve years hinted at. Certainly he had done more in those years than most adults in the Commonwealth.

Nomi felt less than useless, compared to him. Compared to everyone else in Ro's orbit. She leaned back, closing her eyes, and focused on the cadence of her breathing. Sleep wouldn't come, but maybe clarity would.

*

Micah's ears rang in the silence of the bridge. He and Barre traded a look of shared terror and wonder as Halcyone's interstitial engines vibrated below their feet. "You are something else," Micah said, shaking his head. Even in his smoothest days, his father couldn't have done any better. "How did you know Larson would cave?"

Ro stared past them at the display, her green eyes wide. Barre placed a hand on her trembling arm. "Ro?"

"I didn't." The words were a strangled whisper and her face was dangerously pale. "I'm sorry. It was the only way."

Micah exhaled heavily. He wasn't even angry. What good would that have done? She'd done what she had to do. And to be honest, he also wasn't surprised. They had all jumped past the point of caution and restraint. Maldonado had made any other options impossible when he'd taken Dev.

"Okay, then. Let's get out of here," Micah said.

"That's it? No lectures? No arguments?" Ro looked from

him to Barre and back again, almost as if she were pleading for one of them to make a different set of choices.

"No reverse in a wormhole, Cap," Barre said.

Ro shivered and then took one deep, shuddering breath. "Okay then. Okay."

Micah walked over to where she was standing by the main command console and circled his arms around her. She stiffened, but he held on. "We have your back."

Her body shook against his.

"Ro? It's okay. Really." He gripped her shoulders and stepped back. "I'm sorry."

She couldn't catch her breath, but what Micah took for sobs was laughter. Helpless, gulping peals of laughter. Micah shot a concerned look at Barre.

Barre handed her a water bulb. "You going to live?"

Ro wiped her streaming eyes and took a long, slow drag from the container. "Yeah. I think I will. I think we all will, no thanks to me."

"What do you need us to do?" Barre asked.

"Once I configure a tracking routine, can you work with Halcyone to plot our course?" She checked her micro. "Nothing deeper than a four g burn. And even that is pushing it."

"We're working against the clock here, Ro," Micah said. "Your father's not going to react well to any more delay."

"That's all the cushions are rated for. I'm not willing to risk it. And we need to sleep. I don't know about you guys, but I was already running on fumes before this all started."

Risk? Micah wasn't going to point out that if her little gambit had failed, she would have killed them all, making any consideration of their safety moot.

"Agreed," Barre said. "Maldonado won't risk harming Dev before he gets his money. He's ruthless, not stupid."

"Fine. Then what can I do?" Double-checking Halcyone every thirty seconds for a reply from Maldonado wasn't very productive.

"Grab something for us to eat from the galley," Barre said.

"Fine," Micah repeated, but neither Ro nor Barre heard him. He paused at the ruins of the melted door and watched his friends. Ro stood, shoulders back, legs braced apart, chin raised, creating programs out of thin air and light. Barre lounged in the nav chair, his legs swinging over the arms. His hands drummed a counterpoint against his micro.

They had it covered. They were all doing everything they could. Time to fuel their engines.

By the time he returned with a handful of meal bars and more water bulbs, Ro and Barre were talking quietly and pointing at the viewscreen. He slid in beside them and passed out the bounty.

Ro made a sour face. "Only the best for my crew."

Barre shrugged and ate his in three quick bites. Ro nibbled on the edge of hers before pointing with it toward a blinking light on the display.

"We got a hit."

Micah grabbed the edge of the nearest console to steady his knees.

"The tracker uses the ansible carrier currents the way my message program does. So that means he was here." She pointed again to the blob of light circled in orange. "He may still be here, or he may be long gone. But until he passes an ansible node and the tracker pings in, that's the closest I can get."

"What are we waiting for?" Micah flipped the food bar over and over in his hand.

"How's the nav coming?" Ro asked.

Barre nodded at the screen. "We're good. A few burns and four jumps should get us in the same solar system. We'll sleep underway. I have some sedatives if anyone needs them. As soon as we punch back into interstitial space, we'll have to run Ro's tracker again."

It wasn't fast enough by half, but Micah knew it was the best they could do. It wouldn't help Dev if they got shot out of a wormhole into a quasar. Or worse. He tossed Barre his unopened food bar. "Let's do this."

*

Dev jerked awake. Her head slammed into the console behind her and she bit her lip to keep from swearing out loud. She needed real sleep, not this chain of panicked head-bobs and bursts of REM that woke her, groggy and confused, from dreams of being chased into blind alleys through abandoned settlements. Without any external markers, Dev had no idea of how much subjective time had passed, but the little cube's skin had finally absorbed enough UV light to become translucent again. While it definitely served her needs for now, the constant brightness had to be screwing with Maldonado's sleep cycles. It was already making her loopy.

And an unhinged captor was definitely not going to help any.

She repeated her trick on the ocular with Sellen's cube and her wire and smiled. Two down. Time to explore. The room was small. No larger than the galley she'd been trapped in. Three work stations faced the long wall that could probably be configured as a viewscreen. All the displays were dark, silent. The only way she'd be able to tell what they were would be to try to wake them. But even if Maldonado couldn't directly see Dev, he had to have access to the terminals through the bridge.

Besides, she was no hacker; her skills were in the maker realm.

Was there anything here she could use?

It looked like someone had been in the midst of a refit. Two of the three consoles were open. Circuits and wiring lay on the floor in a jumble. Dev smiled. Oh, yeah. Happy birthday.

But even more precious than the components were the tools that had rolled beneath the consoles. Someone had left in a hurry. An array of delicate screwdrivers, each size color-coded. A circuit sniffer. And the ultimate prize: an ultrasonic soldering iron. Dev's mind was already churning out possibilities. With a heat source and a power source, she could really cause some damage.

She loaded her pockets with new toys before retreating through the access tunnels, not even minding the dark. Her mental map took her back beneath the bridge. Above her, silence. Dev held her breath. Where was Maldonado?

Resisting the urge to flee to the galley before he found her missing, Dev forced herself to wait. If he had gone looking for her, rushing anywhere was a mistake. Years of playing 'nought and shuttle with her brothers had taught her the value of patience and stealth. Besides, these tunnels would amplify any sound throughout the ship. If Maldonado was tearing the place apart for her, she would hear it.

As her own breath quieted, she focused in on the sound of the ship's systems. The rhythmic cycle of the air handling reminded Dev of waves lapping against the shore. She closed her eyes to shut out the glow from the grate overhead. A soft buzzing rose over the hum of life support.

Son of a bitch was snoring.

Dev had an almost overwhelming urge to storm into the bridge and kick him awake. If she couldn't sleep, why should he?

Shaking her head, she retraced her footsteps back to the galley, checking the screws she had left at the intersections. Of course they would be there. No one else was here, but old habits died hard. The way back seemed shorter and she was surprised by the square of light traced along the tunnel floor. The galley was directly above her. Maldonado, just a few compartments ahead. Engineering, to the right. The rest of the ship was still blank on her mental map. She'd have to correct that, but she had to rest first.

Emptying her pockets, Dev laid out her new treasures against the tunnel wall. Later. She would work here later. A tired Dev made mistakes. Mistakes on a dig site were dangerous enough. Here they would be deadly. Food. Rest.

Then plan.

Dev nodded before scrambling back up the ladder.

Food. Rest. Plan.

Chapter 19

NOMI WOKE TO a pulsating glow filling her tiny quarters. Her neck was stiff and her eyes swollen. "Lights up, fifteen percent." She yawned as she stretched. Ro's quilt slid from her lap. "Daedalus, local time."

"Zero six hundred forty hours."

Not enough sleep. How Ro got by on three to four hours a night was a mystery. So much about the engineer was. On the end of the sofa, Jem was curled into a small ball, his arms tucked beneath him. Nomi covered him with the blanket and padded over to the head. A shower and a change of clothes would have to stand in for a full cycle of rest. That and caffeine.

Jem was still fast asleep when she emerged from the head and grabbed a cup of coffee. Steaming mug in hand, she knelt in front of him and called his name.

His eyes shifted beneath closed lids.

"Jem," she said again. This time, she gently shook his shoulder with her free hand.

"Go 'way, Barre." His words were slurred. One hand batted at her arm.

Nomi smiled. Daisuke was definitely not a morning person either. She tried again, shaking a little harder this time. If he had been her little brother, her next move would have been to dump him off the sofa. But that wouldn't be fair, especially with his neural still integrating. She glanced up at his waiting program. "Come on, Jem. We have work to do."

His lids fluttered open. He looked up and blinked, his expression dazed. "I was dreaming about Barre." He frowned. "At least I think it was a dream."

"What do you mean?"

"Ever since we linked on Ithaka, I get flashes of what he's thinking sometimes. I keep trying to connect back with him, but I can't figure out how it works."

"What did you see?"

"It's not something I see. More like something I just know." Jem drew his eyebrows together. "It's hard to explain. Barre was on Halcyone, getting snugged down for a jump. He was worried. The music in his head—it was all discordant."

A neural had been well beyond her family's resources. And even if it hadn't, her grandfather had enough stories about the perils of early adopters to quell Nomi's curiosity permanently. Jem's dream could have been a glimpse into Barre's mind, but it could also just have been his own worry. Cosmos knows Nomi's own dreams had had enough fear for all of them.

"There's a clean towel in the head if you want to wash up. Or do you need to check in with your folks?"

"They know they can find me if they need me. Part of the price of my mom finally letting me have the sedatives was promising not to leave the station again." He made a sour face. "Now I wish I'd never given my word."

Sipping her coffee, Nomi checked for messages while Jem cleaned up. Nothing from Ro. It concerned her, but she wasn't going to burden Jem with it.

He emerged from the head, rubbing his short, wiry hair with a towel. "You wouldn't happen to have more coffee, would you?"

"Are you kidding? With Ro around?"

It was the insti-synth stuff, but Jem drank it down eagerly.

"Hungry?" she asked.

"Nah. Let's get to work."

Jem minimized all but the results window and as soon as he interacted with it, the pulsing light stopped. He flicked the display toward her. "Do you mind? I'm still limited in how much scanning and tracking my eyes are willing to do."

"Of course." Nomi started reading. Jem's program had extracted times, places, and circumstances where the public lives of Cam Lowell and Alain Maldonado had a greater-than-random likelihood of convergence. It was a statistical analysis, and was just as likely to report false positives and false negatives. They would have to assess each instance.

"Well, they both spent time on Earth."

Jem didn't even open his eyes. "It's a big planet."

"I know. But for some reason, I always took Maldonado for a born spacer."

"You can drill down for more detail. Just tap and a new window will open."

The file scrolled to fill the entire screen and then some. That was the problem with computers. Too much data. But Nomi was nothing if not systematic. She started at the beginning.

"Well, Maldonado was raised in the NorPac Settlement. At least he has a school record from there." Nomi decided not to follow that particular wormhole for now; she'd be too many jumps from the main navpath soon enough. "But when he was there, Lowell was halfway across the continent on a Commonwealth Reclamation Project Authority gig." So no connection between a kid in the Badlands of what had been the Dakotas and a freshly decommissioned comms officer assigned to a mobile ansible relay network in the new Atlantic Ocean. "Huh. He reupped after the first stint."

"Those CRPA postings were pretty brutal," Jem said. "I can't picture Lowell as that gung-ho."

Nomi thought of what Marchand had said about their boss: it was all about the big score for him. "There was quite a hardship bonus attached. My grandfather had friends who were able to retire after ten years on those rigs."

"If they survived."

"So where's his money?" Jem asked. "If he spent a full tenner at sea, he should have been set for life."

"Good question." Nomi was still sure there was a

connection between the two men, but maybe following the money would lead her to it. She returned to scan the flagged data.

Maldonado had been a brilliant, if uneven student, and had earned a scholarship to Uni in Chicago. Huh. She wondered if Ro knew her father had gone to the same school where Micah got accepted. But Maldonado never graduated and after some redacted scandal, he drifted east and got a job doing maintenance and repair on the ansible rigs.

"I think I got something, Jem," she said, scrutinizing the dates. Maldonado and Lowell could have definitely overlapped on the coastal platforms.

Jem didn't even open his eyes. "Still not enough for critical mass. In the decades following the Drowning and the war, the CRPA was the biggest employer on or off the planet. Bigger even than the mining multis. And if Lowell was rotating out when Maldonado was coming in? Not likely they knew each other."

Nomi sighed and kept digging.

A link to a newsvid story caught her eye. It was attached to each man's dossier. She pulled open a new window. "Hey, Jem, you need to look at this."

It was a still frame from a brief broadcast about a local murder trial. The computer had identified a young Lowell and an even younger Maldonado with ninety-seven percent certainty, highlighting their faces in the image. They were both witnesses for the prosecution. Still not perfect evidence that they had a shared history, but getting closer.

"Keep digging," Jem said. His eyes brightened as he

leaned forward to follow what she was doing. "You're totally on the right track."

It was Jem's program. He'd done all the heavy lifting. Another flick of her fingers and another window slid open. This time, she needed to set up a search for anything available from the trial. Unless it was under a security interdiction, there should be transcripts of the testimony. And even then, there would be official notice.

But there was practically nothing beyond what the program had already scraped. No court records. No transcripts. And no Commonwealth redaction.

"That's not right," Jem said. "Do you mind?"

Nomi slid the windows toward him.

His fingers moved faster than she could track, and it looked like some of the data jumped around even before his hands reached it. He worked silently for several silent minutes before groaning and lying back against the sofa.

"Hey. You okay?"

"Yeah. Give me a nano."

"Here." She pressed a cup of cool water in his hand. Instead of drinking it, he held it against his forehead.

"As far as I can tell, the dead guy was connected to a money-laundering operation. Either he worked for the cartels in their casino business, or ran afoul of them. Maybe both."

"And Maldonado? Lowell?"

Jem massaged the back of his neck. "Connected somehow. But the public records are a dead end."

"Can we get into Maldonado's employee files?"

"Probably archived when they stripped him of his rank. I

don't even think Ro could hack into the data morgue."

"So we need to attack the Lowell angle."

Jem pressed his lips together.

"What?"

"You're not going to like it."

Meeting Ro had already knocked her so far out of her trajectory, she had no idea where she'd land. What was a little course correction between friends? "I already don't like it. But we're here, right?"

"I can put together a little data miner. It's something Ro showed me. Small, lightweight, efficient." He paused, fidgeting with his micro.

"But?"

"Daedalus's systems are kind of analogous to the human body. You know how certain things don't easily cross the blood-brain barrier? Well, private employee files are walled off from the rest of the system like that."

"So what's the problem?"

"The only way this is going to work is if you upload it in comms. On the inside of the barrier, and while Lowell is logged in."

"Oh."

"If it's discovered, there's a chance it'd get tracked back to you."

Nomi drew up her knees and rested her head on them. This was more than passing along information or holding back information. If she were caught, she'd lose everything: her commission, her family, her freedom, her future.

She looked up into Jem's worried expression.

"I'm sorry. If Ro were here, she could probably figure

out a way past the blocks."

His dark face didn't easily show a flush, but Nomi knew he was deeply embarrassed by what he saw as his failings. The boy took too much on his narrow shoulders. He had already risked so much—for himself, for all of them. How could she do less?

"Load it on my micro." If this was going to be her last comms shift on Daedalus, she was going to make it count.

"Are you sure?" Jem's eyes were very wide.

"I'm sure." Nomi glanced up at the high shelf she'd recently set up in the far corner of the living area. It was lined with a tiny round mirror and a handful of stones her grandfather had given her when she'd left home. They had traveled with her ever since, sealed away until his passing. She had hoped that enshrining his kami here would bring her a little of his gentleness of spirit and his quiet joy. Or at least balance. She really should make an offering, but worried that Jem would think it strange.

He nodded and pushed the little hack over. "Okay. It's got my ident all over it. If you get caught, it should be set up to throw me under the afterburners."

"Not a chance," Nomi said. Even if she could sacrifice him, her grandfather would never forgive her. "Go home. Get some sleep." She ushered him out over his sputtering objections. "Keep your ears open. If something goes boom, you'll know. Just don't do anything stupid, okay?"

"Nomi." He paused at the door, turned, and squeezed her hands. "Maybe this isn't such a good idea."

"Too late, kiddo." After she'd pushed him over the threshold, she sealed her compartment and wrapped Ro's blanket around her shoulders, unable to get warm. Ro. Nomi needed to let her know what she was doing and why. In case she wouldn't be able to tell her later.

*

Ro loathed how the sedatives made her brain sluggish and slow, but Barre had insisted. And really, she knew he was right. Their flight plan was efficient without being brutal, but sleeping during the worst of the acceleration was for the best. And without full-on jump berths, it would also make the transits easier.

Sitting on the edge of her small bunk, she broke the tablet in half and set an alarm on her micro. As soon as their deepest burn ended, she wanted to be back on the bridge. If she had to, she could crawl into a snug in one of the emergency niches for a jump. It wouldn't be much less comfortable than this sparse cabin. Barre had surrounded himself with his music and instruments. There was nothing here that revealed her. Everything that mattered was either in her micro, had been poured into the ship's AI, or, if she was being honest with herself, was back on Daedalus with Nomi.

Halcyone sounded the warning tone. Ro dry-swallowed the sedative and fitted herself into the dampening foam. As soon as she could extricate herself, she would reorient the tracking program and contact Nomi.

The foam obliterated any vibration from the growling engines and disconnected Ro from the ship the same way the meds affected her fraying thoughts. Both sensations were unnerving.

She awoke clear-headed a moment before her micro's alarm sounded feeling, if not rested, at least less thin and frayed. The ship's silence settled around her. Halcyone was cruising through interstitial space on their way to their final jump. Barre had cut it as closely as he could, but it still meant several hours of objective travel time. The AI had already calibrated to the Earth-standard clock after their prior jumps. It was first shift on Daedalus. Nomi should still be asleep.

Spacers usually kept their own subjective stream and only reoriented if they were going to spend much time planetside. Ro might have lived outside the Hub her entire life, but now that Nomi was in her orbit, she didn't want to risk timeslipping past her.

Ro splashed water on her face and rinsed the metallic taste of the sedative from her mouth before heading to the bridge. Micah and Barre must have still been secured and sleeping. For now, Ro enjoyed the solitude. The display showed their progress. They had traversed a large chunk of space in just a few hours. Ro was impressed. For someone without a formal navigation background, Barre did good work.

She called up the tracker utility. It would be less accurate while they were underway, but she didn't want to halt Barre's program. Well, a close approximation would be good enough for now. If she got a fresh hit on the ship's location and they needed to change course, she'd have to wake him.

But while she was still alone, she wanted to reach Nomi.

The small messaging program was set to automatically grab the nearest ansible carrier and calibrate. With May's added security, it was as safe as Ro could make it. For Nomi's sake, she hoped it was safe enough.

Even though Ro was hoping for a message, when her micro pinged she yelped aloud on the empty bridge. She raced through Nomi's words, a growing dread spreading through her. Tracking a connection between her father and Lowell made sense, but the risk Nomi was taking by hacking into Daedalus's main systems terrified her. And, even so, she knew the risk was necessary. The safe course was to call off the hack. But safe for whom? And for how long?

Without information, they were all exposed.

She struggled to find the right words to tell Nomi to be careful. Finding the right code and the most elegant command sequences were as natural as breathing, but plain text? Everything she said was weighted down with what she hadn't said until the message was stilted and distant. She signed off with "miss you," hoping it would be enough.

So her father had grown up in the Pacific Northwest settlement. That was more than she had known. Ironic. It was publicly available data, but she'd never run the search. Ro had spent most of her life avoiding confrontations with her father. Until now. There wasn't much she could do to support what Jem had already uncovered. And if there was a direct connection with Lowell, he and Nomi would find it.

But there was a source of information she had that no one else did. Ro had kept her father's memory cube tucked away in a pocket. It was the safest course: If the Commonwealth had known what she had, she would have been charged as an accessory. But that wasn't why she'd hidden it away all this time. Fear had held her back. Prevented her from hacking it as ruthlessly as she hacked anything else in her way.

Nomi deserved better. They all did.

"Halcyone, display countdown to jump Delta."

Glowing numbers winked into existence in the lower left-hand corner of the cracked screen.

As Halcyone skimmed through interstitial space, Ro set the memory cube down on the main command console and got to work.

Part of her mind maintained an awareness of the time slipping away even as she pulled up an ever increasing number of windows to box in the quiet little square. It wasn't the most sophisticated tech ever invented, but sometimes simple was hardest to hack. Nothing she threw at the memory cube stuck.

Ro stood and swept her hair back from her face. She snarled as it slipped back over her eyes. Her father wasn't complicated. Cruel, single-minded, and vicious, yes. But he didn't have the manipulative charm of Micah's father. He had also been so sure of his ability to control Ro, he left the damned thing out in his workspace. She had broken into the room easily enough.

What was she missing?

Their next jump was in less than forty minutes. Her hand rippling with color, Ro snatched up the cube from her ring of virtual windows and flung it across the room.

When she looked up, Barre was standing in the doorway, the cube in his upraised hand. "Lose something?"

"Only my temper. Why are you here?"

"Woke up. Halcyone said you were here."

Ro blinked up at one of the ship's oculars. Did it understand her frustration? It seemed to be learning as much from Barre as he from it.

"I can't crack that thing." She nodded at the cube in Barre's hand. "My dad's." Ro gave him the quick version of Nomi's information.

"I hope they know what they're doing."

"Me too." Ro slumped at the command console and rested her head on her folded arms. "Any genius ideas how to unlock it?"

Barre slid into the station next to her. "Have you considered asking Halcyone?"

She lifted her head and blinked at him. Certainly, Barre had done things with the AI that she hadn't thought possible. In ways she had never even considered. "Well, what are you waiting for?"

He raised his eyebrows.

"Yes, you. My brain hurts. And we have another jump in ..." She checked the countdown. "Twenty-seven minutes."

"Plenty of time," he said, smiling.

His eyes softened when he smiled, losing the guarded look that had seemed to haunt him from the first time she'd met him. Halcyone had been good for Barre. And Barre had been good for Ro. She wasn't sure what she had done to deserve such trust from her accidental crew—her accidental friends. Her father had leaked enough radiation in her life. There was no way in the cosmos she was going to let him poison them, too. Not while she had the con.

Chapter 20

BACK IN THE galley, Dev woke to the same flood of light she had fallen asleep to. It was a wonder she had even slept, but exhaustion trumped any of her other concerns. How long had she been aboard? The relentless brightness played havoc with her body's clock. She counted the wrappers from the emergency rations. Five meals. Two sleep periods. Not long and far too long.

She used her makeshift head and took a quick rag bath. If Maldonado thought that the conditions on the ship would make her feel less than human, he clearly had never been on a dig site. While a change of clothes would have been a bonus, she'd gone without before.

Her secret weapon had been sitting out while she slept and its coating was fully translucent again. Charged and ready to go. And so was she. Dev wrapped it back in its cover before depositing it in her pocket. The first order of the day was to organize her new tools and supplies. She dropped back into the service tunnels under the ship's corridors. If Maldonado was on the move, she'd hear him.

The ship vibrated gently beneath her as it skimmed along in interstitial space and she wondered if he had a destination, or was merely staying on the move. They hadn't taken a jump since that first day, nor had they done any major course correction or burn. How far were they from Earth? Dev was no astronavigator. Even if she found a star map, she wasn't sure she'd be able to make any sense of it. Nor would she be able to get back home. But, she absolutely wasn't going to simply drift in Maldonado's slipstream.

She was sure Micah would be trying to do something. He didn't seem the type to take ultimatums kindly. And there was no love lost between him and Maldonado. So how could she help?

Or, rather, what could she hinder?

That was a much better question.

She squatted on her heels and studied her new tools. Of the implements she'd salvaged, the most valuable was the soldering iron. It was one of the ones rated for vacuum work. Practically indestructible, with a power pack that could charge via kinetic, solar, or isotope energy, it sat in her hand just begging to be used on something volatile.

Blowing up anything on a starship in transit was not necessarily the best idea, and the jump drive was too closely tied to the ship's AI to access without being discovered, but crippling the interstitial drive would at least keep Maldonado off-balance and busy. Maybe, it would even give them a chance to be found. She organized her pockets and headed down the service corridor toward the bridge. As long as her captor was there and certain that she was contained, Dev was free to roam the ship.

She stood beneath the bridge until she got a feel for his baseline routine. Maldonado was a pacer. If she wanted to, she could have braced herself just below the access hatch and been ready with the soldering iron when his feet hit the grate. A fitting payback for the burns that would always scar Micah's feet, but not one she could administer. No. She'd save her destructive impulses for inorganic machines.

Walking aft, she moved out of the borrowed light and into the darkness of the tunnels. The first right-hand branch led back to the room she'd explored earlier. She hadn't yet investigated the other branches. One of those side corridors would have to lead her to the ship's physical plant. No matter how fancy the computer control systems got, or how much AIs evolved, in the end, it all depended on simple mechanics. Those principles hadn't really changed in a century, though the materials and power sources had.

It was up to Dev to throw the proverbial wrench into the works.

*

Barre turned the memory cube over and over in his hand. "He wouldn't have booby-trapped it or anything, would he?"

"I don't think so," Ro said. "I mean, why bother? He had me pretty well locked down and I was the only one even close to having access to his workshop."

"I'd still want to work with Halcyone through a sandbox." He paused to check with Ro. "If you really want me to poke at this."

"I'm too close to him."

Meaning her father.

"I can't find a way in. And I think it's important."

Barre nodded. "I'll do my best."

"Well, so far your best has been pretty seismic."

Heat rose to his cheeks. "Yeah, well, go, team."

"Go, team." Ro smiled, but then checked the countdown and her expression sobered. "Whatever you're going to try, set it up now. I'd be more comfortable knowing you're in your cushioned bunk than a jump snug."

Thirteen minutes to their final jump. He wouldn't be able to do much of anything except wait for normal time and space to start streaming back in the correct orientations, but Halcyone would have cycles to spare. "Go secure yourself. I'll get her started and I promise, I'll watch the clock."

"Are you sure?"

"See you on the flip side."

Ro gave him a quick hug and it startled him so much he nearly dropped the cube. After she left the bridge, he set it down on the console she'd been working on. Halcyone was waiting for his instructions. He fell back into the musical lexicon that formed the basis of so much of his communication with the AI and created a swirling, circular rhythm. It carried the senses of curiosity, urgency, and caution, lots of caution. Halcyone responded by walling off the device from her main program.

Good.

The display kept counting down to jump time. Six minutes gone. He'd have to leave the bridge in three. Barre was no hacker. Ro had already gone through that nav path and wasn't able to break into the memory cube with her toolset. There had to be a different solution. Something Ro hadn't tried. Barre frowned at the impenetrable device. He wasn't the hacker, but maybe that's not what this thing needed.

There were three main pathways to data protection: passwords, biometrics, and environmental conditions. Or some permutation thereof. That was a lot of possible combinations. Too many for his mind to analyze. Barre struggled to tell Halcyone what he wanted. She didn't need to figure out how to open it, only how Maldonado had sealed it. That would at least give them a starting place. Most everything left patterns behind. Clues that you could read, especially if you were an AI with huge computational capacity.

"Warning, jump Delta in four minutes. Secure for jump."

"Give me a nano," Barre muttered.

Halcyone sent an insistent gong ringing through his mind.

"Fine. I'm going. Keep your engines cool."

Her alarm followed him all the way back to his quarters. A sleepy Micah mumbled something at him that made no sense, courtesy of the sedatives. Barre rolled into his bunk and sank into the sophisticated foam.

Halcyone counted down the seconds and then the wormhole swallowed the ship. The jump created strange music in his head—stranger still than even the unusual melodies the AI created. Her music followed rules. It might have sounded like so much discordant noise to Ro or Micah or Jem, but it was still recognizable to Barre. It communicated meaning and emotion.

The sounds that bled into his brain from the quantum weirdness of jumpspace were the auditory equivalent of plasma burns. They seared his nerve endings and created a disharmony within Barre's own tissues and organs. He could feel the pulses in his ears fighting to synchronize rhythm with the beat of his heart and failing. This was vibration well past the spectrum of the human body to manage. It fed forward and back along his synapses, until his skin crackled with a kind of potential energy.

Barre clawed his hands into the temporal foam, wishing he had taken another sedative. The other jumps hadn't been nearly this bad. He squeezed his eyes shut, but this wasn't the kind of sensory input he could wall out. It was inside him, screaming along the pathways enabled by his neural and his own mastery of music.

Sweat beaded across his forehead. The jump seemed to echo on and on. Surely Halcyone wouldn't have entered the wormhole if the quantum calculations hadn't balanced out. But what if he had made a mistake inputting the nav program parameters? What if there was some malfunction because of the Ithaka program?

He struggled to reach the AI past the eldritch sounds. His stomach clenched and he swallowed again and again. "Halcyone." He couldn't hear his own voice. Wasn't sure he was even able to speak. *Halcyone. Please.*

It was an incoherent plea.

Silence rang in his ears.

And then he could breathe again.

Halcyone rang the all-clear and it was as if the painful

music had never been. Barre couldn't even recall a note of it, only how it thrummed through him.

Micah groaned from the top bunk. A normal sound.

"You okay?" Barre asked.

"Yeah, I'll live. Too many jumps all at once. My brain hurts."

"Tell me about it."

"Diagnostics complete," Halcyone announced through his neural.

"Diagnostics?"

"What?" Micah asked.

"Talking to Halcyone. Sorry."

Her quiet voice continued. "Diagnostics complete. Select report: visual or auditory."

"Um. Visual," Barre replied, silently.

"Are we alive?" Micah asked.

"Looks like it." Barre sat up slowly. Halcyone pushed a wall of data directly to him through his neural. It was too much and too fast, but it was about Maldonado's cube. With any luck, it would be something Ro could use. He triggered internal comms. "Ro? Any idea where we are?"

"Even farther beyond the ass-end of nowhere than Daedalus Station, if you can believe that. No sign of any ship."

"Fuck." Micah dropped down from the upper bunk and winced when his feet hit the floor.

"Idiot," Barre said.

"Tracker is active and running," Ro said. "I should get a fix soon. Join me on the bridge when you can."

"On our way. Pushing Halcyone's report on the cube to

your micro."

"Thanks. Got it."

By the time he and Micah got to the bridge, Ro had multiple windows shimmering in the air around her. She lifted her chin toward the viewscreen and pointed at Micah.

"Before you ask me, I'm still waiting for a new sighting. Can't plot a course until we get one."

Micah collapsed into one of the chairs.

There was nothing any of them could do until Ro's locator program finished running. And she seemed fully immersed in Halcyone's analysis of the memory cube. Barre rubbed his temples, still feeling a trace of the headache the jump had triggered. He sat in the station beside Micah.

"Tell me about your friend."

"Dev?" Micah shook his head. "She's a force of nature."

Barre leaned back and propped his long legs on the console.

"She grew up in a settlement."

"So she's tough."

Micah nodded. "And smart. Resourceful."

Life in the settlements did that. Or else it destroyed you. Barre's mother had grown up in one somewhere in the north of what had been the old United Kingdom. Supported by the largest military force in Earth's history, the Commonwealth of Nations had spread its control across the blighted and drowned globe. In those years, before the Commonwealth claimed space, too, you either were a soldier, were corralled in a settlement, or had enough old money to buy your way into the new cities. His mother's childhood was another of the many things she never talked about. Barre had found her settlement ident tucked behind a holo he'd knocked off the wall when he and Jem were little. Even then, he knew some questions were dangerous to ask.

"Dev study plants, too?"

"Not hardly. Materials science." Micah's gaze stared past him. His eyes widened.

"What?"

"She was analyzing this photovoltaic cube. Something she got as part of one of her labs. I think she has it on her and she wanted to make sure I knew it."

A rare smile lit up Micah's face.

"What do you think she's planning to do?"

"I'm not sure, but I'm starting to feel a little bit sorry for Maldonado."

Ro cursed softly from her corner of the bridge. "I hope she knows what she's doing."

Barre slid his feet from the console and turned to her.

"What's wrong?" Micah jumped up.

"Every time I think I understand my father," Ro said, shaking her head. Rapidly scrolling windows of data surrounded her. She stood and looked through them, her eyes unfocused, gently squeezing her index finger.

"You cracked it," Barre said. "How?"

"Thanks to you and Halcyone. It was biometrics. Would you believe he coded in my DNA?"

"What did you prick your finger with?"

She lifted the cube and all the windows winked out. One of the corners glistened with a drop of Ro's blood. "He even included a built-in needle. Thoughtful, right?"

"Wait. He wanted you to have access? That makes no

sense." Micah drummed his fingers on the console.

"I don't think he did, Micah. It was his way of making sure no one else would. His idea of a joke."

"Some joke," Barre said. "What was he going to do? Keep a vial of your blood around?" He would've needed an actual blood sample, or he'd had to have hacked into Ro's medical records and used her DNA fingerprint to create the lock. Either way, it was pretty creepy. It was one thing to use your own DNA, but to use someone else's without their knowledge or permission was wrong in so many ways. It was like he assumed he owned Ro.

"Yeah, well, joke's on him because it's mine, now." Ro held the little device in her hand.

"So what's inside?" Barre asked.

Ro set it back on the command console and waved her hand over the top. Translucent displays popped up in a complete circle around her. "I think I'm going to need a little help here."

"Do we have time for this?" Micah asked.

Barre monitored the tracker program. It was still searching for a fix. "Halcyone will tell us when she finds something."

"And I'll take any advantage over my father I can."

"There may be something about yours here, too." Barre clapped his hand on Micah's shoulder. "Brooding about Dev isn't going to help us find Maldonado's ship any faster. Come on." He steered Micah into the ring of virtual windows.

"There's so much data here and I haven't been able to access its internal search function. Either my dad had other ways to pull out what he needed, or there's some corruption in the cube."

"Can't you have Halcyone help you search it?" Barre asked.

"I don't trust him. I'm not willing to risk linking the AI to this thing."

"Paranoid, much?" Micah asked.

"That's my dad," Ro said, shrugging.

Barre squinted at the display nearest him. Data scrolled across the glowing window at a rapid rate. "Then we'll have to do this the old-fashioned way. Can you slow it down?"

"I can try."

She waved her hands in an arc. The information slowed to a crawl and then stopped. "At least some things work, but you'll have to manually turn pages now. We can split the displays into three sectors." Ro pointed at three windows to her right. "Micah, you take those. I'll take these." She pointed to the ones adjacent. "Barre?"

"Yeah. I'm on it." He moved so that the three of them stood at the center of the displays, facing outward. "Where should we start? I mean, there's a lot here. What are we looking for?"

"Look for anything that references Lowell, for starters."

She was worried about Nomi. Barre turned to meet Ro's gaze and nodded.

The three of them fell silent. Barre was used to noticing patterns. Music was a kind of pattern. He let the words flow past him, scanning them as he might sight-read a score, looking for outliers or repeating sections of melody. There was nothing there about Cam Lowell, but Barre's eyes did stop on a familiar name. Rotherwood.

"Micah?"

"Hmm?"

"Maldonado was planning on selling your dad out." It was all there in glowing pixels. Messages between Maldonado and the cartels. Money received for information. "Oh, man, it wasn't just the weapons buyers he owed money to. Look at this. Seems he pissed off the cartels, too."

Ro and Micah came over to look at his displays.

"No wonder he needs access to my father's accounts."

"Do you think our friend the bartender knew?" Ro asked.

Micah shrugged. "I don't know. Maybe. Is it important?"

"Maybe," Barre said. "If he sells out the tracking frequency to the cartels, then we're going to have to rethink our strategy. We could be flying into a lot worse than an asteroid storm."

"The only thing it changes is that we have to find him first," Micah said.

Ro squeezed his shoulder. "And it tells us that we have more leverage than we thought."

"Does any of this help us find Dev?" he asked softly.

An alert tone rang through the bridge.

"No," Barre said. "But that does." He pointed to the viewscreen. The locator program blinked with a fresh fix.

*

"How in the void do we get him to stay put?" Micah asked. The blinking dot that represented Dev's location could have been half a galaxy away for all it would matter if

Maldonado fled again.

Ro walked through her glowing windows toward him. "Keep him hooked. Offer to make the exchange. But tell him you want to speak to Dev in real time and watch her board an escape pod before you'll authorize the transfer. He'll need to find somewhere with an ansible nearby, somewhere he can park in a stable orbit to set up the vid relay."

"What if we don't make it there in time?"

"That's not an option," Ro said.

Her voice was as cold and as unyielding as her father's and Micah shivered, remembering what the elder Maldonado was all too capable of. But Dev was nobody's victim. He thought back to her short video. There had been absolutely no fear in her eyes. Micah wasn't sure if that was a good thing where her captor was concerned.

"Won't he be able to track our signal and figure out we're coming for him?"

Ro shook her head. "May's modifications made my comms program pretty slippery. It'll act a lot like the ghost protocol. He'll never know we're there. Send your message and we'll set a course. Even if he's gone by the time we arrive, he won't have had time to get too far."

"Fine." Micah woke his micro and thought about what to record. He needed to look beaten. He could do that. But a little defiant, too, or Maldonado wouldn't meet his demands. Well, Micah had been the shuttle often enough to know that sometimes, maneuverability beat out a dreadnought's power and weapons. The trick was convincing the 'nought commander that he had the advantage.

He sat back down and propped his micro on the console.

Barre and Ro edged out of the camera's view before he triggered the recording.

"We've lost our shadow. I have access to the money. My father was a proper son of a bitch and honestly, I don't want a credit of it. I just need to know my friend is unharmed."

Micah ran his fingers through his hair. He knew his eyes were bloodshot. He certainly didn't look like the smooth senator.

"But I am definitely also my father's son."

He could see Barre raise an eyebrow, but Micah didn't take his gaze from the micro.

"He didn't trust you and neither do I. Appended to this message is an account number and one part of a two-part cipher. Once you engage the code, the money is placed in escrow. You can't access it, but neither can I. I'll release the second part of the code once I talk to Dev and watch her board an escape pod off your ship. I give you the code. You give me her coordinates."

That wasn't how it worked, but he was betting Maldonado wouldn't know that. The code Micah included would just lock him out of the account. There would be no second code. It was just one of many fail-safes for the kind of banks people like his father had access to and ones like Ro's father didn't.

"You have Halcyone's node ident. We'll keep a channel open. Rotherwood, out." Sweat beaded across his forehead. He addressed it to the dead drop. "Halcyone, send recording."

"Recording sent."

"Okay. How fast can we get there?" Micah asked, pointing

to the tiny ship icon blinking on the display.

Barre blinked and looked past them all, doing his crazy mind-meld with the AI. Micah and Ro shared a brief smile. He knew she envied the big musician, but she was also a little in awe of him, too. Which was probably good for her.

"Pretty fast. Eighteen minutes subjective time. One decent burn. No jump. The biggest problem is needing to decel and hide before we're in his sensor range."

"What do we know about the neighborhood?" Micah asked.

They were too far out for a detailed scan, but at least they wouldn't be flying in blind. Ro examined the display and zoomed in on a cluster of planetoids orbiting a single star. Farther out, in what looked to be a Lagrange point, were a man-made asteroid cluster and a bunch of abandoned equipment. "Tapped-out mining operation. Lots of places to hide. For both of us."

Would Maldonado run or hide? "Let's get on it, then," Micah said. He wasn't sure what he wanted more—to get there before Dev did anything that might get her hurt, or see what she was capable of. Both. Definitely both.

They set up in the bridge, even though the berth foam was more comfortable than the chair cushioning. Somehow, it felt like they had more control this way. At least they were all together.

Barre set up a countdown. The burn was barely at two g's and lasted all of a minute or so before the weight eased and Micah could breathe again.

"Halcyone, sensor sweep. Map local asteroid clusters. Mirror on forward display." Ro was every centimeter the captain, despite her rumpled coverall and tangled hair.

The image on the cracked screen flickered before shifting from the star map to local space. The tiny solar system's small planets were all too close to their sun to support life. Asteroids—far more of them in a smaller region than what would occur naturally in space—orbited at the far end of the sun's gravitational influence. The mining operation hadn't dispersed the collected rocks when they were done, leaving another local hazard to navigation behind.

"Our shields are for shit, Ro," Barre warned.

His gaze never left the chaos swirling on the display. The large asteroids weren't the problem. Halcyone could account for and avoid them. It was the smaller stuff. From space dust to the equivalent of hailstones. A ship this old wouldn't have the nanotech coating that could heal small breaches. And even if she had, that was scant protection in a field like this. There was debris here with sufficient mass and velocity to penetrate the hull plating

"Well, you can't say the bastard doesn't plan well," Ro said.

"So what do we do?" Micah asked.

"Plan better." Ro turned to Barre. "This'll go faster your way."

"What do you need?" he asked.

"Find a relatively big asteroid. Not the largest, but one that we can definitely match spin to and hide behind. It needs to have a stable course and trajectory. I want Halcyone to be its shadow. Can you do it?"

Barre looked past Ro, his eyes unfocusing. He had to have been "talking" to the ship.

"We can do it," he said and pointed to the display. "That one."

Halcyone circled an irregularly shaped asteroid located in the northeast quadrant of the display.

Ro nodded. "Halcyone, set a course. Place us in the sun's shadow."

If they were lucky, given the trace metals that were likely scattered in the rock all around them and the abandoned mining gear, Halcyone would stay invisible. Of course that meant it would be harder to find Maldonado's ship, too. Except they had the tracker.

"Halcyone, run 'bloodhound,'" Ro said.

For the first time since he discovered Dev missing, Micah let himself hope a little.

Chapter 21

HER STOMACH CHURNING, Nomi made her way to comms, smiling and greeting station personnel on autopilot. This would have been a whole lot simpler if Gutierrez had just acted like they were on the same side. The LC had, at different times, warned her and threatened her. Nomi wasn't sure which she preferred. What she wanted was clarity. What she had was a highly illegal data worm loaded in her micro.

And a freighter's worth of worry.

Ro still hadn't replied. Or if she had, Nomi hadn't gotten the message yet. She was trying not to let her concern goad her into something even more foolish than loading Jem's program into comms. Though at this point, she wasn't sure she could think of anything riskier than that.

At the entrance to comms, Nomi hesitated. This was the juncture Gutierrez had said was coming. The place where to act was to commit treason in the eyes of the Commonwealth, but to refuse to act could very well mean the lives of people Nomi loved.

Nomi wished she could talk with her grandfather. Sofu

had a way of listening and of asking just the right questions that cut through confusion and doubt. What would he ask her now? The corridor was getting congested in advance of second shift and Nomi would start to attract notice if she kept standing at the door to comms.

She raised her hand to the ident pad.

Trust. Sofu would say it was all about trust.

The door slid open.

Cam Lowell stood next to the shift supervisor of the early crew doing handoff. As Nomi slipped into comms, he turned to look at her. His cold gaze trapped her just inside, her back to the door. For a wild instant, as her heart raced, Nomi struggled not to run. Then his usual casual smile erased the momentary menace until she wasn't even sure she'd seen it.

"Morning, starshine," he called out.

Nomi suppressed a shiver. It was just a silly saying, but it was how her parents used to wake her and what she liked to tease Ro with, just to hear the woman growl at her.

It was all about trust.

She trusted Ro. As prickly and as reactive as the engineer could be, Ro cared for her. Relied on her. Trusted her. And Lowell? Nomi wouldn't trust him as far as she could heave him in heavy g's.

Nomi gave some generic greeting and went to do handoff with her first-shift equivalent, barely registering who the man in the chair was. He suspended the comms station and stood to stretch before heading off duty.

She and Lowell had done changeover early. Marchand hadn't gotten in yet, but it was still five minutes to the official start of shift. His definition of "on time" was a bit more casual than hers. For the next five minutes, or until Nomi picked up the headset and logged in, her station was on AI bypass. Daedalus would handle all of her routine traffic and alert comms and command if anything priority came in. She risked a glance at Lowell.

He stood beside the command station, his attention on his micro.

Four minutes to shift change. Simon Marchand would come barreling into comms with barely a minute to spare, earning him the ire of his first-shift mate. And distracting Lowell in the process. She gripped her micro hard enough to warp the thin polymer case.

Trust. She trusted Jem, too. Even after he'd lied to get his message to the black market sent. It had been a desperate move and she forgave him for it.

She slipped on her headset and listened to the pulse thudding in her ears. If Lowell looked her way, it would look like she was logging in early, as usual. He wouldn't take the chair until the exact moment second shift started. This was her best opportunity.

With steady hands, Nomi paired her micro with comms. At the instant she logged in, Jem's worm would deploy and she'd be committed. She took a deep breath. No reverse in a wormhole.

Two minutes to shift change.

Behind her, she heard the door open and Marchand's loud greeting.

Lowell mumbled something back.

Now!

She enabled the login. Her credentials authorized and the

AI's voice greeted her through her headset.

"Nakamura, Konomi, comms turnover in three, two, one. You have comms control."

Her console lit with color. The screen flared to full brightness. Before she started the familiar tasks of monitoring, filtering, and confirming comms traffic, she unpaired her micro and slipped it back into her pocket, praying to her grandfather's kami that Jem's worm had had enough time to deploy. That it would work. That it wouldn't be tracked back to her.

She jerked upright at the touch on her shoulder.

"Hey, Nomi, how's things?" Marchand asked.

"Five by five. You?"

"It's all good," he said as he shooed the annoyed first-shift officer from his station. But no one stayed mad at Simon for long. Which is why he always got away with late turnover.

The hours crawled by, like a slow slog through interstitial space. Every red light and alarm made Nomi start, convinced she'd been discovered. She thought she'd feel better as the time of her shift went on without a tap on her shoulder or a summons to command, but instead, her anxiety climbed with every minute.

At least it would be her break time soon. Though the thought of eating nauseated her, a cold drink and a few minutes of alone time in her quarters would help. And it would let her check for any word from Ro.

"Nakamura!"

Lowell's voice had broken in to her headset and her ears rang with the feedback from his shout. She jerked around in the chair, her mouth dry.

"Sir?"

"Have you been swallowed by a wormhole? I've been calling you. Take your break."

"Sorry. Okay. Thanks."

There was amusement in Lowell's eyes and something else in his expression she couldn't identify. All she knew was it made the skin on the back of her neck crawl.

Nomi logged off her station, pleased to see her hands were steady and sure. Her work would be split between Lowell and Marchand until she logged back in again after break. Would anything in her log files betray the data miner program?

She stood, her spine straight and tall. It wouldn't matter, even if she was discovered. It was a matter of trust and Nomi knew where hers belonged.

*

Dev counted steps as she headed down the dark corridor and found the right turn she was looking for. As before, she trailed one hand along the right side wall. She doubted there would be additional branches off this shorter access tunnel. The ship was probably not that big, but she couldn't be certain and getting lost in its underbelly was not part of the plan.

The floor vibrated. The interstitial engine's growl grew stronger the farther she went until it dampened the sound of her footfalls and her breathing. There were no other openings, no sense of airflow, and no helpful grates letting in light from above. The tunnel dead-ended after she had paced out twelve steps.

She knew there had to be access to the mechanicals from here. If the ship followed any sort of standard design, she was either beneath or over the port nacelle. Given the vibration from below her, Dev was voting on over. Which meant the access had to be through the floor and into a sub-tunnel.

Light would be helpful. Dev turned around, pulled out the soldering iron, and powered it up. The safety light at its tip glowed a dull red that would barely have been noticeable in any amount of ambient brightness, but here in utter blackness, as in vacuum, it became an effective work lamp. As long as she didn't burn herself with it.

Holding the soldering iron in front of her, Dev swept it back and forth looking for the hatch she knew had to be there. Halfway back to the main corridor, she found it set flush into the shiny floor. She set her makeshift lantern down carefully, business end up, and ran her hands along the seam. It took her several times around it to find the small latch. The edge of a square door popped up a few centimeters from the floor. She swung it all the way open. A soft red glow filled the open square and lit the ceiling of the access corridor. The engine noise got louder.

Dev switched off the soldering iron. The precision heating element cooled down almost instantaneously and she slipped it back into her pocket, smiling. She did appreciate well-made tools. The light from the compartment below was enough for her to see the ladder. She climbed down and rode the extension to the compartment's floor. It was a clever design and Dev was grateful for whoever had kept the hatches and the slides in good working order.

She turned in a full circle, examining the room. It was a long, open space, no wider than the galley. The far walls vanished into darkness. A thin track cut a groove down the center of the bay; presumably it and the bay ran the length of the entire ship. The ceiling was only ten centimeters above Dev's head and she had to resist the urge to stoop. Red lights illuminated what she figured was a hold, empty now. There had to be a main entrance for cargo. Probably through the hull. But that wasn't important. Getting inside the engine compartment was.

As far as she could tell, there were no fixed oculars here. Which meant this was probably someone's private ship and not a smuggler's vessel. She wondered where Maldonado had stolen it. In case she was wrong, Dev kept to the shadows along the port-side bulkhead. Three paces aft, she found a doorway. The closer she got to it, the more intense the vibration from the engines became.

It would be even louder inside. Dev took a piece of salvaged jump-snug fabric from her pocket and tore it in half with her knife. Sound-canceling earplugs would have been nice, but she would make do. With any luck, she'd be out of the engine room before she did permanent damage to her ears.

She examined the door and swore—a string of curses that would've earned her a sharp look and a sharper slap from her grandmother. There was no manual release. Only an ident plate set halfway up the doorframe. Mocking her.

Time for a little EMP. She reached for the wrapped cube

and hesitated. If there was a sensor on the door, Maldonado would know something was going on and where. Could she get in, damage the engines, and get back to her prison before he figured it out? She reviewed her mental map. It wouldn't take her long to climb back into the top service corridor level. Then the galley was aft. Maldonado was at the nose of the ship. The question was, how fast were his reflexes?

Hers had better be faster.

Dev took a minute to review her tools. Circuit sniffer, screwdrivers, knife, and soldering iron. The clock would start the instant she fried the door lock.

Repeating her trick with Sellen's cube, she overloaded the ident plate. It was just a standard issue which confirmed that the ship hadn't been built for smuggling. Dev felt bad for the owners. If they ever did get their ship back, it would need a lot of overhauling, some of it thanks to her.

The door released. Dev was glad for the makeshift ear protection, as scant as it was. Shutting out the thrum of the engines as best she could, she stepped inside and took in the machine room at a glance. She wasn't an engineer, per se, but she knew her way around mechanical things. And it was simpler to break them than to repair them.

There was very little space to move around in—just narrow access slots that ran through a floor-to-ceiling mountain of tech. The schematic of a basic propulsion system hadn't changed since the dawn of space travel. What had changed was the power source and the efficiency of the linkages to transmit that power into thrust. Dev wasn't going to directly mess with the aduronium containment system. The isotope itself was fairly stable, except when it was exposed to a quasi-quantum field and then it was in a constant state of near-explosive volatility. Which made it a great power source, but was also one of the reasons Dev didn't much care for space travel.

Wormhole jumps were the other.

So that left either the field generator, or the mechanical linkages to the propulsion system. Of the two, working on propulsion would be easier and maybe a little safer. But if she didn't get it just right, there was a risk of unbalancing the engines and causing a cascade failure. Feedback pressure would make the isotope go critical.

Goodbye, ship. Goodbye, Maldonado. And goodbye, Dev.

Trickier was to interrupt the field, but once it was disabled, the aduronium would revert to its inert state and the port engine would stall. Fail-safes would shut down the starboard engine and keep the aduronium in each shielded and contained.

Dev had studied basic containment systems and design with Sellen last term. If she got out of this alive, she'd have to thank her. Which might shock the old witch into heart failure. Serve her right. Dev grinned and kept moving.

The engine room was an overwhelming mass of interconnected machinery and complex circuits, laid out in concentric circles with a labyrinthine path through it. But, at its most basic, it was no different than the small-scale model they worked with in the lab. Except for the size of the linkages. And the amount of aduronium. It was one thing to work with a gram or less of the isotope. Each of the ship's engines contained several kilograms of the stuff.

But Dev wasn't going to be messing directly with the

radioactive material. Even in its inert state, unshielded, it could cause pretty significant radiation burns. Stripping away the size and complexity, Dev struggled to identify the elements of the engine room as parts of Sellen's simplified schematic. Ultimately, the outcome of any power source was thrust. Since Dev wasn't going to interfere with that end of the system, she could ignore all the linkages from the radioisotope power plant to the mechanics of propulsion.

Turning sideways, she squeezed past the outer rings of machinery. If the full-scale implementation followed Sellen's model, then the fuel containment system and the field generator should be at the heart of the installation.

Something shiny caught her gaze and she stopped to examine a thin wire that snaked its way through what looked like a main linkage. She was painfully aware time was passing and that it was all too possible that Maldonado knew she was here. Or at least that something or someone had broken into the engine compartment. But the silver gleam of the wire bothered her. It didn't belong.

Pulling out her salvaged circuit sniffer, Dev traced along the wire's path. It was definitely not part of the engine design. And it was definitely live. She bit her bottom lip. The old abandoned cities and towns she had spent her childhood poking around in weren't just her personal playgrounds. They were also used for weapons drills and making explosives. The worse the condition of the town, the less likely Commonwealth troops would bother patrolling, and the more attractive it was to radical elements in the settlements. Dev had tripped a bomb once, the summer she was fourteen.

If the explosives hadn't been wired wrong, she would have died. She still had nightmares about it. Since then, she never started poking around an abandoned place without doing a thorough sweep for traps. This was definitely a trap.

She steadied herself and followed the wire to its terminal end. And found a primed power pack from an energy weapon. All it would take was an electrical pulse to set off an explosion that would lead to a chain reaction. Her hands shook as she backed away from the improvised bomb and slammed into the machinery behind her. She turned. At her eye level, another silver wire gleamed. She didn't need to track it to know it would lead to another power pack. Someone rigged this ship into a miniature supernova in the making.

And that someone had to be Maldonado.

Dev jammed her hand in her mouth. Now what? She was no demolitions expert. If she did anything to the circuit, it could blow, taking her with it.

If it was Maldonado, then he had the trigger on him. And she had to believe it would work remotely. He didn't strike her in any way as suicidal. So he also had to have an escape plan. Son of a bitch never intended to let her go. Dev pressed her eyes closed and took a deep, shaky breath. But, she had already known that.

She opened her eyes again. This changed nothing. She still needed to cripple the ship and keep him guessing. And while he was down here assessing the engines, she could be topside looking for his shuttle.

Chapter 22

Ro was about to order Halcyone to show the location on screen, relative to their current position, but Barre must have beaten her to it. The display shifted and recentered. The zoom didn't change.

"He's still here," she whispered, as if he were close enough to hear them. "He's still here!"

"Come on, you son of a bitch. Answer me," Micah said.

"Channel is open," Barre said.

Micah paced the bridge. "Now what?"

"We wait," Ro said. Which wasn't the answer Micah wanted, but the only one she had. If they broke out of their hiding place and her father saw them, he'd run. Suspicious bastard that he was, he'd figure out that they'd tracked him somehow and ditch the ship. They'd never find him, then. "Can you and Halcyone get ready to intercept Dev's escape pod? I'm going to assume my dear father's greed will drive him to accept Micah's terms. I want the AI ready to grab her the minute that ship leaves."

Barre nodded. "We can take the basic code from your

bloodhound program and repurpose it, hooking into Halcyone's sensors."

Ro nodded. It's what she would have done. Micah was still pacing the bridge. "And will you keep still? You're making me nervous."

He glared at her and folded his arms, but stopped moving.

Halcyone broke into the silence. "Incoming transmission."

"Audio only," Ro said.

"Don't flatter yourself, Micah."

Ro recognized the patronizing tone of her father's voice. Rather than make her flinch like it used to, now it just made her want to hit something. Preferably him.

"I see you got my message," Micah said.

It was a little horrifying how quickly he seemed to morph into the late senator, complete with a smile that was at least part sneer and a voice to match.

"You aren't anywhere near as clever and as manipulative as your father, so don't bother trying."

Micah squared his shoulders, as if Maldonado could see him. "So we have a deal?"

"I never wanted the girl. She was simply a means to an end."

Did that mean Dev was unharmed? Would he hold to his side of Micah's bargain?

If Ro hadn't known Micah so well, she would have thought him casual to the point of disinterest. But the lines across his forehead and the rigidity of his spine betrayed him. He kept his voice under control. Ro didn't think she could have done the same in his place.

"And now that you have what you want, I need to see Dev. No vid. A live feed. Or I won't release the second part of the cipher."

Her father laughed and a chill crept down Ro's spine.

"You really believe you're in any position to dictate terms? I thought my daughter would have taught you better than that."

Her cheeks blazed.

"Speaking of ... I assume you're there, Rosalen. How's my ship?"

"Hello, Father. Shall we just get this over with?" She refused to let him goad her. Halcyone was hers. Even if that wasn't true before Barre became her crew mate, it was certainly true now. Unless the man possessed a musical genius he'd hidden all his life, there was no way he could even open a door on the ship.

"Micah, I really do believe it's in your best interest to release that code now."

Micah's face turned an alarming shade of purple. Ro placed her hand on his chest.

Into the silence, a high-pitched alarm began to wail.

"Barre?" Ro's voice squeaked into a higher register.

"That's not Halcyone."

Maldonado's loud cursing burst through the channel before it was abruptly cut off.

"Get him back!" Micah shouted. "Get him the fuck back!"

"I can't!" Barre said.

"Shit." Ro stared at the viewscreen. Her gasp pulled Micah and Barre's attention to her. "Something's wrong."

She swallowed hard and pointed. "Something's wrong with his ship."

It was listing to port.

Ro triggered her micro's interface with the AI and did a sensor sweep. "They've completely lost their port engine. It's cold." As she watched, the starboard engine's temperature also dropped rapidly. The ship slowly drifted out of its parking orbit.

"Holy shit." Micah stared at the view screen. "Now what?"

*

After disabling the containment field, Dev raced back to the main access hatch, scrambled up the crude ladder, and pulled it back into its locked position. She sealed the hatch and ran toward the main service corridor. Unwilling to risk a light, she used her mental map and a hand against the right-side bulkhead to guide her to the turn. Her galley prison was toward the right.

She turned the corner and pressed herself against the near wall, listening. The ship shuddered as the starboard engine shut down, leaving them adrift. If she ever got back to Uni, Sellen would now be her hero.

But, she had to get off this ship first.

Maldonado was yelling. Presumably at someone on the other end of an ansible connection. The metal walls added too much echoing reverb to his voice for her to pick out anything intelligible. But he was still on the bridge.

The safest course would be for her to retreat to the galley, at least until Maldonado headed off the bridge to investigate the problem with the engines. Then she could search the ship for his escape vehicle. Dev was no pilot, but she certainly could get aboard and seal the doors. If Maldonado was trapped on the ship, he wouldn't risk triggering the explosives. It would give her more time to figure out a better plan.

But what if she couldn't? Dev needed a backup. And for that, she needed to have access to comms. There was a chance Maldonado would cross her path in the few seconds she'd need to run up the corridor toward the bridge, but it was a risk she was willing to take. Besides, she had the knife and the soldering iron and he wouldn't be expecting her.

Dev sprinted up the corridor as fast as she dared in the smothering darkness. She nearly overshot the turn. Maldonado was still shouting and swearing on the bridge. Then he fell silent. Footfalls echoed from somewhere above her. Dev held her breath and pressed her spine back against the metal bulkhead, hoping he'd stomp right past her to the engine room.

A clang rang through the corridor and light flared close enough to blind her. Dev blinked rapidly and retreated further down the side passage, her heart hammering against her ribcage. She exhaled silently as his footfalls receded into the distance. If Maldonado was an engineer, he might be able to figure out what she'd done and reverse it. Which didn't give her as much time as she'd hoped for.

She clambered up into the partially dismantled comms station. Private ships were built with idiot-switches for emergencies. If she was lucky, the distress system hadn't been disabled. If she wasn't lucky? She'd think of something else.

It was too much to ask for, but secondary nav control was a mess of wires. No luck there, even if she had known how to fly a ship. But the comms console was still mostly intact. She scanned the mass of controls until she found the distress beacon. There was a basic "everything's gone to shit" setting and a "record a personalized message" setting. Some vague hope that Micah would be searching for the ship convinced her to record a mayday. She set it to a continuous loop. It would definitely let Maldonado know she was roaming the ship, but he'd probably figured that out by now, anyway. Or he would, soon enough.

There was nothing more she could do here. Time to find her ride.

With Maldonado busy in the subsystems, Dev could move around the ship freely. She'd built a pretty decent mental map from the access corridors, and at least here she could see where she was going.

It wasn't rational, but Dev chose to explore the starboard side of the ship first. Maldonado was two levels below her, but she still didn't want to be anywhere near him when he saw the condition of the field generator.

Sellen should give her an A this term for that, alone.

There were two doors opposite the room with the comms station. Each opened to the manual release. Each was a small sleeping cell, empty of everything except a bed frame. She didn't bother to enter. As she turned away from the second room, the ship juddered and a series of loud clangs rang through the corridor from farther aft.

Not her doing.

Dev took a deep breath to steady herself. Now what?

*

The comms crackled back to life. Halcyone's bridge fell as silent as deep space as they held their collective breath, waiting.

"Mayday. Mayday. Mayday. Any ships in the area. I'm on an unidentified vessel and we're adrift. Interstitial engines off line."

"Open a channel! Dev! Dev! It's Micah. We're coming to get you. Are you all right?"

She didn't answer. There was a brief pause and the message repeated twice more and Ro realized it was a recording.

A smile spread across Micah's face. "Dev."

The tension in Ro's shoulders eased. Somehow, Micah's resourceful friend had gotten the better of her father. Wasn't that something. "Let's go get her."

Halcyone broke into their relieved laughter. "Proximity alert. Ship bearing three four one mark seven. Time to engagement T minus four minutes."

"Oh, fuck," Ro whispered. A blinking light representing another ship appeared on the display. It swiftly moved across the viewscreen toward them and Maldonado's crippled ship. "Can they see us?"

"I don't think so."

Then they were going after her father. There hadn't been

enough time for anyone to have responded to Dev's SOS.

"Friends or foes?" Micah asked.

"I don't ... Foes," she said, afraid to meet Micah's eyes.

Barre was silent, his eyes unfocused. Static from comms crackled through the bridge. He nodded and turned back to her and Micah. "Dev left the channel open. I had Halcyone hack into the broadcast."

Ro squeezed his forearm. "Good work."

"Can we reach her?" Micah asked.

Dev was probably not anywhere near comms anymore. If it had been Ro aboard, she would have found a place to hide from her father after that stunt.

"No, but we can listen to their traffic. If Maldonado sneezes through comms, we'll know it."

"How does that help Dev?" Micah shouted.

"We have no weapons and essentially no shields," Ro said. "If we go after her now, without any backup and without intel, we're spaced. And that doesn't help her at all."

The comms channel crackled to life again, startling all of them.

"Maldonado, looks like you're in a bit of trouble."

"Keep your p-suit on, Frint. I have your money."

In the pause that followed, the three of them shared a glance. Actually, he didn't. Not that it mattered.

"I'm afraid it's no longer enough to pay your credit debt. There has been a certain amount of negative publicity and cosmos-wide chatter about our failed arrangement. That's bad for business. You understand."

It sounded like her father was banging on metal pipes in the background. What was he doing? And what had Dev done to take down the engines? Micah was busy pacing again and chewing the cuticles of his thumb. If half of what he had said about Dev was accurate, Ro had no doubt she had sabotaged the interstitials.

"I'm sure we can work something out, Frint. Tell your boss ..."

"You can tell him yourself after we tractor your ship. Wouldn't want anything to happen to it drifting in an asteroid belt."

"Shit," Micah said. "We have to do something. This boat has life pods, right?"

"You can't go after her in a life pod. They're the equivalent of a floating jump snug," Ro said.

"Have Halcyone launch me toward Maldonado's ship."

"What, are you crazy?"

"No. The AI can plot my trajectory, right?"

"This isn't billiards in space, Micah," Ro said. "Without propulsion or the ability to steer, the chances of you reaching the ship and successfully coupling with its airlock are slim to vacuum."

"Damn it, Ro, I have to do something."

Dev was only valuable to Ro's father as long as she served as a bargaining chip. The jilted weapons buyers would have no use for her. They had to stop them. But the same problems remained. Halcyone had no offensive capabilities and the only defense the ship could mount was hiding or running.

"Time to engagement, three minutes."

Her brain was in vapor lock. Every solution came down to equipment or resources they didn't have. Ro couldn't bear to look at Micah.

"Ro? How many working pods do we have left?" Barre asked.

"You can't possibly be agreeing with him."

He was staring at the view screen, his head tilted to one side. "I have an idea, but it means sacrificing a pod."

They had never replaced the one her father had escaped in. "Five. But I don't know what condition they're in." It was something she had meant to check, but had never gotten to.

"It doesn't matter. No one's going to be in it."

"If you have a plan, now would be a good time," Micah said, nearly spitting out the words. He stood near the ruins of the bridge doors, looking like he'd rather be sprinting toward the escape pods.

Barre shrugged. "You said it yourself. Billiards. The pod is the cue ball. We just need it to nudge the right asteroid. Frint's ship? That's the pocket."

Ro stared, her mouth falling open. "Are you utterly insane? Do you know what kind of calculations we'd need to make it work?" Relative velocities were complicated enough without that kind of vector analysis.

"Yeah. About as many as Halcyone solves to make a jump."

"Do it," Micah said.

Barre raised an eyebrow at Ro.

Frowning, she studied the viewscreen. The pod had only so much initial thrust, though a crash might ignite its small store of fuel. Halcyone would have to find an asteroid small enough and close enough to their target that the pod could alter its trajectory. It was crazy, but it could work. The blinking light that represented Frint's ship was edging closer to Maldonado's drifting craft. They didn't have a lot of time.

"Go," she said and balled her hands into fists. This was Barre's job. His partnership with the AI was something she couldn't match, not for this. She would want to tell Halcyone what to do. Barre would communicate the problem. Halcyone would solve it, likely before Ro could have even written the skeleton of a program.

"Time to engagement, two minutes."

Ro held her breath as Barre looked past her, a blank expression on his face. He looked as if he was lost in thought.

Micah came up beside her and gripped the edge of the console. "What if this doesn't work?"

She eased the tension in her fingers and slipped her hand in his.

Halcyone's engine's growled to life. The ship turned in place 180 degrees. Barre stood rigidly, staring at the screen.

The engines stilled. A tiny dot appeared on the viewer, moving away from Halcyone.

"Life pod launched," the AI announced.

Barre swept his dreads away from his face. "If Halcyone did the calculations right, we should see the pod impact a meteor in three, two, one."

The pod's indicator light flared and extinguished. A small green circle glowed in its place. And it was moving.

"Is it going to be enough to stop that ship?" Micah squeezed Ro's hand hard enough to grind the bones of her fingers.

Ro winced. "I don't know. Too many variables. We don't know how big Frint's ship is or how it's shielded. If Halcyone was able to pick a big enough and dense enough rock with a decent amount of velocity? If the pod's momentum was enough to change its trajectory? Then yeah, maybe."

"She knows what she's doing," Barre said.

But Ro noticed the stiffness across his shoulders and the tension in his arms.

"Impact in ten seconds," Halcyone said.

As Halcyone counted down the seconds, Ro silently echoed the AI's voice.

Ten.

Nine.

Eight.

Seven.

Six.

Five.

Four.

Three.

Two.

Impact.

The viewscreen showed the blinking dot of Frint's ship. Micah yanked his hand from hers and swore.

Barre turned to them, his eyes downcast. "I'm sorry. I'm so sorry. I really thought it was going to work."

It should have worked. Barre was right. Halcyone could have done the calculations with half the AI's brain contemplating recursive algorithms. What had gone wrong? And what were they going to do now?

Could they risk trying it again?

"Halcyone, recenter on approaching ship and magnify," Ro said.

"Unable to complete request."

"Ship's a piece of crap!" Micah shouted. He stumbled to what remained of the doors and slammed his fist against a scorch mark.

Barre whistled a brief fanfare. "Halcyone, update time to engagement, target ship."

There was the briefest of pauses. "Unable to complete request."

Cold washed through Ro's body. She held her breath as Barre stepped mere centimeters from the viewscreen.

"Halcyone, zoom out display a factor of five, then return to current magnification."

Ro held her breath, half-expecting the AI to refuse to do this, too. The display pulled back to show a view of the entire solar system. Only the star was easily identifiable at this scale. Then Halcyone redrew the screen as it had been.

Except it wasn't.

"Ha!" Barre shouted.

Micah slowly edged back into the room.

"Look!" Barre pointed to what looked like an empty region of space.

"Halcyone, show sector grid." Ro's heart beat faster. She didn't want to be wrong. A graph overlaid the viewscreen. "Halcyone, recenter on sector twenty-three by negative seventeen."

The display shifted.

Micah returned to his place by her side, but didn't say a word.

"Halcyone, magnify by a factor of two." That should be enough to see the ship, rather than a marker on the screen.

"Where is it?" Micah asked.

Ro nearly collapsed against the console. Halcyone showed them a debris field and the drifting wreck of what had once been a ship, hulled by the collision. Lifepods tumbled away from the Lagrange point in all directions.

"Well, I guess it worked, then," Barre said, turning to them and grinning wildly.

Chapter 23

JEM WANDERED THE corridors of the residence ring until he was certain his parents had left for medical before returning to his quarters. He knew he was avoiding them. He knew it irked his mother, but she had access to his vitals via telemetry and that was going to have to be enough.

He'd agreed to be monitored. Just not harassed and constantly interrogated.

As soon as he got back into his room, Jem found the single sedative dose his mother had left for him. They barely even made him groggy anymore and he wasn't sure if that was a good thing or not, but he would take all the help he could get given the work that lay ahead.

"Okay, nanites, do your stuff," he said as he sat on his bed, leaning against the headboard.

In a few minutes it would be the start of second shift. Nomi was already in comms, looking for her opportunity to load the data miner. Jem bit his lip, wondering if he had made a big mistake, but it was too late for second thoughts. An alert tone sounded in his mind. The worm was activated.

For a terrible moment, Jem thought his double vision had returned before he realized he was seeing the information twice—once on his micro's screen, and again in a virtual display through his visual cortex.

He closed his eyes, leaned his head back, and let the data flow over him. The neural helped him receive and make sense of huge chunks of information as if he were reading rapidly, or scanning his environment. Except it didn't involve his eyes at all. It just felt like it did. As if his mind had created a model based on how Jem had taken in information his whole life until now.

"Seismic," he whispered, wishing Barre was here to talk about it with. He wondered if it worked the same way for him. Or did he hear everything?

Jem refocused on the information flooding into him from the worm. It was perfectly neutral. Unlike all of his sensory input since he woke up with the implant, receiving through his neural didn't bring any weird colors, tastes, or sounds. There was no pressure against his skin. Only the data. Clean and direct. He exhaled deeply, letting his shoulders relax. For the first time since his injury, Jem felt like himself again. He didn't know how long it would last, but he was going to take advantage of it as long as it did.

The little program was designed to burrow into the personnel files, copy anything that referenced Lowell, and transmit it to Jem. So far so good. But the information it was sharing had little value: duty rosters, personal account charges, vacation requests. Jem shoved it all into a data folder on his micro and marveled at how simple it was. The nanoemitters picked up his intention and routed it to the base station, which gave his micro the instructions.

He couldn't wait to send word to Dr. Land.

The data stream from the worm grayed out. Jem scowled. Had he done something wrong? There was no pain or nausea. No dizziness. None of the terrible symptoms he'd been struggling with for months.

Instead, a blank window opened up in his mind. A message template. With Dr. Land's dummy contact information already filled in.

Jem opened his eyes and blinked at the unexpected brightness. His bedroom swam in his wavy vision. So the nystagmus was still there. He winced before closing his eyes again. The unwritten message to Dr. Land still waited for him.

"Not now," he muttered. "Save it for later."

The message template vanished. Jem wondered if there was a way to turn the virtual volume down on how the nanoemitters processed his thoughts. Or maybe that was part of what the team on Ithaka was supposed to have taught him. Well, that ship had jumped and here he was. And there was work to do.

He focused on Lowell and the worm's data-dump became prominent again. The program must have found its way through the comms archives because it was showing him the headers of Lowell's ansible messages: both sent and received.

Jem had no interest in digging through them all. He doubted Lowell would be stupid enough to send or accept anything sensitive to his station account. But he directed the stream of messages into another folder. Maybe later he would run a pattern search on them.

The next chunk of data contained financial records. Jem paid closer attention. The stream slowed down. Station personnel were paid every other cycle. The lab techs were always complaining, especially when they were due emergency bonus pay. Lowell made a decent amount, but then again, he was the senior officer in comms and he'd been doing the job for decades. He also must have saved every credit he'd been paid. His account didn't have the zeros that Micah's dad's did, but it wasn't thin by anyone's definition.

That didn't make sense. Jem's attention traced back to the first folder. Lowell had plenty of charges. He certainly didn't clamp down on spending, even with as little as there was to buy on station. His account showed a ton of import fees on expensive goods from the Hub.

He switched back to the finances. For a long moment, he couldn't focus on the virtual display in his mind without seeing double.

"Damn it," he said, "I need more time!"

He opened his eyes, hoping to reset his mind. This was going to take forever if he didn't develop some kind of stamina. Closing his eyes again, he returned to the financials. He was going to work until he couldn't force his brain to listen to him. A little double vision wasn't going to stop him.

If the nanoemitters provided the data to him using a familiar metaphor, he was prepared to work with that. Jem enlarged the text. Instantly, the financial records came into sharper focus. It wasn't double vision. It was duplicate payments.

Their slippery comms supervisor was getting paid twice.

Jem picked out two credit memos for the same pay period. They looked identical, but he knew that couldn't be true. The Commonwealth didn't make mistakes like that. At least not for long and it looked as if Lowell had been collecting extra money ever since he took the job on Daedalus Station. He carefully traced back the routing for the first deposit. It was the same data path as all Commonwealth payments, even the money Jem had earned doing data collection during his stint as a research intern one term.

The second deposit had to be the mystery one, then.

He studied the memo. It looked just like a normal Commonwealth issue. Except it shouldn't be. But as far as Jem knew, forging Commonwealth credit was as hard as forging diplomatic seals like the ones on the smuggled weapons that had been hidden on Halcyone.

A wave of cold moved through Jem. Sweat beaded across his forehead. It wasn't nausea. It was fear.

Snippets of conversations with Ro, Barre, and Nomi on Halcyone flooded his mind. As did Ada May's warnings. It wasn't Ro's dad or Micah's who had forged those seals. It had to have been someone connected with the Commonwealth. As Ada had said, their tightly controlled military government had everything to gain and little to lose by starting what in all likelihood would have been a tiny war in a far-off corner of the universe. One they would have used as justification and grand security theatre.

One that Ro and the rest of them had interfered with.

Holy mother of the cosmos, what had they drifted into? Jem's mouth dried. Screens of incriminating data glowed in a series of virtual windows all around him, inviting him to dig deeper. Nothing in Lowell's server partition seemed any different than it had only moments before, but Jem started to tremble.

He knew his program was good, but if Lowell was under the control of covert forces in the Commonwealth, their protections would be better. If this was a trap, he had probably already triggered it.

His stomach churned as he carefully backed out of Lowell's credit memos.

Nomi. He had to reach Nomi. Only she could disable the program. If it wasn't already too late.

As soon as he turned away from his internal landscape and back to the confines of his room, his head began to pound. He dry-swallowed something that his mother permitted him for the pain. It wouldn't do a lot, but he hoped it would be enough.

He triggered his micro and accessed Ro's secure messaging program. He marked it urgent, desperately hoping he was wrong.

/Shut it down. There's a recall command in your micro. Do it now./

/too late/

/Nomi? Nomi?/

There was no answer. Jem stared at his micro. The seconds crawled by as the blank screen wavered in his damaged vision.

"Nomi?" he whispered into the room's silence. Swallowing hard, Jem triggered Daedalus. "Locate Nakamura, Konomi."

It seemed as if the station's AI was dragging out its usual response time. When it finally did reply, it wasn't one Jem had ever heard before.

"Unavailable. Please contact command for further information about ..." There was another pause before Nomi's own recorded voice finished.

"Nakamura, Konomi."

Jem squeezed his eyes shut and softly swore.

*

Dev froze at the sounds reverberating through the ship. It sounded like company was coming.

Friends or foes?

It was definitely too soon for her emergency call to have been answered. She chewed her chapped lip. They were definitely being boarded, which could make things better for her, or much, much worse. What would Maldonado do if he felt he was being cornered? He had the explosives. And what if he could reach his ride off-ship from the access corridors?

Shit.

She gripped a tool in each hand to steady them. A soldering iron and a screwdriver. Against homemade bombs and an unknown boarding party.

Their visitors were docking on the port side. So that was where the airlock was. Which meant Maldonado's escape vessel had to be somewhere else. She drew her breath in sharply.

Unless this was his ride.

Dev dropped the tools back into her pocket. They weren't the answer. Information was. There was nowhere she could hide topside and she wasn't going to get any answers back in her makeshift prison.

Maldonado was below her somewhere, but Dev could at least find an effective hiding place in the darkness of the access corridors. And she would be able to hear what was happening above her. As long as she didn't get caught. As long as she was careful.

She turned back to the sleeping cell and opened the floor hatch. Pausing on the ladder, she re-engaged the latch on the cover plate. It clicked softly. She waited, gripping the narrow rungs until her eyes adjusted to the darkness again. Then she slid lightly to the floor and tucked the ladder back.

Calling up her mental map, Dev paused to orient herself. Behind her was the galley and what she suspected was the airlock. If she was correct, it would be the first left-hand turn she had encountered after she broke out initially. The visiting ship was taking its time docking. Random clangs and bangs reverberated through the access tunnels. Though the way sound carried in here, it could also be coming from the engine rooms.

She crept down the corridor, hugging the port-side bulkhead. The first turn she came to led to the port engine. Where Maldonado was. Holding her breath and listening intently, she tiptoed on. She nearly fell into the second juncture. Voices filtered down from above. Dev froze. Two voices. A man and a woman. Arguing.

It was hard to make out the words given the harsh echoes off what was essentially a large metal duct. She crept closer until she was directly beneath the grate.

"I can handle this myself," the woman said.

Her voice was cold and precise. A laugh followed. The man said something she couldn't make out.

"Do you really have that much of a death wish, Taro?"

Dev needed to get closer. The only way was to climb up toward the grate. But there was a good chance they would hear her. She slipped the polymer knife from her pocket and gripped it in her teeth. Then she triggered the ladder and eased it to the ground. Her heart racing, she waited, listening. The two were still arguing. And the woman hadn't stopped her pacing overhead.

"No one's called me that in a long, long time," the man said.

The woman's sharp footfalls fell silent. Her voice dropped to a low growl. "Don't think for a second that I don't remember who you are, Ferryman. You may have changed your name, but you don't get to leave the past behind."

"Is that what you think I've been doing?" The man's voice got louder. His shadow passed overhead.

Dev flattened herself against the ladder.

"I don't give a temporal fuck what you've been doing. May's not here to protect you anymore. You should have stayed on Ithaka."

Ithaka? The planet that either did or didn't exist, depending on which version of the spacer's tales you believed. Who the hell were these people?

"I never meant to hurt you, Emma."

"But you did. And I get to remember every day because of this."

The woman shifted and Dev caught a glint of light on metal from her arm. It was an old-style training prosthesis. Plenty of folks in the settlements had versions of it. Some from the war, others because of accidents. The limbs were cheap and rugged.

"You have to admit, it is funny how the universe works."

The man's voice was gruff and full of suppressed laughter. It didn't make sense. The woman had just threatened him and he wasn't afraid.

"You were the one to disobey orders and you got to go home and play the injured war hero. Me? I tried to follow mine and I got erased from history."

Wait. What? The woman was Commonwealth? Then she was definitely not Maldonado's ride. But who was her companion? And why were they working together?

"I'm going after Maldonado. See if you can locate the girl. And Taro? Watch your back."

So not her captor's associates. But what was a Commonwealth soldier doing with someone so far off the glide paths he may as well be a ghost?

"Fine," he said. "But just to set the record straight, you could have asked the doc for a new arm with less shine and less pointy ends any time."

Her voice dropped even lower. "I know."

She hit the airlock release and the inner doors to the ship opened.

"Rendezvous in fifteen, regardless of what you find," the man said.

"Just do your job. Find the girl."

Dev clamped her jaws down on the knife, trying to

suppress her nervous laughter. If they only knew just how close "the girl" was to them. Their footsteps faded. There was nothing to block the light leak from the grate.

Whoever these two were, they had a ship. Dev needed to get on that ship.

*

Nomi walked silently beside Lewin Holder and Peri Chakrabarti. The two armed officers from Mendez's personal security detail shadowed her as she moved on autopilot through the residence ring toward command. At least they had waited until she was just outside her quarters before surrounding her and asking her to follow them.

So polite. Neither had touched a weapon. Neither had used restraints. They had barely exchanged a handful of words. All Nomi knew was Mendez wanted to see her. To the casual observer, it was just several staff members heading in the same direction. Part of Nomi appreciated their discretion; part wondered if anyone would realize she'd been effectively disappeared.

Well, Jem would know.

After she had texted him, Holder had taken her micro out of her hands. The messages vanished before the security officer could read them. At least that worked. But something must have gone wrong with Jem's program. She didn't blame him.

Nomi looked over her shoulder before they entered the South Nexus. Would she see the station again? She closed her eyes briefly as they stepped through the airlock. Would she ever see Ro again?

Holder and Chakrabarti herded her into command. Work stopped as she entered, personnel looking up from their stations and quickly looking away again. Even her two minders wouldn't meet her gaze. Nomi's heart beat a faster rhythm.

They ushered her through another door and into Mendez's anteroom. Gutierrez's office. Nomi had been here several times before. The first time was the day she'd arrived at the station. It seemed like so long ago. Before Ro. Before Halcyone.

Before Ithaka.

The office hadn't changed. Gutierrez's workstation was as stark as the officer. No personal details gave away any hint about the woman in the uniform. But right about now, Nomi would have appreciated the LC's cold gaze, even as she continually assessed those around her and found them wanting. But Gutierrez was off-station, gone with Charon to help Ro. No matter what else happened, Nomi was grateful for that.

Her fingers twitched, reaching for a micro that wasn't there. If Ro messaged her back, who would receive her texts?

"Please sit," Holder said. "The commander will be with you shortly."

Yes. So polite. So distant. Nomi sat, folding her hands in her lap. The two officers turned crisply and left Gutierrez's office. She had no doubt that they were guarding the door. As if she would make a break for it. Her and what battalion?

Closing her eyes, Nomi leaned her head against the wall

behind her. She wondered if Jem had gotten the information he needed. If not, then she'd just spaced herself for nothing. Gotten detained for nothing. No matter what, she would try to shield Jem from getting his own polite visit from security.

The minutes passed by. Making her wait was all part of the interrogation. Nomi knew that, but it didn't make it any easier to sit there, her anxiety climbing to the stratosphere. She struggled to find stillness in the meditation techniques her grandfather had taught her when she was a child. The last time she had practiced the measured breathing had been during her final boards at Uni. It had helped then, but all she could think of now was spending the next few decades in a military prison. She shivered and tucked her space-cold hands under her armpits.

The Commonwealth might not be at war, but treason was still a serious charge.

The slight whistle as the commander's door opened was as loud as a scream to Nomi's tortured nerves. She jumped up and stood at full attention.

"Nakamura. Inside." Mendez stared at Nomi, her expression severe. Deep lines stretched across her forehead.

"Yes, sir," Nomi said. Her throat was so tight, she could barely get the words out. She walked forward slowly, feeling as if local gravity had suddenly tripled.

Mendez's office was empty except for the two of them. The only illumination in the room was a tiny sculpture of a ship on the commander's desk. Nomi paused at the threshold, wondering why there were no guards in the room.

"Sit," the commander said.

Nomi took the hard chair opposite Mendez's desk. The

commander stood until the door slid shut with a very final sounding click before taking her seat.

"This room is sealed."

"Sir?"

"This room is sealed," the commander repeated. "There will be no record of this conversation."

Conversation. Not interrogation. Nomi gripped the edges of her seat.

Mendez leaned forward into the pool of light provided by the glowing ship's model. It threw stark shadows across her face. "I need you to tell me exactly what you did and what you were looking for."

Her legs shook and Nomi pressed her feet against the floor to keep them still. "I'm confused. Sir." Was this an interrogation? Was she being charged with treason? What could she say that wouldn't knock her farther out of orbit than she already was?

Mendez spoke very slowly. "The program you loaded into comms. What were you trying to accomplish?"

"Am I under arrest?"

"Answer the question, damn it!" Mendez slammed her fist against the desk so hard the little light jumped and fell over. The commander righted it carefully.

This wasn't a Mendez Nomi had ever encountered before.

The commander carefully placed both hands, palms down, on the desktop and stared at her. "I've gone to a considerable amount of trouble and risk to meet with you like this. Don't play the idiot. I've been watching you. You're better than that."

Ro would know what to say. Ro would puzzle out what

Mendez's personality shift meant. But Ro wasn't here. It was up to Nomi, now. And silence wasn't an option.

"Lowell. I was trying to find out what Lowell was playing at." She met Mendez's gaze with her own, just as steady, just as constant.

Mendez nodded. "Do you have any idea what you've done?"

"Sir?"

"I can't shield you from what comes next," she said. There was sympathy in her eyes. "But I'll do what I can in return for access to your data."

Nomi drew a sharp breath. The polite escorts, the private meeting, the sealed room, it was all starting to make some kind of sense. A pattern. The commander's ambition was to land somewhere beyond Daedalus. She thought Nomi's information would grant her some leverage or advantage. If Mendez could make use of it, then this conversation would have effectively never taken place in the eyes of the Commonwealth. But could she trust the commander?

"What will happen to me?"

"You'll be put in detention. There'll be a tribunal. You're lucky. Whoever programmed your hack created it to leave very little evidence behind. In fact, if it hadn't poked itself into certain financial records, it would never have been caught. I know you didn't create it."

"Commander, I ..." Nomi wasn't sure what she was going to say, but she wouldn't implicate Jem. That just wasn't happening.

The commander put her hands out. "I actually don't care who programmed it. I simply need what you found. At least a copy. While it would be safer for all concerned if you gave me everything, I know that's not going to happen. Just take my warning: leave it alone. Walk away."

Nomi exhaled heavily. So the program had worked. Jem had uncovered some sensitive data. The irony was, she would trade what she had for her freedom. But all she had was just a brief warning from Jem and a sense that they had crashed into something very, very big.

"I'm going to need my micro."

Mendez nodded and tapped the surface of her small device. The door buzzed. She walked across the room and stood at the threshold of her office, her hand outstretched. When she withdrew it, Nomi's micro was resting in the commander's palm.

Nomi's hands shook as she reached out for her micro. Her link to Jem. And Ro.

"Don't do anything rash, Ensign."

She didn't think she had done anything rash in her whole life before she met Ro. The slight weight of the micro anchored her. Jem. She had to reach Jem.

She was afraid to use Ro's messaging program, but the risk of going through station channels was too great. And this was the only way Jem would believe it was her. Still, she was afraid to say too much. Afraid to implicate Jem if their texts could somehow be hacked.

/Jem. I'm in a/ She paused and glanced up at Mendez. /meeting./ It was a meeting. Of sorts. /I need that information we talked about./

/Nomi??????/

What could she say that would keep him from asking

dangerous questions?

/*Everything's going to be five by five, but I need you to do what Ro would do and trust me. Upload that data to my server space and send me the link.*/

/*Are you sure?*/

Jem must have suspected she wasn't alone. Did he think she was being threatened? Well, in a way, she was, only not how Jem probably feared.

/*On my grandfather's honor.*/

There was a long pause and Nomi worried that Jem had cut off contact and wouldn't clone the data over. She bit her lower lip and composed one more response.

/*Tell Ro I'll be okay.*/ Tears made her vision blurry. /*Tell Ro I love her.*/

She was afraid to meet Mendez's gaze. Her hands gripped the little computer, already feeling its absence. They'd never let her have it in detention.

A tiny vibration alerted her to a new message. She started and then stared at the screen. Jem had come through with a cloning of the data his worm had collected. His note contained the link and a warning that it was temporary. Nomi exhaled heavily. If this was the last chance she had to access the device, she needed to make sure Ro's messaging program wouldn't betray them. She quickly took a screenshot of the link and disabled the program before passing the device to Mendez.

"The link is set to expire, so best to get your information quickly."

Mendez nodded. "Good."

What side was Mendez on? Nomi couldn't keep from

staring at her micro, sitting on the woman's desk. Her only link to Ro was now gone. She had no idea where in the known universe she'd be when Halcyone returned.

Ro would go nuclear. Nomi closed her eyes and composed herself. She only hoped Ro wouldn't blame Jem or get herself arrested asking dangerous questions.

Whatever happened next, Nomi had done what she knew was right.

Chapter 24

DEV HUGGED THE ladder long after the two interlopers had exited the airlock and moved farther into Maldonado's ship. Her jaw ached from holding the knife in her teeth. Easing her right hand off the metal rung, she grabbed the makeshift blade and swallowed the saliva that had pooled in her mouth.

She climbed to the top of the ladder and opened the access hatch. When she emerged into the airlock, she crouched down and peered out of the port, but both the man and the woman were gone. Were they the only crew on their ship? Dev had no way of knowing just how large their vessel was. It could be the size of a dreadnought; she might be about to try to break into a ship full of armed crew. Which would be monumentally stupid.

But what choice did she have? This place was a reaction about to go critical and she didn't see any helpful rescuers around. To stay here was suicide. Dev checked her pockets, felt for the comforting presence of her tools, stood up, and faced the other side of the airlock. At her touch, the door cycled open.

Dev froze, listening.

The ship rang with silence and the harsh echo of her breathing. She stepped through. The airlock closed behind her. The ship's corridor was narrow and cramped. Bulkhead panels were missing all up and down its length, showing ragged wiring and conduit. No dreadnought, then. Barely larger than a commercial flitter. It was a wonder the thing could fly.

Some escape.

Well, it was better than being blown up.

She pulled out a screwdriver. It felt good to have something to balance out the knife in her right hand. Not that any of her tools would do much against the force of arms.

Exploring here wasn't all that different than prizing the secrets from some abandoned city. Creeping through the ship, Dev poked her head through each of the doorways along the corridor. One small cabin, a cargo hold that wasn't much larger, several jump niches for the unlucky crew, and a stripped-down bridge. Compared to this wreck, Maldonado's ship was a rich citizen's pleasure trawler.

She stood on the threshold of the bridge. There was barely room for a pilot and a copilot. The small viewscreen showed an unfamiliar part of space thick with asteroids and junk. Dev flinched when a large rock swept past. A loud clank from the direction of the airlock echoed through the ship. Shit. It hadn't been fifteen minutes. And there were no hiding places. At least not any she could find before she had unwelcome company. Dev moved to the side of the viewer, squeezing herself beside the copilot's seat. Sometimes the best you could do was choose your ground. She swapped out the screwdriver for the soldering iron and held her breath.

The man stepped through the door, muttering to himself. Dev squared her shoulders and triggered the soldering iron. "I need safe passage."

He looked up. His eyes widened briefly before he smiled. Half his face transformed into wry amusement. The other half was a stiff mask of scar tissue that twisted his mouth and pulled at his right eye.

"You must be Dev," he said, bowing. "I'm Charon. The Ferryman."

"She called you Taro. So which is your name?" Dev gripped her improvised weapons more tightly. "And how do you know who I am?"

"Ahh. You heard that." He smiled again with the intact side of his face. "Both, I suppose. And some friends of yours are worried about you."

Micah. The tension in her shoulders eased. "Then I guess I don't need these." She switched off the soldering iron.

"Well, not unless you plan to work on the overhaul while you're here."

There wouldn't be a lot of time to do anything here. She had no idea how long it would take Maldonado to either undo her damage or decide to cut his losses and blow the place up. "We have to go."

"Yes, that's the general plan," he said, laughing.

Dev shuddered and looked away from the ruin of his face.

"Always such a hit with the ladies."

She shook her head and turned back to the man. "We have to leave. Now."

He dropped down into the command chair, and spun around toward her. "And why is that? I mean aside from the fact that Maldonado's ship is adrift and by the way, good work with that." He nodded to her tools. "That was your work, wasn't it?"

"He's mined the damned engines. And he probably knows you're here. Do you want to wait around and find out if he's bluffing or not? I don't."

Taro or Charon or whatever he called himself swore and whirled around to the console. "Emma! Emma! Abort the mission. Return to the ship."

Dev waited as he listened for a handful of heartbeats. The ship's comms remained silent. He repeated his hail twice more before swearing again and slamming the command console with his scarred fist.

"You." He turned around once more. "Can you fly?"

"No."

"Well then." He returned to the controls. His hands moved over them faster than she could track. When he was finished, he stood up and strode toward the bridge door. He turned back. All traces of humor were gone from his expression. His scars stood out white against the red of his face. "Don't touch anything."

"What are you doing?"

"Going after Emma."

"Wait!"

He stomped over to her and gripped her arms with thickly calloused hands. "I don't owe you anything." A flush spread across his cheeks, making the white ropey lines of scar tissue glow in contrast. He pushed her away and she tumbled into the copilot's console. "The ship is set to engage autopilot in sixty seconds. It'll take you far enough out to avoid the blast radius if the mines go off. You can send out an automated distress call then."

"Why?"

"Because I keep my promises."

"You're going to get yourself killed!"

"Better strap in."

Then he charged down the corridor toward the airlock and was gone.

Dev fumbled for the harness on the copilot's chair, desperately trying to keep a countdown in her head. If Maldonado triggered the mines now, they would all die. Would he really risk that?

A flashing light on the console caught her attention. Was it a malfunction? She hadn't piloted anything larger than a personal skimmer back on Earth. These controls had a level of complexity Dev couldn't begin to decipher.

Several loud clangs startled her. Then Dev was gently but firmly pressed back into the padded chair as the ship separated from Maldonado's. A pitted rock ahead grew larger in the viewscreen. Dev gripped the armrests. Were they on a collision course? How would she know? What could she do about it?

She stared at it as it kept getting bigger. Soon it was the size of an orbital platform and still it continued to fill more and more of the screen. The ship vibrated as it flew, but it was barely pulling more than a single g. Dev was desperate to know what was happening back on Maldonado's ship, but she didn't know how to control the sensors of the viewer.

Details on the large asteroid got clearer and clearer.

It was a mining operation. Probably abandoned, given the jumble of equipment strewn about. She braced herself for a hard landing. Then the ship's engines whined in a higher pitch and the acceleration increased slightly. They veered off. The tapped-out rock disappeared to the right. Dev closed her eyes and let out the breath she had been holding.

The seconds ticked by, and then minutes. The ship was still moving slowly but steadily across the artificial asteroid field. Still no evidence of an explosion. Maybe Taro and Emma together could capture Maldonado and dismantle the bombs. She hoped they had a plan to get their ship back. One that didn't count on her piloting it.

The engine sound changed again, its pitch dropping into a soft growl—and then silence. The light on the console in front of her winked off. Dev sat gripping the webbing of the restraints for several minutes. Now what? There was a steady vibration beneath her feet and air to breathe, so gravity and life support were working. She leaned forward to examine the controls, looking for the auto-distress. "Micah, I hope you're somewhere out there," she muttered.

*

Micah's victory shout thundered through the bridge. He met Barre's smile with his own. "Well, what are we waiting for? Let's get Dev."

Ro looked at the viewscreen and frowned.

"What?" Micah asked.

"This would be simpler if we had a flitter," Barre said.

"We're going to have to match his ship's attitude and orientation in order to dock. And hope my father doesn't regain control in the process."

"Can you do it?"

"Of course I can do it," she said. Then she nodded at Barre. "Or rather, we can."

The two of them huddled together and Micah drummed his fingers on the nearest console. Barre pressed down on his shoulder.

"Hey, leave the percussion to me."

"Both of you should sit," Ro said as she settled herself in the main nav chair. "We'll just be using thrusters, but it could still get a little rocky."

"Like that's never happened before."

"Hey, be nice to Halcyone," Ro said.

Her smile was forced and tight, and her brow was furrowed.

"It's going to be okay. Once we get Dev, there will be four of us and only one of him," Micah said.

Ro didn't look reassured. Micah couldn't really blame her, given what happened the last time they were all on the same ship.

"You ready, Barre?"

"Aye, aye, Captain."

Not too shabby for a musician. Micah smiled. It was good to see Barre come into his own and even better to see how well he and Ro worked together.

The ship's engines powered up and Halcyone slowly maneuvered out of the shadow of their asteroid cover and into the orbiting detritus of what had once been the mining operation. Maldonado's ship grew larger on the display. Halcyone kept adjusting the zoom and center to keep it visible.

"Shit! Halcyone, dead stop!" Ro shouted.

"What? What's wrong?" Micah asked. He dug his fingers into the cushioned arms of the chair.

"Halcyone, zoom in, factor of two."

The ship expanded to take up half the viewer. At first, Micah didn't understand what had triggered Ro's outburst. And then he saw it.

Another ship was docked with Maldonado's. A small scout ship. Light and maneuverable, it must have slipped right past them.

"Shit!" The gun buyers had two ships. Of course they would. No one with half a brain would trust Maldonado. They were outflanked. "Have they spotted us?"

"No way to tell, but it's not like we're hard to see." Ro leaned forward and did something with the holo interface.

The forward screen reoriented and zoomed out. Maldonado's ship became a pinprick. The display showed the sector's wormholes by rings of color.

"What are you doing?"

"Plotting a jump course."

"No!" Micah released the harness and leaped out of his seat.

Barre unclipped and quickly stepped toward him. "We can't fight our way through them. It won't help Dev if we get killed in the process."

He turned to Ro. "Please. We can't just leave her there."

Tears blurred his vision. He swiped them away with the back of his hand.

Halcyone interrupted the tension on the bridge. "Proximity alert. Unidentified vessel approaching."

"Halcyone, display!" Ro shouted. "Calculate time to engagement."

"Unidentified ship moving on forward thrusters. Time to engagement, three minutes."

The screen winked out again and refocused on the scout. It was moving away from Maldonado's vessel at a limping speed. Now that it was closer, it was easy to see it was an older model, one that hadn't been manufactured in decades. At the time, they were the top of the line for speed and stealth; today's flitters could outrun them. "What kind of smuggler uses an old, battered thing like that? It doesn't even have any weapons."

"That doesn't make any sense," Ro said.

"Time to engagement, two minutes."

"What engagement? Neither of us have anything to engage with!" Micah resumed his nervous pacing. "Forget about them. The airlock is clear. We have to get Dev."

"And have a potential enemy at our back? Halcyone, scan for crew. Barre, hail the scout. I'm not going to risk the two of you and this ship going up against my father without more data."

It was the right thing to do. Micah knew that. But if it were up to him, he'd storm aboard that ship and chuck Maldonado out of the airlock without a p-suit. For his sake and Dev's.

"No answer from the scout."

"Halcyone reads one crew member aboard," Ro said.

Dev or Ro's father? Even after Maldonado had agreed to their demands, Micah didn't for a nanosecond believe the man would honor his word. At least not without significantly more incentive. But if it was Dev, why wasn't she answering? And it couldn't be Maldonado. Why would he abandon his ship for the old scout? Or maybe it was someone else. Micah stopped and pressed his hands against the smooth, cool surface of the console.

"What about Gutierrez?" Barre asked.

"Do you think she'd be that subtle?"

"Probably not."

"We have to check it out. If it's Dev, she could be hurt. She might need our help," Micah said.

"Wait a minute," Ro said.

"We don't have a minute!"

"The scout just changed course. Looks like it's in a stable orbit just past the edge of the Lagrange point."

"Which means?" Micah snapped.

"I have no idea what it means." Ro met his frustration with her own, but then her voice softened. She unclipped from her harness and stood next to him, lightly touching his arm. "Does Dev have a pilot's rating?"

"I don't know. Maybe?" He thought about what little he knew about her history growing up in the Midlant Settlement. Not a lot of space-faring opportunity there. "Probably not." Which meant that she wasn't on that scout.

"Whoever's on that ship has it under control. And since it has no weapons, and it's not venting plasma, whoever it is can wait until we assess what in the cosmos my father is up to."

"Okay. Fine." Micah forced himself to breathe slowly and relax his shoulders.

"Barre, have Halcyone resume course."

Micah stared at the viewscreen as the gap between them and Maldonado's ship narrowed. Rescue Dev first, then figure out who was in the scout and what they wanted. Ro was right. The small vessel could wait.

The screen abruptly flared out in a brilliant white.

"Not now," Ro muttered. "Halcyone, recalibrate viewer."

"Viewer recalibrated."

But nothing had changed.

"Zoom out, factor of two."

A brief flicker and the screen shifted. The bright glow receded until it was a tiny pinprick, smaller than the system's primary. Micah stared at the display, trying to sort out what was wrong.

"Collision alert. Asteroids and debris approaching. Bearing zero seven seven, mark twelve."

"Shit!" Ro shouted. "Halcyone, set course three five nine, mark zero, full thrusters."

The ship shuddered. Micah stumbled and slammed his hip against the console. He grabbed onto the back of the chair to steady himself, his gaze never leaving the screen. Where was Maldonado's ship? It should be there.

"Collision alert canceled."

"Shit." Barre picked himself up from the floor.

They watched in horrified silence as debris streaked past them like a comet.

Ro drew her breath in sharply. "Micah, I ..."

He pushed away from the console and stood over her, curling and uncurling his fists. "No. It's not ... It can't be." It wasn't Ro's face he saw, but her father's. His smug smile as he clamped the military restraints on Micah's hands and feet. His satisfaction as he engaged them. A distant alarm wailed through the bridge. He ignored it.

Dev.

Dev couldn't be gone.

A deep pressure clamped onto his arms. Micah thrashed wildly. One of his arms broke free and he connected with a solid wall of Barre. He felt shaky and confused, as if he'd just taken a jump through an unstable wormhole. Barre was calling his name.

"Micah! Micah! Stop!"

Ro stood up beside him. "I'm sorry." Her eyes glittered with tears. "I'm so sorry."

Chapter 25

AFTER JEM HAD uploaded the data, Nomi stopped answering his texts. He stared at his micro until his vision swam, but there was nothing. Heart racing, he ran out of the residence ring toward comms. Just shy of the nexus, he paused and doubled over, short of breath and dizzy. He looked up as station personnel walked by him. No one gave him a second glance. It must be a familiar sight by now. Jem Durbin, curled up and miserable.

What was he doing? Sure, they would let him in comms, it wasn't as if the station was under martial law or lockdown. But once there, then what? He was sure Nomi's "meeting" was detention. She had been arrested, and no one in comms was going to tell him anything. Bursting into command wasn't going to be any more helpful. And it would only call attention to himself.

Honestly, he was surprised they hadn't come for him yet. They had to know Nomi didn't write that program.

It was the only reason she would have been arrested. They must have found traces of the program. And how long would it take them to connect it to him? If any of the worm remained, it would have his ident on it. Jem stood up and trudged back to his quarters. He had been so sure he'd been careful. Just not careful enough. Something had gone wrong. And Nomi was in trouble.

Ro was going to blast him into deep space.

He slipped into his quarters and slumped against the closed door.

"Jeremy? What's wrong?"

Damn it. He did not need his mother interrogating him right now.

Even as he drew breath to tell her he was all right, she was advancing on him, her micro already starting to scan him.

"Stop. Just stop."

"Jeremy." Her voice was a warning.

He could only resist so far or she would admit him to medical.

"Your cortisol levels are high."

A stress hormone. The molecule appeared in his mind's eye in all its beautiful complexity. That was interesting. His own personal encyclopedia. It slowly rotated and the movement made him a little queasy.

"I'm fine. Just tired. The neural is integrating a little more every day. I just pushed it today, is all."

She frowned. It seemed as if that was her natural expression now, even more than usual. "I'll need to scan you again in a few hours. If your levels are still elevated, I'll give you a stronger sedative."

"Fine." The irony nearly made him choke. He'd palm the

meds, not willing to risk losing his edge, even for the sake of his symptoms. "Are we done for now?"

"Jem, I'm trying to help. Please."

He turned away from the uncomfortable and unfamiliar pain in her expression. "I know. I'm sorry. I'll be in my room. You can scan me later."

Maybe by then, he'd be able to sort out what happened to Nomi. But first he had to tell Ro.

He retreated to his room and curled up on his bed, leaving his mother standing in the common space, clutching her micro.

With a mixture of his still-learning neural and voice commands, Jem navigated to the secure messaging program. It was as safe as possible, but he wouldn't believe it was foolproof. Nothing was. Not even things that were supposed to be.

How had they discovered his worm?

No. That didn't matter now. Contacting Ro was all that mattered.

/Ro. I'm sorry. Nomi's in trouble./

He paused. There was no way to avoid admitting his part in this.

/It's my fault. I'm the one they should have detained. I can't reach her. Ro, I'm scared./

The letters vanished from the screen nearly as quickly as they formed.

/You have to come home. I'll keep trying, but I don't know what else to do./

He pulled the pillow over his head and shut his eyes, but he couldn't shut out the dread of having failed his friend.

Maybe he would be arrested, too. He only hoped it would be before Ro could reply to his message. *Keep trying. Keep trying.* His own words mocked him. Comms and command were dead ends. The station AI was a dead end. What else was there?

Follow the ion trail.

Ro's voice was clear in his mind. In this case, it was the data. Follow the data. That's what she would have done. Okay, then.

He still had a copy of everything he'd scraped. And now, so did Nomi's interrogators. Jem stared up at the ceiling and traced the seams in the steel until his eyes crossed. Why had they needed the data? Didn't the Commonwealth already have it?

"Oh, space me," he whispered as equations suddenly balanced in his mind. The port thruster had no idea what the starboard one was doing.

*

Dev leaned forward over the console, straining at the limit of her harness. At least the emergency distress beacon followed the standard interface. It was practically the only one of the controls she felt qualified to touch on the complex panel. Her hand hovered over the button when the ship pitched, throwing her against the sides of the command chair. The harness straps cut into her, first on one side and then the other as the inertial dampers struggled to keep the ship from wallowing.

"What the hell?" Dev looked all around the bridge, but couldn't find any clues to what had hit them. She kept expecting the hull breach siren. How well sealed was the bridge? How quickly would the oxygen run out?

At least on a dig site, Dev could count on gravity and atmosphere. Here, nothing was under her control. "Damned spacers," she muttered.

The ship's perturbations eased and Dev was able to inhale without being strangled by the adaptive webbing. "Now what?"

As if in answer, the ship rocked once more and something metallic banged against the hull. She drew in her breath sharply, as if that would help once the oxygen sats dropped below what could sustain life. What was one more breath at that point? She was going to die in space just like her parents had.

A pressure built up in her chest and threatened to burst from her throat. After everything she'd gone through and done to escape, to die here in a remote asteroid field seemed utterly ridiculous. A wild laughter bubbled up from somewhere deep inside; she clamped her jaws shut to keep it from escaping.

Morningstars didn't belong in the void. They belonged where up was up and down was down. It was what her grandmother had always said when Dev asked about her parents. It was all she would ever say.

Dev hit the record button. Someone should know what had happened to her. Her brothers deserved to know. She wasn't going to be the third family member to disappear off-world without a trace.

It wasn't exactly a distress call, but it would have to be enough.

Blinking back tears, she cleared her throat and began. Her voice seemed steadier than it had any right to be. "This is Devorah Martingale Morningstar, of the Midland Settlement, North America, Earth. I am a student at UCom–NW in the materials science department. I'm currently in a parking orbit on a flitter-sized jump-capable ship, but I have no idea where I am. And I think the ship is hulled."

She paused, listening, but the metallic clangs stopped. The ship was still again.

"Whoever finds this, please have someone contact my brothers. The University will have their information. And tell Michael Chase it's not his fault."

No. That would only pile suspicion on him. She erased that last bit.

"I was abducted from my dorm by Alain Maldonado. I don't know where he is now, but I hope someone finds the son of a bitch and makes him pay."

A sharp hiss pulled her attention from the console.

"Someone did."

A woman in a dark coverall staggered onto the bridge, her face bloody. One arm ended in a prosthetic claw. The other sleeve was ripped open from shoulder to wrist. Her left pant leg was charred and the smell of burned flesh turned Dev's stomach.

Dev froze against the seat restraints, her hand hovering above the control console.

The woman's legs buckled. She tried to catch herself with her artificial hand, but it gave a high-pitched whine and twitched weakly before she swore and crumpled to the floor at Dev's feet. Her breath rasped in the silent bridge.

Swallowing hard, Dev disentangled herself from the seat's webbing and knelt beside the injured woman. It was Taro's companion.

"Maldonado?" Dev asked.

"Fucker ambushed me." Her glare could have ignited a stable isotope.

Dev tore the woman's sleeve away from the intact arm. Or more intact arm. The cut had been made by a very thin, precise blade and it had penetrated clear down to the bone. The edges of the cut were seared, as if she'd been flayed by a laser scalpel.

But by far, the most pressing damage was the burn just below her left hip. The material of her trousers had melted into the bubbled skin and muscle. Dev turned away and gagged.

"You're Emma, right?" she asked, trying to give her mind something to focus on that wasn't blood and burned muscle.

"Gutierrez. Lieutenant Commander Gutierrez." Her voice was clipped and hoarse. She panted in pain.

"I'm going to need to find medical supplies, Lieutenant Commander. Any idea where to look?"

"This was his ship. Charon. The Ferryman."

"Taro," Dev said softly. "What happened to him?"

Gutierrez gave her a withering look.

"Fine. I'll be back as soon as I can."

She closed her eyes.

At least the bleeding from the woman's forehead had mostly clotted. The arm was neatly cauterized already. The burn would need the most attention. If there weren't any med supplies on board, Gutierrez was spaced.

And where were Taro and Maldonado? Given Gutierrez's response, Dev was afraid to ask again.

She ran through the ship flinging open cabinets and drawers in every cabin. In one of the open bulkheads, there was a storage locker with emergency rations and the barest of bare-bones med-kits.

Dev dropped several water bulbs and the med-kit into her pockets and ran back to the bridge.

Gutierrez hadn't moved. Her face was nearly colorless. Dev's breath hitched in her throat and she scrambled over to check the pulse at the woman's neck, but her hands were shaking too badly to feel much of anything. "Fuck."

"Don't toss me out of the airlock. I'm not a corpse yet." The woman's voice was a thin whisper.

Relief nearly made Dev dizzy. "You need a doctor."

"I have you."

"I can't ... I'm not ..." Basic first aid was one thing, but the scope of this woman's injuries was another. "Fuck," she said, again. "I'm going to have to disinfect the burn. It's going to hurt."

Gutierrez's eyes fluttered open. "Been there. Done that."

Dev laid the water and the kit on the floor.

"There should be a preloaded bolus of adrenaline and pain-killer in there. Do you know how to administer it?"

"Yeah." Those things were idiot-proof.

"Then get to it, soldier."

"I'm no soldier," Dev said, as she picked up the automatic syringe. It had the heft of one of her favorite blades and fit comfortably in her palm.

"You are now."

She hesitated for a moment, wondering if she should apologize first, then she leaned over and jabbed the woman's right thigh.

Gutierrez winced, but as Dev watched the sickly gray faded and more normal color returned to the woman's cheeks. Her pulse strengthened. Dev exhaled and let the spent syringe fall from her hand. It rolled beneath the console.

"Thank you. But it's not going to last long. Not with this level of tissue damage."

It was as if Gutierrez were talking about someone else.

"Whatever you're going to do to stabilize me, do it now. Then I'm going to need you to fly this ship."

"Morningstars don't belong in the void," she whispered, but Gutierrez didn't hear her.

Dev took stock of the med-kit. Aside from the booster she had just given the woman, there were sealed bulbs of sterile saline, one set of antibiotic-laced bandages, and a tube of suture glue. Enough to treat a basic cut or a splinter, but not nearly enough for this.

The pants would have to be cut free of the burn, but the kit didn't contain sterile scissors. Dev took out the knife she had sharpened from the water-bulb polymer. One of the advantages of the material was that it was antibacterial on a nano-cellular level. Which was fortunate, because the only thing Dev had to sterilize it with was her soldering iron, and that level of heat would melt the blade into a puddle of uselessness.

"Brace yourself," Dev warned as she leaned close with the blade in her hand.

Gutierrez's injured hand grabbed hers. Dev could have opened the woman's fingers with very little effort, but she covered them with her other hand instead. "I'm sorry."

The lieutenant commander looked away and relaxed her grip. "Just do it."

Dev cut a circle in the woman's pants wide enough to clear the burn by several centimeters in every direction. Then she cut below the level of the damage and down the seam. Gutierrez would need something to keep her warm, but Dev figured she'd need the material for bandaging. The only way to remove the fabric melted into the burn was to wash it out.

It was going to hurt.

She hoped the bandages in the med-kit had anesthetic in them as well as the antibiotics.

Gutierrez sucked in her breath and grimaced, but she didn't move. Not even when Dev jostled her leg. The saline sloughed off bits of burned skin, fabric, blood, and clots of tissue. It ran out before the wound ran clean.

Dev rocked back on her heels. What did any of this matter? She was in the middle of nowhere in a ship she couldn't fly with a desperately injured companion. A companion who would likely die before any help came for them. She wanted to collapse on the floor beside Gutierrez. Instead, Dev let the leg air-dry for a minute or two before gently patting the bandage over the weeping burn.

Still Gutierrez didn't flinch or cry out. The edges of the bandage auto-adhered to the intact surrounding skin. It wasn't enough, but it was all she had.

"I need to look at your arm," Dev said. There was little else she could do, but if she could make the woman more comfortable, she would.

Gutierrez met her gaze and nodded.

There were no more bandages, antibiotic-treated or not. The cut was clean. Whatever had sliced open the lieutenant commander's arm was sharp and hot. Probably sterilized it on its way through. She thought of her soldering iron and shuddered.

"I'm going to seal this with the glue. It should keep anything bad out of the wound."

Gutierrez grunted her assent. Her eyes were clouded. She'd probably already burned through whatever pain-killer was in the injection.

Dev snapped off the tip of the glue nozzle and ran a line of it down Gutierrez's arm like caulk. It filled in the sharp edges of the cut, drawing the flesh together in a ragged seam. Then she wrapped the fabric she'd cut from her pants leg around the arm to protect it from bumping against anything.

It was the best she could do.

"Well done, soldier," Gutierrez said. "Too bad you don't have anything to fix up my other one." The prosthetic arm twitched once against the floor.

"I'm better at mechanics than first aid, but I don't think I have the right kind of tools. Sorry." Maybe back at Uni. But then, if they were back in the Hub, Gutierrez wouldn't need Dev and she'd have at least a chance to survive.

"Well, I've done without before. Help me up."

"I don't think that's a good idea," Dev said, putting a hand on Gutierrez's chest.

"It's not our job to think. Get me up. That's an order."

It would probably have had more impact if Gutierrez's voice hadn't been husky with pain.

Dev sighed and helped boost the injured woman to sitting. "What happened back there?" If they were going to die, she thought she deserved to know.

"Maldonado is no longer a problem." Gutierrez's lips pressed into a thin, colorless line.

"Where is your ..." Dev trailed off. Taro didn't seem to be her friend, but they did have history. That much was clear from their eavesdropped conversation. "Where is the Ferryman?" It seemed safer to refer to him that way.

Gutierrez's face paled again. Dev couldn't be sure if it was from shock or pain.

"Shepherding one final soul to the underworld."

That made no sense and by the look Gutierrez gave her, it was clear she wouldn't tell her anything more.

"You're going to need to strap me in."

"What?"

Gutierrez repeated herself slowly, the annoyance clear in her voice. "Strap me in. The command chair."

Dev wasn't sure the woman would be able to make it there, even with her help. But it was either that or drift here forever. "Don't put any weight on that left leg."

Gutierrez smirked. Some of the fire had returned to her eyes. "How do you think I got here, soldier?"

"Adrenaline and stupidity," Dev snapped back before she wrapped her left arm around the woman's waist and hauled her to her feet. The three steps to the command chair had to have been agonizing, but Gutierrez set her jaw and kept silent.

"Don't underestimate the power of adrenaline and stupidity, soldier," Gutierrez said, panting. "Now the webbing. Then strap yourself in." She lifted her chin toward the copilot's seat. "And we won't be needing your distress call."

"No, sir," Dev said as she watched Gutierrez take command of the ship one-handed, functioning by the grace of battlefield boost and the force of her relentless personality.

Chapter 26

RO STARED UP at the viewscreen long after the debris cloud of what had been her father's ship dissipated. Somewhere in that cloud, her father was vaporized. And so was Dev.

Micah sat slumped in his chair with his head in his hands. Barre stood beside him, a hand on his shoulder. Ro couldn't move from her rigid stance in front of the display.

Her father had done this. And he deserved what he got.

So why did Ro feel as if Dev's death was her fault?

Into the strained silence on the bridge, Ro's micro gave a cheery beep. The three of them started. Micah blinked and looked away.

Ro checked the message. At least it was something to do.

The words scrolled across the screen and at first, Ro couldn't force them to make any sort of sense. And then they did and dread turned her insides cold.

"We have to go back," she whispered. "We have to go back to Daedalus now."

Barre looked up, frowning.

"It's Nomi. She's been arrested."

"Ro? I'm sorry, but I think we have more immediate problems."

She stared at Barre as if his language, too, had suddenly become unfamiliar and indecipherable.

"That scout ship just started moving again. And it's headed our way."

Micah leaped from his seat. "If they had anything to do with—" He shook his head, unable to say it. "Anything to do with that, they're going to answer for it."

The finality in his voice broke through Ro's fear and replaced it with fury. They needed answers. And not just for Micah's sake. If Nomi, too, was going to be a casualty of this fucking supernova of a failure, then by all that was vast and terrifying in the void, they would make someone pay. She would make them pay.

"Plot an intercept." Ro hardly recognized her own voice.

Barre nodded, his eyes very wide.

"Full thrusters." She'd see how much they liked playing galactic chicken.

"Ro?"

She ignored Barre's concern and repeated her command.

"Collision warning. Ship bearing zero zero seven mark zero. Time to impact, forty-seven seconds."

She ignored Halcyone as well. The opposing pilot had to have seen them by now. Had to realize they were on a collision course. The question was who would blink first.

Well, whoever it was, they didn't know her. Didn't know

how far she was willing to go.

A strident alarm sounded through the bridge. "Collision warning. Time to impact, thirty seconds."

"Ro?" Barre's voice cracked.

"Maintain course and speed."

"Collision warning. Time to impact, twenty-five seconds."

There was still a universe of time to avoid contact. Ro watched as the small scout ship converged on them. What was the captain thinking?

"Collision warning. Time to impact, twenty seconds."

"Ro, this is crazy!" Barre shouted.

"Open a channel."

"Channel open."

"Collision warning. Time to impact, fifteen seconds."

"Shut up, we know," Micah muttered.

"If you don't want to end up a smear crushed between this ship and a handy asteroid, I would advise you to power down your engines. Now."

"Collision warning. Time to impact, ten seconds."

"And dent your pristine hull? I can't imagine you would do that to your beloved Halcyone." It took Ro several heartbeats to recognize the faint voice that emerged through the ship's old speakers.

"Halcyone! Reverse thrust. All stop!" Ro shouted.

The ship seemed to shudder in place. The collision alarm stilled, leaving them in a stunned silence.

"Well, Lieutenant Commander Gutierrez. To what do we deserve the pleasure?" Ro was certain her sarcasm would carry across the comms channel.

"What did you do? What did you do to her?" Micah's voice was thick with rage and pain.

"Michael? Micah, is that you?"

He blinked. His mouth fell open, but nothing emerged except for an incoherent stammer.

"Dev." He slumped against the nav console. Barre guided him to a chair.

A warmth burned through Ro's chest. They hadn't failed. Not at everything. "Welcome back from the dead, Dev. We're Micah's friends and it's a pleasure to meet you."

"There's a small matter of logistics, Captain Maldonado," Gutierrez said.

It didn't even bother Ro the way the LC said "captain." "What do you need?"

"My helper here can't fly and there's a flitter taking up the airlock."

"Move to the flitter and dock with us. We'll get to the scout later."

Silence and static filled the comms channel for a long moment. "But there's a slight problem." Gutierrez sounded distant.

"Problem?" Micah asked. "Is it Dev? Is something the matter with Dev?"

"I'm fine, Micah. Really. It's Emma."

Emma? Since when was anyone on a first-name basis with the lieutenant commander?

"She's pretty seriously injured. Honestly? I don't think she could even reach the flitter, much less fly her. Even with my help."

"What kind of injuries are we talking about?" Barre

asked, already in medical mode.

"Her prosthesis won't respond. Her other arm is pretty deeply cut, but the worst is a burn on her upper leg. I did the best I could with the supplies on board, but I think she's going into shock."

Despite the frantic edge to her voice, Dev sounded just as capable as Micah had described. Maybe even more so.

"I can do what's necessary," Gutierrez said.

Barre caught Ro's gaze and shook his head.

Ro nodded. Triage first. Equipment later. "Jettison the flitter, Lieutenant Commander. We can go after it later. Cut your engines. We'll come get you."

"Aye, aye, Captain." Gutierrez's reply was weak and thready, but the mockery was still clear.

The flitter floated away from the small ship's airlock. Ro had Halcyone track its course before setting up a docking intercept. Unless it smashed into an asteroid, they'd be able to get it back at some point.

"You good here?" Barre asked.

There might have been a time when Ro would've been insulted at Barre's question, but they were a crew now. "I'm good."

He nodded. "I'm probably going to need your help, Micah. If the LC is as bad off as it sounds, I'll need to stabilize her on their ship before risking transport. Are you up for this?"

Micah gathered himself from where he'd been staring at the ship on the display. "Hell yeah."

"If you need another set of hands, I can have Halcyone take the helm," Ro said. "I'm looking forward to meeting your friend." Besides, the sooner they got Gutierrez squared away, the sooner they could get back to Daedalus.

And to Nomi.

*

After her unsettling conversation with Mendez, Nomi was escorted from command by Holder and Chakrabarti. She kept her eyes downcast, hoping no one would notice or try to stop to talk to her. It was the only way she could hold on to any sense of her own dignity.

She was being arrested. How could she explain to her parents? They had been so proud of her when she'd gotten accepted at Uni. When she'd taken her Commonwealth commission. Even when she'd received her orders to Daedalus Station, despite it being so far off anywhere's jump paths.

Now Nomi was going to lose her position here. There was even the chance she'd be tried for treason and stripped of her citizenship. Which would leave her parents in debt for her education. It was a debt they would likely never be able to repay. And what would happen to Daisuke? Her disgrace would spill over on him to taint his future.

Still, she would make the same choices again. How could she do otherwise? She blinked back tears.

Her guards stopped suddenly and Nomi looked up from where she had been staring at the subtle geometric patterns stamped in the metallic floor. She knew the station had a brig, just not where it was.

And this definitely wasn't it.

They were standing outside the door to her quarters.

"What's happening?" Nomi asked.

"Please remain inside until the commander contacts you," Chakrabarti said. "You'll have restricted access to the station AI and are cleared from the duty roster until further notice. Your meals and any other necessities will be delivered." The woman triggered the door to open.

"Am I under arrest?"

"Daedalus has your status as under quarantine."

So no visitors either. Well, Jem would be safer out of contact with her. "Thank you." It wasn't their fault she was in this mess and they had been professional and polite.

"Is there anything you require right now?"

Nomi shook her head. The only thing she wanted was her micro and to see Ro. Neither of which was likely to happen.

Her minders waited until she'd stepped over the threshold before they closed her in. Nomi didn't even bother to try the door. She filled a glass and drank deeply, water sloshing over the rim as her hands shook.

"Daedalus, message Durbin, Jeremy."

"Access denied. State override authority."

"Shit." Nomi collapsed on her sofa and dragged Ro's quilt over her lap. Did Ro even know what had happened? Surely Jem sent her a message. Unless he was in detention, too. But they couldn't have arrested him—he wasn't of age.

Nomi's thoughts chased one another around her mind until she wanted to scream with frustration.

Her door chime sounded. Before she could respond, the door opened and Commander Mendez entered. Nomi jumped up, about to demand to know what was happening when Mendez stood aside and the taller, more imposing Targill stepped inside.

Mendez gave her a stern look Nomi couldn't interpret. It was a warning of some sort, but for what? And why? And what was Targill doing here? Since his role in tracking down Halcyone during her wild ride, he'd been here on Daedalus and communicating with Mendez more than seemed necessary, given how much of an outpost this place was. Their one small wormhole wasn't strategic enough to warrant a larger station or more than the minimal amount of troops to guard it.

So what was this decorated war hero doing here with his fast cruiser? And why was he interested in her?

She glanced up at her grandfather's kamis for strength and was reminded of his endless capacity for patience and courtesy. Nomi centered herself. "Please come in. Can I offer you some tea?" She was pleased that her voice remained steady.

Targill gave her a look that mixed a certain curiosity with surprise, before his expression closed down to his usual military neutral. Mendez just shook her head.

"Please sit down," Nomi said, still channeling her grandfather's hospitality. At least until she knew what was going on, politeness was the safest course. And if it confused them, so much the better. She returned to her place on the sofa.

Targill nodded to her and took a stool from the galley area. Mendez stood at the edge of the rug that delineated the common area of Nomi's small quarters, her arms behind her back. Her sidearm reflected the light. "Ensign Nakamura. Thank you for your cooperation. I suspect you have some questions. We just need to talk to you about an irregularity that showed up in the personnel files during your shift in comms."

Nomi blinked in confusion. This was clearly not for her benefit, given the conversation she'd just finished with Mendez. What was going on between her commander and Targill? Well, she could certainly play dumb. It's not like she knew what their game was. "Why am I under house arrest?"

"You are not under arrest, Ensign," Targill said.

The "yet" was more than implied.

"We have confined you to quarters as much for your own protection as anything, Nakamura," Mendez said.

"Protection? From what, sir?"

Targill leaned forward. "Tell me about your comms supervisor."

"Cam Lowell?" Nomi wished she'd had the opportunity to review the data Jem's worm had unearthed. She was flying this flitter blind. "He complains a lot about the work. And he's obsessed about an old spacer's myth. Other than that? I don't know much about him. Until last week, I hadn't even been on shift with him."

"An old spacer's myth that your girlfriend seems to know more than a little about," Targill said.

Nomi blinked up at Mendez, but the commander didn't give her any hint of what was safe ground here.

"If Ro had discovered Ithaka, she wouldn't be flying around in a forty-odd-year-old transport with more broken than working." Nomi hoped Halcyone wouldn't take her disparagement personally.

"She and the ship are off-station. Don't you find that curious?"

Wait. Was this about her and the data breach or Ro? Did Targill think Ro had hacked the files?

Nomi kept her voice soft and conversational. "She had some work to do on Halcyone that required a bay and some equipment more readily available on Eurydice. I suspect she filed a flight plan. Why don't you ask her yourself when she gets back?" The reality was, they had no evidence on which to arrest Ro nor could they compel her to answer their questions, since unlike Nomi, Ro didn't have a Commonwealth commission. And Nomi had no idea when they'd return or if they'd have Dev and Micah with them.

That would make things an entire dimension's worth of complicated.

"We certainly will, Ensign," Targill said. "But if you have any information that links Ms. Maldonado with the data breach in comms or to Ithaka, it will certainly help clarify your connection to the matter."

Well, that couldn't be clearer. Targill wanted Nomi to throw Ro beneath the afterburners. And by implication, he would make sure she had a smooth landing if she did. She raised an eyebrow at Mendez. The commander stared straight ahead and wouldn't catch Nomi's gaze.

What was in the data they found? Jem knew and so did Mendez. So what was Targill's connection?

Was he building a case against Ro? Then why ask about Lowell? The only thing that connected them all, as far as she could tell, was Ithaka itself.

"I'm sorry, Commander Targill. I really wish I could help you."

"It would be much simpler if you shared what you knew. Before we examine your micro for evidence."

Nomi focused on her breathing and the outward expression of her grandfather's calm. Did Targill have her micro now? Would his technicians find any of Ro's modifications or programs? She scowled at Mendez. Nomi didn't think a ship's captain would outrank the commander of an entire station, but if Mendez had more power, how could she have let him take the micro?

What was Mendez up to? Damn it, Nomi needed to know what was in those scraped files.

Wait. Mendez knew, but she hadn't told Targill. Why? All Nomi knew for sure was if she said the wrong thing, she could set off a chain reaction that would make an aduronium explosion look like an oxygen-starved flame.

Trust. It was always a matter of trust and Nomi was clear on who she trusted and why. That had not changed, despite her confusion.

Chapter 27

"IT'S GOING TO be okay," Dev said into the silence of the cockpit. She said it as much to convince herself as to keep Emma Gutierrez focused. There was no answer. The woman's eyes were closed and she slumped over, hanging limp from her harness. All the color had drained from her face.

"Shit." Dev unstrapped the restraints and hurried over to her. The medical kit was useless. She kicked it across the room. Gutierrez's eyes had rolled back and she was unresponsive.

If Micah and his friends were going to help, they'd better do it fast.

Gutierrez's pulse was weak and rapid. That was not a good sign. Making an executive decision, Dev freed the woman and lowered her to the floor. Her shallow breathing didn't change and she didn't make a sound, which were also not good signs.

The ship's engines stilled; the last of the vibrations died away. There was no rescue team. Where the hell were they?

As if in answer, a series of metallic clangs rang through the ship. Dev exhaled heavily. She looked up as the bridge door hissed open. A tall, broad-shouldered man with deeply bronzed skin and shoulder-length dreadlocks stepped through carrying a larger version of the med-kit she had used up. On his heels was Micah.

Dev tried to scramble to her feet, but her legs were trembling so badly she couldn't stand.

Her accidental roommate stopped short at the threshold of the small bridge. "Hey," he said softly. "Oh, this is Barre. He can help."

Relief flooded through her. "She's in rough shape," Dev said, as Barre knelt down beside Gutierrez.

"Are you hurt?" Micah asked.

"Your friend's fine," Barre said. "She can talk and she's upright. Which is more than I can say for our LC."

Dev met Micah's gaze and was surprised at the intensity of emotion she found there. For someone she hadn't known very long, he was surprisingly easy to read and right now, he was nearly radiating a mix of fear and guilt.

"Hey, it's not your fault," Dev said. "Thanks for coming after me."

"I think you did all the heavy lifting."

"I had some help along the way." She nodded at Gutierrez. "She had a friend, too. I don't think he was so lucky."

"Charon?" Barre asked.

"That's what she called him." An image of the scarred man filled her mind. For all that they'd had a single, brief conversation, Dev would never forget him. "She won't tell me what happened, but I think Maldonado killed him."

"Well, you don't have anything to worry about from him

anymore," Micah said. "His ship exploded."

Dev nodded. If it hadn't been for Taro, she and Emma would be elemental particles now. She should have tried to disarm the mines. Then Taro wouldn't have had to sacrifice himself for them. She pressed her hands against the floor to steady them.

Micah dropped his gaze to his feet. "We thought you were aboard. Are you sure you're okay? He didn't hurt you?"

His concern was both a little sweet and a little irritating. Dev reached into her pocket and brushed her hands across her tools. "Worry about Emma. I can take care of myself." Her voice was as sharp as a blade.

Micah flushed a deep red and went over to kneel beside his friend. "Anything I can do, Barre?"

He had his med-kit open beside him and had put on sterile gloves. "This your handiwork?"

Dev nodded.

"You did good. But there's not much more I can do. Not until we reach a real doctor and a full medical bay."

"You're not a doctor?"

"She'll be okay. Barre's a good field medic."

"Nope," he said. He smiled broadly as his large, capable-looking hands examined Gutierrez. "A musician. But if we can get her back to Daedalus, my folks are the station doctors and they can take it from there."

"How's it look, Barre?" Their captain's voice came through the still-open comms channel.

"She's lost a lot of blood and the burn is a serious one. No fractures. I'm going to start an IV and then she'll be safe to transport."

"What about jumps?"

"It's a tough call, Ro, but I'm not sure we have a lot of options. She won't have much of a chance if we delay."

Ro. Gutierrez had called her Captain Maldonado.

"Okay. I'll get Halcyone started on plotting a course with the shallowest interstitial burns possible."

"That would be good. I don't think her wounds can stand a lot of g forces, even with cushioning."

So who was Ro in relation to Alain Maldonado? Could she risk asking? If the woman was Micah's friend, did it matter?

Barre removed his gloves. "Okay. I've done as much as I can for now. Let's get her on Halcyone. Micah? On three."

They were going to lift her. Dev frowned, thinking of Micah's feet. "I think you should grab the med-kit and take care of the airlocks. I got this."

Barre gave her an appraising look before nodding. She headed over to relieve Micah by Gutierrez's legs. He stepped back.

"Anything you need from this ship?" Micah asked.

"No." She patted her pockets. They were heavy with Sellen's cube, the tools she'd made, and the ones she'd salvaged. They would find a place of honor with her grandmother's blades. "I'm good."

Micah slipped from the bridge ahead of them.

Barre folded Gutierrez's arms across her chest, tucked the IV bag beneath them, and shook out a transport sheet. "Help me roll her onto this."

Together they got the LC centered on the sheet. It was more like a shallow hammock with handles at each end.

"Okay, count of three. Ready?" Barre said.

She nodded.

"One, two, three."

Barre lifted Gutierrez from the head. Dev took the foot end. It didn't look all that comfortable for their patient, but she was barely conscious and there wouldn't have been room to use a gurney even if they'd had one.

They set down their patient just shy of the airlock while Micah cycled it open.

"These don't look like they were designed for emergency evac," Dev said. If Gutierrez could stand, it would be no issue to move all of them through the lock at once, though it would be crowded with four. But there was no way to bring her through on the transport sheet.

"Medical override," Barre said. "Opens both sides at once. Works fine. As long as you trust your seals."

Dev studied Charon's ship. If the missing bulkhead panels were any indication, she wouldn't trust the seals. But what choice did they have?

"Micah. Take Dev on ahead. I'll manage with Gutierrez."

"No fucking way," Micah said.

Dev's "no" overlapped his.

Ro's voice interrupted them all. "Don't be an idiot, Barre. Have Dev help with Gutierrez. I'm on Halcyone's side with emergency air. Micah, stay on the scout's side. If there's a problem with the seals on your end, you'll have to manually shut the door and repressurize once they clear it. You can cycle yourself through after."

"Aye, aye, Captain."

Dev looked up. Through the two sides of the lock, she could see the silhouette of a petite woman and not much else.

"Ready?" Barre asked.

She nodded. They picked up Gutierrez. Micah triggered their side of the lock to open. Ro finished the medical override. There was a staccato clank followed by a low hiss.

"Seals holding," Micah said. "Mostly."

"Let's go," Barre said.

They hustled the injured woman through the first lock. Dev paused to look out at the expanse of starlit darkness visible from the transparent membranes that spanned the ship's airlocks. It was dizzying and made Dev feel as if she were falling from the top of a building to a ground that kept receding from her. Between one step and the next, she nearly lost her footing. Her stomach fluttered. Her sense of up and down wavered and she gasped.

"Steady," Barre said. "Gravity will stabilize as soon as we hit Halcyone's field."

Dev squeezed her eyes shut and kept moving. It only took another step before her body settled and her equilibrium returned. At least she hadn't let go of her side of the transport sheet.

And then they were on the other ship.

They set Gutierrez down. Dev leaned over and caught her breath.

"Welcome aboard," the captain said. Ro, her friends called her. Ro Maldonado.

Dev gave her an appraising look. Slender, petite, with long blonde hair that hung past the tip of her shoulder blades, she certainly didn't look dangerous. As Ro met her gaze, Dev noticed her bright green eyes, so like Maldonado's it made her step back and gasp.

"I'm not my father," she said.

"No. You're not."

Micah cycled through the airlock right behind her.

"Ro? Devorah Martingale Morningstar. Dev? Rosalen Maldonado."

"Let's finish the introductions once we get my patient secured."

"Where should we put her, Barre?" Ro asked.

"Her best chance will be in a jump snug and temporal foam. Let's put her in my cabin. I'll take Jem's bunk. That way I can check her in between each leg home." He nodded to Dev. "Once more?"

She nodded and took the handles by Gutierrez's feet. Grunting with the effort, she managed to carry the LC through a corridor that looked a whole lot better than Charon's ship.

Micah held the door to Barre's quarters open while Dev and Barre wrestled their patient into a jump snug.

Dev stared at the instruments crowding nearly all the floor space. She didn't even recognize some of them. "You really are a musician."

"Guilty as charged," he said, before turning to Ro. "Can you handle the trip home without me? I'll need to monitor Gutierrez closely." He had already moved away from them and started rummaging through his medical kit again.

"I got this," Ro said, before turning to Micah and Dev. "Follow me. You'll both have to use the jump niches on the bridge. We're running short on accommodations."

Dev fell in behind Ro, with Micah last. She felt vaguely

uncomfortable, as if she were being herded off to some unknown doom.

"And Ro? I haven't had time to look at Dev. I don't think she's in shock or anything, but at the very least, she's going to need some fresh clothes and something to eat and drink before we head back."

Dev stared down at her torn shirt and grubby pants. Her hair felt lank and greasy against the back of her neck. She'd been in the same clothes for what, three days? And she would just about sell out one of her brothers for the chance to really wash up. Food was not even a close third.

"You got it, doc."

"I'm sorry, I should've thought of that," Micah said.

If he was going to keep apologizing, Dev would have to return to the smaller ship.

Ro studied her for a moment. "Micah, there's some freeze-dried soup in the galley. Grab a mug and a meal bar and meet us back here."

Dev must have made a face because Ro apologized this time.

"It's all we have aboard. I promise, we'll get you a real meal on Daedalus. As far as clothes, you won't fit into anything of mine, but I think I have a coverall that will do."

"Ro, I—" Micah was hovering near them, rocking back and forth on his feet.

"Oh for cosmos's sake, Micah, I'm not going to space her."

Dev was grateful for Ro's brusque humor. It was easier to handle than Micah's guilt.

He mumbled another apology and sprinted down the corridor.

Ro led her to the door opposite Barre's cabin. Unlike the musician's space, this room was devoid of any hint to its occupant's identity. A bed, a desk, and a storage locker comprised the sum total of Ro's home aboard ship.

"Like what you've done with the place," Dev said.

Ro's lips twitched into a half-smile. She rummaged in the locker and handed Dev a coverall. "It should fit. I always have to roll up the sleeves and legs on mine."

Dev looked from her clothes to the clean, albeit worn, garment.

"Oh," Ro said, "here's a towel. The head's through there."

"You've just become my new best friend," Dev said. She washed and dressed as quickly as she could, rinsing the worst of the stink off her. A real shower would have to wait. Emma Gutierrez came first. The ruined clothes could get shoved outside an airlock for all she cared, but she carefully transferred all of her tools to myriad pockets on the coverall. Having them made her feel safer.

When she emerged from the head, rubbing the towel over her damp hair, Ro was manipulating virtual windows through her micro faster than anyone Dev had ever seen. "Wow."

Ro tossed all of the data back onto the device. "I have our course to Daedalus Station locked in. We should get to the bridge."

"Do you really think that's a good idea?"

"Gutierrez needs medical attention. And ..." Ro's voice hitched. "I have an urgent personal matter to attend to."

"No. I mean me. Me and Micah. If you show up with us, won't there be questions that'll be awkward to answer?"

"Any more awkward than the ones you don't want to ask me about my father?"

Dev's face heated up.

"She's right," Micah said. He stood outside Ro's door, a steaming mug in one hand, a meal bar in the other, and handed them to Dev. He met her gaze directly and something had changed in his stance.

"What choice do we have?" Ro asked.

"There's a jump-capable ship attached to our airlock. I propose Dev and I take that ship back to the Hub."

"Where you'll have your own set of awkward questions waiting for you."

Micah got very quiet. "I've spent a lifetime watching my father wriggle out of worse than that. Besides, there's a lot of discretion his money will buy us."

Dev tilted her head, studying him. Who was his father? Well, some of those questions would be coming from her, and awkward or not, he was going to have to answer them.

"Go home. Help Nomi. We'll be okay," Micah said.

Ro winced. "Okay. You're right. Is there anything you need from Halcyone?"

Micah looked at Dev. She shook her head.

"No. And I'm sorry I got you into this mess."

"It wasn't you, Micah. It was my father. And for the record? I'm glad he's dead." Ro gave a startled Micah a quick hug. Then she turned and did the same with Dev. "Good luck. Contact me when you've landed."

Micah laid a hand on Ro's arm. "She'll be okay."

"She has to be."

Dev realized they weren't talking about her. There was a

fierce expression on the young captain's face that was uncomfortably familiar.

Chapter 28

HIS ROOM FELT a lot more cramped than usual with Gutierrez in the lower bunk and the med-kit spread out across the floor. Barre asked Halcyone to keep the door open. He knelt to examine his patient. Most of one bag of enhanced fluids had already emptied into her. He swapped it out for a full one. When he reached behind him for the med-kit's basic scanner, his fingers brushed against the strings of a guitar. Dissonant chords filled the room.

Gutierrez's eyes fluttered open. Her right hand grabbed Barre's wrist. The scanner fell out of his grip and clattered to the floor.

"It's okay. You're safe," Barre said. He covered her hand with his other one. "Relax. I don't want you to reopen your wounds."

She glanced around his quarters, her gaze clouded by pain and confusion, before she finally focused on him. "Barre Durbin. How did I get here?"

He let his hand fall away as she loosened her grip. "What's the last thing you remember?" He reclaimed the scanner even though it wouldn't be able to tell if she'd sustained a concussion.

"Passing out on Charon's ship. Where's Dev?"

"She's fine. On Halcyone's bridge with Ro and Micah."

"Halcyone. An unlikely name for a ship that keeps finding so much trouble."

Barre waited as he finished his scan. Her vitals were as stable as they were likely to get, short of treatment in a full medical bay. "I didn't name her."

"He was an idiot."

"Who?"

"The Ferryman." She gazed past him. "Taro."

Barre nodded. "What happened?"

"It doesn't matter." She turned her face toward the wall. "I swore I'd never forgive him for what he did."

There was nothing he could do for guilt. "I can give you something more for pain, but treating the burns is going to have to wait until we get back to Daedalus." Barre riffled through the basic meds stocked in his kit.

"No." Gutierrez grunted and Barre turned back as she was struggling to sit up. Her prosthetic arm was tangled in the jump snug and she couldn't extract it.

Barre pushed her back down into the temporal-damping foam with one hand on her collarbone.

"I need to get up." As weak as her voice was, it still rang with command.

"You need to listen to me." Barre echoed his mother's absolute authority.

She cursed and fought against his restraining hold.

"You may be second in command on Daedalus," Barre

said. "But here, you're my patient. And you're in no condition to be up and around."

"Don't be an idiot."

That might have bothered Barre a few months ago, but not anymore. He whistled for Halcyone to open a channel to Ro.

"When do we leave, Cap? We have a patient here who needs to be transported as soon as possible."

Gutierrez stopped pushing against him. Barre lifted his hand away.

"Stand by," Ro said. "Change of plans."

"Barre? Dev and I are taking Charon's ship and heading back to the Hub."

"Wait. You're leaving?"

"Of course they're leaving," Gutierrez said. "What do you think would happen if Rotherwood and his companion returned to Daedalus with you?"

"She's right," Micah said. "Too many questions we don't have the right kind of answers for."

"Emma? I mean Lieutenant Commander?" Dev's voice broke in. "Thank you. I'm sorry about ... sorry about your friend."

"He wasn't my friend," Gutierrez snapped, but Barre saw the flash of pain and regret in her eyes.

"And I'd like to give Dev the once-over before you head off," Barre said.

"There's no time for that," Gutierrez said. "You weren't the only ones that bartender sold Maldonado's tracking frequency to."

"So that's how the buyers were able to find my father's

ship."

"And it's how we tracked it. By the way, Captain Maldonado, what you did to your father's business associates? That was very well done." Gutierrez seemed completely sincere in her praise. "I don't believe we should wait around until others find us here. Eventually, you'll run out of escape pods."

"But my father's ship is destroyed," Ro said.

Again, the LC winced. "The tracker will have pinged this system as its last known location. We need to move."

"Sorry, Barre, no time for big goodbyes. I'll check in when we're back in New Chicago."

"Thank you," Dev said. "Micah is lucky to have friends like you."

"Take care of yourself—both of you." There was so much more he wanted to say, but there wasn't time.

The comms link dropped and Barre stared past Gutierrez toward the door as if he could see all the way to the airlock.

"And it's time for me to go, too," Gutierrez said.

"Go? Go where? You can hardly sit, much less stand."

"If you thought you would face uncomfortable scrutiny for having the two of them on board, what do you suspect will happen when you return from your supposed refitting trip to Eurydice Station with me here, injured, and without my companion?" Her face soured at that last word.

"Charon. You knew him."

Gutierrez's voice was very still and quiet. "I knew him. His name was Taro Odachi. He abandoned it a long time ago and no one is left to mourn the man he was."

"Will you?" Barre asked.

"No."

Barre checked her IV bag even though he knew it was all set, but it gave him an excuse to avoid making eye contact and gave her privacy. Using his neural as if he were composing music, he drafted a quick message to Ro.

/Situation here with Gutierrez. Hold return program. Will keep you apprised./

When he looked up, tears glittered in Gutierrez's dark eyes.

"What happened?"

She glared at him. "I need to get off this ship before we all end up as space debris. Or worse."

"And where will you go?"

"I need you to grab the flitter. I'll make it back to Daedalus on my own. "

"You and what pilot?"

"I'll manage."

"Your right arm is barely functional. If you use it, you'll start bleeding again. Your prosthesis doesn't respond to your commands anymore. And you're going to manually fly a flitter back to Daedalus?"

"It's jump-capable and I've done more with fewer assets."

"There are quicker ways of committing suicide, Lieutenant Commander," Ro said. "I don't recommend any of them, but they do exist." She stood on the threshold, frowning. "We can dock with the flitter, but there's no way I'm going to let you fly it all the way to Daedalus."

"You don't really have a choice, Maldonado."

"Actually, I do. I'm captain here. Your authority through Daedalus doesn't supersede mine on this ship."

This could be interesting. Even as injured as she was, the LC was a formidable opponent. But Ro wasn't in the habit of backing down.

Gutierrez rolled her eyes. "It's not about whose plasma rifle is the longest. Think, Ro. Having me aboard is dangerous. For me. For you. For Ithaka."

"Fine. Even if you could manage at the helm—and that's up to Barre to decide, not me—what story will you tell them that they'll believe?"

"That Charon ... That Taro and I went after your father, acting on an anonymous tip."

Again, Barre saw the flash of pain in her expression.

"That Taro had a grudge against Maldonado and he came to me because we served together in the war."

He wondered how much of that was the truth of their history together.

"That I boarded Maldonado's ship and attempted to capture him, but he had been prepared. That he disabled me and had mined his own engines, planning to escape in the flitter before blowing up the ship. That Taro rescued me, shoved me aboard Maldonado's flitter, and went back to ensure the smuggler would die in his own trap. "

"Along with Taro," Barre said softly.

"Yes," Gutierrez replied.

"Will they buy that?" Barre asked.

"I'm a decorated Commonwealth war hero and have served in one capacity or another for over forty years. Besides, look at me."

Certainly, Gutierrez had served. But not only for the Commonwealth. "And if there's even a hint of suspicion about you?"

"Then my coming in alone is in your best interest."

"Barre, we don't have time for this," Ro finally said. "If the LC wants to be a martyr, there's nothing we can do to prevent her. We have to get back. I have to help Nomi."

Gutierrez again tried to sit up.

"If you open the dressings on your burn, I swear, I will sedate you," Barre warned.

She slumped back on the bunk. "What have you powered into this time?" she asked.

"I don't know. But Nomi's been detained on Daedalus," Ro said. "Do you have any intel on her?"

"It's obvious, isn't it? Someone higher up in the chain of command has decided it's time to get to you through your greatest weakness."

"If you're not willing to help us, then I want you off my ship." Ro turned to Barre. "Can you get her in any condition to travel?"

"I don't advise it, Ro."

"I didn't ask if you recommended it," she snapped. "Can you do it?"

Gutierrez closed her eyes. "I warned you. More than once. And I warned Nakamura, too. The path you're traveling is one full of painful decisions and necessary sacrifices."

"Nomi is not a sacrifice!"

"Then Ithaka will be. Are you willing to risk all those lives and the outbreak of a galactic war for one person's safety? I knew May was wrong to trust you."

"So that's it? You won't help us? Nomi doesn't deserve this and you know it," Ro said. Her voice cracked.

The LC turned her face to the wall.

"Fine. I have half a mind to throw you out of the airlock. See how far that gets you."

Gutierrez turned back to stare at Ro. "So there are some hard decisions you're prepared to make."

"Ro," Barre warned. Getting into a sparring match—even just a verbal one—with the LC was a bad idea.

"You might have been able to trade Nomi's safety for your father, but he's dead. As far as the Commonwealth is concerned, you have nothing of value except your knowledge of Ithaka and I can't let you betray her."

"But no one knows we found it," Ro said.

"Oh, they know you found it. They just can't prove it. There's a difference."

Barre narrowed his eyes and pursed his lips, thinking. "We do have something worth trading."

Ro and Gutierrez stared at him, Ro's gaze full of a desperate hope, the LC's skeptical.

"Your father's memory cube. We can offer it in exchange for Nomi's freedom."

"And where will you say you got it? Found it laying around on Eurydice?"

"I stole it from his workshop on Daedalus," Ro said. "So what?"

"So it ties you to him and whatever information's on it in ways you don't really want," Gutierrez said. "Especially for Konomi's sake."

"We can't just do nothing!" Ro's shout set the instruments in Barre's room vibrating in sympathy.

"Please," Barre said. "Don't punish Ro for what you've

lost. I don't think that's how Ada would want to honor Taro's sacrifice."

"What do you understand about sacrifice?" she said and turned her head to the wall once more.

Ro looked ready to snap back at Gutierrez. Barre pushed her into the corridor. "Go back to the bridge. You're not helping here."

She opened her mouth and closed it again as Barre shot her a warning look.

"Fine."

Barre returned to Gutierrez's side. "I know about loss. And guilt." His sense of responsibility for his brother's injury was never far from Barre's mind. "But I also know about forgiveness."

"You're as bad as Ada," she said.

"Do you want to talk about it?"

Gutierrez faced Barre once again and he had never seen her face look so open and so vulnerable before.

"No," she said. "But I'll help Konomi if I can."

"Thank you."

They sat in silence for a moment.

"You can say you found it."

Gutierrez blinked up at him with pain-clouded eyes.

"The memory device. Tell them you found it on Maldonado's ship. Hand it over to the Commonwealth. It'll give them something more useful to chew on than Nomi."

"Your captain doesn't trust me."

Barre sighed. "I'll take care of that."

"Now, what can you do to get me ready to fly?"

He could give her another adrenaline boost, but it would

only be temporary and wouldn't last the entire way back to Daedalus. Besides, she would fare better during the jumps on Halcyone.

He had the AI open a comms channel to the bridge. "Ro?"

"What." She sounded resigned and more than a little mad at him.

"Can you push your proposed flight parameters to me? I have an idea."

"Fine."

Barre knew from the tone in her voice that it wasn't fine, but she would do it anyway.

"You're different from the belligerent child you used to be," Gutierrez said.

"Guilty as charged. But she's changed, too. And not just because she's free of her father." He didn't need to name Nomi. Gutierrez understood. "Okay," Barre said, after he'd quickly scanned Ro's flight plan. "I can boost you enough to function for about an hour or two. Beyond that, there are consequences both to your heart and your wounds that I won't risk."

Gutierrez started to protest, but Barre put his hand on her chest again.

"We'll stop in interstitial space one jump before Daedalus. Then we'll strap you into the flitter and program the autopilot. You can take it from there."

She stopped struggling against his hold and exhaled. "For a musician, you're not such a bad negotiator."

He gave her a lopsided grin. "You should see me program."

Chapter 29

"ARE YOU SURE you don't want Barre to take a look at you before we leave?" Micah asked, glancing at Dev from the pilot's seat of Charon's well-worn scout.

She was fumbling with the copilot's harness. Micah had to resist the urge to get up and adjust it for her.

"No. I'm fine." She finally dogged down the harness and Micah exhaled. "And will you stop staring at me like that?"

Micah turned away to hide the heat rising to his face. "Like what?"

"Like I'm going to vanish or maybe fall apart. I'm not. On either score."

He didn't bother to apologize this time; it would only infuriate her. "Fine." The comms channel between the scout and Halcyone was still open. "Ro? Will you have Halcyone double-check our course? I've managed to link my micro to this ship's AI, but it's primitive. No voice integration."

There was a long pause before Ro responded. "Your course back to the Hub looks good. Are you sure the command chairs will provide enough protection?"

"They're actually top of the line. And so are her engines." Which was odd, given the appearance of the rest of the ship and the stripped-down AI interface. There were a couple of jump tubes built into the corridor, but they were probably original to the scout. The chairs and the drives were definitely retrofits. "Honestly, it'll be a more comfortable trip than either the one from Daedalus or the outbound one to Eurydice."

"Then you're clear to disengage. Be safe out there."

"I'll do my best."

"Send a secured message when you've arrived."

"Roger that. And Ro?" He didn't wait for a reply. "Nomi will be okay."

Ro didn't respond.

"Micah?"

He turned to Dev. Her dark eyes were narrowed and her normally animated face, expressionless and stiff.

"How much of what you told me in the biodome was the truth?"

He had been dreading this conversation. "All of it. I just couldn't tell you everything then. It would have betrayed confidences I needed to keep."

Dev nodded. "And now?"

Micah delayed answering and busied himself for launch. It was trickier because he couldn't use direct voice commands, but, while he wasn't as proficient in gestural controls as Ro, he could get the job done. "We're going to take a shallow burn. Are you ready?"

She nodded again.

"Disengagement and launch in ten." He counted down

the seconds.

A loud clang reverberated through the ship before it hurled itself into interstitial space, pushing Micah and Dev into their cushioned seats. The burn lasted for only a handful of minutes, but they always seemed endless to Micah. The scout skimmed along at just under a single gravity. They would reach their first wormhole in less than an hour.

"We need to figure out what to tell our respective programs at Uni," he said.

"No. You need to tell me the full story first."

There was no threat in her voice, only a terrible weariness that Micah also felt in the deep ache in the muscles of his neck and the relentless throb of his damaged feet. He was so damned good at lying and evading, but she deserved better. He owed her better. "It's complicated." He struggled to pull his thoughts together.

"What part of getting abducted and threatened and nearly killed isn't complicated?"

Micah winced. "I'm sor—"

"Stop. Just stop. No more empty apologies. I think we owe one another the truth, Micah Michael Chase." She paused. "Is that even your real name?"

"The Michael is. Only no one's ever called me that. It's always been Micah." His mother started calling him that when he was a toddler. It was how he had pronounced his own name and it stuck, despite his father's dislike of the nickname. Maybe it was childish, but he couldn't let go of the last vestige of his mother in his life. "Chase was my mother's family name. She officially changed it when she married my father."

"That's a little old-fashioned. Was she a traddie?"

"Not really." It was something his father had asked her to do for the sake of his political career, and she had done it. She'd done everything for him. At one time, that would have infuriated him. Now, he just felt tired. Micah stared down at the controls, even though the ship was perfectly stable and on its flight path. He dreaded her reaction. "My name is Micah Rotherwood."

Dev remained silent.

Micah took a deep breath. Was she waiting for him to spell out his humiliation? Fine. He would own his past. "As in Senator Corwin Rotherwood."

"Oh."

He risked a glance at her face. She looked puzzled more than repulsed.

"Wasn't he put on trial for something illegal a few years back?"

"Um, yeah," Micah said. "You could say that." He shook his head and then he started to laugh.

"What?"

It took several minutes for Micah to get himself under control. "That's really all you know about my father?"

"We really don't pay much attention to politics in Midlant."

"Wow. That's actually kind of refreshing." The laughter was still pressing against his chest and he swallowed hard.

"It's hard to care about scandals when you're worrying about survival." She shrugged. "In a way, growing up in the settlements was a little bit like being on an outer colony. If it doesn't bring more food to the table or credit to your account, it's not all that important."

"Serves him right."

"Who?"

"My father. He always had an inflated sense of his own importance."

"Maldonado said he was dead."

He would always picture his father the way he'd looked in the generic body bag on Daedalus's sick bay. The slack face had been gray and empty of the manipulative charm that had defined him. "It's a long story."

"I think we have the time."

Micah checked the flight plan displayed on his micro. Fifty-two minutes left until their first jump. But where should he start? With his mother's illness? The bittergreen he'd smuggled in for her? Or Halcyone and Maldonado?

"So you and Ro have father issues," Dev said into the silence.

"You could say that." And now they both were without fathers. Which was for the best, on both counts. Maybe he should start with Maldonado and work backward. "Okay. So Ro, Barre, and I all know each other from Daedalus Station. It's a small outpost guarding a pretty insignificant wormhole. That ship we were on? Halcyone? She was an old, crashed freighter that the original station had been built around." It seemed so simple in the retelling. So logical. As if it had all happened to someone else. "For me, it was a botany lab. For Ro, a chance to prove herself to Uni if she could fix its damaged AI. For Barre, a way to escape his folks.

"We were all aboard—me, Ro, Barre, and Barre's brother, Jem—when something Ro did triggered the AI to reboot and make an emergency lift-off from the station." This quick and dirty explanation left out the fear, the anger, and the distrust that had flared among them. "The ship was out of control. We got banged around pretty badly. Jem was hurt the worst."

In his memory, the acrid scent of urine linked taking care of Jem with taking care of his mother as she was dying. At least Jem was getting better. He was glad his father's ill-gotten money had led to some good.

"And Ro's father? How does he fit in?"

It was harder to talk about this part without reliving the pain of the cuffs and the brutal choice Micah had made to blast his way free of them. "He and my father were using Halcyone's storage bay to hide the weapons and military supplies I told you about. When the ship took off with us, it also took their goods."

"And they wanted them back."

"Ro's father was on the ship that tracked us down. He got aboard and threatened us."

"Even his own daughter?"

Micah nodded. "Trust me, Ro won't be mourning him anytime soon."

Dev winced. "I'm sorry."

"Don't be." They both fell silent for a long moment. Micah wondered about her missing parents, but he didn't think he'd earned enough of her trust to ask. "The part about the restraints and my burns you already know." He closed his eyes, willing away the memories. The smell of Gutierrez's burns had nearly triggered a panic attack when he'd stepped into the cockpit earlier. He thought he'd gotten better.

"What happened to the weapons?"

That was an easier question to answer, one that was a little bit removed from his charred feet. "Ro managed to trap her father in engineering on Halcyone, but he escaped in a lifepod. We got the ship back to Daedalus and traded the contraband and information about our fathers for immunity and citizenship."

"Your father. How did he die?"

Micah replayed the audio in his mind: his father trying to bluster his way through their accusations and then his incoherent shouts followed by the sound of weapons firing. As far as he knew, there was still a discolored spot in Commander Mendez's office to mark the place where his father had killed a security officer and then shot himself. "He deserved to spend the rest of his life in prison. Instead, he took the easy way out." Not like his mother. The good senator made sure he didn't suffer.

"I'm sorry."

"Don't be," he repeated. "I'm not." Micah couldn't decipher the expression on Dev's face, but it made him examine his anger in a way that nothing else had—not his friends' sympathy, not Dr. Leto Durbin's attempt to convince him to see a therapist. This definitely wasn't the time to delve into his complicated relationship with his late father.

"So Maldonado abducted me trying to punish you?"

"Sort of. The Commonwealth stripped him of citizenship and his assets. Which happened to include the first half of the payment for the weapons. And the Commonwealth also had the weapons. Maldonado's buyers were less than thrilled. My father, on the other hand, given his connections, had been able to hide his share of the money."

"Then Maldonado was going after you."

Micah curled his toes in his shoes and winced. "Yeah. My father left him holding the proverbial bag. I'm betting he was looking forward to another chance at me."

A long silence fell between them. Micah checked their time. Another thirty-two minutes to the jump.

"I'm sorry you got tangled up in this. I never thought ..." What could he say? He never thought he'd have a roommate or find in her a friend. It seemed like he wasn't a very safe friend to have.

"And that's it?"

"What do you mean?"

"We go back to Uni and head to class, like nothing happened?"

Micah had honestly not thought that far. Hadn't really thought beyond what he was going to tell Dr. Parrish about his absence. And then get back to his work with the bittergreen. "What is there to do? Maldonado's dead. He can't hurt anyone anymore."

"And the buyers? What happens when they pick up where Maldonado left off?"

"They won't."

"The hell they won't! I may be just a settlement rat, but I'm not stupid. I know smugglers. I know how they operate. Your father cheated them. They won't stop until they're satisfied you've paid his debt. One way or another."

"I paid them off."

"With what? From what I can tell, you have a fast micro and a few cases of belongings. Unless you're hiding a bittergreen stash, I don't see what you could hope to sell to pay off that kind of obligation."

"Not hardly." Bittergreen. That was rich. In reality, that's what got him into this mess in the first place. "Well, since you may be the only person in the cosmos who doesn't know about Corwin Rotherwood and his myriad crimes, I guess I have to tell you." He summarized his father's financial exploits: his connection with the cartels, his propensity for cheating people out of their hard-earned credit, his ability to slither his way out of most of the consequences. "I used my father's money to pay off Maldonado's debt. It seemed fitting." Micah didn't think the buyers would be eager to throw more credit into revenge even after Ro destroyed their ship. It was bad for business.

"Well, I get why you changed your name."

If only he could as easily separate himself from the guilt he carried about his mother and the drugs he'd gotten for her pain during her long illness. It didn't matter that he knew the cartels were looking for any way to hook the senator and that he had simply been a convenient means to that end. From the perspective of this side of the wormhole, Micah understood that in the senator's own twisted, self-centered way, his father must have loved him. Otherwise he wouldn't have gone to such lengths to protect Micah all these years. Or maybe it was just the way he protected his own name and perceived legacy.

It didn't matter. He'd never know the truth now, anyway. Dev had fallen silent. He wondered what she was thinking.

"He changed his name, too."

"Huh?"

"Charon. Emma Gutierrez called him Taro. She said something ... about him changing his name, but not being able to leave the past behind." Dev drew her brows together, concentrating. "She threatened him. Said they weren't on Ithaka anymore."

Micah pretended to busy himself with the controls.

"I may not have heard a lot about your father, but I know what Ithaka was." Her eyes widened and she drew in a sharp breath. "Or is. And you and your friends weren't surprised to see Gutierrez. You knew the two of them were coming. What aren't you telling me?"

That was definitely not his story to tell. But he wasn't sure how he could explain that to Dev without losing the tenuous trust they'd seemed to have developed. "It really is complicated. And I wasn't part of it. That's something you're going to have to ask Ro or Barre about."

A slow anger burned in her gaze.

"I'm not trying to put you off. I swear. You're part of this now, even if you don't want to be, and you deserve to know everything."

Her dark eyes softened. The skin beneath them was puffy and discolored. She needed a full-body med scan, a hot shower, a real meal, and a few days' real rest. Micah feared they'd have a lot of questions to answer and very little else.

"I'm sorry. There are too many lives at stake and even I only know the barest part of the story."

"Then tell me what you do know." Dev blinked back tears. "Tell me Ithaka truly exists. Tell me that the Commonwealth doesn't control everything in the damned universe."

Her passion and her anger stunned him.

"You really have no idea what it was like to grow up in the settlements."

The history was something he had studied in school. The building of the thousands of settlements world-wide was one of the greatest public works programs in the history of the planet, and evacuating the cities post-Drowning was Earth's greatest diaspora. But Micah had never lived on Earth before coming to Uni. Had never seen the new cities that grew out of the settlements or met someone who had been raised in one, though such places couldn't have been pleasant.

"Tell me Ithaka isn't an old spacer's tale and I'll show you where I grew up." She blinked and looked away. "And maybe you'll understand why I need to know."

He hoped that Ro would understand. "Yes. Ithaka exists. Charon was from there. So was this ship." Which could pose a problem, once they return to Earth.

Dev's soft gasp filled the cabin. For several moments, she remained silent.

Micah checked the countdown. They had only another ten minutes before their first jump. "We're going to have to tell them something. We've both missed several days of classes."

"I know." She laughed and it was tinged with bitterness. "They'll probably think I washed out like my brother. It's what they expect from a settlement rat."

"Hey. Stop that."

She looked at him with such defeat in her expression that Micah nearly turned away. "You are one of the most resourceful and resilient people I've ever met. And if you truly got to know Ro Maldonado, you'd know what a compliment that is. When we get to someplace safe and you've had a chance to recover, I want to hear what happened on that ship. I suspect my opinion of you will go even more stratospheric."

Dev's cheeks flushed a deep bronze.

"First things first. We can't just land this ship at New Chicago's spaceport. There's a chance it could be linked to Ithaka and we can't take that risk." Micah drummed his fingers on the console. "But there are private docks available. And I haven't quite expiated my father's guilt.

"Then there's the matter of my healing wounds. I do have orders from my treating physician back on Daedalus for follow-up. I had a problem with the grafts dealing with Earth gravity and needed to consult with him. How does that sound?"

"What if they check with the doctor?"

"Why would they? But just in case, I can have Ro or Barre figure out something once they're back on station." What Barre could do now with the ship's AI was astonishing. Barre was astonishing. Micah hoped he knew that.

Dev played with what looked like a translucent blade with a thick handle. "I suppose I could have had a family emergency." She sighed. "They probably won't care enough to check. After all, if I fail and drop out, they'll replace me and pocket the scholarship money."

"Did you make that?" Micah nodded toward the knife.

"Maldonado left me a case of water bulbs. His mistake." Dev pulled out some other tools from the pockets of Ro's coverall. "Some I made, others I found. And I was able to use Sellen's cube to trigger local EMPs."

"Huh. Too bad you won't get life experience credit for

your mini-course aboard his ship."

She met his smile with her own and this time the light was back in her eyes. "And after this, nothing Sellen can throw my way will rattle me."

"No, I guess not." His micro blared a sixty-second warning. "Your harness set?"

Dev nodded.

"See you on the other side."

They sat in silence, watching the countdown. At the ten-second mark, Dev called his name. He blinked and looked up from his micro.

"Thank you," she said.

He nodded.

And then there was no more time for words as time and space involuted and the little ship jumped.

Chapter 30

As Ro waited for Barre's signal, she checked and rechecked the fight plan. If it had been only her on Halcyone, Ro would have had the AI calculate the deepest burn and most direct jump path, but Barre would shove her out of the airlock in a leaky p-suit before he'd let her put his patient at risk.

Worry for Nomi kept fragmenting her concentration. Would they transfer her off station? How would Ro find her? Regardless of the consequences, Ro was going to find Nomi. And secure her freedom. Even at the cost of her own.

She patted the command console, glad Barre wasn't here to see her. Though Ro was the one who mocked his anthropomorphizing of the AI and the ship, she understood Halcyone was more than the code and mechanicals that allowed it to fly. The ship was also an expression of Ro's own creativity and passion. But having Halcyone meant little without Nomi.

For the first time in Ro's life, she was enmeshed in a rich

web of relationships and for a brief moment, she wished she could have gone back to her old, isolated life. It may have been cold and empty as vacuum, but she wasn't sure she could live with the pain of losing her friends. Of losing Nomi.

Barre's voice broke into her racing thoughts, startling her.

"We're secure. I'll stay with Gutierrez until it's time to transfer her to the flitter. Unless you need help on the bridge."

"No. Halcyone has already plotted an intercept." Ro's hand hovered over her micro, ready to go.

"Okay. See you on the other side."

"Roger that."

She triggered the program and Halcyone's maneuvering thrusters fired in short bursts.

"Come on, come on, come on," she urged.

The ship moved with such excruciating slowness, it was hard for her not to wrest control from the AI and fly the ship manually. But Ro knew she'd most likely overshoot the flitter and take twice as long to match trajectories. It seemed to take another age for Halcyone to dock securely with the small ship. As soon as she got confirmation of lockdown, Ro sprinted for her cabin. Once trussed in her bunk, she set the route toward Daedalus in motion.

The short burn was simply an annoyance. The first jump sent her anxiety over Nomi into overdrive. Two more jumps with brief trips through interstitial space and they would be somewhere they could safely jettison Gutierrez in the flitter. Then one final short jump and they'd be back. Daedalus Station. Nomi.

Her stomach roiled, and not from the temporal travel.

A few hours of subjective time later Halcyone finally came to a dead stop, signaling the all-clear. Ro rolled out of her bunk and ran to the bridge.

"Halcyone, display current position and scan for ships."

The view screen brightened to life, showing an empty starscape. "No ships currently within hailing distance in local space, Captain Maldonado."

"Internal comms. Durbin, Barre."

"Open."

"Barre? Whatever you're going to power up Gutierrez with, now would be a good time."

"Working on it."

"Can you get her to the flitter?"

"Yeah. Just get the ship's flight plan programmed. I'll meet you aboard."

"Ro, out." While Halcyone was drawing up a flight plan to Daedalus for the flitter, Ro snatched her father's memory cube from her coverall pocket and turned it over in her hand. Just a dull, metallic box, a few centimeters tall. Such a harmless-looking thing. Her father had never been harmless.

For the entirety of her life, he'd been an isotope always on the verge of critical. The fact that no one seemed to realize his volatility made Ro constantly question herself all the while she worked to contain him. She slammed the cube down on the nav console and pressed the heels of her hands to her eyes.

The tears weren't for him. The truth was, Ro was more afraid now than when he'd been the major threat to her life. She'd expected to feel more satisfaction at the bright, hot explosion of his ship.

Barre was right. Having Gutierrez turn over the cube would divert suspicion from Ro and by extension, Nomi. But she wasn't going to hand it over without cloning its contents.

She scrubbed the wetness from her cheeks and tapped the box. A slender needle emerged from the far corner and she jabbed her index finger on it. A single drop of blood was all it needed to unlock. It would be interesting to see how long it took the Commonwealth to figure that one out.

After setting the cube down, Ro pressed her thumb against her index finger until the bleeding stopped. Then she slid her micro from the pocket and created a virtual machine where she could quarantine a copy of the data.

There was some old Greek myth about a box. Pandora's box. And what was inside brought chaos to the world.

There was no doubt that her father's data would do the same.

Halcyone had finished the flight plan several minutes before Ro was done with the memory device and the AI's alert tones took on increasing urgency as if it was growing impatient.

Now she was seeing the AI the way Nomi did. Her almost-smile died as suddenly as it appeared. Halcyone passed the flight parameters to Ro's micro and she raced to the airlock. Barre appeared nearly simultaneously, his arms supporting the LC as they stumbled along the ship's corridor.

Ro wasn't sure Gutierrez could manage to sit in the command chair, much less fly the flitter. But Halcyone would ensure she didn't have to.

"Here, let me help you," Ro said. She cycled the airlock. The three of them squeezed inside. Ro brushed by

Gutierrez's prosthetic arm and it swung at the woman's side, like a pendulum.

Barre grunted with the effort of supporting the injured LC, but waved off Ro's assistance. "Just get the damned door."

Gutierrez remained silent, her face lined with pain and as gray as regolith. Ro opened the flitter-side of the lock. She looked up at Barre, afraid to ask if the LC was going to make it back to Daedalus alive.

Sweat beaded across Barre's forehead and the cords of his neck stood out as he lurched with Gutierrez toward the pilot's chair. The woman gave a muffled grunt as Barre half-lowered, half-dropped her into it. She swayed when Barre let go of her to take a syringe from his pocket. Ro rushed forward to support her, realizing almost too late that Gutierrez had little use of either of her arms.

How was the LC going to do anything on this flitter except die?

"You'd better remove the dressing on my arm."

"Not a good idea," Barre said.

"It's conceivable for me to have dealt with the burn one-handed, but to dress my only functional arm? I don't think so."

"Fine." Barre carefully unwound the dressing. "They'll notice the glue."

Gutierrez grimaced. "Maybe my arm gave out after I sealed the cut."

"I don't like any of this."

"Secure the webbing, Captain." Gutierrez's voice was frayed.

Ro hurried to stabilize her in the chair before loading the program from her micro to the bare-bones AI on the flitter. Like the computer on Charon's ship, this one had no manufactured personality and no synthesized voice. But it could manage the quantum calculations needed for wormhole travel.

"Okay. Done." She tried to catch Barre's gaze again, but he had gone back to frowning down at Gutierrez.

"I'm not happy about this," he said, tapping the syringe with his index finger.

"Happy isn't part of the equation, Mr. Durbin." Gutierrez tried to straighten her spine, but she just slumped against the webbing. "The longer you delay, the worse my chances get."

Barre swore softly under his breath.

"Do you have your father's storage device?"

"If you betray Nomi, I swear I will end you." Ro tucked it inside the webbing with shaking hands.

"Get in line," Gutierrez said. "Now, if you please, Mr. Durbin."

"Good luck," he whispered before leaning over her to inject the cocktail into the base of her neck. Gutierrez didn't even wince.

Ro did.

"See you on the other side," the woman rasped.

Barre stood, passing the empty syringe from hand to hand.

"Clock is ticking," Ro said.

"She's right. You've done all you could do. Don't waste this."

Ro took the syringe from him and gently turned him toward the airlock. And Daedalus. And Nomi.

*

Jem paced the confines of his room muttering to himself. "Follow the data. Follow the damned data." He was going to have to burn through whatever concentration he had left if he was to be any help at all to Nomi. The info dumped from the worm was organized into three virtual folders on his micro. One for basic station personnel data, one for Lowell's communications, and the one with his suspicious financials.

Combing through them all manually would take more time and more focus than he had. Maybe he could program a scan-and-sort routine. But what was he going to look for?

He stopped and collapsed on his bed, his arms folded across his eyes. Where to start? Okay. There were some things they knew for sure: Lowell was getting hidden credit by way of some Commonwealth source. To do something. According to Nomi, he also said he'd done some work with Ro's father. Which was likely related to the smuggling operation or something else equally illegal. He was hot to find Ithaka and ostensibly claim the prize money.

But what if that wasn't the only reason?

Was Lowell controlling both ends of the wormhole?

So Jem needed to look for links between him and Ro's father for a start. Accessing his neural, Jem set up a search parameter for Maldonado's name. He directed the utility to the folders on his micro. At least he could rest his brain while it did its work. He got why Ro kept her library of little programs at the ready.

Jem rolled over onto his stomach, waiting. His micro beeped at the same instant he noticed a flashing light at the corner of his closed eyes. All it took was a brief glance toward the signal and three virtual windows opened in his mind.

There was nothing in the financial records that hinted at any connection between the men. Nor were there any messages that referenced Maldonado or were sent to or received from him. A dead end. He quickly scanned the third window with the results from the personnel records.

"Huh."

He paused the scroll and went back to the top of the page.

There were work orders. A lot of work orders. All initiated by Lowell and all for minor or routine issues, mainly in comms. They had all been logged as completed during third shift. And they stopped abruptly just a few months ago. After that, the work orders changed. They became less frequent, and they were for issues inside Lowell's quarters, instead.

Jem had a hunch and checked the dates on Lowell's work orders against Nomi's service record. The work orders in comms had stopped after Nomi arrived at the station and command changed the comms duty schedule.

He didn't need to check against Lowell's work history to know that all the work orders would have been closed out during his periodic stints on third shift. That's how they shared and passed information.

But who was Lowell's money source? Who was he reporting to?

Okay. So Lowell was in charge of comms. That meant he

had access to the ansible logs. How easy would it be to divert messages or alter the headers? Impossible for most station personnel, but probably not hard for the comms supervisor. If Jem was right, there might be a way to assess whether messages were tampered with. He probably wouldn't be able to read them, but if there was a pattern to the changes, it might tell him something.

Jem rolled back onto his back. His head ached. "Not now," he muttered. He reached for the cup of water and package with the sedatives on the bedside table. It was the last dose he'd be able to get for hours.

Waiting until the meds took effect wasn't in the program. Jem sighed and set up a new search. Every file had its metadata. All he had to do was find ansible messages with a discrepancy between when they arrived, when they were logged, and when they were last accessed by comms personnel. The vast majority of traffic should have all three occur on the same date and at the same time. Whoever was communicating with Lowell wouldn't necessarily always know when he was on shift. So there had to be messages that arrived that he altered to some other time.

There had to be a pattern. There had to be.

"Jeremy, you were supposed to be here nearly an hour ago for your scan."

He jumped up as his mother's voice filled his room. Shit. "On my way."

She wasn't above sending a security detail for him if he didn't come voluntarily. Jem tucked his micro in a pocket and headed to medical. The search program would alert him when it was complete. Until then, he needed to placate his mother. Ro hadn't contacted him yet. For Nomi's sake, he hoped she was on her way back. And for his own, he'd better find something in Lowell's records that would help.

He nodded to the tech on call who smiled and pointed to the back of medical, where the treatment rooms were. His mother was waiting for him, her arms folded across her chest, her foot tapping the floor. Having her act as parent, doctor, and parole officer was intolerable, but Jem didn't know how to get out of the agreement he had made. Under duress, to be sure, but he had agreed.

"I want to do a full scan."

"Fine." Jem hopped up onto the padded table.

She slipped a visor over his head. It was similar to what Dr. Land had done during the neural implant procedure.

"Focus on the blinking light at the center of your visual field."

"Fine." He stared straight ahead. Eventually, his eyes would start their mad dance. His mother would be measuring how long it took for the nystagmus to start, along with its frequency and amplitude. Jem knew it had gotten better, but she wouldn't be satisfied until he was quantified and recorded.

"When was your last dose of the neo-benzo?"

"About a half-hour ago."

"That's too soon."

He knew that, too, but how could he explain to her that he needed to function. "Yes, Mom."

An alarm wailed through medical and Jem jerked his head away from the visor.

"Emergency. Flitter crash on south launch pad. One

occupant. Response team Alpha on scene."

"Patch me through to the team," his mother said in her rock-steady voice.

Jem pushed the visor away from his face and sat up.

"Stay here," she warned.

His father's voice filled the small exam room. "Emmaline Gutierrez. Multiple injuries. Patient in shock. Prep the burn chamber."

Fear thudded through him. What had happened out there? He gripped his micro. The secret data was suddenly real and deadly—no longer just a hack, just a challenge. Had they found Ro's father? If anything had happened to Ro, Nomi's future was in his hands alone. Shit.

Jem wouldn't have left medical even if his mother had kicked him out. He stood back as the entire staff prepared for the incoming patient. It was a well-practiced choreography where every person knew their role. There was no haste and no unneeded chatter. In less than two minutes, medical was transformed into an urgent response unit.

They wheeled Gutierrez in on a PCU, its monitors beeping their warnings. A central line was already pouring fluids in her as fast as it could. They had cut away her clothing and her body was gray against the white sheet they had thrown over her. Except for the silver gleam of her prosthetic arm. The sheet slid away from her left shoulder, revealing the juncture between puckered, damaged flesh and cybernetic implant.

Jem looked away, uncomfortable with how vulnerable the old soldier looked.

The staff rushed her past him, through the UV pulse

generator, and into a sterile surgical suite. Jem knew the drill. If she had an open airway and wasn't in danger of bleeding out, they would have to manage the burns first.

He stood outside the suite, watching as his father handed Gutierrez over to his mother. She directed one team to the LC's leg and one to her intact arm. His father moved to her head and took point on the monitors.

What happened? Where was Charon? Jem frowned down at his silent micro. He wanted to jump out of his own skin or run into the room and demand answers from Gutierrez. Instead, he leaned his head against the glass wall and watched the silent medical ballet. A blinking light in the corner of his eye distracted him. He turned toward the alert, wondering what was happening to the LC, and realized it was from his search program.

His heart sped up as he reviewed the results. There were messages with discrepancies in the header time stamps. And they were all from Hephaestus.

Targill's ship.

Chapter 31

RO WATCHED BARRE communicate with Daedalus and envied his outward calm. The closer they had gotten to the station, the more anxious Ro had become. She hadn't trusted herself to message Jem, for fear of saying something to him she would end up regretting. It wasn't his fault, even if it would be convenient to have some target for her tangled emotions.

"Halcyone, you are cleared to land. Please be advised, there is an ongoing emergency on the south launch pad."

"Thank you, Daedalus." Barre closed the comms link.

"So she made it back," Ro said. It hadn't been a sure thing by any means.

"She's a fighter."

Ro nodded. Gutierrez deserved her admiration and despite the LC's continual reluctance to help them, she had nearly died to rescue Dev. Charon had. "Do you think she'll survive?"

"My folks will do all they can."

"All right. Let's get this boat docked." Ro let Barre glide

Halcyone in for a landing. The reality was, he could probably fly the ship without her. The reverse might not be true. It didn't bother her as much as it once might have.

As soon as they reconnected with Daedalus, Ro queried the station's AI for Nomi.

"Unavailable. Please contact command for further information about ... Nakamura, Konomi."

Her breath caught in her throat at the sound of Nomi's voice at the end of the message. *Unavailable. Shit.* Had she already been taken off station? She started at the weight and warmth of Barre's hand on her shoulder.

He stood behind her on the bridge, a comforting, silent presence.

Ro reached up and squeezed his hand. *Think, Ro, think.* She couldn't hack into Daedalus's main security system: it would be too heavily firewalled. So how was she going to find Nomi? It was highly unlikely they'd let her keep her micro, but it was worth a shot.

Chewing on her lip, Ro typed a quick, generic message. /*Hey, Nomi, we just got back.*/ If anyone else had confiscated the micro, she wasn't giving anything away.

There was no reply.

She wasn't surprised at that, but she hadn't expected the crushing disappointment and the angry tears that blurred her vision.

There had to be another way. Ro stared at her micro. Then she smiled up at Barre.

"What?"

"The ghost program."

"But you're not trying to hide Nomi. You're trying to find

her."

"I left a back door. So I could locate any of you when I needed to."

"Why am I not surprised." But he was smiling.

Her little program worked via two ways—tracking their micros and working off the same ident system that the AIs used to keep tabs on them. Theoretically, Ro could find Nomi and her micro, though the little machine was not her first priority.

She opened the program in a virtual window and reached in to activate the tracker utility. If Nomi was on station, it would find her. If. A second window opened beside the first, this one showing a schematic of the entire station. Small lights indicated Ro's and Barre's position parked on Halcyone. Another light blinked in medical. That was Jem.

Barre met her gaze and raised an eyebrow. They would sort out his brother after they found Nomi.

The map winked out and redrew itself as Ro held her breath.

If they had taken her off station, Ro didn't know what she was going to do. But it wasn't going to be pretty. And it probably wouldn't be safe or wise. Barre hadn't moved from his spot behind her. His hand anchored her to the command chair, the ship, and her fragmenting thoughts.

A fourth locator light brightened on the station map and Ro remembered how to breathe.

Nomi. She was still here.

Barre leaned forward until he was nearly on top of her. "Ro? Isn't that her quarters?"

The tears that she had struggled to hold back dripped

down her cheeks. "Got you!" She wriggled out from beneath the hulking Barre and hugged him.

"Okay, Cap. Now what?"

What would happen if she just walked up to Nomi's quarters and requested entry? It didn't seem as if she was officially under arrest. Would they have revoked Ro's access? And how would they explain keeping her out, since she wasn't even supposed to know Nomi had been detained?

Barre patted Ro's spine awkwardly and stepped back. "I think she's safe for the time being. And the less attention we bring to ourselves or to Nomi, the better."

Heat rose to her face.

"Think, Ro. Let Gutierrez work her end of the bargain."

"What if she doesn't make it?"

"We'll traverse that wormhole when we get there. For now, we have a reason to check medical. Jem's there."

She hated admitting it, but Barre was right. "Give me a nano." At least she could set up an alert on the ghost program. If Nomi moved more than a few meters in any direction, her micro would tell her.

Hold on, Nomi. We're coming.

*

Her little apartment's lighting program had cycled through more than an entire day since Nomi had been escorted to her quarters. She wondered who they placed on her shift in her stead. And what would Simon think? What about Lowell?

She must have walked several kilometers back and forth across the living area this morning. Neither Mendez nor Targill had returned, though her polite minders had delivered meals. At least they weren't making her subsist on emergency rations. She'd had enough of those on Halcyone with Ro.

Ro. Where was Ro?

She'd hardly gotten more than a few hours of fitful sleep, interrupted by dreams where she was adrift in a lifepod, lost in a silent void. It wasn't hard to figure out where those images had come from. Her stomach gurgled. Somehow, it felt wrong to sit down to a meal when everything else seemed so disordered, but she had to at least try to eat.

Several trays littered the surface of her small galley's counter and Nomi uncovered the most recent one. The smell of hot peppers and aromatic spices filled the room. She picked up the bowl and frowned. This didn't come from the commissary. It was gumbo. Simon Marchand's recipe. On a commissary tray, on commissary dishware.

Which meant he knew she was under house arrest. Or quarantine. Or whatever they were calling it. Was he telling her that she couldn't just vanish without someone kicking up a fuss? She blinked back tears, absurdly comforted by the gesture.

It was a huge risk to take for such a subtle message. Why would he do that? They were friendly, to be sure, but he wasn't what she'd consider a close friend, though she enjoyed his humor and his company. And aside from his penchant for late shift turnovers, he was a good comms officer and was happy to share his experience with Nomi and the rest of the newer staff.

She examined the bowl. So why this?

There was some bad blood between Simon and Lowell. She was sure of it. Nomi just didn't know what it was and what it meant. Shit, Lowell was annoying and arrogant. That could have been enough.

Except, she couldn't convince herself that was all. She was sure he'd been trying to communicate some kind of warning to her about Lowell at breakfast a few days ago. Now, Simon had gone out of his way to cook his homemade gumbo and slip her a bowl of it, disguising it on a commissary tray. Which meant he knew she was trapped in here and under guard. There had to be a deeper message.

Whispering a brief apology to the gods of good cooking everywhere, Nomi dumped Simon's gumbo in the sink. A small slip of permapaper stuck out from the chopped celery, peppers, okra, and chunks of replicated sausage. She picked it up and rinsed off the grains of sticky rice and thick stew that clung to it. It had three words written across it.

override: alpha epsilon

She sent a pulse from her micro through the permapaper to clear it, but she still didn't feel safe. Her heart thudding, she disposed of the note along with the gumbo. After a glance at the silent door, Nomi squared her shoulders and triggered the station's AI.

"Daedalus, contact Marchand, Simon."

"Access denied. State override authority."

"Override: Alpha Epsilon."

"Stand by."

Nomi gripped the edge of the counter. Could she have

been wrong? Was this some kind of elaborate set up?

"You figured it out." Simon's voice emerged from the internal comms speakers and Nomi jerked away from the counter.

"Simon. I don't understand."

"We don't have a lot of time before my temporary disruption gets fixed by the station's AI. I know Mendez set you up as Lowell's watchdog and she got a lot better than she bargained for."

"What?"

"Just listen! She may not be able to protect you from Targill, but I can."

None of this made any sense. "What do you mean?"

"The data you mined. It's worth a lot to the right people and I'm the closest you're going to get to those people. I know you cloned whatever you gave Mendez. She has good instincts and she wants to do the right thing, but it's going to blow up in her face."

"And you?" Nomi whispered. This wasn't at all the jovial comms officer she knew. The one who no one ever got mad at. The one who was counting the days until retirement so he could return home and cook to his heart's content.

"I'm your best chance at getting out of this unscathed. But you're perilously close to knowing too much for everyone's good. Have your little friend hand over the data and walk away."

"What about Targill?"

"I can point him in another direction. But only if you do what I tell you."

Nomi shivered and wrapped Ro's quilt around her

shoulders. Even if she wanted to walk away, she knew Ro never would. Too many lives depended on keeping Ithaka safe. Not the least of which were their own.

"Simon, I—"

A burst of static blasted through her apartment and in the ear-ringing aftermath, the speakers went silent. Nomi glanced toward the now empty sink. *Holy mother of the cosmos. What was going on?*

*

Barre paused at the Halcyone's airlock and signaled Ro to wait. She was practically vibrating with impatience.

"Hang on." Medical was probably a madhouse right now. They got very few true emergencies here on Daedalus and it's pretty much what they lived for. Barre felt a little sorry for Gutierrez. He knew what that kind of attention felt like. Barging in to find Jem would only incur his parents' wrath. And probably get them thrown out anyway. "Let me try something."

"Barre ..."

She sounded like Jem used to when he was little and didn't get what he wanted. He ignored her.

He hadn't even tried to reach his brother during the chaos of the past few days. There was no reason he shouldn't have been able to, but since he still didn't really know how it all worked, it was very much a trial-and-error thing. So far, more error than trial.

"I don't want to walk in blind. The more we know, the

better position we'll be in to negotiate for Nomi."

"Fine," she muttered and stomped off down the corridor, staring down at her micro.

Barre tried to clear his mind, but it was impossible. He was weary and grubby. Between meals grabbed on the go, too many sleepless nights, and more jumps than he wanted to think about, it was a wonder he could think at all. So he closed his eyes and concentrated on his music instead.

Phrase by phrase, he built what he thought of as "Jem's theme" and let it fill him. The music swelled and vibrated through his whole body. Maybe someday, he would notate it and play it for his brother.

"Barre!" His brother's shout surged over the music, bringing the sense of his fear and relief with it. *"Shit, that's loud. Turn it down, I can hardly hear myself think!"*

Barre grinned and let the song fade away.

"Are you okay?"

"Me? I thought you were dead. Is Ro with you? Are you all right? Gutierrez is in medical. She's ..."

Jem's worry threatened to overwhelm their tenuous link. *"I know. We're okay. It's a long story."*

"What about Micah? Did you find Dev?"

"Yeah. They're probably back on Earth by now."

There was a brief pause, before Jem spoke again. "Charon?"

"He didn't make it."

"Oh."

"We found Nomi. She's confined to her quarters. Ro's—"

"Barre—I found something. We found something. I'm sorry. There was no other way to get the worm in the

system. *It should have been me they arrested. It's my fault. I'm so sorry—*"

Jem's words came pouring in so fast, Barre could hardly separate them into coherent thoughts.

"Whoa. Slow down. Found what?"

There was another pause and Barre thought the connection was gone.

"This."

A link to a text file glowed in his mind.

"Wow. I didn't think you could do that!"

"Me neither. Barre? Tell Ro ..."

Jem's voice faded just as the file opened. Barre reached for him the way he used to grab his little brother's hand to keep him from wandering off, but there was nothing to hold on to.

"Barre?" Ro was looking up at him, concern in her bright green eyes.

"I think you need to see this."

"See what?"

Barre pushed the file Jem had shared with him to his micro. "This."

They scanned it together. Ro drew her breath in sharply. "Son of a bitch."

So someone on Hephaestus—and probably Targill—was passing intel to and from Lowell. And paying him. All the while he was also working through Ro's father with the black market and looking for Ithaka. He whistled low and long. "Now what?" Barre asked.

Ro tugged her hands through her tangled hair. "I have no idea."

Chapter 32

FROZEN AT THE airlock, Ro read and reread the file Jem had given them. There wasn't enough Maldonado paranoia in several galaxies to deal with this.

Lowell was some kind of double agent. And it looked like Targill was his handler. And he'd probably been some kind of silent partner in her father's schemes. All her interactions with Lowell since she'd been promoted to Chief Engineer had been superficial. No work orders. No attempts at a secret handshake.

The only odd thing was what Nomi had told her—that Lowell had wanted Ro to know he'd worked with her father. He must have been feeling her out and when she didn't respond, figured she didn't know anything about their side dealings.

"This is explosive," Ro said.

"And it could blow up in our faces."

"Or we could use it to break Nomi out." She had this incongruous image of a data stream burning a hole in the door to her quarters.

"Everything we have navigates dangerously close to Ithaka."

"I know." Ro's body vibrated with barely controlled fear and fury. This was what Gutierrez had warned her about. The point where she had to weigh her loyalty to Ada May and the secret of Ithaka with Nomi's safety. She squeezed her eyes shut and leaned against Halcyone's bulkhead.

"Besides, leverage only works if you know how to apply it. Who do we tell? How do we know who to trust?"

"I wish I knew," Ro whispered.

A loud clang echoed in the corridor as Halcyone triggered the inner hatch. Ro and Barre looked up. Jem was leaning over in the airlock, breathing hard, his face flushed.

As soon as the door swung open, Ro yanked him aboard so fast, he tumbled into her.

He looked up into her face, his eyes wide. "Ro, I'm sorry. I didn't mean to get Nomi in trouble. I—"

"Shut up, Jem. If jettisoning you in the void would make Nomi's problems go away, I might consider it. But the fact is, we're going to need every one of us to figure this out."

"Oh," he said. His eyes started to skitter back and forth and he looked away, reaching for the support of the bulkhead. Barre steadied him.

"Okay. Everyone in engineering. We need to plan."

They piled in to where they'd had all their group meetings. Only Nomi was missing. Ro checked her ghost program and she hadn't moved. Good. If the two of them had had neurals, maybe Ro could have figured out a way to communicate with Nomi the way Barre and Jem did. Though that could get a little awkward. Heat rose to her cheeks and she focused on the problem at hand.

"How's Gutierrez?" Barre asked.

"They're still swarming all over her. But from what I could see, her vitals were stabilizing."

"Good."

"I need all your raw data, Jem," Ro said. "We have to integrate everything we've got. Including everything you pulled from the files. And everything you and Nomi discovered." There would be time to tell him the whole story of Dev's escape, her father's death, Charon's sacrifice, and the LC's injuries after they cleared Nomi. Ro gripped her micro and felt the polymer deform. They would clear Nomi.

"Here." He pushed his micro over to her. "Take what you need. My brain's mush. I'm just going to sit over here and close my eyes for a bit."

She didn't even spare a glance for him, but grabbed his device and triggered the pairing with hers. In seconds, she was surrounded by glowing windows and scrolling data. "Jem? You programmed this?"

"The worm? Yeah. You could have the decency not to be so surprised."

"Don't be an idiot, Jem. It's very good. You're very good. I'm just surprised it got noticed."

"Well, it did. And then Nomi got arrested."

"Not exactly," Barre said. "She's not been formally charged, and according to Daedalus, she's just unavailable. If she'd been arrested, they'd have put her in the brig."

"Which means there's some room to negotiate," Ro said, nodding at Jem's data.

"But with who?" Jem asked.

"Well, that's the million-credit question," Barre answered.

"We know Gutierrez was tracking Lowell." Ro and Jem had found the connection between the LC's postings and Lowell's when they were digging into Gutierrez's records. The LC had tried to minimize the man's importance, but she'd been looking at him for a reason. Was she trying to find who in the Commonwealth was filing Lowell's flight plan?

"Gutierrez isn't in any position to help us right now." The "if ever" was pretty clear in Barre's voice. "And we can't betray her connection to Ithaka."

Ro rubbed her eyes. "I know."

"Then who is?" Jem asked.

Ro paced the narrow central walkway in engineering. Who could they trust? No. That wasn't the right question. Who had enough authority to divert suspicion from Nomi? "Mendez."

Jem flushed and turned away. "That won't work. The commander already has a copy of the raw data. How long do you think it will be before she balances all the equations?"

Ro dragged her hands through her hair. What could they use? There had to be something that wouldn't force her to give up Ithaka. There had to be. Her father wouldn't care who he'd have to burn to get what he wanted. For the first time in her life, she regretted not being able to be him. She looked up into Barre's worried expression. "Wait. My father."

"What about your father?"

"I have his data. Unencrypted."

"But Gutierrez—"

"We can't wait for her." Even if she survived, it could be a long time before the Commonwealth hackers could get into the DNA-encrypted data cube. Especially if they thought it needed a sample of his DNA, given he was elemental particles now. "We give it all to Mendez."

"She's Commonwealth. What makes you think she's not working with Targill?" Barre asked.

"Possible, but I don't think so. She set Nomi to spy on Lowell and got Jem to give her data she'd already have access to if she were part of this."

"Okay, but then we're going to implicate a decorated Commonwealth officer. A war hero. In a conspiracy involving Ithaka. I don't know."

Ro knew Barre was thinking of Gutierrez's accusations on Halcyone. Her words echoed in Ro's mind. *I warned you. More than once. And I warned Nakamura, too. The path you're traveling is one full of painful decisions and necessary sacrifices.* The LC wasn't wrong. "I think this is one of those necessary sacrifices. Mendez already knows Ithaka exists and we have a connection to it. This doesn't tell her any more than that. Besides, it's not a matter of trust, but, like you said, of leverage. Mendez is ambitious. She doesn't want to be stuck on this rock forever. This could get her out of here."

"Or it could get her court-martialed."

"Well, that's not our problem, is it?" Ro asked.

"That's cold, Ro, even for you," Barre said, shaking his head.

"And?"

"And you're right."

"Ro?" Jem looked up from where he'd been resting his

head on a console.

He still looked fatigued. "Hmm?"

"You could reconfigure my worm to deploy in an anonymous message to her. That way there'd be no direct connection to us. And if she got it while Nomi was in solitary, then she'd have to know it wasn't Nomi who was responsible."

Ro smiled broadly. "You're not so bad for a drone." Not that Mendez wouldn't be suspicious of them, but at least it gave them all some degree of plausible deniability.

Jem matched her smile with his.

She tossed him back his micro. "Go rest. We got this."

"Are you sure?"

"You're not the only genius Durbin brother, you know."

"Yeah, well, Barre will do, I guess." His eyes sparkled, even as they continued their shifting dance. "I'll be back in medical. Mom was in the middle of a scan when Gutierrez came in. She'll want to finish with me as soon as the LC is stable. And I'll keep an eye on things there."

"Thank you," Ro said.

"We're a crew, right?" Jem asked.

"Yeah." They were just short a member or three.

*

Nomi's tea had gotten cool again and bitter. She made a face and poured it down the sink before glancing up at the shelf containing her grandfather's kami. "So, now what, Sofu? I wish you were here. I could really use your wisdom."

Nothing made sense anymore. And everyone was part of a conspiracy. Even Simon Marchand. After his link dropped, Nomi had tried to use his internal comms override to get in touch with Jem, but Daedalus had locked her out again. Either Marchand had programmed it for a single use, or the AI had discovered it.

Or maybe Marchand had also gotten arrested.

Too many conspiracies. Lowell and Ro's dad. Gutierrez and Lowell. Targill and Mendez. Everything about Ithaka. Nomi was an ansible network with a major node down: all her thoughts kept re-routing themselves in circles.

The door chime sounded and Nomi jerked around, slamming her hip into the counter. As she stood swearing softly, it rang again. That was odd. Her guards would simply come in after signaling. It was a small courtesy, but Nomi had appreciated it. The chime rang a third time and Nomi authorized the door to open, her heart beating double time.

"Hey."

Nomi drew in her breath sharply. Ro stood at the threshold. "Ro," she whispered, hoarsely and looked around for the guards. There was only Ro. "How did you ...? Am I free?" She was afraid to move away from the door, afraid it would close again and not reopen. Afraid that Ro would be trapped on the other side from her.

"It's okay. It's going to be okay." Ro stepped inside.

Nomi shuddered as the door shut behind her.

"Hey," Ro repeated again. She took Nomi's hands in her own. "You're cold as space!"

Nomi pulled her hands free and circled her arms around Ro, shivering against her.

Ro nestled her head in the hollow of Nomi's collar bone. Her pulse slowed and matched Ro's measured heartbeat. It seemed to take forever until she stopped trembling.

"I thought I'd never see you again," Nomi whispered, laying her cheek against the top of Ro's head. Strands of long blonde hair brushed against her face.

"Yeah. Me too. Let's not do that again, okay?"

"Deal."

Ro lifted her head and smiled up at her. She looked as weary as Nomi felt. Could they even talk here? Would the door open if she tried to leave? "Ro, I have to tell—"

"Later," Ro whispered in her ear. "I'll tell you everything later."

The warmth of her breath made Nomi shiver. There was a lot of everything she had to tell Ro, too. "Micah and his friend?"

"Safe."

"Your father?"

"I don't want to talk about him now." She reached up and cupped Nomi's cheeks with her work-calloused hands. They were a strange combination of rough and gentle and Nomi felt a warmth glowing in her core. "I can't lose you."

Nomi leaned into Ro's touch and closed her eyes, hoping they could stay like this forever. Ro's kiss was fierce against her lips. Their hearts sped up again, but this time there was no fear.

They curled up on the sofa, legs and arms entwined. Ro tucked her quilt around them both and Nomi felt like she could finally breathe again. Every time Nomi tried to ask a question about what happened or tell Ro what she knew, she would be answered by another kiss. The two of them finally collapsed in a heap of laughter, kisses, and tears.

Ro gently wiped the wetness from Nomi's cheeks. "Better?"

Nomi let her breath out in a shuddering sigh. "Yeah."

"Hungry?"

Her stomach rumbled, right on cue, and they both laughed again. She hadn't done more than pick at the trays her guards had brought her and a day's worth of crackers and tea had left her ravenous.

"Come on. Dinner on Halcyone."

Of anywhere, it would be the safest place to talk. Nomi stared at the door to her quarters, still not convinced it would open for her.

"It's okay." Ro took her hand and towed her toward the door.

It slid open.

Nomi exhaled heavily and stepped into the corridor, still clutching Ro's hand. The whole way to Halcyone, Nomi kept glancing over her shoulder. The fact that no one was following them wasn't entirely reassuring. She didn't relax until they were aboard the ship. Just inside the airlock, Nomi halted and patted the bulkhead.

"Come on. Barre's in engineering. I think Jem's back, too. There's a lot we have to catch you both up on."

There was more than Ro thought. Conspiracies within conspiracies. "It's never going to be the way it was, is it," Nomi said, her voice dropping.

Ro sighed. "No."

Life had been a whole lot simpler before Ro. "If you knew

what waking up this ship was going to lead to, would you still have gone ahead?"

There was a long silence. Ro stared directly into Nomi's face, her green eyes bright. "It led to you. Yes."

Nomi blushed and turned away. "That's not what I meant."

"I know."

"I'm afraid."

Ro started to answer but Nomi stopped her with a touch.

"Not just for me. This isn't just about us anymore." It really never was. "We know too much and too many people know that. How will we figure out who to trust? How can we just keep on as if nothing had happened?"

"We can't. You're right. I'm sorry." Ro reached for her hand again. "I'm not sorry I'm not alone in this mess. But I am sorry it's such a mess."

"Hey, dinner's getting cold." They both jumped at Barre's voice behind them.

Jem stood next to Barre, smirking at her and Ro. Nomi squeezed Ro's hand more firmly before slipping free and hugging each Durbin brother.

"It's going to be okay," Barre said. "Ro has the best crew in the cosmos."

Were they good enough? They were all going to have to become very, very skilled at 'nought and shuttle, but even not knowing all the details from the past few days, she had the feeling Ro was already a master. Nomi looked from Barre to Jem and smiled. "Yes, she does. And she's damned lucky to have us."

"I'll do my best to remember that," Ro said, "but feel free

to remind me, okay?"

"Deal," Nomi said.

"Deal."

"Deal."

Jem and Barre echoed her and their shared laughter reverberated along the corridor.

"Some crew," Ro said, shaking her head. "Come on. We have work to do."

She tried to look affronted as she swept past the three of them, but Nomi could see the effort Ro was making not to smile. Nomi linked arms with Jem and Barre as they followed her toward engineering. No reverse in a wormhole, and perhaps their course had been set even before Nomi had struck up a conversation with an engineering intern at breakfast a few months ago.

No reverse in a wormhole. Time to see where this latest jump had landed them.

Acknowledgments

To be able to return to Halcyone Space is a privilege. These characters and their world have become a kind of second home over the past few years and that's thanks to the readers who have inhabited this universe with me. Thank you. You have encouraged me and supported me on this journey and for that I am truly grateful.

Writing does not happen in a vacuum (see what I did there?), no matter the romantic vision of the author working alone in a freezing garret. I am beyond grateful to my community of writers, the women of the SFWG and the members of the Sooper Sekrit Clubhouse (I could name them, but then, dear reader, I'd have to kill you ...). In large ways and in small, they have all kept me from wobbling out of orbit.

This story actually began on the front porch of an old house by Lake Champlain in Vermont. My gratitude to Ilyanna Kreske for giving me the space and support when I was mourning my father and wasn't sure the words would be there anymore.

411

To my generous cadre of beta readers who were willing to take a rough cut of this novel and help me polish its jagged edges: Roland Boykin, David Litster, Donna Desborough, Bryce Alexander, Becket Morgan, Richard J. Kendrick, Cathy Pelham, John Redcat, Nightwing Whitehead, Sally Smith, and Bobbi Fox. Thank you for your time and your feedback. I appreciated both knowing what moved you in the story and where I wandered off the rails.

The Materials Science community on Google+ was patient and extremely helpful in answering my questions about EMPs and polymers; all useful to Dev during her capture. I know she is grateful!

To my partner-in-crime-and-life, Neil, who is honest with me even when I might wish he were otherwise: You make me better. In all ways.

To Chris Howard, who continues to astonish me with his artistic talent: Thank you. There is no one else who captures the world of Halcyone Space like you do.

And finally, to Karen Conlin, my editor: I am learning to make new mistakes. Lucky for me, you catch them.

The adventures of Halcyone and her crew will continue.

LJ Cohen
June 2016

About the Author

LJ Cohen is a novelist, poet, blogger, ceramics artist, and relentless optimist. After almost twenty-five years as a physical therapist, LJ now uses her anatomical knowledge and myriad clinical skills to injure characters in her science fiction and fantasy novels. She lives in the Boston area with her family, two dogs, and the occasional international student. DREADNOUGHT AND SHUTTLE (book 3 of the SF/Space Opera series Halcyone Space), is her sixth novel. When not doing battle with a stubborn Jack Russell Terrier mix, she can be found working on the next novel, which often looks a lot like daydreaming. LJ is a member of SFWA, Broad Universe, and the Independent Publishers of New England.

Connect with LJ online:

Homepage: www.ljcohen.net/
Blog: www.ljcbluemuse.blogspot.com/
Facebook: www.facebook.com/ljcohen
Twitter: @lisajanicecohen
Tumblr: www.ljcohen.tumblr.com
Google+: www.google.com/+LisaCohen
email LJ: lisa@ljcohen.net

Sign up for Blue Musings, an occasional email newsletter complete with free, original, short fiction offered in a variety of drm-free formats. (www.ljcohen.net/contact.html)

32504217R00266

Made in the USA
Middletown, DE
06 June 2016